W9-API-241

Return to Summerhouse

BOOKS BY JUDE DEVERAUX

Jude
Deveraux

Return to
Summerhouse

Pocket Books
New York London Toronto Sydney

Pocket Books
A Division of Simon & Schuster, Inc.
1230 Avenue of the Americas
New York, NY 10020

Cover design by Lisa Litwack; Image © Jupiter Images

Manufactured in the United States of America

ISBN: 978-0-7394-9935-1

Return *to* Summerhouse

Part One

One

❧

Amy closed her suitcase and looked around the bedroom she shared with her husband, Stephen. Everything was neatly in place, just the way she liked it. Stephen teased her that she'd fall down dead if the clock showed eight A.M. and she didn't have all the beds made. But he didn't fool her; he liked the house to be clean and neat as much as she did.

She sat down on the buttoned bench at the foot of the bed and sighed. I can't do this, she thought for the thousandth time. For that matter, *why* was she being made to do it? She wasn't good with strangers, wasn't good in social situations where she had to meet people and make chitchat. She liked going to the same places, seeing the same people, and talking about their same lives. So what was wrong with that? If it made her feel safe, so what?

Just because Stephen and his father knew some therapist and she suggested that Amy get away for a while didn't make it necessary. Besides, what gave that woman

the right to tell other people what they should do with
their lives?

"You have on your sulky face again," Stephen said
from the doorway.

It flashed through her mind that this was her last
chance to show her husband how much she hated being
sent away, so she tried to keep her look of anguish. But
it didn't work. He was leaning against the doorway,
wearing dark gray trousers and a crisp white shirt. Sunlight was coming in from the window across the stairs
behind him, making the light hit his dark blond hair
in a way that made a halo around his head. When he
smiled, his blue eyes seemed to emit starlight. She could
feel her body growing limp.

"Don't give me that look," he said. "The kids are
downstairs diving into their Froot Loops and we don't
have time to . . ." He gave a little one-sided grin and
nodded toward the bed.

It took Amy three whole seconds to react. "You gave
them Froot Loops? Do you know what's in that stuff?
Sugar!" She was running toward him and the doorway
when he caught her about the waist.

"That got you out of your stupor," he said, pulling
her to him. "They're not eating anything illegal." He
nuzzled his face in her neck. "They're having one of
those sawdust cereals you buy for them."

She pushed away and glared at him. "But I bet that
the minute I'm out of here, you'll let them have everything they want."

"Why not?" Stephen said, smiling, still holding on to her. "I'll be the good guy and you'll be the dictator."

She twisted out of his grip. "That's not funny."

He dropped his hands to his sides and his face became serious. "Amy, we've been over this a thousand times. I'm not going to leave you here alone."

"Then stay with me. Or go with me."

"No," he said firmly. "I promised the boys this camping trip and I'm going to do it." He smiled a bit. "You're welcome to go with us."

Amy rolled her eyes. She loved her husband and two young sons passionately, but camping? During the one camping trip she'd gone on, three years ago, she'd been so nervous that she'd made all of them miserable.

There had been an open campfire and a toddler. She stayed awake for the first three nights, terrified that her youngest son was going to wake up and walk into the fire.

There had been bugs, dirt, and no bathrooms. When they finally hiked out of the place, she had fallen asleep in the car, exhausted and relieved that the ordeal was at last over.

During the following year, neither Stephen nor their oldest son mentioned that Amy had spent the entire week complaining. But the next summer when Stephen spoke of another camping trip, before Amy could say a word, he said, "I vote that this year we leave Mommy at home." Both had agreed.

After that, Amy's extreme hatred of camping had

become a family joke, and she had laughed along with them. The second year, she'd helped them pack nutritious food, buy the best camping gear, then she'd happily waved them off. She spent a luxurious week repainting both of the boys' bedrooms and going to the gym. When they returned, all four of them were happy to see one another and had had much to talk about. Amy had been in such a good mood that she'd laughed when she found her homemade, good-for-you food still in the cooler, right next to a bag full of empty wrappers for every disgusting, high-sugar, high-fat thing they could find at the local convenience store. It took the boys nearly three days to come off their sugar high. But then, it had taken Stephen the same amount of time to come down, and since he expended his energy in the bedroom with Amy, she didn't complain.

This year was to be their fourth camping trip, their third without Amy, but now things were different. Four months ago, she had miscarried their third child, a little girl, and Amy had not been able to recover from her grief.

Everyone said that she was young and she could "try again," but nothing consoled Amy. She had reacted by closing into herself, not wanting to get out or see anyone.

Through it all, Stephen had been wonderful. He'd done the grocery shopping and he'd been the one to go to the boys' last teacher conference. At church he'd made excuses for why Amy wasn't there. He said she had the flu, then bronchitis. Not one person believed him. They patted him on the arm and said, "Give her time."

Stephen had gone home, battled with the boys to get them out of their good clothes before going outside, then told Amy every word the people at church had said about her absence. For the last two Sundays, she'd still been in bed when they returned.

But a few weeks ago, things had changed. His father called him at work and asked him to go to lunch with the wife of a friend of his. She was a therapist. Stephen had thanked his father for the offer, but said he couldn't possibly go. Between all that he had to do at work and his new responsibilities at home, things that Amy usually took care of, he was overwhelmed. The day before he'd put on socks that didn't match and a new client had noticed. For the ten years that they'd been married, Amy had always put out his clothes for him. The truth was that he didn't know where his socks were kept.

But his father knew how to get his son to do what he wanted. "Are you saying that you don't want Amy to get back to her true, bossy little self? Do you want to spend the rest of your life with a woman who can hardly get out of bed? Do you want to start dressing yourself?"

Stephen sighed. He knew he'd lost this argument before it began. However, he had the presence of mind to ask about the woman. He didn't want to be conned into sending Amy to somebody who rang bells and burned incense. According to his father, the woman had credentials "a mile long." "She works with some big names," his father said. "I can't tell you who they are because—"

"I know," Stephen said, "breach of trust. I just don't want to waste my time with her if all she's going to tell me to do is sit down with Amy and reason with her. I've tried that and it doesn't work."

His father hesitated. "Are you saying you want to give her drugs?" There was horror in his voice.

"No, of course not! I want . . . I don't know, maybe I'm looking for magic."

His father snorted. "Good luck on that! But do give Jeanne a try."

"I'll give her anything I can, but it's Amy who won't listen to anyone."

"Sometimes, son, you just need to be the man of the house."

Stephen looked at the phone and grimaced. "Sure, Dad, I'll club her over the head and drag her around by her hair."

"The good ol' days are gone, son, and all of us men have to face that."

His father said the words so seriously that Stephen laughed. "Okay, point made. I'll listen to the woman and do whatever she wants us to do. I just hope we don't have to sit in a candlelit circle with a bunch of strangers and tell our innermost fears."

His father chuckled. "From what I've seen of Jeanne that would be *her* worst nightmare. She's pretty down-to-earth and she tells it like she sees it."

"Oh great," Stephen groaned. "Dr. Phil on hormones."

"I'm glad to see that you haven't made up your mind about her."

Stephen started to reply but his secretary tapped on the glass wall of his office to let him know that the meeting was starting in three minutes. "I have to go, but I'll see her. It can't hurt to talk to her."

"At this point, nothing can hurt."

Stephen put down the phone, slipped on his suit jacket, and went to his meeting. The next day, he met with Jeanne Hightower at a restaurant near his office. Later, he was ashamed to admit to himself that he'd gone to the lunch with a certainty that it was going to fail. He knew that Amy would refuse to go to a stranger and talk about her problems. She'd think that going to a therapist meant she was one step away from being committed to an insane asylum. But then, Amy loved historical novels and often tended to think in nineteenth-century terms.

Stephen had been startled at the look of the woman. She was quite a bit overweight and looked like someone's grandmother, not a therapist who dealt with "celebrities," as his father had told him in a second conversation.

Stephen braced himself for a long, nerve-racking luncheon in which he'd be asked all about the state of his marriage and whether he and Amy were faithful to each other. Instead, as soon as he sat down, Jeanne pushed a folded piece of paper toward him.

"I think we should get business out of the way first. Your father told me about your wife and I think she should spend a few days at my house in Maine."

"What?" was all Stephen could manage to say.

"Your father told me that you and your sons go on a camping trip every year and that Amy usually stays home and works on the house."

Stephen's back stiffened. The woman was making it sound like Amy had to fix the plumbing on a shack. "She usually does some decorating, yes," he said.

Jeanne smiled at him. "While you and your kids go camping, get your wife to go to this place on those dates. I have a couple of other women who'll be there and I think the three of them will mesh."

Stephen opened the paper, saw the address in faraway Maine and the dates of his camping trip. He smiled at her in a patronizing way. "Amy has a mind of her own and she would never agree to spend time alone with strangers. For that matter, I'm not sure I like the idea either."

"Okay," Jeanne said and picked up her menu. "What's good to eat here?"

Stephen frowned. "Is that it? You're just going to drop it?"

Jeanne looked up at him with twinkling eyes. "You could always tell me about your wildest sex experience. Unless it's boring, that is. But if it's a good one, I'd like to hear about it."

All the stiffness left him and he smiled. He realized

that she had seen and felt his reluctance, and she'd quickly managed to relax him. "You are good, aren't you?"

"The best. In fact, I'm so good that if you tell me you'll use all of your gorgeous six feet to persuade your wife to go to my house in Maine, I'll not mention another word about it and you and I can have a nice lunch together. You don't happen to like baseball, do you?"

"Love it," Stephen said as he slipped the note into his shirt pocket and picked up his menu. With his head down, he said, "By the way, it's two."

She blinked at him for a moment, then smiled. "Right. Six feet *two.* Are you *sure* you wouldn't like to tell me about your sex fantasies?"

"Fantasies?" he said, his eyes on the menu. "You mean like the one where I wear tall black boots and ride a black horse and Amy is—?"

"Your wife?" Jeanne said, her eyes wide. "Your sex fantasies involve your *wife*?"

"Always have, always will," he said. "We met when we were just three days old and we've been—"

"If you spend my lunch hour telling me your life story I swear I'll charge you double my hourly rate."

"Even if I tell you about the sword?"

Jeanne hesitated. "Okay, I'll have my secretary call yours and I'll schedule you for next week."

"In your dreams," Stephen said.

It hadn't been easy for him to persuade Amy to

agree to go to Maine. They didn't usually argue—his father said it was because Stephen let Amy make all the rules—but this time they did.

"I do *not* want to go to some faraway state and spend weeks with a bunch of women I've never met. Women *you* heard about through a therapist."

She made the last word sound like "witch doctor."

Stephen was determined to not let her wear him down so he stood his ground. "You cannot stay here in this house alone while the boys and I go camping."

"Then I'll go with you."

That idea horrified Stephen so much that he'd taken a step back from her. His reaction set Amy off into the tears that were always near the surface these days.

He threw up his hands in futility. "Amy, other women would kill for this chance. You get to get away from us and this house that you work on like a galley slave and you—"

"Is that what you think of me? As a . . . What did you call me? A galley slave?"

"You're not going to twist this around so I'm the villain. I think this is a good thing for you to do."

"I don't know these women and neither do you. Who knows what they're like? They're in therapy. For what? Murder?"

"Amy, calm down. It's true that we don't know them, but Jeanne does and she—"

"And I guess *you* know this Jeanne person?"

Stephen thought back to their luncheon and the two subsequent phone conversations and he couldn't help smiling. For all that she was old enough to be his grand-mother and as wide as she was tall, there was something sexy about her. When his secretary heard him laughing on the phone she had raised her eyebrows.

"What does that smile mean?" Amy asked, advancing on him. "That's a sex smile, isn't it? There's something more going on with you and her than just therapy, isn't there?"

Stephen stopped smiling. "How did you guess? I've been having an affair with Jeanne Hightower for weeks now. Great sex. She likes my sword the best. And the tall leather boots." He left the room before Amy could say another word.

That argument had been a turning point. That night Amy put on her prettiest lacy nightgown and snuggled up against him. They hadn't had sex in weeks. But Stephen knew what she was doing and he was having none of it. It took all his resolve but he'd moved away from her and gone to sleep. Never before had he turned down her invitation for sex.

The next morning Amy got up early and made them breakfast. She didn't say much during the meal, and it had been a solemn occasion. Usually, the boys were talking on top of each other and kicking each other under the table, but that morning all four of them had been quiet.

As Stephen left for work, Amy told him she'd go to Maine. It had been a victory for him, but he hadn't liked being a bully to make her do what he wanted her to.

Since she'd told him she'd go, she'd done everything she could to get out of her promise, but Stephen remained steadfast. He saw how she was pretending to be more cheerful, but he also saw how she would stand and look out the kitchen window for half an hour at a time. He had known her all his life and he'd never seen her like this. When her mother died six years ago, Amy had mourned then moved on, but since the miscarriage she seemed to have stepped back from the world.

Stephen couldn't see how a few days at a summerhouse in Maine with some strangers would help, but he had no other ideas. Every day, Amy seemed to move deeper inside herself. Slowly, he seemed to be losing her.

And he knew that if he lost Amy, he'd lose his life. She was his life. She had been everything to him for his entire life, through kindergarten, elementary school, high school, college. She had always been there, always with him. When they were six, one day over milk and cookies, she'd said, "Let's get married right after we get out of college. I want a big wedding, and I want three children: two boys, then a girl. Okay?" Stephen had nodded in agreement. They had never talked about it again but it was exactly what they'd done.

The only flaw in the plan had been the miscarriage, and with the break in Amy's perfect life she seemed to have lost something that she couldn't get back.

Now, he had to work to keep from giving in to her. He knew that if he said yes, why didn't she forget about Maine and go camping with them, Amy would explode in happiness. She'd throw herself at him for a moment, then she'd bustle around to hurry and get everything and everyone ready. Amy the dynamo of energy, happiest when she was organizing people. Their pastor once said that he didn't know if he could run the church without Amy.

But Stephen knew that Amy's happiness wouldn't last long. By the time they got to the campground she'd be staring out the window, her mind only half on what was going on around them.

And, of course, there was the horror of a camping trip with Amy. Cleaning fish was not her idea of fun. Campfires scared the wits out of her, and he didn't want to think about her lectures on what could be crawling inside a sleeping bag. No, camping was for him and the boys. No bathing, no shaving, no eating anything that was remotely good for them. Last year he'd won the belching contest but he feared his youngest son might win this year. He meant to practice on the drive to the campground. He and the boys were going to buy one each of every cola they could find and see which one produced the most gas. The big contest would be on their last night out. The winner got the plastic vomit that was hidden at the bottom of his backpack.

No, he didn't want Amy with them on the camping trip. But if she was at home, with no reason to get out of bed, he'd never enjoy himself.

"All packed?" he asked cheerfully. Amy gave him a pleading look, but he ignored it. "Dad should be here soon to take you to the airport." His father said that Stephen would cave if Amy shed even one tear at the airport, so someone other than his son had to drive her there.

"Yes," she mumbled in such a sad voice that Stephen almost gave in to her. But he squared his shoulders, picked up her suitcase, and left the room. Amy scuffled along behind him.

Amy said nothing on the way to the airport with her father-in-law. She knew from long experience that she wouldn't get anywhere with Lewis Hanford. When she was four, he'd watched her and Stephen playing in the sandpile and he'd said to her, "You're as bossy as they come, aren't you?" Amy'd had no answer for that so she'd just blinked up at him. He was a tall man, with broad shoulders and a hard, flat stomach. She didn't know it then but he'd played semipro football until an injured knee had sent him home. He wasn't the easiest man to live with, nor were his three eldest sons who were just like him.

Amy looked up at the man, utterly unafraid of his size or his gruff manner. "Stephen and I are going to get married."

Lewis looked at his youngest son, the incredibly beautiful, blond Stephen who had a temperament just like his mother's. He was always in a good mood, always happy, very easy to get along with. "I think you two will do very well together," Lewis said, then went into the house. Neither he nor Amy spoke of the matter again. To them, it had been settled that day.

Now, in the car, she confronted him. "I'll never forgive you for making Stephen send me away," she said under her breath.

"Add it to the list you already have against me."

"That list fills up a roll of paper that is now too heavy for me to lift."

She knew how to get to him and he smiled. "You'll be fine," he said gently. For all of their arguments over the years, he loved her as the daughter he'd never had. His three eldest sons had all married and divorced and their lives were now full of exes and steps. But Amy was a person who made up her mind and never swayed from her decisions. And she was still unafraid of him.

"Oh, so you've met these women who have to go to a therapist for whatever horrible things have happened in their lives."

"Like losing a baby?" he asked softly.

Amy turned to look out the side window. "I didn't go to anyone for that."

"But you should have."

She looked back at him. "Like you should have when Marta died?"

"Yeah, I should have," he said loudly. "I should have gone to talk to someone instead of drinking myself into a stupor every night for a year and trying to run my truck into a tree."

"All right," she said in a tone meant to calm him down. "I was willing to go talk to someone—" His look made her backtrack. "Okay, so maybe I wasn't willing to talk about what was a very private matter to me, but going to spend time in a house with strangers . . . I don't see how that will do me any good."

" 'Spend time,' " he said. "You make it sound like you're off to prison. What do they sell up in Maine?"

"Sell? I don't know. Lobsters. Blueberries."

"You better bring back some food. Stevie and the boys will be full of the junk they're taking on the camping trip and they'll need something good."

"If you're trying to make me angry, you're succeeding."

"Good. I like you angry better than weepy." He stopped in front of the departure area of the local airport.

"I still don't see how my Stephen could be related to you."

She waited for him to reply but he just sat there. Obviously, he wasn't going to help her with her suitcase. Again she thought how Lewis and his three eldest sons were Neanderthals. Stephen opened doors for women, carried anything that weighed more than their handbags, and sang in the church choir. Lewis and the "boys" smashed beer cans on their foreheads.

She got out, opened the back, and hauled her heavy bag out. Before she closed the door she said, "Ever think that maybe Marta came to her senses and Stephen isn't yours?"

When Lewis looked at her with fury on his face, Amy gave him a sweet smile and slammed the door shut. He took off so fast she had to grab her hand back.

She went into the airport to start the long security check.

Two

When Amy at last landed at the Bangor airport, a driver was waiting for her, holding a sign with her last name on it. "That's me," she said, smiling.

He was an older man with gray hair and he didn't smile back. Instead, he looked her up and down as though trying to figure her out.

Amy's face turned red and her body rigid. She was sure that he knew she was a guest of a therapist, a person who dealt with disturbed people. What would she say when he asked her what she'd been sent there for? If she told him that she'd never even met the therapist, would he believe her? Of course not!

As they went past the ticket counter, Amy thought about running toward it and getting on a plane home. The thought of seeing her father-in-law's smirk and her husband's disappointment held her back.

I can do this, she told herself. She was a grown

woman, thirty-two years old, and she could handle this. She would be able to get through it.

"Jeanne said I was to give you this," the man said as she got into the backseat of his black Town Car.

Amy took the envelope and opened it as he shut the door. It was a single sheet, with a photo of a very cute little house at the top, then a few paragraphs about its history. She scanned the text. The house was built by a ship's carpenter in 1820 and lived in by only two families before Jeanne Hightower and her husband bought it in 1962. Using old photos, they had restored the house to look as original as possible.

At the bottom was what Amy was interested in. In the year 2000 Jeanne had lent the house to a patient of hers to use for her fortieth-birthday celebration, and the woman had invited two friends to join her. The extraordinary success of that weekend on the lives of all three women had encouraged Jeanne to extend the invitation to other people. She added that two years ago the house had been remodeled so there were now three bedrooms instead of two.

"More room for other insane people," Amy muttered.

"Yah?" the driver asked as he looked at her in the rearview mirror. It was that sound that only someone who has lived in Maine all his life could make. "You all right?"

"Yes, fine, thank you," Amy said. "Tell me, do you pick up all the women who visit Mrs. Hightower's house?"

"Mostly, I do. Some of them drive."

"So she lends the house out a lot, does she?"

"No more than needs to be, I guess," he said.

Amy wanted to ask if the people were screaming lunatics, but didn't know how to say that politely. She looked back down at the paper in her hand. It didn't tell much else, just that there would be some food in the house, but the guests were encouraged to walk or drive around town and find things for themselves.

Amy looked out the window but she was too nervous to really see anything around her. The little town looked old and she was sure that if she were there with her family, she'd think it was adorable. They passed several little shops where she thought she could buy souvenirs for the boys. She'd look for something educational.

Or bloodthirsty, she thought. That's what they'd really like. She wondered if they sold pirate gear in the stores. Didn't Stephen say something about a sword? Maybe she'd get one for him. And maybe she'd go to a bookstore and buy herself half a dozen novels, stay in her room, and read them. When enough time had passed, she could go home—and rave about all she'd seen and learned.

The man stopped the car in front of a lovely little house that dripped gingerbread. Amy itched to get her camera out and take photos to show the boys. Behind her the driver put her bag in front of the door and Amy gave him a five-dollar tip. He nodded toward her, still no smile, and said, "Keys under the mat," then left.

She stood there for a moment, hesitating before she

entered. If the key was under the mat, that meant she was the first one there. If she was going to leave, this was the time. She could pull her bag behind her, call a taxi, and go right back to the airport. Then she'd—

Thinking what she'd do next was the hangup. Go back to Stephen and admit she'd chickened out?

Bending, she pulled the corner of the mat up and looked under it. No key. She lifted the whole thing and was looking all around the tiny porch when the door opened.

"Are you the other one?" said a young woman, early twenties, who had on lots of eye makeup, black nail polish, and glossy black hair. "I thought I heard a car but when no one knocked . . ." She trailed off and stood there looking at Amy, who was still holding the mat in her hand.

"I assume you're also one of Jeanne's Crazies," the girl said slowly, as though she had to enunciate every word.

It was all Amy's fears put into one sentence. "I . . . I've never met her," was all she could mumble.

"Really? Come on in and I'll tell you all about her."

Amy hesitated. Did the entire tiny town think of them as "Jeanne's Crazies"?

"Come on," she said again as she held the door open wide. "We don't bite. We might give you electric shock treatments, but no biting."

"You're scaring her," said another voice, and Amy looked past the first woman to see an older one, probably in her early fifties, coming from inside the house.

"Please come in," the woman said, moving to stand in front of the first one. "I'm Faith and this is Zoë. I've only been here a few hours, but I've already seen that she has a sense of humor that is an acquired taste."

"Me?" Zoë said, grinning.

Faith took the handle of Amy's suitcase and started wheeling it toward the back of the house. "I hope you don't mind that we decided on rooms before you got here."

"We cut cards for them," Zoë said.

Amy looked at Faith questioningly and she nodded. "You'll be happy to know that you won the new room, which has an en suite bathroom. Zoë and I share a bath."

Amy hardly had time to look about the house at the mix of antiques and used furniture. It was all lovely but looked a bit worn. She got the idea that the house had had some hard use in the last few years. For a moment she had a vision that some kind of therapy went on in the house. Was this a sort of rehab house where they'd be awakened at four A.M. and made to go hiking?

"This is fine," Amy said when Faith opened the door to a pretty little room done in rose-patterned chintz. It was exactly to Amy's taste and she hoped it would help her survive the next few days.

Turning, she looked at Faith. "I think I can manage now." The woman had her salt-and-pepper hair pulled into a bun low on the back of her neck, and she wore a flowered cotton dress with a little white collar. She looked sweet and lovely. Amy wondered if she was a mass murderer.

"Sure," Faith said slowly. "Let us know if you need anything. We thought we'd have dinner together. About six?"

"I have a bit of a headache so I might stay in," Amy said.

Faith couldn't cover the frown that passed across her face, but then she smiled. "Sure. If I don't see you any more, have a good night."

❧ ❧

"*I don't like* her," Zoë said. "I mean, I really and truly don't like her."

She and Faith were at a local seafood restaurant. Before them were plates full of clams and lobster, and to one side were huge sheets of glass that allowed them to see the beautiful Maine coastline. A wooden pier ran out into the sea.

They were an incongruous pair. Zoë, with her shiny black hair, gobbed-on makeup, and her layer of black clothes ranging from leather to lace near her throat, made people do double takes. Faith drew no attention from anyone. She was shorter, rounder, and had a bend to her back that made a person think she'd spent her life bent over—which she had.

"I don't think you should judge her so harshly," Faith said. "Jeanne said that all three of us had been through a trauma and she thought we'd be good for one another."

"Speaking of that," Zoë said, as she dipped a piece of lobster in warm drawn butter, "what is *your* trauma?"

Faith smiled in a way that let Zoë know she wasn't telling anything. "We agreed to wait until we were all together, then we'd talk."

"But Little Miss Perfect said she'd never even met Jeanne."

"When did she say that?"

"When I opened the door to her. She was standing there holding the doormat, and she looked at me as if I were an insect she wanted to squash."

"Aren't you glad I talked you into taking out the nose ring?"

"Not really," Zoë said. "If I'd known the third prisoner was going to be a judgmental, uptight little snot, I would have had a dozen more piercings."

"I really don't think you should make judgments before you get to know her."

"Why not?" Zoë asked, taking a deep drink of her soda. "She made lots of judgments about *me*. I could pretty much read her mind. In fact, I could read her *life*."

"Come on," Faith said, frowning. "You're not being fair. No one can read another person's life."

"Okay," Zoë said, wiping her hands on a napkin. "Let me tell about you." She didn't wait for Faith to answer. "You grew up in a small town, loved by everyone, went to church all the time, had adoring parents— What?" She broke off because Faith had started to laugh.

"I think you should clean your crystal ball. You could not be further from the truth."

"So how am I wrong?"

Faith started to speak, then smiled. "No you don't. I'm not telling my story until all three of us are together."

"Do you think that Miss Perfect is going to come out of her room in the next few days? No way. She's going to stay in there until she thinks it's safe to leave, then she'll go back to her loving family, who will protect her from whatever nastiness she thinks has happened to her."

"Maybe Jeanne should have sent you to a camp where they teach courtesy," Faith said, glaring. "We don't know what happened in Amy's life and I don't think you should set yourself up as judge and jury. How would you like it if you were judged by how you look?"

"But I am. And so are you. We all are."

"And you want people to know that you're . . ." She trailed off as she looked at Zoë's makeup and hair.

"I'm what?" Zoë said daringly.

"If you're so determined to talk, please do so. Tell me all about your rotten childhood and how you grew up hating everyone because of something awful that happened to you. What was it? An uncle that visited you in the night?"

Zoë blinked at Faith for a moment. "You can give it out, can't you?"

"You mean that I can be as hateful as you? You may think you know all about me but you don't. For your information, when I was a teenager, I was considered the wildest girl in town. I drank too much, rode in too many fast cars, and had sex with lust and abandon."

"What changed you?" Zoë asked softly.

"Marriage to a good man," Faith said quickly, then picked up the bill off the end of the table. "Shall we go? Or do you want to sit here and cut other people to shreds?"

They paid at the register without saying a word to each other, and when they walked back to the summerhouse, Faith kept ahead of Zoë, not speaking to her. She unlocked the front door and went in, still saying nothing to the younger woman. Faith stayed in her bedroom with the door closed and waited until she heard the water running in the bathroom, then she slipped out the back door and into the little garden.

As soon as she was outside, she flipped open her cell phone and called Jeanne. "This isn't working," she said without preamble.

"What isn't?" Jeanne asked, her mouth full of food.

"Don't pretend you don't know what I'm talking about. This. All of it. The three traumatized strangers staying together in one house."

"Okay, tell me everything," Jeanne said.

Faith told her about being the first to arrive and how she thought the town and the house were both lovely. She didn't know what was supposed to be accomplished there, but she'd had high hopes.

"That is until Zoë arrived. How could you have

thought that that aggressive, opinionated girl and I would get along?"

"Did she tell you about herself?" Jeanne asked.

"Not a word."

"That's because she doesn't know much about herself. She was in a car accident that split her head open and she doesn't remember anything after she was about sixteen. All she knows is that she woke up in a hospital and an entire town was furious at her."

"Why?"

"She doesn't know."

"But surely *you* could find someone who knew her and you could ask them."

"Of course I did."

"And what did they say?" Faith asked.

Jeanne was silent.

"Well?"

"Patient confidentiality. Why don't you ask Zoë?"

"Cute," Faith said, "but you're trying to entice me to like her."

"Not like her, but have some patience."

"That's not easy," Faith said. "Zoë says she can't stand Amy and wants nothing to do with her."

"How is she?"

"Amy? Zoë opened the door to her and she looked scared to death. She took her suitcase into the new bedroom and we haven't seen her since."

"I feared that. She doesn't want to be around anyone she hasn't known for twenty years."

"Jeanne's Crazies," Faith said quietly.

"What?"

"Zoë calls us Jeanne's Crazies."

Jeanne laughed so hard she nearly choked. "I think I'll get a plaque carved with those words. Think I should hang it over the door?"

"Wonderful idea," Faith said. "I'd sure want to be a visitor to a house with a sign like that."

"Okay, I won't do it," Jeanne said, "but I'll never be able to look at the house again without seeing that sign there." Her voice changed to serious. "Look, Faith, none of you are crazy. I don't put disturbed people together. Each of you has been through a great personal trauma and I think it would do you good to talk about what happened to you to someone other than a professional. It's that simple."

Faith sighed. "My husband died after a very long illness. I still don't see that as a trauma. It wasn't as though his death wasn't expected or planned for."

Jeanne was silent.

"Stop it!" Faith said. "I mean it! Stop it right now! I can see the look on your face. You want to say that if it wasn't such a trauma why did I take a bottle of pills? And why did I attack my mother-in-law at the funeral?"

"You tell me," Jeanne said.

"I *have* told you!" Faith said, her voice rising and filling with exasperation. "I spent an entire year telling you why I did both of those things, but you've never believed a word I've said."

"Faith," Jeanne said, "how old are you?"

"You know how old I am." When Jeanne said nothing, Faith sighed. "I am thirty-eight years old."

"When you stop looking fifty and look your true age, I'll begin to think we've made some progress. As it stands now, I don't think you and I have achieved anything. How's your former mother-in-law?"

"Dead, I hope," Faith said before she thought.

"I rest my case. Faith, the truth is that I've made more progress in less time with people who have been declared criminally insane than I've made with you. For the last year, every day I've expected a call in the middle of the night telling me that you've committed suicide."

"That's absurd."

"Is it? What's in your handbag?" When Faith didn't say anything, Jeanne said, "I hope Zoë makes you furious. I hope she makes you so angry that you tell her things that you've never told me."

"I think I may have already," Faith said softly, as she remembered telling Zoë that she'd been a wild child in high school. She hadn't told Jeanne that in their therapy sessions.

"Good!" Jeanne said, then lowered her voice. "Faith, I shouldn't tell you this, but you three are very much alike."

"They've had to deal with long-term illness?"

"No," Jeanne said. "All three of you hide what you feel and tell no one anything. I wish you could get the women to talk."

"If you tell me that because I'm the oldest *I* am to get these girls together and play therapist, I'll leave tonight."

"Yes, Zoë's young, but for your information, there isn't that much age difference between you and Amy. She looks so young because she has a drop-dead gorgeous husband, so she takes care of herself. You look old because . . ."

"Because why?" Faith asked, interested.

"I've been making you pay me for a whole year so you'll tell me why, but you won't."

Faith took a deep breath. "Okay, let's deal with the present. What do I do tomorrow to keep Zoë from offending Amy and me?"

"There's a big blue cabinet in the living room. It's full of art supplies. Show them to Zoë and they'll keep her busy. You need to get Amy out of her room and take her shopping for her kids and husband. If you ask her about them, she may talk."

"So how much are you going to pay me to do *your* job?"

"If you leave there and aren't satisfied with what's happened to you, I'll refund every penny you've paid me. And Faith?"

"Yes?"

"Take all business cards from everyone."

"What?"

"Just do it. Don't throw away any business cards. And call me tomorrow and tell me what cards you have."

"Is this some new therapy for especially damaged people?"

"Yes and no. Just let me know, will you?"

"Sure," Faith said, puzzled by the request. They said goodbye and Faith went into the house. Zoë was out of the bathroom and there was no light under her door so maybe she was asleep. Faith thought about knocking on Amy's door because she did see a light, but she didn't. It had been a long day and she wanted to rest.

She went into the bathroom, meaning to take a shower, but instead, she filled the tub with steamy-hot water and got into it to soak. Lying in a bathtub of very hot water had been one of her few relaxations in the many years it took her husband to die. He always encouraged her to spend as long as she wanted in the tub, and every bath had been a hedonistic rite that involved heat and delicious herbal smells and candles. Eddie used to tease her that when she was in the bath-tub she went away to a fairy-tale kingdom.

But as Eddie grew worse and she began to be afraid that her every second with him would be their last together, she'd stopped the tub baths and settled for quick showers.

Eddie was dead now. He'd passed away over a year ago, and just as Faith feared, she'd been out of the house when it happened. At the very end, Eddie'd had a pro-fessional nurse who came for three hours a day, but it was still left to Faith to do the errands. Never mind that they lived in his mother's house and she had four ser-vants, Faith was still sent to the drugstore, the grocery, to wherever her mother-in-law wanted her to go.

Faith had returned from the grocery, full of stories

about the outside world, to find that the nurse had pulled a sheet over Eddie's dear face. His mother had been with him in his last minutes. She had held his hand and said goodbye.

It was late when Faith let the water out of the tub, dried off, and put on her nightgown and robe. She was heading into the bedroom when she thought she heard a sound in the house. An intruder?

She opened the door a bit and could see the third woman, Amy, in the kitchen. Faith wanted to go to bed, but she also wanted to get to know this woman.

"Hello," Faith said softly, but Amy still jumped as though a firecracker had gone off. "I'm sorry. I didn't mean to startle you."

"I'm fine," Amy said quickly. "Sorry I woke you. I just wanted a cup of tea."

"Did you have any dinner?"

"I bought some sandwiches at the airport so I had plenty, thank you." Amy started toward her bedroom.

"I talked to Jeanne tonight."

Amy stopped and turned back to her. "I've never met the woman. Without even meeting me, she heavy-handed my husband into sending me to . . . to this place."

Faith gave a small smile. "That sounds like her. I think all three of us are trauma victims and she thought we might like to talk to one another."

"Trauma?" Amy said, and gave Zoë's darkened room a quick glance. "What sort of trauma?"

"You mean did either of us murder anyone?"

When Amy heard it said out loud it did sound preposterous, but at the same time she didn't know either
of these women.

Faith got a tea bag out of a box, put it in a cup, and
poured boiling water on it. She took her cup to the
wooden table and sat down. "I don't know about you,
but I have *no* idea why I was sent here."

Amy's eyes widened and she took the few steps back
into the kitchen. "Me either."

"My husband died, but he'd been ill for a very long
time. It wasn't traumatic at all. I expected his death. I
keep telling Jeanne that a person needs *time* to get over
a death, but she seems to think I should snap out of it
yesterday and start wearing red dresses."

"I like your clothes," Amy said as she sat down across
from Faith. "They suit you."

"I guess they do," Faith said absently. "What about
you? Why are you here?"

Amy took a deep breath and glanced into the dark
living room, as though she were checking to see if Zoë
was there. "I had a miscarriage," she said softly.

"A long time ago?"

"Four months."

"But that's not enough time to get over anything,
much less a death," Faith said.

"I agree completely!" Amy said. "But no one will
listen to me. I was sent off to this place—" She waved
her arm around the room. "I was sent here to be with
strangers—no offense—and I don't see why."

"We have something in common," Faith said as she finished her tea. "But we have to please other people so we must stay."

"Exactly," Amy said.

"I think we should make the best of it."

"What about . . . her?" Amy asked, her voice lowered.

"Zoë?" Faith got up and went into the living room to the blue cabinet and opened it. When she turned on the light, she saw that it was packed full of art supplies: paint and canvas, Cray-Pas, chalks, huge pads of paper, watercolors, lots of brushes.

"Please tell me we don't have to draw our secret selves," Amy said from behind her.

"I hope not. Jeanne said to open this cabinet in front of Zoë and she'd stay busy for days."

"Glory hallelujah!" Amy said under her breath, then smiled at Faith. "Shall you and I eat breakfast out?"

"I'd like that," Faith said. "I'd like that very much."

Three

❦

"*Did you two* have a good time?" Zoë asked, and they heard the animosity in her voice. "Did you do a lot of bonding?" She was in the garden behind the house and on the metal table were two watercolors.

"These are good," Amy said in wonder as she looked at them. "In fact, they're very good." She held up a watercolor of three little kids struggling to pull a canoe onto a rocky beach. "If I saw this in a store, I'd buy it." She looked at Zoë with different eyes.

"The queen has spoken," Zoë said, and made a little bow toward Amy.

"However, if I'd met the artist I'm sure I would have changed my mind."

Zoë laughed. "*Did* you two have a nice day out? Buy lots of stuff?"

"Amy bought half the town," Faith said as she sat down by the table and looked at Zoë's paintings. "You must have spent a hundred years in school to do this kind of work."

"Actually, I never went to art school," Zoë said. "Would either of you like something alcoholic to drink? I could make a pitcher of margaritas." When neither Amy nor Faith said anything, Zoë said, "Let me guess, you two angels of middle-class America don't drink."

"Give me the tequila." Amy shook her head at Zoë. "Do you ever say anything *nice*?"

"Not if I can help it," Zoë said as she headed for the kitchen. When she looked in the refrigerator she was glad to see that it was packed with a dozen little carry-out boxes. She'd been sure that they'd go to dinner by themselves and leave her out of it, but they hadn't. She couldn't help feeling betrayed. She and Faith had been at the house first and Amy had arrived later. If sides were going to be taken, shouldn't it be Faith and Zoë against Amy?

As Zoë started squeezing limes, she could almost hear Jeanne asking why it had to always be someone against someone else. Why couldn't they all be on the same team?

Minutes later Zoë had filled a pitcher, salted three glasses, and put it all on a tray. For a moment she paused in front of the window and watched as Faith and Amy looked at the paintings she'd done that day. It was gratifying to see them shake their heads in wonder. Faith had said that Zoë must have spent a lot of time in school learning how to paint. But no, Zoë had woken up one morning with metal staples in her head and no memory of the preceding years of her life. It was when she was handed a ballpoint pen and a pad of paper to write on because her throat was sore, that she'd drawn portraits of all the people around her. The people consisted of the medical staff. No relative and no friend came to see her.

She took the tray outside and set it on the table. Faith moved the watercolors into the house, out of danger of the damp, then returned to pour the drinks.

"It's lovely here," Amy said, looking at the roses hanging over the fence. "I can see why Jeanne sends traumatized patients here."

When Zoë's heavily made-up eyes narrowed on Amy, as though she meant to say something hateful, Faith spoke up. " 'Traumatized' doesn't mean insane."

"I think snooping Jeanne might disagree with you," Zoë said in a sneering tone.

"If you don't like her, why do you go to her?" Amy asked.

"Court ordered." When the others said nothing, Zoë ran her hand through her hair. "Half of this isn't mine. It's extensions. I was in a car wreck and the top of my head was sliced open. The doctors sewed me back together but . . ." She shrugged. "Something happened inside my head. I can't remember part of my life."

"At least you kept your talent."

"I don't think I had it before the accident."

"You don't think? What did your family tell you?" Amy asked.

"My parents are dead. I only have a sister and she hates me."

Faith gave a little grunt. "From my observation, I think all sisters hate each other. Pure jealousy. I think that if one sister is homeless and the other lives in a McMansion on Long Island, if the homeless one has curly hair, the other sister will be jealous and hate her."

Both Amy and Zoë were looking at her in astonishment.

"Just my personal opinion," Faith said, putting her drink up to cover her mouth.

"When I first saw you," Zoë said, "I thought you were the most boring person I'd ever met, but I'm beginning to change my mind."

"Is there a compliment in there?" Faith asked.

"If there was one, I didn't hear it," Amy said, but she was smiling.

"I suggest that we spread dinner out here on the table," Zoë said, "and that Faith entertain us with her life story. I want to hear the part where you were born on the wrong side of the tracks."

Amy looked at Faith with interest. "Is that true?"

"More or less, but I married the son of the richest man in town."

"Is that why you wear a twenty-thousand-dollar watch?" Zoë asked.

Faith put her hand over the watch, then made herself remove it. "Eddie bought this for me five years ago. I told him not to and I wanted to take it back to the store but he'd had it engraved so I couldn't."

"Why are you frowning?" Zoë asked. "Not good memories?"

"From Eddie yes, but his mother threw a fit about the watch. You see, no matter that I went to college and got a degree, no matter that I dedicated fifteen years of my life to caring for her son, to Ruth Wellman I was never anything but poor white trash. The lowest of the low. Scum."

"So tell us," Amy said. "We have nothing else to do except listen."

"There isn't anything to tell. I grew up in a small town, fell in love with the son of the richest family in town, and we got married."

"Big wedding?" Zoë asked.

"Tiny, but nice."

"Was that because of the mothers?" Amy asked quietly.

"Yes and no. Actually, mostly yes. Mrs. Wellman, who was, is, an extremely rich widow, insisted that the bride's family pay for the wedding. My mother was also a widow but her husband, my father, died in debt. My mother worked sixty hours a week just to feed, shelter, and clothe us."

"Yet your mother-in-law made her pay for the wedding," Amy said.

"And I assume this was to keep you from marrying her son," Zoë said.

Faith nodded.

Amy got up and went into the kitchen to get the carry-out food she and Faith had bought that afternoon. She hadn't planned to spend any time with these other women who had been labeled as "trauma victims," but the day spent with Faith had been fun. Faith said she had no people to buy gifts for and that had made Amy give a shiver of horror, but then Faith had asked so many questions about Amy's family that the tension disappeared.

Since Amy tended to stay with people she knew, she didn't often have the opportunity to talk about her family. First, she told Faith about her sons, mentioning how smart they were and how good they were at sports. "I'm sorry, I'm bragging," she said.

"Go ahead. It sounds wonderful. Tell me more."

Amy did most of the talking and Faith helped her choose gifts for both her boys. It was when they sat down to lunch that Faith said that Amy hadn't even mentioned her husband. There was a tone in her voice that suggested she thought all was not well between Amy and her husband.

Amy reached into her handbag and pulled out a little photo album, flipped to a picture, then handed it to Faith.

"My goodness," Faith said, eyes wide. "Does he really look like that or it is just a good photo?"

"He looks better in person," Amy said, then showed the other pictures of her handsome sons.

"They are all as beautiful as movie stars," Faith said, smiling. "One time—"

"What?"

"Oh, nothing," Faith said, looking at her menu.

"No, tell me," Amy encouraged.

"Last night Zoë said some things to me and—"

"Hateful things?

"Of course. She's Zoë," Faith said with a smile that Amy didn't return.

"What happened?"

"Zoë reminded me of some things that happened a long time ago, and now, seeing your husband brought it all back."

Before she could say anything else, the waitress came to take their orders. They both got the lobster salads. When the waitress was gone, Amy leaned toward Faith. "What were you going to say?"

"Nothing important. When I was a kid I was in love with a young man who looked a bit like your husband, except he had dark hair and eyes."

"Really?" Amy said in disbelief.

"Yes, really," Faith said. "But I get the idea your husband comes from a good family, and—"

"Good is how you look at it. Sometimes the wrong people are put into families. My husband has a father and three older brothers who are as primitive as they come. They think tractor pulls are high art. But Stephen is at ease in a tuxedo."

"Tyler was more of a tractor-pull person," Faith said. "He didn't even finish high school. He usually had grease on him from some car he was overhauling, and he rarely ate anything that wasn't wrapped in paper. He really was the most crude, most . . ." Trailing off, she looked down and was silent.

"Were you in love with him?" Amy asked softly.

"With all my heart."

Amy reached across the table and put her hand on Faith's wrist. "So what happened to him?"

Faith laughed and the faraway look in her eyes disappeared. "I don't know. Nothing. Ran away, I guess. Who knows? When you get down to it, you don't actually *marry* the Tylers of the world, now do you?"

"I guess not," Amy said with a sigh. "I was lucky that the man I loved had everything going for him. He's smart and funny and considerate and a hard worker. He's perfect."

As the waitress put their salads in front of them, Faith said, "Come on, there has to be something about him that you don't like. Even if it's a small thing."

"No, nothing," Amy said honestly. "I wanted to throw the pots and pans at him when he told me he wanted me to go on this trip, but I'm coming to think that he was right."

"You aren't going to tell him that, are you?"

"Of course not," Amy said. "*He* may be perfect, but *I* am not."

The two women laughed together and finished their lunches. The rest of the afternoon they spent chatting about their lives, but neither of them told anything revealing.

Now, Amy put the food and plates on a tray and carried them outside. Faith and Zoë were sitting in silence, sipping their drinks, both staring off into nothing.

This is ridiculous, Amy thought. We can't spend our time like this. "Zoë," she said sharply, "go make a big pitcher of iced tea. Faith, help Zoë, then get the knives and forks and napkins and bring them out here." When neither of the women moved, Amy said, "When we get everything out here, Faith is going to tell us a story about a man named Tyler."

"Her husband?" Zoë asked, her voice bored.

"No. Tyler is the blindingly handsome young man who she let slip through her fingers. It's a love that haunts her and pulls her back into time. It is the chain that binds her to the past. It is the love that was to be but never happened."

Both Faith and Zoë were looking at Amy with their mouths open in astonishment.

Go!" Amy said as though she were speaking to her young children. They scurried into the kitchen with the urgency of schoolkids. As Amy set out the food, she smiled. Maybe this time here in Maine wouldn't be so bad after all.

Four

❦

"*Will you two* stop looking at me like I'm the village storyteller," Faith said as she took a sip of her wine. They'd finished dinner, cleared up, and moved inside to the living room. Zoë had opened a bottle of chardonnay, poured glasses full, and they were seated and looking at Faith in expectation. "I really don't have anything to tell." She gave Amy a look that let her know she'd betrayed a confidence and Faith didn't like it. It was one thing to tell something to a normal person, but to Zoë? No, thank you!

"Aren't we supposed to talk about our traumatic lives and do Jeanne's work for her?" Zoë asked.

"All right, then you tell us about you," Faith said.

"Fine," Zoë answered. "I woke up one day in a hospital with most of my body in bandages, and casts on both my legs. I didn't remember what happened to me and I still don't."

"Who visited you in the hospital?" Faith asked, smiling sweetly.

"Jeanne has a big mouth," Zoë said.

"What did I miss?" Amy asked, looking from one to the other.

"All Jeanne said was that an entire town was angry at Zoë. What I want to know is why."

"I have no idea," Zoë said.

"You asked them, didn't you?" Amy said.

"No."

Faith and Amy looked at each other.

"You mean that you have family and friends, they're all angry at you, you don't remember why, but you've never asked them what you did to make them hate you?" Amy asked.

"Strong words," Zoë said. "Hate. Anger. No, I never asked anybody anything. When I didn't remember a big part of my life, the court assigned me to Jeanne. I've been seeing her for over a year. Really boring."

"But what about where you grew up? Do you have parents? Siblings?" Amy asked.

"I have a sister, but she wants nothing to do with me, so I want nothing to do with her. Could we stop this? I'd rather hear Faith's story about love being lost."

"What about a boyfriend?" Amy asked.

"That is another question I don't know. I didn't have one at the high school prom and that's the last thing I remember. But then, there are a whole lot of years that I don't remember. I woke up in a hospital with my head stapled together, and didn't remember anything of the years after my prom."

"Why—?" Amy began, but Zoë gave her such a hard look that she closed her mouth.

"Faith," Zoë said, "you're on. You entertain us while I make a few sketches."

She picked up a big sketch pad and a pencil, drew up her knees, and looked at Amy as though she meant to start drawing her.

Amy jumped up, got her little photo album from her handbag, and handed it to Zoë. "Can you draw from photos?"

"Sure," Zoë said, then her eyes widened as she looked at the pictures. "Is this your family?"

Amy smiled.

"They make Hollywood families look ugly. I'm not sure I can capture such perfection on paper."

"Zoë, I might be able to find some things to like about you after all."

Zoë groaned. "Oh no! Don't say that. My reputation will be ruined. And don't tell Jeanne that. She'll raise her prices and take the credit for making me into a better person."

Amy settled down on the chintz sofa and looked at Faith. "I think you should tell us your story."

"Really," Faith said, "there isn't a story. The love of my life was my husband. Now if you'd like to hear about him I'll tell you, but—"

"I want to hear about the gorgeous hunk that got away," Amy said. "What about you, Zoë?"

"I want to hear about your sex life with this man," she said as she looked at Stephen's photo.

"Hold your breath," Amy said, making the women smile. "Faith?"

"Okay, where do I begin?" she said as she looked down at her wineglass. "Maybe I should start when I got home from college. Ty and I had been buddies all our lives, all through grade school."

"That's like Stephen and me," Amy said. "Even when we were kids we knew that someday we'd get married." She looked at Faith. "Sorry. Go on."

"I bet you had family problems," Zoë said, not looking up from her sketch pad.

"No, not really," Amy began. "Oh, sorry again. Faith, did you have family problems?"

"Did we! I lived alone with my mother who did everything she could to give me the best life possible. She worked long hours at her job, which meant I was unsupervised a lot. I was supposed to stay at home and study, which I did most of the time. I made mostly As in school. I was always well dressed and I never got into trouble. Until high school, that is."

"What about Tyler?" Amy asked.

"Redneck heaven," Faith said. "I never knew how many kids were in his family, and Ty would never tell me. When we were little, I only saw his house once. It was set back in what I thought was a forest. I lived where the houses were close together and we had sidewalks, but Ty's run-down old house was surrounded by trees, old cars, and dogs that were chained to steel stakes."

"What did your mother think of you and Ty being friends?" Amy asked.

"About like you can imagine." Faith gave a sigh. "My mother was a social climber. She used to tell me that she took a step down when she married my father. Then he did a low-class thing like die and leave us with no insurance money. She never forgave him."

"What did she do to support you?" Zoë asked.

"Beauty treatments. She went to the house of any rich woman within fifty miles of our little town and did hair, nails, faces. She plucked eyebrows, gave permanents, did body wraps. I think that half of our problems were caused by my mother spending all her time surrounded by luxury. She'd go to the house of some woman who had a maid to open the door, a cook to make lunch, and my mother felt that that was where she belonged. I don't think there was a day when she didn't tell me that her big mistake was in marrying for love."

"Ah," Zoë said.

"What does that mean?" Faith asked.

"That's why you married the richest man in town."

"I married for love," Faith said stiffly. "My husband, Eddie, was the love of my life. The trauma I experienced came from *losing* him. He was my world."

Amy gave Zoë a hard look, but she didn't look up to see it. "Let's keep this light, shall we?"

"In that case, we should hear *your* story," Zoë said to Amy. "From what I can see, you've never had so much as a hangnail in your life. Married to Mr. Beautiful, two gorgeous kids. I bet you live in a brand-new house with granite countertops in the kitchen. And one of those six-burner stoves. I bet every bedroom has its own bathroom."

Amy didn't answer because Zoë was a hundred percent right. "And I'll wager that you didn't do just one horrible thing to the people in your hometown but hundreds. I bet they just used your accident as a time to break away from you forever."

Zoë laughed. "You're probably right."

"Faith," Amy said, "I apologize for the interruption. Please continue with your story. What happened when you returned from college?"

"I don't know," she said, looking down at her hands. "I mean, I do know, but at the same time I don't know. I've never been able to figure it out. My mother found out where Eddie was going to college so she sent me there too."

Zoë gave Amy an I-told-you-so look.

"It wasn't like that!" Faith said. "Eddie and I were as much friends as Ty and I were. In fact, all through elementary school we were a threesome, even if we were a bit odd. Ty said that we covered all the ground from rich to poor. Whatever we were, it worked in spite of all Eddie's mother could do to break us up. She used to give big birthday parties for Eddie and not invite Ty or me."

Pausing, Faith smiled. "On Eddie's sixth birthday he

was so angry that his mother wouldn't let him invite us, that he sneaked into the kitchen, opened the door for Ty and me, and we stole the birthday cake. Eddie's mother was so upset they had to call the doctor to give her a sedative. While she was down, he slipped out and joined us. We ate so much cake we were sick. After that his mother had the parties at restaurants."

Faith smiled in memory. "But it all changed when we entered high school. Eddie was in the debating society and head of the math club, while Ty had to work after school, and he missed a lot of days because his father often needed him for something or other—we never knew what and Ty never said."

"And what about you?" Amy asked.

"I'm afraid that I sowed a few wild oats. Mostly with Tyler. He had a souped-up convertible and I had red hair. It was a dangerous combination."

Amy looked at Faith and had trouble seeing her like that. Now her hair was pulled tightly back, her dress hanging below her knees, and her spine was bent. She looked as though she'd never done anything even remotely interesting in her entire life.

Faith laughed at Amy's expression. "I was only wild for a while, just the last two years of high school, really. I was sick of being locked inside my house with my mother who never stopped complaining, and, well, I'd learned a bit from all her beauty work."

Zoë looked up from her sketch. "You're telling us that you were a knockout."

"More or less," Faith said. "I was certainly the best-looking thing in *that* town."

"Good for you!" Amy said.

"I calmed down after high school—I had to. I went to the same college as Eddie and that's where we really got to know each other. We were pinned by the second year and we knew we were going to be married. We didn't make it official because we both dreaded telling his mother. She'd already picked out Eddie's bride, a third cousin of his who looked like the horses she loved."

"So you chose Eddie over Ty," Amy said softly.

"Riches over love," Zoë said.

"Actually, I didn't choose. Ty dumped me."

"Okay," Amy said, "now I for sure want to hear every word."

Faith took a moment to consider. It had been a matter of pride to her that she hadn't told Jeanne about her first love affair with her hometown's best-looking dropout. But, like Zoë, Faith hadn't wanted to go to a therapist. She'd been blackmailed into going because of what she'd done at Eddie's funeral. Her mother-in-law had pressed charges and Faith was facing time in the local jail and having a criminal record for the rest of her life. It had taken a lot of effort, but she'd finally worked out a deal with Eddie's mother that if she, Faith, would leave town and get some "help" the charges would be dropped. So Faith rented an apartment in New York, and went to the therapist her mother-in-law told her was the only one she'd accept.

But it hadn't really worked. From the beginning, Faith had connected Jeanne with Eddie's mother—and that meant she had to protect herself at all costs.

"All right," Faith said, "I'll tell you. I think the relevant part of my life started . . ." She counted the years. "It's hard to believe but it was only sixteen years ago. It feels like a hundred. I'd just come home from college and my mother was angry at me because I didn't have a ring on my finger. I was dying to tell her that Eddie and I were as good as engaged, but I knew she'd tell her first client and five minutes after that, it'd be all over town. Eddie needed time to tell his mother, then keep her from dying of a heart attack.

"I was in my bedroom, unpacking my clothes, when Ty shoved the window up and stuck his head inside. For a moment I couldn't get my breath because he was even better looking than I remembered."

Five

SIXTEEN YEARS AGO

"Hey!" Ty said as he shoved the window of Faith's bedroom up and started to climb inside.

"What do you think you're doing?" Faith ran toward him, meaning to push him back out, but he was already inside. She looked out the window to see how many people had seen him enter her bedroom. But the big wisteria vine was still there and still covered the view.

"Not bad," Ty said as he gave her an appraising look when she bent over.

"Stop it!" she said as she straightened up and slammed the window shut. "We're not in the third grade anymore."

"I didn't look at you in that way when we were in the third grade," he said as he turned away and looked at the posters on her bedroom wall. "If I had, I would have been locked up."

"Just cut it out," Faith said, her hands on her hips as she glared at his back.

"Cut what out?" he said in that lazy way he had. It was a way that attracted lots of girls to him, Faith included. For all that she didn't want to, she couldn't help noticing how he'd changed in the three years since they'd last been together. It seemed that every time she'd returned from college, something had kept her from seeing him. During those years, his father had died and she'd heard that most of his siblings had left town. Last summer she'd been told that now only Ty and his mother lived in the old house back in the woods. Faith had meant to visit him, but she hadn't. She knew that he'd stopped by her house and called her a few times, but she'd never called him back. Maybe she hadn't visited him because she knew he'd ask her about her and Eddie and she didn't want to tell him. She could lie to her mother and the town, but Ty would see through her.

"We're not kids anymore and you can't just jump into my bedroom anytime you want," she said sternly.

"Is that so?" He stretched out on her bed. It was covered in the pink, ruffled spread she'd chosen when she was nine years old, and he looked even more masculine on it. He was taller than she remembered and his feet passed the end of the bed. She didn't mean to, but she couldn't help comparing him to Eddie. Whereas Eddie was blond and blue-eyed, with a look of innocence and sweetness about him, Ty was dark and lean and . . . And sexy, she thought. It was as though her childhood bedroom had been invaded by something that children should know nothing about.

What Faith wanted to do was lie down on the bed beside him and snuggle against him. Could he still kiss as well as he used to? He had been her first lover and their last two years of high school had been passionate. She could still feel the leather of his car seats on the back of her bare thighs.

"So?" he asked. "What do you think? You're looking at me awfully hard."

"I was wondering how you could presume so much after all this time."

"Right," he said. "And that's what I think when I see you too. You look good. You look like you have some muscle on you."

"Sports," she said. "At college."

She'd meant the word as a put-down, but Ty just smiled. He was wearing jeans and a black T-shirt that showed off his muscles, but she wasn't going to comment on it.

"I think you should leave," she said as primly as she could manage.

"And I think you should take off that fancy dress, put on some Levi's, and go with me."

"Where to?"

He shrugged, a gesture that was very familiar to her. "Just for a drive. I spent the weekend tuning up the old convertible and it's outside. Wouldn't you like to ride in it with me, with your hair streaming out the back? What did you do to your hair anyway? Is it still there?"

"It's here," she said, putting her hand up. "It's just that it's better to pull it back. It's more tidy that way."

"And who told you that? Edward?" As he sat up, he picked up the photo on the bedside table. It was of the three of them as children, their arms around each other, happy. They were all three filthy and laughing as they held up strings of fish they'd caught that day.

Back then, Faith had seen only the joy of that day, but now she remembered the grown-up part of it. They'd given the fish to Ty because they knew his big family always needed food. Eddie's mother had punished her son for getting dirty and smelly; he'd not been allowed out of the house for two weeks. Faith's mother had cried at the sight of her dirty daughter and lectured her for two hours about being "a lady."

Faith stepped toward Ty and took the photo out of his hand. "I think you should leave."

Before she could step back, his arms went around her waist and he put his head against her belly. "I've missed you," he said softly. "Every minute of these years, I've missed you. I thought I'd die when you came back and wouldn't see me. I didn't think I'd make it until you left that damned school and came home to me."

She knew she should push him away, but she couldn't. Her hand came up and touched his hair. It was thick and full and soft and it reminded her of the warm summer days they'd spent together. She remembered every night that she'd buried her face in his hair and smelled of it, inhaling deeply, letting the scent soak into her.

He looked up at her. "Go with me to the lake. Just for the afternoon. I've got a cooler full of food in the car."

"I . . ." she began. She knew that she had a lot to do. Eddie had things he wanted her to do with him, and her mother had scheduled her for half a dozen events around town, but at the moment she couldn't seem to remember what any of them were. "All right," she heard herself saying.

Ty stood up, his body moving up the front of her. "Good. Get dressed. I'll see you outside in five minutes. You take six and I'll come in after you." With that, he planted a quick, sweet kiss on her lips, then opened the window and climbed out.

For a full minute, Faith stood there looking at the window in confusion. She'd just finished four years at a Northern college where she'd been Edward Wellman's girlfriend and she'd worked hard to be worthy of his attention, his friends, and his name.

Her freshman year had been difficult. She'd attended her first classes wearing a skirt so short it was almost cheeky. Her hair was in fat curls down about her shoulders, and she had on a tank top that fit like skin. As she'd strode across campus, young men had patted their hearts and dramatically fallen to the ground near her feet. She'd laughed at them and enjoyed every second of it.

It was when the girls saw her that she encountered the sneers. When one girl with her straight brown hair pulled back with a headband made a remark about "Southern hicks," Faith realized how they were seeing her. She understood that in her rebellion against her mother and Eddie's, she'd gone too far the other way.

The next day she'd had her hair cut, and she went to class wearing what the other girls wore: jeans and a modest top. It had taken the rest of the year to redo her image, but she did it by studying harder than anyone else. Her high grades made her sought after as study help in the classes. When she graduated with an honors degree in English lit, she was well respected by both her teachers and her peers.

Best of all, she was sure she'd changed herself so much that Eddie's mother would accept her. And to achieve this approval, she knew it was imperative to stay away from Ty when she was home. She could *not* be seen riding around town in a convertible with one of the Parks kids. What Faith wanted most in life was to be seen as a demure young woman who had a right to be Eddie Wellman's wife.

But right now her girlish bedroom was filled with the scent and raw sexuality of Ty, and it was as though the four years of college and behaving herself had never happened. Without conscious thought, she pulled the pins from her hair, then the tight band, and let it loose. Her hair was thick and a natural dark auburn and she knew that if she let it hang loose it made men think of sex—or that's what Ty used to tell her when she'd lie in his arms and look at the stars.

What was it about bad boys? she asked herself as she nearly ripped off her dress and pulled on a pair of jeans that she hadn't worn in two years. She and Eddie had agreed that they'd wait until they were married before they went to bed together. There was a small group of kids on campus who had signed pledges to do the same thing. They hadn't done that—"No one's business but our own," Eddie said—and they'd done a lot of heavy petting, but they hadn't gone "all the way."

Faith was sure Eddie knew that she and Ty had been lovers, but he never mentioned it and she certainly didn't either.

When Faith was dressed, she started to open the door to her bedroom, but when she heard her mother in the kitchen, before she knew what she was doing, she was climbing out her bedroom window. As she did so she felt young again—which was absurd as she was hardly over twenty. But sneaking out to be with Ty—as she'd done so many times before—made her feel sixteen.

She heard the deep rumble of Ty's car before she saw it and she knew he'd parked around the corner where Faith's mother couldn't see him. Her mother had always disliked Ty. Not because he wasn't polite and respectful and had mowed their lawn for free since he was eleven, but because of his family. "Born from nothing, will always be nothing," was her pronouncement.

Faith felt her long hair bouncing around her shoulders as she ran, and she knew that the neighbors were watching. She also knew that they'd hurry to tell her mother, but she didn't care. As she ran she felt the four years of being in a straitjacket falling away from her.

"Baby, you look great!" Ty said as she got into the car beside him. Then, as he always had done, he put his hand to the back of her head and kissed her on the lips. They both laughed together and Ty revved the engine, put it in gear, and laid a strip of rubber as he peeled away from the curb.

Faith threw back her head and laughed, exhilarated at the feeling of freedom. She was free to laugh, to shout, to go and do and see—all the things she'd kept bottled inside her at school.

"Did you learn anything in college?" Ty asked as he turned onto the highway and shifted into third.

"Everything. Ask me about Shakespeare or Wordsworth. Ask me about Hawthorne."

"No, thanks," Ty said, turning to look at her. "You look better than when you left. Is that possible?"

"If my looks hadn't got me in such trouble at school I'd call you a liar."

"What does that mean?"

"It was a very conservative college," Faith said, her eyes closed, feeling the wind on her face. "Big-busted redheads aren't what they want to see."

"I do," Ty said as he leered at her.

They laughed together.

She opened her eyes in time to see him turn off the highway. "This isn't the way to the lake. Unless they've moved it while I was away."

"They had enough time," Ty said, letting her know how very long she'd been gone. "I want to show you something."

He drove down an old road that had grass growing

through the pavement, and he had to slow down to a crawl to keep from tearing out the underside of his car.

"So what do you want to show me?" she asked. "Some isolated place that no one else has ever seen?" She wiggled her eyebrows at him.

"Can't wait for me, can you, baby?"

Some part of Faith was sane and knew that now was the moment when she should tell him about her and Eddie, but she didn't say anything. She felt better than she had in years and she couldn't bear to ruin it. She knew Ty well and if she told him she was going to marry Eddie, he'd take her back to her house and leave her—and she'd probably never see him again. One time she'd said that he was ninety percent pride. He'd replied that that was because he didn't have much else in life.

The road they were on cut through a field that had once had dairy cows but was now full of weeds. The man who used to own the land died when Faith was just a girl and his heirs lived in the East so no one had done anything with it in years.

Ty pulled off the road into the graveled area in front of an old brick building that had three open bays. At one end was a falling-down old office. It had once been an automobile repair shop, but now weeds had broken the concrete in front of the buildings. There was nothing around them and the wind whistled through the buildings and the trees. It was a lonely, desolate place.

She watched Ty get out of the car and look about with an expression on his face that she'd never seen before. She wanted to leave, but she got out and went to stand beside him.

"Why did you bring me here?"

"You remember this place?"

"Sure," she said, rubbing her arms. It was a hot day but getting out of the wind was giving her goose bumps. "I don't like it here."

He put his arm around her shoulders and drew her to him, but he didn't take his eyes off the derelict old building. "That's because you don't know what it is."

"Something that's waiting to collapse?"

Smiling, he tightened his grip on her for a moment, then let her go and walked to the building. He ran his hand down the side of it in a caressing, loving way. "It's mine."

She blinked at him. "Yours? Don't tell me you bought this awful old spot?" She wanted to ask him where he got the money, but she didn't.

"You remember old man Nelson I used to work for?"

"How could I forget? You missed a hundred weekends with Eddie and me because you were his slave."

"Yeah, well, it paid off."

"He gave you this?" She looked at him as though to say, What was second prize?

"*Gave* me?" Ty said. "You have to be kidding. That man never gave anything to anyone. His whole family despised him, and when he died he left them nothing. He gave everything he had to the church. He said they deserved the money more than his lazy kids did."

"Nice man."

"No, not a nice man, but what no one knew is that on his deathbed he gave *me* something."

"In gratitude for all the years you gave to him? I remember seeing you on Sunday morning so tired you couldn't stand up because you'd been digging or doing something for him until ten at night—and this was when you were just twelve years old."

Ty shrugged. "He paid me for every hour and I always needed the money." He was silent for a moment, still looking at the old buildings with love.

"So?" she said. "What did he give you?"

"Information."

She saw that he was teasing her, drawing out what he wanted to say to make her beg him to tell her. It was a game they'd played all their lives. Ty used to make her and Eddie ask him about something until they were ready to pummel him.

"I give up!" she said. "What did that awful old man tell you?"

"That the state is planning to put a road through here."

"Here?" Faith asked, looking about the place.

"They're going to put in a major highway that will link the two Interstates."

As she thought about it, she knew it made sense. All her life she'd heard adults complain about having to drive around the lake and across side roads to get to the big highway. There had always been a rumor that the state was going to put in a new road but . . . "I've always heard that," Faith said. "What he told you wasn't news."

"Yeah, but old man Nelson had a date and a map. It'll start next year, and I own a lot of the land where they're going to put the road. The contracts have been signed."

She could no longer contain her surprise. "You bought land?" she blurted. "How?"

"With you and Ed gone, I had nothing to do but work. And with Dad and my leaching brothers gone, it didn't cost much to support Mom and me, so I saved what I could and put it in land."

She watched him shrug as though to say that it was nothing, but she could almost see all that he'd done these last four years. He must have worked without stop on weekends, holidays, and into the night.

She thought about what he'd done and wondered why he'd given up so much of his life in the pursuit of money—but she knew why. He'd done it for her. She couldn't help glancing at his jeans. If she knew anything about him, she was sure that in his pocket was a diamond ring. An engagement ring. It wouldn't matter to Ty that they hadn't seen each other for years. Nor would it matter that she'd been dating other men, and she was sure that he'd been out with lots of women in that time. Ty had made up his mind about the two of them long ago and he was sticking with it.

Part of her thought that if she had any brain at all, she'd tell him about her and Eddie right now. But she didn't do that. Instead, she smiled. "Okay, so show me and tell me everything. If you leave anything out, I'm going to start quoting poetry."

She saw the tension leave his body. He grabbed her about the waist, lifted her up and twirled her about. "You're still my girl!" he said. "You always have been and always will be. Come on!" He put her down, then grabbed her hand and began to pull her through waist-high weeds toward a dilapidated old house that was a quarter of a mile from the garages.

It was a two-story farmhouse, tall and big and in need of major repairs. He pulled her up on the porch as she picked briars off her shirt. "Watch that board," he said when she stepped to the side of the door.

He didn't need a key as the door was swollen shut, but he knew how to open it by pulling up on the door-knob, then shoving hard. He had to hit the door with his shoulder three times before it opened, and when it did the doorknob stayed in his hand. "Have to fix that," he mumbled as he went in ahead of her. She heard some rustling of feathers—birds living in the house—then he came back and held out his hand to her.

Inside, the house was dirty and some kids had spray-painted their names on the walls. Faith recognized the names of kids they'd gone to school with. She nodded toward one. "I could believe he'd spend his spare time vandalizing an old house."

Ty ducked his head when she saw his name painted on a wall. Grinning, he led her through the house.

Faith looked at the house as an adult, thinking about

how one could live here. It had large rooms with high ceilings and she thought that cool breezes would flow through it. There were beautiful ceiling moldings and, on one wall, under the paint, was what looked to be a splendid fireplace. In its day, it must have been grand.

He led her upstairs to see four bedrooms and a bathroom. "It could be remodeled up here to have more bathrooms," he said, holding her hand and leading her from one dirty room to another. Layers of wallpaper were peeling off the walls and she could see the different patterns going back from the 1950s to, probably, before the Civil War.

"You aren't thinking of living here," she said. "If that highway is built it would be horrible."

"No," he said slowly. "Not here."

She waited for him to say more, but he didn't. He led her to the window of the master bedroom and showed her where the new highway was to go. It was only a few feet outside the house.

She thought about what he'd said. Not *here,* he'd said. "You're thinking about moving this house to another location, aren't you?"

Ty gave his shrug that she knew meant he didn't want to tell something for fear of being ridiculed. His pride again. "You like the house?"

Faith drew in a breath. Again, she knew that he was planning for a life with her. This house could be hers, and she knew that Ty had the knowledge and experience to remodel it. "Yes, I like it," she said honestly.

He started to take her in his arms then, but she pulled back. "Ty, I think there's something I should tell you."

He dropped his arms and took a few steps away. "You mean that you're planning to marry Eddie?"

"How do you—?" she began, then took a breath. "You've talked to him, haven't you?"

"No," Ty said. "I haven't talked to him any more than I've talked to you over the last four years. You two went off to college and dropped me, remember?"

"It wasn't like that," Faith said, but she could feel her face turning red.

"Yeah, it was just like that and I don't blame you a bit. You two needed to get away from here, get away from Eddie's mother. And you needed to get away from your mother."

Faith felt her spine stiffen. "It's not like you didn't have some relatives that *you* needed to get away from."

"Nah," he said. "They never had any control over me. I always saw what they were, what we were, that is. I know how the town looked at us. I was always separate from them, but you and Eddie . . ." He trailed off and shook his head as though in disbelief. "You two were controlled. You two were ruled by your mothers."

"I was not! The last two years of high school I was everything my mother didn't want me to be. Remember how I ran around with *you* all the time?" As soon as she said it, she wished she hadn't. It sounded as though Ty were the lowest of the low and she'd degraded herself by dating him. "I didn't mean it like that."

Ty grinned. "I know you didn't. Your mother tried to make you into a snob, but she couldn't. Although Eddie almost made you into a nun. When I first saw you yesterday, I thought I might as well set a torch to this house. I thought he'd overcome you and beaten you down into a replica of his mother."

"He did no such thing!" Faith said, but she couldn't help smiling. "So what made you think he didn't succeed?"

"When you first got back, you didn't see me, but I saw you. You were with Eddie and your mother, and so prim and proper that I hardly recognized you. At first I thought maybe you'd cut your hair, but then I saw you'd just tied it back. Anyway, you were standing outside with them and I told myself to go home, that you were a lost cause. But then a little yellow convertible drove by and I thought you were going to melt right there on the street. It was only for a second, but I saw the lust in your eyes."

"Hardly lust," she said as she remembered seeing the car. A girl was driving it. She was wearing a sleeveless blouse and her hair was flowing out behind her. Faith had been wearing what felt like twenty pounds of clothes and sweat was running down her back and under her bra. When she saw the girl in the car she'd envied her so much she'd wanted to run after her and jump in the passenger seat.

"Okay, so it was lust," she said, smiling again. "It was hot and the girl looked cool. But really, Ty, I do have an unspoken arrangement with Eddie. He and I have talked about marriage for two years now."

"But he ain't told Mommy yet, has he?"

"No," Faith said, "but you know what she's like."

"She's a bully and people have to stand up to her. Eddie and you could never make her back down."

"But I guess you could."

"I can and I have," he said matter-of-factly.

Faith turned away for a moment but she knew what he was talking about. Yes, Ty had stood up to Mrs. Wellman many times when they were growing up. Eddie and Faith were scared of her, but Ty never was. She remembered one time when he'd stood in her kitchen and looked her in the eye while she told him what he'd heard so many times before: that he was nothing and would never be anything. Ty calmly said how it was easier to put a camel through the eye of a needle than for a rich man to get into heaven. Mrs. Wellman grabbed a broom and chased Ty out of the house. Later, Eddie and Faith had sat by the lake with him and marveled at his audacity. Ty said, "What's a broom? It's when a person runs after you with a knife that you have to worry." Eddie and Faith had looked at each other with wide eyes, but they'd asked no questions. Besides, they knew that Ty wouldn't answer them.

"Okay, so I'm caught on every count," Faith said. "I'm terrified of Eddie's mother, only slightly less afraid of my own mother, and I like to ride in convertibles. What other onerous character flaws do I have?"

"Onerous, heh?" Ty said.

"It means—"

"I know what the word means," he said. "Or I can guess. You know, Faith, you don't have to have a college education to be worth something in the world."

"Of course not," she said quickly, but she could feel her face again turning red.

"Quit looking like you have pity for me," he said as he started downstairs. "Ready to go to the lake?"

"Actually, I've been gone for quite a while already, and I didn't leave a note for my mother, so maybe I should go home."

"Okay," he said quickly. "Whatever you want."

He went to the front door and waited for her to leave ahead of him. She stood on the porch for a minute while Ty wrestled with getting the door closed, and took a deep breath of the air. She had been cooped up inside for four long years, her nose always in a book. It seemed that she hadn't been out of sight of concrete in that entire time. When she'd returned home, her mother had always had a long list of things for her to do. The last two summers Faith had gone with her mother to do beauty treatments. She'd hated every minute of it-especially giving pedicures.

"Maybe . . ." she began.

"Yes?" Ty asked, looking at her, his handsome face showing nothing.

"Well, since we're so close to the lake and it is lunchtime, and since I am starving . . ."

"Go on," Ty said.

"You can be a real jerk at times, you know that? So what did you bring for lunch? If it's fried chitlins, I'm leaving now even if I have to walk back."

"Corn pone," he said seriously. "Possum. All the things I grew up on."

"Then it'll be McDonald's," she said, turning away from him.

"Come on. I'll race you back to the car." He took off running, Faith right behind him.

When they got to the car, she was drenched in sweat, but Ty looked as cool as if he'd just stepped out of the shower.

"Out of practice, aren't you?"

"Completely. I haven't raced a boy back to the car since I was . . . What? Ten?"

"I knew you'd missed me!" Ty said, smiling as he turned the ignition in the car.

As he pulled out, he stopped so she could see the house silhouetted against the bright blue sky. With some work, it could be a beauty. When she turned to look at Ty, he was smiling in a way that made her think that he knew she was a done deal. As he turned onto the road, she thought that she had to emphasize to him that she was going to marry Eddie and nothing would change that.

Ty drove them to the lake and she knew before he got there where he was going. It was "their" place. It was the place they'd gone with Eddie to catch fish, and later it was the place she and Ty went to make love.

She stood by the lake and looked out at the water as Ty unpacked the car. She made no effort to help him. In a way, it was as though she'd never been away from this tiny town. Today it felt as if all her time at college hadn't happened. If it weren't for the books that were rattling around in her head and for the many thousands she owed in student loans, she might think she'd never left.

Turning, she watched Ty spread the old blanket on the ground under the enormous willow tree that they had considered theirs. Like them, the tree had grown and aged. She could still see the place where they'd tried to carve their initials with the little penknife that Ty always carried. The blanket he was spreading was the same one that they'd made love on the first time.

He glanced up at her, and as he often did, he read her mind. "Don't worry, it's been washed."

Smiling, she sat down on the edge of it while he emptied the cooler and put out the food. There were tuna salad sandwiches, cut-up fruit, and homemade cookies.

"You didn't make this, so who did?"

"Mom."

Faith looked at him with wide eyes. "Ah, the mother you rarely mention. You know, I don't think I've seen your mother more than a dozen times in my life." She was teasing, but she was serious also.

"She was there," Ty said, his face solemn. "She and I've always been friends. She said we got along because I was like her and not like my dad."

He stretched out on the blanket on the other side of the food and looked out at the lake.

"Is it true that all your family is gone?" she asked quietly as she stretched out across from him.

"My brothers are." He picked up a sandwich half and glanced at her. "It was the oddest thing. After my dad died my three oldest brothers got job offers in Alaska."

"In . . . ?" she began, then grinned. "I see. That is indeed a coincidence. Imagine that. Three offers for three brothers."

"It was extraordinary, wasn't it?"

She picked up a sandwich. "Only three brothers? What about the rest of them?"

"They all decided to try their luck in Alaska, so they all went. I gave them my double-cab truck and off they drove."

"But I guess they write often."

"Every week. And they call Mom and me every Sunday evening."

Faith laughed. "You're terrible!"

He smiled at her in agreement as he reached for another sandwich.

Faith opened the plastic container of fruit salad. "So who cut this up? Your mother?"

Ty nodded. "I think you should spend some time with her. She's a nice woman."

For a moment her mouth hung open in shock. Was he inviting her to his home? In all her life she'd never been to his house. She'd seen his father and his brothers around town, but she, like everyone else, gave them a wide berth. "Okay," she said at last. "I'd love to."

Ty said nothing as he turned to look at the lake. But she knew he was pleased. "So tell me about that college you went to," he said.

An hour later, they had eaten every bite of food and cleared it all away. They were lying on the blanket, their hands behind their heads, and looking up into the willow tree.

"How about a swim?" Ty asked.

"No suit," Faith said, then before he could speak, she said, "and I don't do skinny-dipping."

Ty rolled to his feet and went to the car. He returned with a canvas bag and tossed it to her. "See if you can find anything in there."

She unzipped the case to see four swimsuits in different sizes. One was a tiny bikini, but the other three were one-piece. One looked old and too big, but a red one was her size. "If I asked you where these came from, would you tell me?"

"What do you think?"

"I think I don't want to know." She picked up the red suit and went into a little grove of trees to put it on. When she emerged, she had the pleasure of seeing Ty's face show what he thought of her in a swimsuit. In college she'd found out that her tomboy childhood had helped for the required sports courses. By her senior year, she'd earned a minor in physical education. All the exercise had toned her body and she knew she looked good.

Ty had on a pair of trunks and was waiting for her, but when he saw her in the swimsuit, his eyes widened. "Your legs," he managed to choke out.

"What about them?" she asked innocently. She'd been told many times that she had the long, lean legs of a dancer. "Too fat?" she asked facetiously as she turned around. "Too thin? Too long?"

Ty recovered himself enough to shake his head at her. "I bet you gave those Yankees a hard time."

"Actually, I did what I could to become one of them."

"A lost cause if I ever heard one," he said as he held out his hand to her, and they ran into the lake.

The water was just as cool and as calm as she remembered it from childhood. But even better, Ty was just as playful and fun. He swam underwater and chased her. She climbed on his shoulders and dove off. They had a major splashing match that Ty won easily. When they saw a motorboat approaching and it was a family with four young children, Ty stood on the bottom just so his head was under, while Faith climbed on his shoulders and stood there and waved to the wide-eyed, pointing children. Faith looked to be standing on top of the water.

"You nearly drowned me," Ty said when the boat had passed and she let him up.

"You never could hold your breath for very long," she said, splashing him as she swam out into the middle of the big lake. Ty was right behind her.

When she got to the middle, she turned and treaded

water as she waited for him to catch up with her. When they were kids, Ty had always been the strong one, but Faith had been a natural swimmer and, in water, she'd won every race. When Ty reached her, they both turned to look back at the shore and she half expected to see Eddie standing there. When they were kids, she and Ty often swam far out into the lake, then they'd turn and look back at Eddie and wave. Whenever she and Ty got too rowdy or too energetic, Eddie always stayed behind. He'd lie on the blanket, a book in his hand, as Faith and Ty tumbled over each other in the water like a couple of dolphins.

"I miss him too," Ty said, treading water beside her. "I didn't see him any more than I saw you in the last years. You two left town for college and you left everything, including me, behind."

She looked at him. "Are those tears of self-pity I see?"

"Pity, but not for me. I feel sorry for ol' Ed when you marry me and not him. Think he'll be my best man?"

The idea was so preposterous that Faith splashed him with water. "Marry you?" she said. "Of course I won't marry you. How can I live in a shack in the woods?" She regretted the words the second she spoke them, and when she saw Ty's face, she was almost frightened. Turning, she started to swim back to shore, but he caught her arm and pulled her to him.

"I'm not the scum you've been made to think I am." His face was close to hers, their bodies together. "Just because you spent a lot of time with snobs doesn't change who *you* are."

She struggled against him, but it was a halfhearted attempt to be released. His body was so familiar to her, and she'd had long years of frustration with no relief.

He held her to him and when he put his lips to hers, she hugged him back. His kiss was long and hard. She clung to him and it was as if the last years hadn't happened. She was once again seventeen years old and she and Ty were alone and about to make love.

They forgot about treading water and began to sink down into the water. They were holding each other, their bodies close, legs wrapped around each other, their arms entwined, their lips together.

It was Ty who saw the bottom of the motorboat that was fast approaching them. If they stayed where they were, the propeller would cut through both of them. Ty kicked out, and, still holding Faith, he dragged her down deeper into the water.

She didn't see the boat and since she could no longer hold her breath, she began to fight him. She wanted to go to the surface and breathe, but Ty was pulling her down. It went through her mind that if he couldn't have her he was going to make sure that no one else did. He intended it to be a murder-suicide, Faith thought as she tried to push away from him, but he held her tight. She hit his chest with her fists, kicked against him. Her nails clawed at his neck and she felt his skin tear. But Ty wouldn't let go of her. His arms around her were a steel grip as he kept going down.

When they were nearly at the bottom of the lake and Faith was about to pass out from lack of oxygen, she saw the bottom of the boat go over their heads. It was a big boat and sat deeply in the water. If Ty hadn't moved them, they'd be dead now.

When he saw that she knew what he was doing, he let her go and at last she went up. When she hit the surface, she took air into her burning lungs. She didn't know how long they'd been under, but she was sure it was the longest time she'd ever held her breath.

Two seconds later, Ty came up beside her. He gave her one hard look, then he swam to shore, Faith behind him.

He grabbed towels from the trunk of his car and, without looking at her, tossed her one.

"I'm sorry," she said to his back as he dried himself off. "Ty, look at me. I'm sorry that I fought you. I thought—"

He turned to her, his face showing his rage. "Yeah? Exactly what did you think? That I was trying to kill you?" He put his hand to his neck and it came away bloody from the scratches she'd made.

When she didn't say anything, he looked at her again. "By all of heaven," he said softly, "you thought that if I couldn't have you nobody would, so I was killing the two of us."

It was exactly what she'd thought and her face turned the color of her hair. "No, of course I didn't think that," she whispered.

"Like hell you didn't," he said as he tossed his wet towel in the back of the car, then pulled his jeans on over his wet trunks. "So you and Eddie went away to some ritzy college way up North and you come back here to look down on us in the South. Never mind that you and I practically lived in each other's pockets all our lives. Never mind that you and I used to screw like rabbits. Now you've elevated yourself—and, yes, I do know what that word means—and you think you're better than us hillbillies."

He paused for a moment, then looked back at her. "You know something, Faith, I was wrong about you. You *have* changed. You're selling your entire future. But for what? To live with a guy who you think will please your mother? Do you think that if you marry rich Eddie that you'll rise up into another class of people?" He didn't wait for her to answer or explain. "But you know what you're going to get, Faith? You're going to marry Eddie's mother. *She* rules him. Always has, always will. And you will *always* see yourself through *her* eyes. And that means that no matter what you achieve in life you'll never be good enough."

He opened the car door, got in and sat there, staring straight ahead, saying nothing. Faith quickly pulled her clothes on over the wet suit, picked the blanket off the ground, and got into the passenger side of the car.

Ty didn't look at her as he grabbed the blanket and threw it out of the car onto the ground. "I never want to see that thing again. Too many bad memories." He started the car and they drove home in silence.

Six

"What happened after that?" Amy asked when Faith didn't say anything more. "You can't leave us dangling. I know you married Eddie, but what happened to Tyler?"

"I don't know," Faith said, finishing her glass of wine and pouring herself another one. "I honestly don't know what happened."

For a moment, Amy and Zoë were quiet.

"What did you do after the fight?" Zoë asked.

"Ty let me off at my house and I went inside. My mother was waiting for me with her sharp tongue to bawl me out. She said I was no better than a street-walker, and that I looked like one with my wet clothes and my hair in a tangle. But for once in my life I didn't defend myself. I went to my room, changed my clothes, and went to bed. I was so depressed I think I would have stayed there for the rest of my life if Eddie hadn't come to rescue me the next day. My mother was so glad to see him that she let him into my bedroom."

⚜

"Go away," *Faith* said, pulling the covers over her head. "I don't want to see anyone."

"I'm not anyone," Eddie said as he gently pulled at the covers.

But Faith kept her face covered. "Leave me alone. I look horrible."

"Like I've never seen you look bad," he said. "I've seen you with mud all over you. And what about the time you and Ty rolled in the poison ivy? You were more than ugly then."

"Don't mention his name to me."

"Ah," Eddie said as he sat down on a pink-upholstered chair across from her. "Tyler. I thought as much." His voice lost its humor and became dull, dispirited. "So what happened between you two this time?"

Faith pushed the covers away, sat up in bed, looked at Eddie and almost smiled. He was pleasingly familiar to her and he fit well in her childish room. She had an idea of what he'd look like when he was an old man. He'd be bald, of course, because his father had been, and his mother's hair was quite thin in places. And he'd have a little paunch and he'd wear glasses.

"Why are you looking at me like that?"

"I was just imagining you as an old man."

Eddie didn't smile like she thought he would. "I want to know what happened between you and Tyler."

"The same ol' thing," she said, pushing her hair out of her eyes. She hadn't taken a shower since she'd been out with Ty the day before and she could smell the lake water on her body. Her hair was frizzy and greasy at the same time.

"Meaning that you two got along perfectly until one of you said something that the other took the wrong way, then you started fighting."

"More or less," Faith said, not wanting to look in his eyes. She couldn't tell him the circumstances of the fight because that would involve telling Eddie about the underwater kiss.

He got up, went to the window, and looked out. "I thought that it was all over with him," he said softly. "I thought that the years you and I spent together would have wiped Ty out of your mind. But I can see that it didn't."

"Nothing was wiped out of my mind except that I can't be around Ty for very long at a time."

Eddie looked back at her, his face in an unpleasant scowl. "I seem to remember when you two spent a lot of time together."

Faith looked away and tried to keep her face from turning red. After a moment she looked back at him. "All right, so we did, but I didn't stay here with him, did I? I left with you."

"Only because your mother filled out your college

application and paid someone to write your entrance essay for you."

"Okay, so maybe I was reluctant to go to a college a thousand miles away from everyone I knew."

"Away from Ty. He's the only one here who matters to you. You would have applied to go to school on the moon to get away from your mother."

Faith ran her hands over her eyes. "You're not making this any easier for me. It's true that back then I didn't want to leave Ty, but I did want to get an education so I wouldn't be stuck in a house changing diapers for the next twenty years."

"And for me."

"What?" she asked. "Oh right. I wanted to go to be near you. Eddie, you have always been my friend as much as Ty has."

"Yes, I have, but certainly not in the same way as he has."

At that Faith narrowed her eyes at him. "If you're referring to sex, that was *not* my fault." In her third year at school, when she and Eddie were talking about marriage as if they'd already said their vows, one night when her roommate was away, Faith had planned a candlelit dinner for the two of them. Her idea was that he'd spend the night with her.

But it hadn't happened. Eddie had walked in, taken one look at the scene, and his back had become rigid. Throughout the meal he'd looked like a soldier at attention. He wouldn't touch the wine Faith served and as soon as he'd eaten he practically ran from the room. Faith had been so hurt that she couldn't bear to look at him for nearly two weeks.

During those weeks, Eddie had drowned her room in flowers, but she still couldn't look at him. When it started on the third week, he'd caught her by the arm as she was walking across a remote area of campus, and he'd made her sit and talk with him. That's when he told her that he wanted them to save themselves for their wedding night, then he'd given her a three-carat diamond ring. Oddly, he hadn't said the words "Will you marry me?" But Faith assumed that's what the ring meant. As she started to slip the ring on her left hand, Eddie said he wanted her to wear it on a chain around her neck—he'd even bought her a chain. He didn't have to say that he feared that if she were seen wearing the ring, someone would tell his mother.

In spite of the secrecy, the beautiful ring had been enough to make Faith forgive him, but there had been several times when she'd mentioned the way he'd turned down her invitation for intimacy. No matter that he'd worked to make it right, it still stung.

"Yes, it's all my fault," Eddie said, his eyes blazing. "I'm not like Ty, with his great good looks, his flashy cars, and his ease with women. I've never been like him, but I always thought that you knew me well enough to know that. And I thought things were decided between us."

Faith flung back the covers—she was fully dressed in

sweatpants and a T-shirt—and went to the dresser to pick up her hairbrush. "By 'decided,' do you mean our engagement? Do you mean, have I picked out my dress yet?" Before he could speak, she turned on him. "Look, Eddie, I don't know what's going on with me right now. I thought my life was settled, but I'm not sure it is."

"What are you saying?" There was a note of panic in his voice. "You aren't calling off the wedding, are you?"

Faith put her hands to her temples. "Sometimes I feel like I'm in a one-act surrealistic play." She looked at him. "Eddie, I know you gave me a ring and I've worn it around my neck for nearly two years, and I know that you and I talk about marriage as if we did the deed years ago. But the truth is that you never officially asked me to marry you and I never accepted."

When she started to speak, she put up her hand. "No, just listen to me. I need some time before I decide what to do with my life."

"Damn him!" Eddie said under his breath. His fists were clenched at his sides.

"Wait a minute! I thought Ty was your friend as well as mine."

"Not when it comes to love," Eddie said, his blue eyes cold and hard.

When Faith looked at him, she took a step back. Eddie's eyes were as angry and as hate-filled as his mother's.

Faith opened the little enameled box on top of her dresser and took out Eddie's ring on the chain. "I think you should keep this until things between us are more certain," she said quietly.

"Faith, you can't let one afternoon with Ty change your entire future."

"How do you know how much time I spent with him?"

"Do you think you can do anything in this town without everyone knowing?" He stepped toward her. "You and I are engaged, but you went out with another man."

"We will only be engaged when you tell your mother and we toast with champagne at your house."

Eddie stayed where he was and said nothing.

Faith gave him a smile, then dropped the ring into his shirt pocket. "Let's give this some time, shall we? When you're ready to go public with us, then I'll be ready to listen. But for now, I think we should . . ." She wasn't sure what to say.

"We should what? Just be friends? Is that what you want to tell me but can't make yourself say? We've spent the last four years together, but you blow me off after you spend just a few hours with your ex-lover? Is that what I'm supposed to understand?"

"Eddie, I really don't like your tone."

"And I don't like what you're doing with my life. We had it all planned. But now you're throwing it away." He took a deep breath and calmed his anger. "Faith," he said in the voice of a man giving advice to a child, "you're one of the smartest women I've ever met and right now you need to think about what you're doing. You can't throw *me* away for someone like Tyler Parks."

"What does that mean? That you think you're a higher class than he is?"

"Don't be absurd. But I am thinking of practical matters. If you marry Tyler, where will you live? In that shack of his out in the woods? Will you get pregnant on your wedding night and spend your pregnancy working at the local Burger King?"

"For your information, Mr. Edward Wellman, while you and I have been at college having a good time, Ty has been here earning money. Not only that, but he's bought me a house."

"A house?" Eddie said, his voice low, his eyes wide. "What kind of house?"

"That big old farmhouse just past the Carsons' place."

Eddie frowned for a moment as he thought. When he remembered the house, his frown deepened.

His expression made Faith smile. She didn't want to betray Ty's confidence and tell about the new highway, but it was nice to see that Eddie knew the house and knew that it wasn't just a "shack in the woods."

Eddie recovered himself. "What has Ty been doing to earn money?"

There was a hint of something in his voice that Faith didn't like. She also didn't like the way this argument was going. She'd had very few disagreements with Eddie in her life. As kids she and Tyler had been the ones with the ideas. They'd come up with plans for the exciting things they did, such as putting pennies on the railroad tracks.

Eddie had always been a follower, the one who was up to doing anything they wanted to, but when it got too strenuous, Eddie had stayed far enough away from them to watch, but not participate.

She would have said that she knew everything there was to know about Eddie, but now she was seeing a different side of him. She was seeing what she recognized as his mother in him. She'd never thought about it, but it was inevitable that he would have picked up some of his mother's snobbery. What was making her sick was that Eddie was directing that snobbery at their friend Ty. Considering that Ty had twice saved Eddie's life when they were kids, he shouldn't snub him. But then, the first time Eddie'd been saved, he said that if it hadn't been for Ty he wouldn't have been there in the first place, so in a way, it was Ty's duty to save him. Ty had punched Eddie in the nose. The second time Ty saved him, Eddie said, "Thank you."

Now, as Faith listened to Eddie, she thought that she wanted him to leave her house and never come back. Instead, she said, "I think it would be better for both of us to take the summer to think about what we want to do with our lives."

"I've known what I wanted to do with my life since I was six years old," Eddie said softly, the anger gone. "I've wanted you since you lent me your blue crayon."

"Because yours was broken," Faith said, smiling at the memory. "You opened your new box of crayons and the blue was broken. I thought you were going to start crying, so I lent you mine."

"And you lent Ty all of them, yours and mine, because he didn't have any crayons," Eddie said.

Faith smiled more broadly. There really were strong ties between the three of them. Her anger at Eddie left her. "We'll take this summer to think about things, all right? You work on your mother and try to get her used to the idea that I might be part of your family, and I'll—"

"You'll what? Spend your days with Ty? Your nights with him?" Eddie spat out the words.

Again, she stepped back from him. "He never wants to see me again so you don't have any worries on that part. I think I'll . . ."

"You'll do what?" Eddie asked, but softer this time.

"I think I'll get a job." She'd not thought of it before, but she suddenly realized that in the last two years she'd been so absorbed in the idea that she was going to be Eddie's wife that the idea of getting a job was new to her. But now that she'd thought of it she liked it. She could start making a dent on her student loan debt.

"Doing what?" Eddie asked.

"I don't know," Faith said, her good mood recovered. "Maybe I'll become a marriage counselor." She put her hand on Eddie's shoulder and pushed him toward the door. "As much as I've enjoyed this jealous fit of yours, I

want you to go away now, so I can think about what I'm
going to do this summer."

"And after the summer?"

"I don't know," she said. "Maybe I'll marry Mr.
Tucker."

Eddie gave a bit of a smile. Mr. Tucker was a handy-
man, had no teeth, and was over eighty. He was also the
biggest flirt in town.

"Can I give you away?" Eddie asked, deadpan.

Faith laughed and pushed harder on his shoulder, but Eddie didn't leave. Instead, he turned around,
grabbed Faith in his arms, and gave her the most passionate kiss he'd ever given her.

When he released her, his eyes were bright. "There
are some things that I can do as well as Tyler Parks can."

Faith just gave him a little smile, then opened the
door and watched him walk out. Her mother was standing a few feet away and she glanced at Faith's left hand
in speculation. Would she be wearing an engagement
ring? When she saw her daughter's naked hand, she
gave a sigh that let Faith know she'd again disappointed
her mother.

Faith closed the door behind Eddie and leaned on it
for a moment. "No you can't," she whispered in reply to
Eddie's statement. He couldn't kiss as well as Ty could.
She'd kissed Ty and had been so taken over by his lips
that she'd not realized that they were underwater and
that a motorboat was heading toward them. If it hadn't
been for Ty's awareness, they'd both be dead now.

She was thinking about everything that had happened in the last few days as she went to the bathroom to take a shower.

❧❧

"*What happened?*" Amy asked.

Faith took a breath. "It seems like so much longer than just sixteen years ago. Ty packed up and left town."

"He did what?" Amy asked.

"He left town. He was never seen again. When I didn't see him for about three weeks, I went to visit his mother and she said he'd come home wearing wet clothes, then he'd changed and left in his convertible. To my knowledge, no one in our town ever saw him again."

"That's odd," Amy said. "You'd think he would have fought for you."

"No," Faith said softly, "I think that that afternoon he saw me as he thought I had become, and he wanted nothing more to do with me."

"Or maybe he was in a car wreck and lost his memory," Zoë said, not looking up from her pad. "It does happen, you know."

Grimacing, Amy looked back at Faith. "What happened with you and Eddie?"

Faith gave a bit of a smile. "Everything changed. It was as though he saw that it was possible to lose me, so he fought the dragon."

"And the dragon was his mother," Zoë said.

"Oh yes. A few days after our confrontation in my bedroom, Eddie told his mother he was marrying me and that was it."

"So you married in a tiny wedding that was paid for by *your* mother, and afterward, what did Eddie's mother do to you?" Zoë asked.

Faith put her head back and made a groan that came from inside her soul. "She made my life a living hell. While Eddie was sick—"

"When did he get sick?" Amy asked.

Faith looked down at her hands.

When she took so long to answer, Zoë looked at her. "He was always sick, wasn't he?"

Faith didn't look up, but nodded her head.

"Oh!" Amy said. "That's why he never participated in sports with you and Ty. It's why he always held back." She paused for a moment. "But you didn't know that when you married him, did you?"

"No," Faith said. "His mother was the consummate snob and she couldn't bear for anyone to know that she'd been able to produce only one child and he had a defective heart. She took him to doctors far away from our small town so that no one knew he had anything wrong with him. And she lectured Eddie daily about keeping his bad heart a secret."

"She probably didn't want him to marry a lusty redhead for fear that you'd kill him in bed," Zoë said.

Faith smiled. "That may have had something to do with it, but I think her real objection was that, in her mind, I was of a lower class than her precious son was."

"Was his illness why he didn't go to bed with you before you were married?" Amy asked.

"Yes," Faith answered, and there was a quick flash in her eyes. "I was pretty angry about that. Eddie knew that I'd been to bed with Ty and he assumed that Ty was a good lover, so Eddie didn't want any comparisons with him. Eddie wanted me tied to him legally before I found out that he . . ."

"He what?" Zoë asked.

"Before I found out that he was . . . What is the kindest thing I can say? Premature in bed."

"You were lied to and tricked into marriage," Zoë said, "so why didn't you divorce him?"

"I thought about it. Three times I tried to leave him. One time I even had an affair with another man, but in the end, I always went back to Eddie. He needed me so very much and I . . ." Her head came up. "The truth was that I loved him. I'd loved him since I was a child and we had a lot of history between us. On the days when Eddie felt good, we laughed and enjoyed ourselves. There was very little sex, true, but there were other things."

When Zoë and Amy looked at each other, Faith continued, her voice urgent as she defended herself. "I know I've made my life seem horrible, but it wasn't. At least the first years weren't. You can put it down all you want, but Eddie was rich. The first five years of our marriage, we traveled. I mean traveled in the old-fashioned sense, not one of those things where you go to six countries in six days. Eddie and I went on ocean liners and stayed in first-class hotels. We stayed a month in Venice, six weeks in Paris."

"It also got you out of town and away from his mother," Zoë said.

"And, besides," Amy said, "what was there for you at home? Your true love wasn't there."

"True love," Faith said. "Is that what you think Ty was?"

"Yes," Amy answered, but Faith said nothing.

"What happened about the road across Ty's property?" Zoë asked.

Faith shrugged. "The road was built and the money for the land was paid to Ty's mother. She also left town and I never heard from her again. I don't know what happened to her, but the gossip was that she went to live with Ty."

"What about the house he was going to remodel for you?" Amy asked.

"It was torn down. Eddie offered to buy it for me and move it anywhere I wanted, but I couldn't bear to look at it, much less live in it."

"So where did you and Eddie end up living?" Zoë asked, her eyes on her drawing pad.

When Faith didn't answer, both women looked at her.

"Don't tell me you lived with Eddie's mother," Amy said. "You couldn't have done that. Tell me you didn't."

"We did. Eddie said it was just temporary until we got

our own house, but once we were in there, he said that his mother was alone and that he'd be torn in half thinking about her in that big house by herself." She shrugged. "By that time I was already so beaten down by the two of them that I didn't make much of a protest."

"What happened to her?" Amy asked.

"Nothing. She's still alive and still hates me."

Zoë gave a low whistle. "You've put up with that battle-axe for your entire life?"

"Yes," Faith said, but she gave a little smile. "But I hit her. I hit her hard."

"With what?" Amy asked. "Some information?"

"No," Faith said, smiling broader. "At Eddie's funeral I hit her in the face with my fists, first a right, then a left. Pow, pow! It was wonderful. Of course I was hauled away and spent a night in the local jail, but I still remember it as one of the high points of my life."

"Too bad you didn't do that before you married Eddie," Zoë murmured.

"But you loved Eddie," Amy said. "I can understand a lot of what you did because, in spite of everything, you loved him."

"You really are a romantic, aren't you?" Faith said.

"If I had her husband I'd be a romantic too." Zoë turned the sketch pad around and showed them her drawing of Stephen. If it was possible, she'd made him look better than he did in real life. Since the drawing was black-and-white, you couldn't see his blond hair. Zoë had portrayed him as having dark hair and eyes, and his eyebrows were arched in a way that said he was used to getting what he wanted.

"My goodness," Faith said, eyes wide.

Amy reached out and took the pad from Zoë. "I think I might have to fly home tonight," she said, looking at the picture.

"Can I go with you?" Zoë asked. There was such sincerity, such lust, in her voice that the three of them laughed.

"May I buy this from you?" Amy asked, holding on to the pad as though her life depended on it.

"No, but you can have it."

"You can't—" Amy began, but stopped herself. "Thank you. Thank you very much. I'll owe you for this." Reluctantly, she handed the drawing pad back to her.

Faith gave a yawn. "I don't know about you two, but I need to go to bed. This has been a four-hour therapy session."

"Won't Jeanne be proud of us?" Zoë said as she put away her drawing supplies.

"Oh yes, speaking of her," Faith said as she got up, "did either of you receive any business cards today?"

"Business cards?" Amy asked as though she had no idea what they were.

"Not me," Zoë said. "I didn't buy anything except lunch and no one gave me any business cards."

"Why do you want to know?" Amy asked.

"I talked to Jeanne yesterday and she said we were

to take all business cards that were offered to us. She seemed to think it was important."

Amy looked at Zoë and they shrugged. "Sorry, can't help," Amy said. "We'll go out tomorrow and see what we can find. Maybe she collects business cards."

"Nah," Zoë said. "She probably has a crazy patient who uses them for—"

"Building model houses," Amy said quickly before Zoë could come up with some disgusting use for the cards.

"Sure," Zoë said. "I'm off to bed. You want the bathroom first?" she asked Faith.

"I'd like to take a shower, if you don't mind."

"Ha!" Zoë said. "You'd like to spend an hour in the tub. I saw those jars of smelly stuff you bought."

"That takes too long," Faith said. "I'll just shower and—"

"Use the tub!" Amy said in a commanding voice. "Zoë hasn't finished the drawing of my son and she can use my bathroom. Go and enjoy yourself."

"Okay, I will," Faith said, then left them.

When they were alone in the room, Zoë went to the kitchen, Amy right behind her. "So what do you want to talk to me about?" Zoë asked as she opened the refrigerator and took out a bottle of white wine.

"What makes you think I want to talk to you?" Amy asked as she washed their wineglasses.

"You lied to Faith about the drawing that I haven't even started and you're in the same room with me. Alone. So what do you want to say?"

"I don't know," Amy said. "It's just that Faith's story upset me. What do you think really happened to Tyler?"

"He left town. That's what she said. He hung around that town waiting for the woman he loved to come home from college, and when she did, he saw that she wanted someone else. So Ty did the smart thing and left."

Amy held out her glass for Zoë to fill from the bottle she'd just opened. "I don't know. There was something creepy in her story that bothered me."

"You mean the way Eddie lied, cheated, and manipulated in exactly the same way that his mother did?"

"Yeah, that's what I mean. Poor Faith," she said, leaning against the countertop and sipping her wine. "I feel so sorry for her. She still says that Eddie was the love of her life but how could he be?"

"So what's in your clean little mind to do? Take her to a hairdresser and give her a makeover?"

"Would you stop it?" Amy said, glaring at Zoë. "I'm beginning to be able to see through your tough-girl act."

"I guess I'm just a scared little girl under a lot of face paint."

"Is that what Jeanne said about you?"

Zoë smiled. "Yeah, it's a direct quote."

Amy looked toward the bathroom door where she could hear water running. "I wish there was something we could do for her. It's hard to imagine all that's happened to her in these past years. She went from being a—"

"Busty redhead," Zoë said.

"Yes, a busty, lusty redhead, to a . . ." She looked at Zoë.

"To a worn-out, beaten-down old woman who isn't even forty yet."

"I wonder what happened to her mother?"

"Died years ago," Zoë said. "Faith told me before you arrived. I bet the old bat died happy."

"Why not? She'd badgered and bullied her only child into marrying a man with a defective heart and—"

"And had a mother-in-law with no heart, but she was *rich*."

"I swear that I'll let my children marry whomever they want," Amy said.

"Oh yeah? And what if one of your beautiful, college-educated sons comes home with a bleached-blonde high-school dropout on his arm and he tells you he wants to marry her and adopt her three illegitimate children?"

"Good point," Amy said, looking out the window at the garden. It was late and she should go to bed, but she kept thinking about Faith's life that had been thrown away. "I wonder if we could find Ty?"

"We? When did you and I become 'we'?"

"When you drew my husband as the sex god that he is."

Zoë laughed. "I bet the truth is that he drinks and fornicates."

"No, that would be his brothers. They're on second and third wives. But Stephen is perfect."

"Isn't that a bit boring?"

"Of course not!" Amy said, then drained her glass and washed it out. "I think that tomorrow I'll check out some of those search engines that help you find people."

"What do you know about this man Ty that you'll be able to find him?"

"His name, the town where he grew up, and that his brothers moved to Alaska. I think I can piece together enough to find out something. Okay, I'm off to bed. See you in the morning."

When Amy was gone, Zoë stood in the kitchen for a few minutes, then she went into her bedroom and got her laptop. Even though it was close to midnight, she wasn't tired. Since she'd been in the hospital she'd had trouble sleeping and rarely got more than four hours of rest a night. Usually, she stayed up painting, but tonight, she thought she might see what she could find on the Internet. As her computer warmed up and the wireless Internet came on, she poured herself another glass of wine and sat down.

"Well, Mr. Tyler Parks, if you still have the same name, I'm going to find you," she said to the screen as she began typing.

Seven

Amy was dreaming.

She was in bed, but it was different from her own. The covers enveloping her were heavy and there seemed to be a foot-tall stack of them. Yet in spite of them, her nose was freezing. She pulled back under the covers, trying not to let any of her body be exposed. The room seemed to be unheated. She stuck out her foot to feel for Stephen. Maybe she could get him to turn up the thermostat.

In the next second, she sat upright. The boys! If their room was cold, so was the boys'. As she sat up, she hit her head on something hard. Rubbing it, she turned and put her feet on the floor, but instead of her soft bedroom carpet, she felt something rough that hurt the bottoms of her feet. "What in the world have the boys spilled on the carpet while I was in Maine?" she murmured as she ran her hand over the foot of the bed, looking for her bathrobe, but it wasn't there.

It was so cold in the room she could see her breath. She glanced at the window and saw that it had panes that were diamond-shaped, not the Colonial windows that she and Stephen had chosen when building the house. What had they done while she was away?

With her hands on her upper arms, trying to protect them from the chill, she walked across the rough carpeting and headed for the door. "Stephen!" she said when she got to his side of the bed. She could see the top of his head, but nothing else. "Stephen!" she said louder. "Something's wrong with the furnace. You need to call someone.

"And I'm sure they'll come out in the middle of the night," she said under her breath. She saw her husband move a bit, but he didn't look out from under the covers.

"Men!" she said under her breath as she went to the door. It was dark in the room, with only the moonlight shining through the window illuminating it. But she knew the room well so she didn't need to turn on the light.

When she got to the door she reached for the brass doorknob, but her hand came in contact with an odd contraption that was more like a latch for a barn than for a bedroom. "What is going on?" she said aloud, while wondering what she was going to say to her family for making changes while she was away.

Annoyed, she lifted the latch and went into the hall. It was darker there than in the bedroom. Where were the night-lights that she kept all over the house? She knew the boys sometimes got up at night, so she'd wanted them to be able to see where they were going. The fixtures were supposed to be light sensitive, coming on only when it was dark, but they weren't on now. Amy wondered if the electricity had gone out and that's why the furnace had stopped working.

She hurried the few steps down the hall to her oldest son's room. Again when she reached for the knob, there was just a latch. Frowning, she opened it.

She lifted the latch, but before the door opened, a strong arm reached out and grabbed her.

"I would not do that if I were you," said a man's voice above her head. His voice was deeper than Stephen's and it had an old-fashioned English accent, like something from an old black-and-white movie.

"Stephen?" she asked. "What are you doing? Let go of me and go down and check the furnace. It's freezing in here." She turned back to open the door.

The man put his hand over hers. "Nay, do not."

"Will you stop it!" she said, pushing his hand away.

"Ah, I see. You are not who I thought you were. I see now that you are in your nightdress. Go on, then. And mayhap you will come to my room later."

"Great," Amy said. "The house is an ice cube and you want to play sex games. Tell me you didn't put on those ridiculous tall leather boots you bought."

"Boots?" the man said. "Aye, my boots are leather."

Amy couldn't help laughing. "Stephen, you have the strangest timing. Go downstairs and see what you can do with the furnace. I'll get the boys and put them in bed with us. Go on now and do it!"

For a few moments the man didn't say anything. "You are mad, woman," he said. "Your mind is deranged."

"It'll arrange itself back once it's above fifty degrees in this house."

She heard him moving—it was too dark to see anything—then a match was struck, he lit a candle, and he held it up. Amy's eyes widened as she looked not into the face of her husband but at a stranger. He was as dark as Stephen was fair. His black hair was long, ending just at his collar, and his eyes were dark, with thick lashes above them. His brows were black and shaped like a bird's wings.

She stepped back, her hand at the neck of her gown. "Who are you and what are you doing in my house?"

"Your house?" the man asked. "I think the landlord would disagree with that." Turning, he lifted his arm and the light illuminated some stairs. Amy glanced over the railing and below she saw what looked like a tavern resembling the ones they'd seen in Williamsburg.

Amy took a step back from the man. He was as tall as Stephen but he looked bigger, broader, and he didn't have Stephen's sweetness of expression. "I don't know who you are or what your game is, but if you don't get out of my house this minute, I'm going to scream for my husband to call the police."

The man stepped farther away from her. "Please do call your, uh, what is it? Your husband, wench. I will see to him." He flipped back his heavy black cloak to show the long, silver sword in a scabbard at his waist.

Every newspaper account of every horror Amy had ever read about came to her mind. "Please don't hurt my children," she whispered while thinking that he'd already harmed them.

Her eyes wide with terror and her heart pounding, she put her hand behind her to open the door to her son's room. In one swift movement, she opened the door, ran into the bedroom, then shut the door and leaned against it. She didn't know what she was going to do if the man pushed against the door; she'd never be able to hold it against him. But when the door stayed still, her only concern was to find her son and get him out of the house. They'd practiced fire drills and Amy kept rope ladders rolled up in the cabinet under the window seat.

She ran to the bed. "Davy?" she whispered urgently. "Get up. Get up now. You have to get out of the house. There's an emergency." When the boy didn't move, she threw back the covers and put out her hands to wake him.

"Oh, this is a nice surprise. Come here, honey," said a man's voice, and the next second Amy was being pulled into the bed by a pair of strong arms. The man smelled as if he hadn't had a bath in a year, and in addition to being frightened, Amy felt nauseous.

"Let me go!" she said, kicking out at him, which, unfortunately, made her nightgown go up above her knees.

"Just like I like 'em," the man said, his hand on her knee and moving upward. His mouth was near her face and he had breath like a cesspool.

"Stop it!" she said as loudly as she could, but her voice was muffled by his hand, his face, and his body that was moving on top of her.

In the next second, someone lifted the man from her and she heard him hit the wall.

"Stephen!" Amy said, her arms going up to him. "It was horrible! He tried to— The boys! Our sons! We have to get them."

"I do not know who Stephen is," the man said, "and I do not know of your sons. I was not aware that you had a husband."

It was the dark man. She could see his face outlined by the moonlight coming in through the window. "You!" she said. "What have you done with my husband and children?"

The man stood up straight as the other man groaned in the corner. "Unless you want him to be your companion for the night, I would suggest that you go back to your own bed. Perhaps on the morrow you will be less insane."

Amy just sat on the bed and looked up at him in confusion. The bed was so soft that the mattress nearly surrounded her. "I don't know who you are or what you're talking about. This is my home and I live here with my husband and two sons. What have you done with them?"

Even in the darkness of the room, she could see the man shake his head, then roll his eyes. In the next second, he bent and lifted her into his arms.

Amy struggled to get away from him.

"If you do not be still I will drop you and I can attest that this floor is very hard." When she quit struggling, he carried her down the hall and through the doorway of the room she'd awakened in, and dropped her onto the bed.

When Amy landed, there was a high-pitched scream and a woman stuck her head out from under the covers.

"What by God's teeth is this?" the woman said, sputtering and fighting her way out from under the covers. She looked at the man. "Oh, it's you, my lord. Do you need something?" As she said this, she was kicking at Amy and trying to get her off her legs.

The man used flint and a striker to light a candle by the bedside. "Aye, I do," he said. "Keep your sister in bed unless it is your plan to hire her out to the men in your keeping."

"Why not?" the woman said. "She's of little other use to us. She is weak and slow-witted. My father despairs of her."

Amy stopped struggling against the legs kicking at her and looked at the woman. She was pretty, but in a slovenly way. Her dark hair looked as though it hadn't been washed in a while and there was dirt on her neck. The worst thing was the way she was looking at the man looming over them. Pure, undiluted lust.

"Might there be something I can do for *you*," the woman said, her tone suggestive.

"Nay, not tonight. Just keep your sister in the room. Tie her to the bed if need be."

"Ah," the woman said, her voice low and purring. "I might like to be tied to the bed."

Amy grimaced at the forward manner of the woman and looked up at the man, but his dark face gave no hint of what he was thinking. She'd thought he was Stephen but he wasn't. He looked a bit like him, but—

"You look like Zoë's drawing," Amy said. "You're Stephen, but distorted."

"I am not your husband," the man said, but his tone was more amused than angry.

"Of a certain you are not," the dark woman said as she swung out with her fist and hit Amy on the arm.

Amy fell back into the heavy covers and grabbed her arm. "That hurt!"

"It was meant to," the woman said, never taking her eyes off the man. When she started to get out of bed, the man stepped back, obviously wanting to get out of the room.

"I will leave you to it, then," the man said as he opened the door, then he was gone.

Amy sat where she was, still too stunned by the last few minutes to understand what had happened. She turned to the woman in the bed beside her. "My name is Amy Hanford and I seem to have . . . Actually, I don't know what's happened to me, but I need to find my husband and children. If you could—"

She didn't say another word because the woman hit her in the face with her fist. Amy went sailing back into the bedcovers, and when she put her hand up, her nose was bleeding.

"You're my stupid sister!" the woman yelled into her face. "You have no husband and no children. You have no *men*! You understand me? The men belong to *me*. And especially Lord Hawthorne. He's mine and not yours, so don't go followin' after him to try to get him in bed with you. You understand me?"

"Perfectly," Amy said. She was looking for a box of tissues, but saw none. As blood ran down her arm, she grabbed a gray piece of cloth and held it to her nose.

"You're washin' that, not me," the woman said.

Amy realized she was holding a corner of the sheet. "I'm sure I'll be the first," she said, but was glad that her stuffed nose kept her from being understood. She didn't want to be hit again.

The woman blew out the candle. "Now let me get some sleep."

"Happily," Amy muttered, then lay down in the bed beside the woman. By now she'd decided that she was at home and dreaming and the faster she went back to sleep, the sooner she'd wake up and laugh with Stephen over her ridiculous dream.

Or would she wake up in Maine and share the dream with . . . ? She smiled. With her new friends. It was a nice thought in the midst of a truly awful dream, and Amy believed in nice thoughts.

She closed her eyes and gave herself over to the memory of the day she and Stephen and the boys had gone to the zoo. That had been a lovely day. After a while, her nose stopped bleeding and she went to sleep.

Eight

❧

"What happened to you?" Zoë asked when Amy walked into the kitchen the next morning.

Zoë was sitting at the kitchen table, an empty plate in front of her, her sketch pad on her lap. Faith was at the sink, washing dishes.

Amy opened the freezer door and got out a tray of ice. "I think I rolled over and hit my nose on the bed-side table. At least that's all I can think of that would do this. Does it look really bad?" She wrapped the ice in a dish towel and held it to her sore face.

"Awful," Zoë said. "One side of your face—"

Faith put her hand on Zoë's shoulder. "She's been up all night, so don't listen to her. You look fine. A little makeup and some—"

"Plastic surgery," Zoë cut in.

"Don't make me laugh," Amy said. "My whole face hurts. I got blood all over Jeanne's sheets and they're in the washer now, but I don't think the stains will come out." She looked at Faith. "Maybe we could buy her some new ones today."

"Sure," Faith said as she accepted the invitation.

Amy looked at the woman. "Is there something different about you today?"

"She looks five years younger, doesn't she?" Zoë said. "I noticed it right away. Now you, you look like you spent a couple of rounds with a boxer."

There was a mirror by the dining table and Amy looked in it. Since she'd been up, she'd done little but stare at her reflection, but each time it still looked like she'd lost a fight.

"I think we should take you to a doctor," Faith said. "Your nose could be broken. Why didn't you call out when you hit the cabinet? I'm a light sleeper and I would have heard you."

Amy sat down at the kitchen table and gingerly touched her nose. "Actually, I did call out, but only the man heard me."

"Man?" Both Faith and Zoë stopped and looked at her.

Amy took Zoë's drawing pad and flipped the pages to the sketch of Stephen—Stephen the Dark, she thought. "Him. He heard me in my dream."

"You had a dream about *my* man?" Zoë asked. "I'm not sure that's legal. I think that if I conjured him, he's mine. You already have one hunk, so you can't have mine."

"What was your dream?" Faith asked, her face serious as she sat down opposite Amy. "And was he the one who hit you?"

Amy glanced at the two women and saw that they both had lost their look of amusement. "No, no, and double no," she said. "The man didn't hit me. No man, not in life or in a dream, has ever hit me, so you two can stop looking at me like that. It was my sister—the sister in the dream, that is—who hit me and I was in bed with her."

Zoë and Faith were silent for a moment, then Faith said, "I'll get the eggs out while you start talking."

Amy groaned. "No, really, it was just a stupid dream. I'm sure it's not part of Jeanne's therapy that we have to tell our dumb dreams."

"Are you kidding? She loves dreams," Zoë said. "I got to the point where I made them up just to entertain her. I liked to see how fast she could write to get them down."

Faith gave Zoë a look of disgust. "And you wonder why the court ordered you into therapy." She looked back at Amy. "Even if Jeanne hated dreams, I think I can speak for both of us by saying that we'd like to hear your dream about being in bed with your sister and that man."

"He wasn't in the bed."

"Oh," Zoë and Faith said in unison, and they sounded so disappointed that Amy laughed—but that hurt her swollen, bruised face, so she stopped.

"Okay," Amy said, "I'll tell, but it was nothing, really."

She smiled. "Stupid. That's what my sister kept calling me. I think she really hated me."

"All sisters do," Faith said as she broke eggs into a bowl.

"That's the second time you've said something rotten about sisters," Amy said. "What makes you so down on them?"

"When my mother died, I found out that my father had been married before and had two daughters older than me. Let's just say that when they found out I'd married a rich man, they were all over me."

"Were they in your bed and did they hit you?" Zoë asked.

"No."

"Then I'd rather hear Amy's story," Zoë said.

Actually, Amy didn't mind telling her dream because she hoped that the telling would take it out of her head. Even though she was now awake and in the sunlight and it was the twenty-first century, it still felt real.

"Interesting," Zoë said when Amy had finished talking. "My guess is that you had the dream after you hit your nose. It was a story to explain the accident."

"I guess so," Amy said, looking down at her bowl of cereal. "But I've never had a dream that had odors in it. I can still smell that horrible man's bad breath. Yuck!"

"What about the hero's breath?" Faith asked.

"Hero? Oh, you mean the—"

"The tall, dark, and handsome demigod," Zoë said.

"Hardly that," Amy said as she carried her empty

bowl to the sink and washed it. "What shall we do today besides buy sheets?" Turning, she looked at both of them, but neither Zoë nor Faith spoke.

"Did I miss something?" Amy asked.

"Actually, Faith wants to spend the day with a hairdresser and get her hair cut and dyed flaming red."

"Really?" Amy asked, eyes wide.

"I thought I might," she said shyly. "I mean about the cut part, not the flaming red."

"I think that's wonderful. And what about you, Zoë?"

"Sketching," she said, holding up her pad. "I have a few things in my head and I'd like to walk along the coast and get some ideas."

Amy wanted to protest that their plans left her alone, but truthfully, she didn't mind being by herself. She wanted to go to the bookstore she'd seen yesterday. She looked at Zoë. "Did you really stay up all night?"

"Sure, I do it often."

"She was still on the computer when I got up," Faith said. "Maybe you should take a nap today."

Amy looked at Zoë in question, and she gave a quick nod to let Amy know that she'd been on the Internet looking for something about Ty. Her eyes said that she'd found something, and from her look, what she'd found wasn't good.

"Well," Amy said, "I think I'll go look for replacement sheets for Jeanne, and I'll sightsee around town."

"We saw all of it twice yesterday," Faith said.

"Maybe I'll spend the morning in that little used

bookstore we saw. Remember? It's down that alley by the pizza place."

Faith had her head turned and Amy was looking at Zoë, who nodded. She'd understood Amy's message that Zoë was to meet her there and tell her what she'd found out about Faith's former boyfriend.

"All right," Amy said, "I think I'll finish getting dressed. Shall we meet back here for dinner? Maybe we should cook something."

"I make a mean zabaglione," Faith said. "Think I can find vin santo here?"

"You could use Marsala," Amy said.

"Deliver me," Zoë groaned. "I'm trapped with two housewives."

"When you're home, what do you eat?" Amy asked. "Don't you cook?"

"I not only don't cook, I don't have a home."

"What?" Faith asked.

"Since the accident, I've made my living by painting portraits of rich people and their kids. I stay in some mansion for three to six months and do watercolors and pastels of the whole family. I have become a 'must have' of the wealthiest people in the country."

The way she said it, with a tone that said it was all ridiculous, made Faith and Amy smile.

"If you're never in one place, how do you see Jeanne?" Faith asked.

"Computer setup. Video, audio, the works."

"You have a therapy session by long distance?"

"Yeah, sure," Zoë said. "What's wrong with that?"

"Nothing," Amy said. "It's just that sometimes I feel very old." She left the kitchen to go to her room. Before she left the house, she took the sheets out of the washer and she could see that they were still stained. That much blood would never come out.

As she put them in the dryer, she again thought about her dream. She'd made light of it to the others, but the truth was that it had deeply upset her. Usually, dreams faded during the day. A person could wake up still half in the dream, but by breakfast the images had dulled.

But not this dream. Right now it was almost as though she could remember the dream more clearly than she could remember her own family. She'd called Stephen this morning, catching him just as they were leaving on their camping trip. She spent about three minutes with each of her sons, but they were so excited about the trip they couldn't focus. When Stephen got on the phone, the first thing she asked him was if he knew whether the name Hawthorne was in his family tree.

"I have no idea," Stephen said. "What makes you ask a question like that?"

"I had an odd dream and you were in it and you were named Hawthorne." She crossed her fingers at the lie.

"Yeah?" Stephen said. "That sounds interesting. You'll have to tell me about it when you get back."

There was a pause from Stephen. "Is something wrong?"

"Not at all. In fact, I think I may have made a couple of friends."

"Friends? The last time I talked to you, you were complaining that one was a goth and the other an old maid. You wanted to get on the first plane out."

"I know, but things have changed. Faith has had a hard life and she's going to get her hair cut today."

"That's my Amy," Stephen said, chuckling. "You've persuaded her to have a beauty makeover."

"I didn't do it," Amy said, not liking what he'd said. It made her sound as though she thought of nothing but makeup and clothes. "Zoë did it."

Again Stephen paused. "Honey, are you all right?"

"Fine," Amy said. "I'm just fine. What about you and the boys?"

"We're great. Dad came over last night and we watched sports on TV."

When he didn't say anything else, Amy knew it was her cue to ask him if Lewis had smoked in the house, if they'd put wet beer cans on the wooden furniture, and if they'd cleaned up the pizza she knew they'd eaten. But Amy didn't say anything. All that seemed truly clear in her mind was her dream.

"I don't think you are all right," Stephen said. "Hey! I have an idea. Why don't I let your dad and mine take the kids camping and I come up there? I could be there tonight—"

"No!" Amy said, then drew in her breath. The last thing she wanted was for him to see her face as it was, but there was something else. She was enjoying her time alone and . . . "I mean, no. I have to play this out. I have to do what I'm supposed to do."

"Supposed to do?" Stephen asked. "Amy, what's going on up there?"

"Nothing. It's nothing. It's just . . . I don't know, it's interesting. Look, you better go with the boys. They'd never forgive me if I ruined their trip."

"Sure," Stephen said slowly. "But Amy, if you need anything, I'm here. You know that, don't you? And you know that I love you, don't you?"

"Yes, of course," Amy said quickly, then hung up. She realized that she'd not told him she loved him and she almost called him back, but she didn't. It was better to let them leave on their trip that they so looked forward to. A trip without her.

Amy got dressed quickly, spent fifteen minutes doing all she could to cover the bruises on her face, and left the summerhouse before the others did. She had an idea and she wanted to research it. What she wanted to do was see if she could find out anything about an Englishman named Hawthorne. Of course, the sensible thing would have been to stay in the house and search on the Internet, but there was something that seemed to be pulling her to the little bookstore.

When she opened the door to the shop, a bell rang and she smiled. The place looked like something out of an old movie, just as she hoped it would, with books piled everywhere. There were shelves full of them, and chairs and tables were covered. She could see that underneath the books the furniture was antique. She smiled as she thought that from the look of the place the furniture had been new when it was put in the store.

"May I help you?"

She turned to see an old man with white hair and a straight carriage that made her think he'd spent his life in the military. "I'm looking for something about the history of England in . . . I guess it would be the eighteenth century, the time of Williamsburg. Personal history. I'm not interested in the kings and queens."

"I think we have what you need," the man said as he started walking toward the back of the store.

He led her into a room that had been set up like a study in someone's house. There was a deep-set window with a cushioned seat beneath it, half a dozen old pillows on the seat. A big comfy chair sat in a corner with a brass reading light above it. A coffee table in the middle was covered with books and even a pair of reading glasses.

"Here we are," he said. "I think that if you look in this section, you'll find what you need." The bell on the front door sounded. "Ah, if you'll excuse me, I will see to them. Take your time," he said. "Take all the time you need."

"Yes, thank you," she said, as he left the room to go into the main part of the store.

Amy liked the smell of old books and she liked the look of the shelves bowing under the weight of what had to be thousands of volumes. She went to the far wall and began to read titles. That case seemed to be about medieval history. But what she'd seen in her dream was later than that.

Turning, she looked out the window. There was a field full of wildflowers behind the store and the sunlight on them was beautiful.

As she looked back at the room setting, she thought how much she loved it. Stephen had often told her that she'd read so many historical romances that she should start writing them. "Maybe I should," she whispered as she looked at the book titles.

She spent an hour happily rummaging, pulling one book after another out and looking at it, then sliding it back into place. Even though the store was in a tiny town in Maine, the owner certainly did have a good collection of titles on English history. They went from the Norman conquest to the Mitford sisters.

As Amy looked at the books, she thought she'd like to take the entire selection—and the room—home with her. She'd like to just pick the whole thing up and move it back to her own house.

I'd have my own summerhouse, she thought. Last year Stephen had said something like that, that they could build a little house in the back for her. "Why would I want that?" she'd asked.

"Just to get away from us," he'd said.

"I don't want to get away from you. You three are my whole life."

Stephen had frowned at that and she didn't know

why. But today she thought maybe she did understand it. Did she hover too much? Did she boss them around too much? Was she too possessive? Stephen's father rarely visited them because he said Amy had too many damned rules for his taste. He wanted to have a good time and he didn't want to be told what to do.

For the first time in days she thought of the baby she'd lost. Had her sadness been about the baby or because her plans hadn't been realized?

Frowning, she put the book she was holding back onto the shelf. There were tall volumes at the top, but she couldn't reach them. She looked about and saw a little stool in a corner, picked it up, moved it in front of the case and climbed on it. She still had to stretch to see the top shelf.

They seemed to be genealogy books. How to find your ancestors, that sort of thing. She wasn't interested in them and was about to step down when a name caught her eye. A small book with a spine no more than a half-inch wide had a single name on it. All she could see was "awthor" but it was enough to pique her interest. She reached for it, stretching as far as she could. She had just touched it when she lost her balance and fell.

When she hit the floor, she put her arms over her head, expecting the entire case to come tumbling down on her, but it didn't. Instead, the book she'd been trying to reach neatly fell into her lap.

"Good shot," she said aloud as she picked up the book and opened it. It had been published in 1838 and its title was *The Tragedy of the Hawthorne Family As Told by Someone Who Knows.*

For a moment Amy just sat there staring at the title page, then she got up and went to the window seat and began to read. The sun came in bright and clear and she read, fascinated.

"There you are!" Zoë said, frowning at Amy.

She looked up, blinking. Zoë had on a raincoat and water was dripping off her shoulders.

"I've been looking everywhere for you."

"I've been here for—" She looked at her watch. It was nearly three P.M. "My goodness, I've been here for hours. I just finished the most interesting book. I think I found the man I dreamed about."

"You have a dreamboat, remember? I get the imaginary one. Have you had lunch?"

"No," Amy said, uncurling herself off the window seat. "It was so nice here, with the sun shining in, that I lost track of time."

"Sun? Are you out of your mind? It's been raining for hours. If it keeps on like this the ocean level will rise."

Amy glanced out the window and, sure enough, it was raining. Besides that, she saw that there was an ugly old stone warehouse just a few feet out the window, not the field of wildflowers that she'd seen every time she'd glanced up.

"Are you okay?" Zoë asked impatiently.

"Sure," Amy said, but still blinking in bewilderment. Between what she'd read and the oddity of the rain and no rain, she was feeling a bit dazed.

"Faith wants us to meet her for tea at some shop about a half mile from here. We'll have to walk through mud to get there. You look funny."

"I know," Amy said. "I'm sure the makeup's worn off."

"No, you can hardly see that. It's just . . ." She trailed off, then shrugged. "I've been around Jeanne too long and I'm reading too much into everything. Do you want to go or not?"

"Oh yes, I want to go." She opened the little book to the front end papers to see if there was a price on it. Of course she'd have to buy it no matter what it cost. It was five dollars.

"What's that?"

Amy saw that Zoë was looking at something on the floor. "I think it fell out of the book." She picked it up and looked at it. It was a business card.

Futures, Inc.
"Have you ever wanted to rewrite your past?"
Madame Zoya can help
333 Everlasting Street

"If that's a business card, take it. It'll be our first one for Jeanne."

Amy slipped the card back into the book and held

on to it as tightly as she held her children's hands when they crossed the street.

At the front of the store, Amy paused to pay the old gentleman while Zoë waited outside under an umbrella.

"Did you find what you needed?" he asked politely.

"Yes, I did," she said. "And I especially enjoyed the sunshine and the field of wildflowers."

The man took a moment to reply, as though he were trying to decide what to say. Act as though he had no idea what she was talking about? Or acknowledge what she'd said?

When he looked up at Amy, his eyes were twinkling. "We do so like to please our customers."

"You have pleased me very much," she said as she took the receipt from him. She paused at the door. "If you should come across a book that has some designs for summerhouses in it, I'd like to buy it. I want something old-fashioned, Victorian maybe."

"With or without plumbing?"

"With, certainly," she said.

"I'll see what I can find and send it over to Mrs. Hightower's house."

Amy gave him a radiant smile. "Thank you."

The old man smiled back as she left the store.

"What was that all about?" Zoë asked. "I thought you were going to ask him out on a date."

"No, I was just asking him about another book I want."

"We'll have to share the umbrella," Zoë said as she started to walk, but Amy held out her hand.

"I think the rain's stopped."

"Great!" she said as she closed her umbrella. "It was raining so hard that I couldn't find this place. I hadn't seen it before and you gave me directions about the pizza place, but I still couldn't find it. I found the pizza parlor, but no bookstore, not even an alleyway. And the idiot girl in the shop on the corner said she didn't know of a bookstore except the one down the street. When I finally found the place, I wanted to drag her here to see it. What a day!"

"Sorry," Amy said, but she felt no guilt. She knew magic when she saw it, and she knew she'd just experienced it. But Amy had an idea that Zoë wasn't one to believe in magic. In fact, she didn't think that Zoë believed in much of anything.

"Did you find out anything last night?" Amy asked.

"Yeah," Zoë said, then lowered her voice. "I had to pay to subscribe to an online newspaper, but I found out that—" She looked around as though Faith might be behind them. "You can't tell Faith about what I found out because I think it would upset her a lot."

"What did you find out?" Amy asked.

"Six months ago two teenagers in Faith's hometown found a skeleton at the bottom of a cliff. It's been identified as Tyler Parks."

"He died?" Amy asked as she stopped walking. "That poor, poor man. I wonder—"

"No," Zoë said. "You're not understanding. He didn't die, he was murdered."

"Murdered? But—"

"The article said that the skeleton was years old, at least fifteen."

"Fifteen? But that means that he died not long after Faith saw him."

"Not died," Zoë said louder. "*Murdered.* There was a hole in his skull, like someone hit him on the head with something heavy, like a rock, maybe."

Amy took a moment to think about all this. "Are you sure Faith doesn't know about this?"

"Yes. I called Jeanne but she was no help. She had never heard of Tyler Parks."

Amy looked at Zoë in disbelief. "Faith didn't tell her therapist about this man who meant so much to her?"

"I guess not. I tried to get Jeanne to tell me some things about Faith, but she'd only tell facts. After her husband died, Faith moved away from that little town where she grew up, and she's been living in New York for the last year and going to Jeanne three times a week. It wasn't easy to get info out of Jeanne, but she told me that if Faith hadn't agreed to therapy, her mother-in-law was going to press charges and keep her in jail for as long as her money could buy. It seems that Faith didn't just punch the woman a couple of times; she went berserk and attacked her with everything she had, including a few plates. The old woman was in the hospital for two weeks."

"Our quiet little Faith?" Amy said, looking down the street to where they were to meet her.

"It seems that Faith has a great deal more anger inside her than she lets on."

"She has reason to be angry," Amy said, "but I haven't seen it. Faith seems so down-to-earth, so sane. I can't imagine her attacking anyone." She started walking, but Zoë caught her arm.

"There's something else."

"What?" Amy asked.

"Jeanne didn't say anything directly, but she kept asking me what kind of mood Faith was in. Happy? Despondent? In despair? That sort of thing."

"Okay, so now you're giving me the creeps. We don't have to bolt our bedroom doors, do we?"

"No, I think that Jeanne was hinting that Faith tends to take her unhappiness out on herself."

"You mean suicide?"

"That would be my guess," Zoë said, then when she saw Amy's face, she said, "So help me, if you let Faith know we know this, I'll . . . I'll tear up that drawing of your husband."

"If you do, I'll have this one." Amy took the book she'd bought out of the little bag and flipped it open to a photo of an oil painting. The caption under it read *Lord Tristan James Hawthorne, Sixth Earl of Eastlon, 1763–1797.*

Zoë's mouth dropped open at the sight of the portrait. The man was an exact likeness of the one she'd drawn. She looked at Amy in astonishment. "Where did you find this?"

"In the bookstore. He's the man in your drawing *and* the man in my dream."

"What . . . ?" Zoë began. "How . . . ?"

"Come on, let's go meet Faith. Let's get her to talk so we don't have to tell her that you were snooping into her life."

Zoë ignored Amy's jibe. "If Faith ever visits her hometown again, or looks on the Internet, she's going to find out."

"Gee, that reminds me of someone else I met recently. If *you* ever went back to your hometown or searched on the Internet, I bet *you* would find out a lot about what happened to you."

"I don't think I like you very much," Zoë said, glaring at Amy.

"That's funny, because the more time I spend with you, the more I like you." She smiled at Zoë's frown. "I'm starving, so let's go get something to eat, then we'll go to the grocery and get something for tonight. With the way you pack away the wine, we'll need four bottles."

"I want to borrow that book," Zoë said.

"Hold your breath," Amy said, laughing as she walked ahead toward the place where they were to have tea.

Nine

"So *what did* you two do today?" Faith asked as she ate a buttered scone.

Zoë and Amy could only stare at the difference in her. Faith's hair was now shoulder length and it had been dyed to a deep auburn. She had on makeup and her green eyes glistened. She'd also bought a new outfit of dark brown trousers and a cream-colored shirt. She'd topped it with an expensive-looking red leather jacket.

"Where did you get those clothes?" Amy asked in awe. "I haven't seen anything that didn't have a duck embroidered on it."

"The hairdresser told me about the place. It's really a woman who sells out of her house. She said she hates tourists so she sells only to people who have been recommended to her."

"Your hair looks great," Amy said.

"She did do a good job, didn't she?" Faith said as she touched her hair.

"Okay, enough of that," Zoë said. "I think Amy's going to sell her firstborn kid to go to that dress shop. Amy, show Faith what you found."

"Okay." It took Amy a few moments to collect herself enough to remember what she'd done all day. She took the book from the bag and opened it. "I went to the nicest little bookshop, with the nicest little man running it. I told him I was interested in an English family named Hawthorne and—"

"How did you know they were English?" Zoë asked.

"Didn't I tell you that everyone in my dream spoke with an English accent?"

"No," Faith said, "but tell us what you found."

She handed the open book to Faith.

"But this is Zoë's man," Faith said. "He looks just like the man you drew. And he—" She broke off. "Of course. Now I see it. I knew there was something about him that I recognized."

"What?" Amy asked.

"The real Hawthorne," she said. "Nathaniel Hawthorne. This man looks a lot like the man who wrote *The House of Seven Gables.* It's not him, of course, but there is a strong resemblance. It was said that Hawthorne was so beautiful that people stopped in the street to look at him. It made him a recluse, which is good for us since while he was hiding away, he wrote. With the names the same, they have to be related. I'll bet some Ph.D. students have written papers about the families."

She handed the book back to Amy. "Do you think you read about the man somewhere and incorporated him into your dream?"

"You sound just like Jeanne," Zoë said. "I think Amy was his wife in a past life, and they were so in love that he now haunts her in her dreams."

"And you say *I* am a romantic," Amy said as she put the book away. "Anyway, Zoë, what you said can't be true. Lord Hawthorne died young. And he had no wife or children. The title died with him and his nephew got the estates and squandered them on cards in just two years. There's nothing left of the family today."

"Did you read the whole book?" Faith asked.

"Every word of it," Amy said. "I curled up on a window seat with the sun streaming in and read the whole book." She gave them a look that dared them to tell her it had been raining all day.

"What's more," Amy said, "this was in the book." She produced the business card with a flourish.

Faith took it first, read it, then handed it to Zoë.

"Cute," Zoë said as she handed it back to Amy. "I don't know about you guys, but I think we should leave now before it starts to rain again. There's a grocery about a block away and we can—"

"That's it?" Amy said. "Neither of you are going to comment on this card?"

Faith looked to Zoë for help. "Look," Zoë said, her voice full of patience, "I know Jeanne told us to look for business cards, but I don't think she meant she wanted us to see something about a psychic. Jeanne is a woman who studies."

"She's a scientist, actually," Faith said in the same extra patient voice.

"That's ridiculous!" Amy said. "Nobody's a scientist when it comes to the human mind."

"Okay, so I agree with you about that," Zoë said. "You know what I think she wanted us to look for in business cards?"

"What?" Amy asked.

"A Realtor."

"Why a Realtor?" Faith asked.

"I thought about it yesterday and it makes sense. Faith, you and I have no homes. I'm sure it says in some psychology textbook that patients must have homes. So Jeanne conned you and me into coming to this cute little town, told us to look at business cards, knowing that Realtors have their cards everywhere, and voilà! the spirit hits us and we buy a house here. Or two houses, that is. I don't think we should live together, do you?"

Amy was so flabbergasted by this that she could say nothing.

Faith blinked a few times before she replied. "If I were going to buy a house, it would be in Florida or southern California, not in Maine. It's beautiful here, but their winters are not for me." She leaned toward Zoë. "What I want to know is how you know that I don't own a house."

"You told us," Zoë said, the lie slipping quickly and easily off her tongue.

"I think we should go," Amy said. She wasn't going to let them see her disappointment at their reactions to the card. Let them think that the therapist meant for them to buy a house here, but Amy thought otherwise. Between her dream and the bookstore and the book, she was beginning to think that this trip was part of her destiny.

When she glanced up, the other two were looking at her. "What?"

"You just said the word 'destiny' and we wondered why."

"Oh, nothing. It's just something I've thought about. Nothing important."

"I'd like to hear it," Faith said, then glared at Zoë to keep her from making a sarcastic remark.

"Yeah, me, too," Zoë said, but there was a tone of facetiousness in her voice.

"It's nothing," Amy said. "It's just that years ago I read something that stuck in my mind. Everyone has heard about predestination, that before we're born our lives are planned out for us."

"And whoever believes that please raise their hand," Zoë said.

Faith gave her another glare and Zoë closed her mouth.

"Anyway," Amy said, "I thought about it because when I was very young I knew that Stephen was my destiny. I don't know how to explain it, but I *knew* that my destiny on earth was to marry him and have three children, two boys and a girl. When I miscarried the girl I was upset, true, but it was deeper than that. I was afraid that I had somehow accidently changed my destiny."

"If it's predestined before you're born, how can it change?" Zoë asked.

"That's what I always thought, that it couldn't change, and I guess it wouldn't if you were the only person on earth. Well, actually, that would change your destiny for sure, but, anyway, I read an article in some magazine that said that people and events can change your destiny. Like you, Zoë, that car accident could have changed your destiny."

"How do you know the accident wasn't in my destiny?"

"I don't, but since you're so angry about it, maybe your destiny was to do something else, but the accident sent you in another direction."

Zoë didn't say anything, just looked at Amy.

"And me," Faith said. "Maybe my destiny was to marry Tyler."

It took all Amy could do not to look at Zoë. If they looked at each other, it would give too much away.

"Murder must change a person's destiny," Zoë said.

"Murder?" Faith asked. "What brought that up?"

"Here!" Amy said quickly. "In this book. Lord Hawthorne was killed in his sleep. Someone plunged a knife in his heart."

"What a waste," Zoë said. "Are you two finished? I

think we should leave." She looked at Amy. "Unless you have another fascinating word to whisper."

"No, destiny is my word for the day. I'm ready if you are." She picked up her handbag and her book, then reached for the business card on the table, but Faith held on to it.

"Interesting come-on this woman has," she said. "To rewrite one's past."

"And if you could, what would you do?" Zoë asked, standing and looking down at Faith.

"Probably nothing," she said as she stood up. "I think my destiny was decided for me by Tyler Parks. I think that if he'd climbed in my window a second time I would have run off with him." She shrugged. "But he didn't. He ran off, true, but it was probably with a blonde."

When Faith looked at the other two, they weren't smiling. "It was just a joke. Don't you two have a sense of humor?"

"Sure," Amy said. "Wait until tomorrow when I tell you about the dream I'm going to have tonight."

Amy and Zoë left the shop in front of Faith. "You have to tell her," Amy said under her breath. "She needs to know."

"Why? So she can go back in time and change her destiny?"

"You can laugh at me all you want, but I think she needs to know."

"Who needs to know what?" Faith asked, coming up behind them.

"What she's going to put in the salad she's going to make tonight," Amy said quickly.

"Yes, of course," Faith said, but they could tell she knew they'd been talking about her. "I'll help you choose," she said, then walked ahead of them.

Amy glared at Zoë. Tell her! she mouthed. Tell her.

Ten

Again, Amy was dreaming.

The man was getting on a horse. It was pouring down rain, she was standing in a mud puddle, and looking up at him. To her left was the tavern.

"Someone is going to kill you," she said as she tried to keep the water out of her eyes while she looked up at him.

The man smiled down at her, rain dripping off his hat. "I thank you for the warning," he said, amused. "It is most kind of you."

"No!" Amy said, moving closer to him. "You have to listen to me. Someone is going to kill you in your bed. They're going to put a knife through your heart while you sleep."

The man frowned at that. "I do not like soothsayers," he said. "They go against God. Beware who you tell your evil predictions to or someone may remove your head." He reined his horse away, obviously wanting to get away from her.

"Is she botherin' you, my lord," said a man from behind Amy. He was short and fat and wore a leather apron. Before the man on the horse could answer, the fat man gave Amy a backhand slap that sent her sprawling in the mud. "Get back to work," he shouted at her.

The older man looked up at Lord Hawthorne, blinking against the rain. "She be me own daughter but she's a worthless lot. I'll see that she don't bother you no more, sir."

Lord Hawthorne reached into his pocket, pulled out a coin, and tossed it to the man, who caught it easily. "Don't beat her. If I return here and see bruises on her I'll hold you responsible."

Smiling, the man winked at Lord Hawthorne. "Oh, aye, me lord, I'll be careful that the marks don't show."

Lord Hawthorne looked at Amy standing behind her father. Her nose was swollen from the blows of her sister and now there was a bruise growing on her jaw from where her father had just hit her. "How much for her?"

The man licked his lips. "For the night?"

"Nay, to take her with me."

"Two guineas," the man quickly said.

Lord Hawthorne reached into his pocket, found the coins, and tossed them to the man. He looked at Amy. "Climb into the cart if you want to go. I will not wait for you to gather your flea-ridden goods."

Amy didn't lose a second before she jumped onto a two-wheeled cart. It was packed so full of trunks and cases that she could hardly find standing room, but that didn't bother her. She just wanted to get away from the place where people were free to hit her. She managed to squeeze herself in between two trunks and sat down on a third one. The rain was coming down hard in her eyes, but she could still see that the man who was supposed to be her father didn't so much as look after her long enough to wave goodbye. She looked up at Lord Hawthorne as the man leading the old cart horse began to move, but he didn't look at her. She was wet and her face hurt, but once she'd made herself a cavelike space between and under the trunks, she realized how tired she was. The sound of the rain and the moving of the cart soon lulled her to sleep.

⚜⚜

The next morning, Amy took her time getting dressed and she did what she could to cover the new bruise on her jaw. It hurt to open her mouth and she was sure her eye was going to turn black.

"What truck hit you?" Zoë asked when she saw Amy.

Faith stared for a moment, then pulled out a chair for her. "You don't look good."

"Thanks," Amy said. "My mirror didn't have enough bad to say about me, so you two told me more." She sneezed.

"Are you catching a cold?" Faith asked.

"No," Zoë said, looking up from her sketch pad, "she's had another dream."

"Have you?"

" 'Fraid so," Amy said, and sneezed again.

Faith handed her a glass of orange juice. "You want to tell us about it?"

In between sneezes and gulps of juice, Amy told them about the second dream. "When I woke up from it, it was the middle of the night, my nightgown was soaking wet, my hair sopping, and my jaw hurt like heck."

"From where dear ol' dad smacked you," Zoë said in wonder.

"I was either in the eighteenth century or I was sleep-walking and jumped in the shower with my clothes on," Amy said. "Take your pick."

"Shower," Faith said.

"I like the man on a horse. Please tell me it was a black horse," Zoë said.

"Like midnight," Amy answered.

"Were you reading that book again last night?" Faith asked. "Before you went to sleep?"

"Yes," Amy said, blowing her nose. "But I nearly always read before I go to sleep and not once have I dreamed about the characters in a book."

"Maybe you should go to Madame Zora and get your future told," Zoë said, her tone teasing.

"It was Zoya, not Zora."

"Whatever," Zoë said. She turned her sketchbook around so Amy could see what she'd drawn. She'd made a full-length portrait of the Dark Stephen, as Amy thought of him.

Taking the pad, Amy looked at the drawing. There was the man wearing his black clothes, complete with long cape and silver sword. His hair was long and hung about his eyes—eyes that were intense but kind at the same time.

"He is perfect," she whispered. She was looking at the drawing so she didn't see the way Faith and Zoë glanced at each other, as though they were concerned about her but didn't want to say so. "It's hard to believe you drew him so well just from my description."

"How could I not?" Zoë asked. "You described him in such detail I could see every inch of him. Maybe if I slept in your bed I'd have a dream about him. I could stand that."

"She had a little help from this," Faith said, handing Amy a copy of *The Scarlet Letter*. In the back was a photo of a portrait of Nathaniel Hawthorne, a truly beautiful man.

"It does look like him," Amy said. "But there's something different about the eyes of my man."

"Your man?" Zoë said, raising her eyebrows.

"I'm beginning to think he's part of me," Amy said softly as she reluctantly handed the drawing back to Zoë.

Faith put a bowl and a spoon in front of Amy and she poured herself some cereal.

"Do you think that if I called Jeanne she'd know anything about this?"

"No!" Faith and Zoë said loudly in unison.

Faith recovered first. "I'm sure Jeanne would love to hear about a woman who has dreams so real that if it rains in the dream she wakes up wet, but . . ." She looked at Zoë for help.

"You'd end up spending the next several years of your life going to therapy and talking about what you could just as well tell your friends."

Amy thought about her friends at home. Without exception, they were like her. It was true that some of them had been through divorces and they'd had their share of grief, but all in all, not much supernatural had ever happened to them. Most of them said they didn't believe in ghosts. If Amy told them of her very realistic dreams, she doubted that they'd ever speak to her again.

"Do you know why your therapist sent us here?" Amy asked.

"She wouldn't tell me a word," Zoë said. "She just said I was to consider it a vacation and that if I did it, she'd give me a good report to the court."

"Isn't that blackmail?" Amy asked.

"As black as it gets," Zoë said, "but she knows I'll do most anything to quit having to check in to my parole officer, so to speak."

"I don't understand why a court ordered you to seek therapy if you didn't want it," Amy said. "Losing your memory isn't a criminal offense."

"Actually, I wondered about that too," Faith said, and both women looked at Zoë.

When about three minutes went by and it didn't

seem that the two women were going to relent in their staring, Zoë sighed. "Okay, so maybe there was more to it than just losing my memory. Let's just say that I was a bit angry that the people I'd known all my life weren't speaking to me."

"So?" Faith asked.

"So nothing," Zoë said as she picked up her pad and started to leave the room.

She got halfway out before Amy spoke. "Next time I have a dream I'm going to tell Faith but not you."

Zoë glared at Amy and was about to say something, but she closed her mouth. "Okay," Zoë said at last, "I told you that the last thing I remembered was the high school prom?"

"Yes," Faith said.

"When I woke up it was, well . . . A bit disconcerting to be told that not one person had come to see me in the hospital. Not my sister, not any of my cousins, not all the girls I'd giggled with in high school. Nobody."

"White-hot rage?" Amy said.

"That describes it. At first I tried not to care, but as I healed, I began to get angry. In fact, I think rage may have been the fuel behind my rehabilitation."

"So what did you do to get the attention of the court?" Faith asked.

"I . . . Well, I sort of, well . . ." Zoë put on a look of defiance that dared them to judge her. "I had the car I crashed in hauled to the center of town and I set it on fire."

At first Faith and Amy just blinked at her, then Amy started to laugh. A second later, Faith joined her, and after that, Zoë began to laugh. They were falling over one another. Faith made hand motions of the car, then yelled, "Kaboom!"

"Was it a big fire?" Amy asked, still laughing and holding her face to keep it from hurting.

"Huge. Enormous. I dumped four gallons of gasoline on the thing and it went up in a great blast. I think the tank was still full."

Faith was holding her stomach laughing. "Did they come out to see it?"

"Everyone did," Zoë said, laughing. "The whole town. Bells went off, people screamed, and everyone was flapping their arms."

"Anything else burn?" Amy asked, pausing for a moment.

"Just grass. I put the wreck smack in the center of the town square. There weren't even any trees nearby. I wanted a clear spot where everyone would see it."

"I can visualize the whole thing," Faith said, grinning.

"Where were *you*?" Amy asked.

"I was standing as close as I could get without getting burned," Zoë said. "Like this." She stood with her legs apart and her arms crossed over her chest. Her face had an expression of defiance that dared anyone to mess with her.

"I would have stayed away from you," Amy said. "What about you, Faith?"

"Wouldn't have got within a hundred feet. But did they? Surely, someone must have approached you."

"No one," Zoë said with pride. "Well, not until the police showed up and they, well, sort of touched me."

"Handcuffs?" Amy asked. "Read you your rights?"

"Yup," Zoë said. "But it was worth it. I saw my sister in the crowd, and when she saw me, she ran away as fast as she could. She couldn't face me."

"Or her guilt," Amy said.

Zoë stopped smiling and sat down. "You know, when I saw her run, that's just what I thought, that she looked guilty. If the car hadn't exploded right then and the fire department hadn't pulled up with their sirens blaring, I might have run after her."

"Interesting," Amy said. "I wonder what she told people and what the truth was?"

"Don't get me started on sisters," Faith said, then shook her head at Zoë. "I understand why you did what you did, but I'd never have the courage to do something like that."

"You should have stood up to your mother-in-law while your husband was alive," Zoë said. "You shouldn't have let her beat you down until you exploded." Zoë stopped when Amy's look reminded her that they weren't supposed to know how serious Faith's attack on her mother-in-law had been—or the consequences.

"Yeah, sure I should have," Faith said, her eyes not meeting Zoë's. She got up and went to the sink.

Amy looked at Zoë. "Even after all that, you still

didn't find out what happened just before your wreck?"

"No," Zoë said. "I spent a few days in jail, then had to do some community service, and—"

"In your hometown?" Amy asked.

"No." All the humor left Zoë's face. "That's what the judge wanted, but the mayor refused to have me. I ended up working at an old-age home."

"I bet you drew for them," Faith said.

"Sure did. It was better than cleaning bedpans. I took the photos of their grandkids and made portraits. It was through them that I met their rich kids and started my job as an itinerant portrait painter."

"Destiny," Amy said, and Zoë groaned. "No, maybe it was your destiny to meet those people and draw their grandchildren, and through them—"

"Yesterday you said that my destiny had been changed and that's why I was so angry."

"What do I know?" Amy said. "The only destiny I'm *sure* about is my own. I was supposed to marry Stephen and have three children. There's a little girl's spirit just waiting for me to make a body for her."

Faith smiled at Amy. "I wish I had your conviction," she said. "I've never been sure about what I was supposed to do."

"Murder your mother-in-law," Zoë said quickly, then looked at Amy. "If Stephen is your destiny, then why are you having these fabulous dreams about another man?"

"I don't know," Amy said.

"Maybe it's what Zoë said about past lives." Both Amy and Zoë looked at Faith in puzzlement. "What if Stephen is your destiny in this life and this Hawthorne is your destiny in a past life?"

"I'm not sure I believe in past lives," Amy said, but she was thinking about what Faith said.

"I think you should find out as much as you can about this man Hawthorne, and if you have another dream about him, you should do what you can to change his fate," Faith said.

"But that doesn't make sense," Zoë said. "If she changed what happened to the man, would the books change? The print? How is that possible?"

"I don't know," Amy said, then put her hand to her face in pain. "If it weren't for the physical evidence, I'd think I'd made it all up." She looked from Faith to Zoë and smiled. "I want to thank both of you for not making fun of me. If I'd told anyone else what was happening to me, they'd—"

"Think you'd hurt yourself and send you to therapy," Zoë said quickly. When Amy and Faith looked at her, she said, "Not that I know about self-mutilation. But, anyway, Amy, I'm glad you're telling us all this because they're great stories. I think that today I might add some paint to these pictures of Nathaniel Hawthorne's English cousin or whoever he is."

"What about you, Amy?" Faith asked. "Any plans for today?"

The way she said it made Amy know that Faith

wanted to do something on her own. But that was good for Amy because she had her own plans. "I didn't buy those sheets I owe Jeanne," she said, "so I think I'll get them. Thank heavens she has good mattress pads on the bed or it would have been soaked last night."

"If that had happened, Jeanne would ask you so many questions that you'd end up telling her about your dreams," Zoë said.

"She's that persuasive?"

"Yes and no. If you work at it, she can be got around," Zoë said.

"Okay," Amy said, standing up. "I'm going to go exploring on my own today. I'll get sheets and . . ." She shrugged. She knew exactly what she wanted to do, but she wasn't going to tell them.

Thirty minutes later, Amy was dressed and the bruises on her face were covered as best she could. She'd taken two pain tablets to dull the ache. When she left, Zoë was bent over her sketch pad and Faith was on the Internet. They hardly looked up when Amy said goodbye.

As soon as she was outside, Amy looked again at the card in her hand. Madame Zoya, 333 Everlasting Street. She didn't remember seeing the street but she was determined to find it. She didn't want to ask directions from anyone for fear they'd laugh at her for going to the local psychic.

Amy thought she was doing well around Faith and Zoë because she wasn't letting them see how much the dreams were beginning to upset her. The idea that she was living these dreams to the point where she woke up with signs of them on her body was enough, but there was more than that. They were disturbing her inside, in her mind. The man Hawthorne seemed to mean something to her. Yes, he resembled Stephen, but it went deeper than that. She felt something between them.

She told herself it wasn't love. Now, in the bright sunshine of a Maine morning, all she could see was Stephen and her love for him and their children. She had no love for any man other than her husband. But when she was in the dreams, it was almost as if she were another person. She could remember Stephen, yes, but he seemed far away. When she was there, when she was looking at the dark man, all she could really see was him.

She hadn't told the other women, but in the second dream she'd felt a longing for the man that she hadn't felt since when she'd first met Stephen. A lot of people laughed at Amy when she told them that she'd known since she was a young child that she and Stephen were going to be married and spend their lives together. "How boring," said a young girl at their church. "If I thought I was only going to meet one man in my life and stay with him forever, I'd shoot myself." Amy wanted to tell the girl that she had no romance in her soul, but she didn't.

In all the years she'd been with Stephen, Amy had never felt as though she were missing something. She'd been to bed with one man and she'd never wanted more.

But now that she'd been having these dreams, something was happening to her. Not in her present world, but in his. In his world she could feel herself changing, being pulled to this man who wasn't her husband.

As she puzzled over what was going on in her life, she walked about the town, and when she saw the sign for Everlasting Street, she went down it. Immediately, she was surrounded by beautiful forest. Turning, she looked back to see the shops and the cars, but the farther she walked, the trees closed in around her.

Abruptly, the road turned right and there was the prettiest Victorian house that Amy had ever seen. It wasn't overpoweringly large, but every bit of it was exquisite, and the painting was art. It was done in three colors of green, brown, and a neutral taupe. The pretty porch was draped with blooming wisteria and a tall hedge of lilacs ran along the side. Amy could smell the flowers.

The numbers were in shiny brass on the side of the house, and she knew it was the place she'd needed to find. She wanted to talk to a woman who claimed she could rewrite a person's past. Of course Amy knew that couldn't true, but she hoped that maybe the woman had talked to enough people that she could answer some of Amy's questions. Maybe the woman had heard of other people who dreamed as realistically as Amy had.

She stepped onto the porch and noticed how clean and neat it was. She pushed the button for the doorbell and within seconds it was opened by a pleasant-looking little woman. She was short and round and could have posed for a portrait of Mrs. Claus.

"Are you Madame Zoya?" Amy asked.

"No," she said sweetly, holding the door open. "I'm Primrose, her sister. Do come in. Maybe you'd like some tea."

As Amy couldn't resist seeing the interior of the house, she stepped inside. She was glad to see that there was no hard, uncomfortable Victorian furniture. Instead, it was English country, which she loved so much. In her opinion, John Fowler, the famous English interior designer, should be canonized.

"Beautiful," she breathed. The walls were covered with fabric, a grayish silk that made the room look rich and comfortable at the same time. Truly beautiful. This room and the one in the bookshop, she thought. That's what I'd want for my own office.

"I thought you'd like this room," Primrose said. "It suits you. If you'll have a seat, I'll make us some tea."

"Yes, thank you," Amy said absently as she went into the living room. She always carried a little notebook with her and she couldn't help making notes about the colors and patterns of the fabrics. She sat down on the pretty sofa and made a sketch of the layout of the furniture and the placement of the windows.

Just when she'd finished, Primrose returned with a big tray with a pretty porcelain pot, cups, and a plate full of warm cookies. She set it on the coffee table, then took a seat across from Amy on the chintz-covered chair.

"Now, what can I do for you, dear?" Primrose said as she poured the tea.

"I . . ." Amy wasn't sure where to begin. "I found a card from your sister, Madame Zoya, and I . . ." She what? She wasn't sure what to say.

"You want to go back in time and change your life," Primrose said knowingly.

"No!" Amy said quickly and much too loudly. "I mean, no, I don't want to change even one day of my life."

"Then why were you given a card?"

"Given a card?" Amy said. "Oh no, I wasn't given your sister's business card, I found it by accident. It was in a book that I bought at the bookstore." She tried to remember the name of the store but couldn't. "The store down the alleyway."

"I know which one," Primrose said with a smile. "But, you see, my sister doesn't allow just anyone to get her cards. They must need them."

"Need them? I don't understand. Don't you need to . . ." How could she put this delicately? "You need to run a business, don't you?"

"Oh, I see. Money. You want to know how we support ourselves if we just give out a few cards." Primrose smiled. "We have money from our father. He provided for us, so we don't have to worry. But I'm curious. If you were given a card, but you don't want to change your life, why are you here?"

"I wanted to talk to someone about something odd

that's been happening to me and I thought that maybe a psychic might understand things better than I do."

"But my sister isn't a psychic," Primrose said. "She doesn't read minds."

"I'm not asking anyone to read my mind. I just . . ." Amy hesitated, and when she tried to talk again, there were tears in her eyes and her throat was closing. "I'm sorry. I've been through a lot in the last few months and I'm not myself."

Primrose poured Amy another cup of tea. "Why don't you tell me everything? Starting from the beginning."

"You mean, from when I lost the baby?"

"I think that would be a very good place to start."

It took Amy thirty minutes to tell her whole story. During that time Primrose sipped tea, ate half a dozen chocolate-dipped cookies, and never said a word, but Amy could feel the intensity of her listening.

"And that's where I am now," Amy said, putting down her cup. "For the second morning in a row I had to put my sheets through the washer. And look at my face!"

"You can hardly see the bruises," Primrose said, but she was no longer smiling. "I must say that I've never heard a tale like yours. Usually, the people who receive my sister's cards are like the women you're staying with. They desperately need to change their lives."

"But they haven't received the cards."

"Yes they have," Primrose said. "They may not have

seen them yet, but they've received them. That poor, poor girl. What is her name?"

"Zoë."

"She had so much taken from her life. And the other one. I saw her after the hairdresser worked on her. She's so much better now, but she's still an old woman. Misery wears one down."

"You seem to know us well," Amy said.

"Oh yes. Such interesting people stay at Jeanne's house."

"Do you know her?"

Primrose smiled. "You want to know if *she* has received a card."

"And I thought you couldn't read minds."

Primrose laughed, but she didn't answer the question. "Of course I see all of my sister's clients, and I must say that they are an unhappy lot. Without exception, they have all had dreadful lives."

"Their destinies have been misdirected by other people," Amy said quietly.

Primrose looked as though someone had pinched her. "You are exactly right, dear. The truth is that my sister merely puts their destinies back on track. It's like a train that's been derailed. Sometimes the train goes off in a different direction, on a side track, but sometimes it falls onto its side and just lies there in the dirt."

"That's Faith and Zoë," Amy said. "Zoë acts tough but she's not. She makes her living by staying in other people's houses and painting portraits. Faith lives alone in an apartment in New York and visits a therapist three times a week. Neither of them have lives."

"Like you do?"

"Like I do," Amy said. "Am I strange because I like my life? I wouldn't trade my husband and children or even my house for any other."

"Yes, dear, you are a rarity. You are a person who is content with her life. When you speak of your family it's as though your entire body glows."

"So why did *I* receive a card from your sister?"

"I would imagine it's because of your dreams. I think your destiny in another life was derailed."

"That's just what Faith said."

"Perhaps you should go back and fix it," Primrose said.

"Go back? You mean as in a hypnotic regression?"

"No. What my sister does is a great deal more than that. She has a gift where she can send people back to any time in their lives for three weeks."

"Three weeks?" Amy asked as she tried to comprehend this concept. "What could a person do in three weeks?"

"It only takes a small thing to change a person's life. Say no to a marriage proposal. Say no to getting into a car at a certain time. Or say yes to an opportunity."

"All right," Amy said, "say you go back and change something, but then what happens?"

"Why, everything changes, of course."

Amy blinked a few times. "Changes? You mean your whole life?"

"Of course."

"How could that be? What if, say, a person had written a book about a trip he took, but the second time around, he didn't take that trip and so didn't write the book. What would happen to the copies of that book? And what about people's memories?"

"Then the book would not exist and no one would remember that it ever had. It can be quite disconcerting that you remember something that no one else does."

Amy opened and closed her mouth a few times. "But how . . . ?"

"I don't know," Primrose said. "Nor does my sister know how it works. It's a gift she's had since she was eighteen. Something . . . well, rather unusual happened to her and since then she's been able to send people back to the past."

"Why hasn't the world heard of this?" Amy asked softly.

"We're careful that people at large do not hear. And . . . Well, my sister can change the past."

"Oh!" Amy said. "You mean that if someone told the secret your sister could go back and change it?"

Primrose shrugged. "I couldn't know, now could I?"

"Of course, because you wouldn't remember. Could a person go back and change a big thing?"

"You mean things like disasters and plane crashes, don't you?"

"And assassinations that start wars," Amy said.

"Alas, no. My sister tried that. She wanted to go back

and stop Eve from eating that forbidden fruit. But it didn't work. Her abilities are wonderful, but they're limited to the personal problems of individuals."

"But what if I want to go back, not to my immediate past, but to before that? To another life I may have had?"

"I don't know," Primrose said. "I've never encountered this situation before."

"What I want to know is if changing my destiny in the past would change my present life. If, say, there were a way to change what happened to a man in the past, say I kept him from being killed, would that change *me* today?"

"Very interesting question," Primrose said. "I can't give you an answer, but in my experience, true love usually wins over everything."

"True love didn't win in Faith's life and I don't think Zoë has ever experienced it."

"If that were true, she'd have no need of my sister's services."

Amy blinked for a few seconds. "You mean that Zoë loved someone but that person hasn't come forward?"

"Perhaps," Primrose said as she glanced at the clock. "I really think I've said too much. My sister will cut off my chocolate for a week. Hmmm, it seems that the teapot is empty."

Amy knew that was her cue to leave, but she had a thousand questions that needed answering. "All of this is so new to me," she said. "Since I lost my baby nothing has been the same in my life."

"Perhaps your daughter didn't want to be born to someone whose destiny was off track."

"If my destiny *is* out of balance it's not because of anything I've done in this life." Her head came up. "How did you know I was to have a daughter?"

"Intuition. You have a house full of men. Tell me, what does your husband do for a living?"

Amy sighed. "He runs the trucking company that his father started. It's not Stephen's choice of careers, but it makes good money. His three older brothers are . . ." She tried to think of the kindest way of describing them. "They like adventure and excitement. They never seem able to settle down to any one thing, not a job, a wife, or anything."

"Hotheaded speed demons?" Primrose said so pleasantly that Amy laughed.

"That's about right."

"I'm not a trained therapist and I'm no psychic, but it seems to me that while your destiny may be on track, maybe the destinies of the people close to you are not."

Amy well knew that Stephen wasn't as perfectly happy as she was. He loved her and his children, but his job was not of his choice. But Stephen wasn't a complainer and he was a man of honor. When his eldest brother refused to take over the family business, it had gone to the next son, who had also refused to take it on. Too much work, too much responsibility, not enough excitement, was what they said. Stephen had also wanted to turn down the job, but he hadn't been able to stand the disappointment in his father's face and voice. When he was just weeks out of college, he'd gone to work for his father. Over the years he'd expanded the business and had made a very good living, but sometimes Amy had seen him looking at his brothers with envy. They went from one job to another and took off when they wanted to. When they got behind on child support payments, they "borrowed" from Stephen. After all, he was running a *family* business. To their minds, the profits belonged to all of them.

It was Stephen in his unlikable job, and the callousness and ingratitude of his father and brothers, that made Amy often drive herself to exhaustion. She wanted everything at home to be peaceful and perfect for Stephen.

Amy looked at Primrose. "Do you think that if I could change the destiny of this man who looks like my husband that I could change Stephen's circumstances in *this* life?" Her eyes lit up. "Could I change his brothers? Maybe even change his father?"

"I really don't know," Primrose said. "All I know for sure is that my sister only gives out her card to people who need her and that true love is always involved. Now, if you'll excuse me, I have some things to do." She stood up.

Amy wanted to stay there all day and ask the woman questions, but she knew she was being dismissed. When she stood up, she glanced out the windows at the sunlight. "Do you think it's pouring down rain out there?"

Primrose laughed so hard that Amy was afraid the little old lady was going to choke. "You have brightened my day, my whole week," she said to Amy at the door. "And I shall think about the questions you've asked me."

"If I do want to . . . do this, I mean, do what it says on the card, what do I do?"

"The three of you come back here together and my sister will meet you at the door and she'll tell you what to do." Primrose lowered her voice. "I shouldn't give you any advice, but I really think you *must* do whatever you need to to get your destiny back on track. And, dear," she said in a warning voice, "you need to choose the time carefully. There have been mistakes made and some people return to the wrong time and don't change a thing. My sister doesn't allow them to try again."

She patted Amy's arm. "But I think you know what time you want to go back to. And oh yes, each of you should bring one hundred dollars. That's what she charges."

Amy stepped onto the porch, then turned back. "Could someone go with me?"

"With you?" Primrose asked, surprised. "You mean go back with you to change *your* life?"

"Yes. I wish Zoë could go with me. I think that right now, the way things are, even if she had a chance to return to the past, she wouldn't go. I've never seen anyone with so much anger inside her."

"You have the most extraordinary ideas," Primrose said. "Let me talk to my sister about this. She'll have the answers when you return. But I would think that if anyone is to go with you, she'll have to want to."

"Don't worry. Zoë would go back just for the man's horse."

Again Primrose laughed. "What is it about beautiful men on beautiful horses? Would that *I* could go back with you."

"Why don't you?" Amy said, her eyes alight.

"It's your destiny," Primrose said as she stepped back into the house. "Your destiny, not mine," she said as she closed the door.

"Mine or Stephen's or the dark man's or even Zoë's," Amy muttered. "I can't figure out what belongs to whom."

Eleven

❧

"*Poppycock!*" *Faith said.* "That's the most absurd thing I've ever heard in my life."

"I've looked through everything I have and I have no business card from your magic woman," Zoë said.

"She's not mine," Amy said, exasperated. She had made dinner tonight, a lovely chicken dish that she often made for guests at home. She'd bought all the ingredients and done all the work by herself. Her plan was to tell the women about her visit to Primrose once they'd each had a few glasses of wine.

But Zoë thwarted her. As soon as they sat down, Zoë asked, "So what do you want?"

"Whatever do you mean?" Amy asked in her most innocent voice.

Faith and Zoë just stared at her.

"Okay," Amy said, "I went to Madame Zoya's house today." She then proceeded to tell them what she wanted them to know of the visit. She left out anything that she feared would upset them.

Neither Faith nor Zoë believed a word of it.

"It's not possible," Faith said. "No one can change the past. You can't go back."

"And I wouldn't want to," Zoë said.

Amy looked at her in astonishment. "You wouldn't want to go back to three weeks before your accident and stop it from happening?"

"No," Zoë said. "That accident was the best thing that ever happened to me. I found out who really loved me and I started drawing. The doctors said they thought parts of my brain were hit in a way that made me forget some things while others were enhanced. I'd rather draw than deal with a lot of people who never really cared about me in the first place."

Amy didn't know how to deal with logic like that.

"Besides," Faith said, "we don't have the cards so we're not invited. Why don't you go by yourself?"

"I got the idea that if the three of us don't go together, nothing can be done. It's all of us together or no one gets to change her destiny." This was the lie she'd come up with on her walk back from Primrose's house. If she could go back in time—which was, of course, impossible—and she could take Zoë, then why not Faith too?

But nothing Amy said changed their minds. They had no interest in going to a "charlatan" as they called the woman Amy had met. They didn't want to talk to her and certainly didn't want to pay money for her ridiculous claims.

After dinner Faith and Zoë practically ran into the living room, leaving Amy to do the cleaning up.

"If this keeps up, we'll achieve nothing," Amy muttered as she filled the dishwasher. She had a feeling that by tomorrow the other women would start talking about going home. And Amy knew that if her family were at home and waiting for her and not on a camping trip, she'd want to go home too.

But she also knew that she was the only one who'd had dreams so real that they haunted her even when she was awake. She was the one who sat in sunshine when it was raining. She was the one who'd talked to a little old lady and come away feeling that changing a destiny that had gone in the wrong direction was a perfectly feasible idea. And most of all, she was the one who had a place and time so fully in her head that she sometimes got confused as to where she was. But no matter what she said, she couldn't get Faith or Zoë to agree with her.

On the other hand, everything had been shown to Amy, not to Faith or Zoë. So how could she expect them to want to participate?

When she finished in the kitchen, Amy went into the living room, but Faith didn't look up from the TV show she was watching, and Zoë's eyes never left her sketch pad. Amy could see that Zoë was drawing Faith. She wasn't making sketches of the man on the horse.

"I think I'll go to bed," Amy said. The others didn't look up as they said good night.

She went to her bedroom, took a long shower, then got into her nightgown and slipped under the covers. It was still early, but she was tired from what she'd been through that day. It took a lot out of a person to be beaten up during the night, then to wrestle with destiny questions during the day. The worst had been trying to talk to Faith and Zoë.

Friends, she thought as she turned out the light. She'd really begun to think that Faith and Zoë were her friends, but they had looked at her just like Amy thought a person off the street would look at her at the mention of time travel and destinies—as though she were demented.

As she fell into sleep, Amy thought that maybe she was losing, if not her mind, certainly her touch with reality. She had everything a person could want in life, so why was she considering fooling around with it? Why was she trying to change things? Not that she could change anything, but . . .

She drifted off to sleep.

The dream came almost instantly. The man was dead and everyone was crying. Amy, wearing a long dress of blue and white print, was too stunned to know what she was doing. She had a set of keys in her hand but she didn't know what they opened. There seemed to be people asking her what they were to do, but she couldn't focus enough to understand them. He was dead. Killed during the night with a big knife stabbed through his heart.

She could hear crying all through the house. A woman was crying loudly, and as she went up the wooden staircase, she heard a man sobbing. She opened a door and looked inside to see a gray-haired man in bed. He was thin, as though he were wasting away from some disease, and his face was red with his weeping. "Go! Leave me!" he ordered.

She saw two young women who looked to be maids and their eyes were red. Behind them a door was open and Amy went to it. She felt unreal, as though she were in her body but not in it.

Inside the room were three men, all dressed formally in black coats, white shirts, and tight black trousers. Two of them wore wigs. They were talking quietly among themselves while taking frequent glances at the man on the bed.

Amy went to him. He looked like he was sleeping, his face calm, peaceful, as handsome as always. He was wearing his clothes and looked as though he'd lain down for a nap. If it weren't for the dark stain where his heart was, she wouldn't have known he was dead.

"Who did this?" she asked the men.

"We do not know," one man said. "He was found that way this morning. By the coldness of his body, it must have happened yesterday. Did you see anyone?"

Amy could only shake her head. The truth was that she didn't remember anything that had happened since she climbed on the cart. How long had it been? By the way she was dressed and by the keys at her waist, she'd been given the job of housekeeper. For all she knew, it could have been years ago that she got on the cart.

Reaching out her hand, she smoothed his hair back from his brow, then kissed his cold cheek. The men were watching her, but she didn't care. Her tears began and they dropped onto his face. She'd never again see him laugh. Never again argue with him. She'd never tell him that he was wrong and had no idea what he was talking about.

As she looked down at him, she realized that memories were coming back to her. She had never been subservient to him. She'd always stood up to him and told him what she thought. Many times he'd told her that he understood why her father had sold her. "And I paid too much!" he'd shouted at her.

But through all the arguing, through the constant clash of wills, he'd elevated her to a high status—and he hadn't sent her away.

As she stood there a pretty young woman came into the room. From her dress she was of the same class as the man. It took her a moment, but then Amy remembered that the young woman was his sister, and that the man had loved her very much.

The young woman bent over the man from the other side of the bed. "What will I do without you, Tristan?" she whispered. "How can I live without you?" She looked across him to Amy. "What will we do? How can we live without him?"

All Amy could do was shake her head that she didn't know. Her throat had closed and the tears had begun in earnest.

❦❦

"Amy!" Faith said, her hands on Amy's shoulders. "Wake up! It's only a dream. You're safe. Wake up!"

Amy opened her eyes and saw the two women hanging over her, but she couldn't leave the place she'd been in her mind. "He was dead," she cried. "Someone killed him." She put her hands over her face and kept crying.

Zoë stood beside Faith. Both women were fully dressed so it wasn't late.

"There was a girl there," Amy said, still crying hard and her face still covered. "She was his sister and I could feel her pain. I could feel that she wanted to go with him. Who could have done such a thing? Why was such a horrible thing done to him? He was a good man."

"Amy," Faith said softly as she pulled her hands away from her face, "look at me. It was only a dream. You're safe now and you're here. The dream will go away."

"It will never go away," Amy said, looking up at her. "Don't you understand that it's real? It's real and I'll never be able to change it. I know I *must* go back and stop him from being murdered, but I *can't* go. Primrose said I had to show up with both of you but you won't even *try* to go!"

The two women were silent for a moment, then Zoë spoke. "Faith, if we don't agree to go with her to see some witch doctor we're going to be here all night."

Faith sighed. "Okay. Amy, Zoë and I will go with you to see that woman tomorrow." When Amy didn't stop crying, Faith said it louder. "Did you hear me? We'll go."

"But it's too late," Amy said. "He's already been killed. Murdered in his sleep. There was a man in a bedroom, crying. He was very ill. I don't know who he was, but I don't think he was going to live much longer." She looked up at Faith. "I think he was Tristan's father. No, he was an uncle. Yes, that's who he was and he was dying. He—"

"Amy!" Faith said loudly. "Stop it! I mean it. It was just a dream."

Zoë had picked up the old book from the bedside table and opened it. "It says here that Tristan Hawthorne was stabbed to death in 1797 by an unknown assailant."

"So long ago," Amy said, tears still rolling down her cheeks.

"Yes and no," Zoë said. "Maybe if you can go back in history you could go to a time before 1797 and save him. You could prevent his death."

"How? I don't know who could do such a thing," Amy said. "You should have seen it. Everyone was crying, even the maids. He was a man who was loved by everyone."

Zoë sat down on the bed in front of Amy. "You need to get hold of yourself. Something is causing these dreams, and no matter what you think now, they *will* go away. I know because after I was in the crash I had horrible dreams."

"About the wreck?" Amy asked, sniffing and wiping her face with the tissues Faith handed her.

"No, about things that made no sense to me. I saw a man shoot himself in the head. I saw it over and over. I'd wake up screaming and the nurses would come running. After a while they gave me pills so strong that I had no more dreams."

"But Zoë," Amy said, blinking back her tears, "don't you see that that might have really happened? Maybe seeing that is what made you drive a car too fast or whatever made you crash. Maybe—"

"I have one therapist I don't want, so don't *you* start on me," Zoë said. Her words were harsh, but she picked up Amy's tear-soaked hands and held them. "Tomorrow morning bright and early, the three of us are going to this woman you met and see if her sister can help you. Maybe she can hypnotize you deeply enough that you can get rid of these dreams. Faith and I are getting tired of every morning seeing you with bruises all over your face."

Amy looked at Zoë and managed a bit of a smile. "You're a very nice person, aren't you? And without all that makeup you're quite pretty."

Zoë stood up. "Now go back to sleep and don't do any more dreaming, you hear me?"

"Will you go with me?" Amy asked.

"I said we would," Zoë answered.

"No, I mean back to the past."

Zoë gave a little laugh, but Faith looked at Amy in wonder.

"You can't possibly believe that that woman can really—" Faith began, but Zoë stopped her.

"Yes, we'll go back with you," Zoë said. "Won't we, Faith?"

"Oh sure, why not? Better the eighteenth century than going back to New York and spending my days trying to make Jeanne believe that I am *not* suicidal."

"Do you promise?" Amy said.

"Cross my heart and hope to die," Zoë said, making the gesture.

Amy looked at Faith.

"I promise," Faith said. "If you go back in time, Zoë and I will go with you."

"All right," Amy said as she moved down into the bed. "I feel better now. The three of us will go back and save him. We'll find out who hates him and we'll stop them. I think I'll turn that knife on the killer and jab him in the heart with it."

Zoë stood up, turned out the bedside light, and she and Faith left the room.

As she closed the door, Faith said, "What in the world have you done? I don't want to go to some two-bit psychic and have her tell me my fortune."

"Me neither," Zoë said as she walked into the living

room. "My real fear is that she'll tell me what happened in my life."

Faith looked at her. "Did you really see a man kill himself?"

"I don't know, but I dreamed it often enough. I figure that I saw it as much as Amy saw an eighteenth-century man lying on his bed dead."

"Did you tell Jeanne about your dreams? Not the ones you made up, but the real ones?"

"Not a word," Zoë said.

"I see," Faith said.

"Don't start sounding like Jeanne. And what do you mean by 'I see'?"

Faith smiled. "I think you and I have some things in common. I never told her my dreams either."

Zoë smiled back. "I'm beginning to see why Jeanne sent us up here together. I guess she knows that I have a few things I refuse to tell her and so do you."

"More than a few," Faith said, and her smile widened.

"Isn't it odd that even though Amy is the one with the cute little life, she's the one having the bad dreams?" Zoë said.

"Until tonight, I thought they were good dreams."

"Me too," Zoë said as she picked up her sketch pad off the couch.

"You don't think there's any truth to what Amy seems to believe, do you?" Faith asked.

"You mean about going back in time?" Zoë smiled. "Not in the least. None whatsoever."

"That's what I think too," Faith said as she looked about the room. It was tidy, nothing left out. She turned out the light as she and Zoë went to their bedrooms.

❧❦

The next morning, Amy was the only one who was chipper. She'd had a good night's sleep after her bad dream, and she felt good. She'd even braided a few strands of her hair, intertwining it with a narrow ribbon her oldest son had painted for her. "I think we should go the first thing this morning," she said as she flipped pancakes on the grill.

Zoë was huddled over her sketch pad and Faith was looking at her plate.

"Come on, you two," Amy said as she put a tall stack of pancakes on the table. "This will be fun."

"I don't think so," Faith said.

Amy sat down beside her. "What is it that you two are so afraid of? Being trapped in the eighteenth century? I told you that Primrose said we'd only be there for three weeks."

Zoë looked at her. "I think I can speak for Faith when I say that, no, we're not afraid of being trapped in the eighteenth century." Her voice dripped sarcasm.

Amy ignored her tone. "Then why are you two so glum?"

"We're afraid of what we'll be told!" Faith said loudly. "You may have a wonderful past and a truly glorious future, but I don't. If this woman is a psychic she might see things that I don't want to see, she might tell me things I don't want to know."

"Primrose said her sister isn't a psychic. She—" Amy broke off. They didn't believe her and Amy wasn't sure she did either. "Maybe she'll see something good."

Faith just snorted.

"Glass half empty," Amy said under her breath. "What about you, Zoë? Are you afraid of the same things?"

"More or less," she said. "I know that I did something truly bad in my past and I really don't want to know what it is."

"So you're going to spend the rest of your life hiding, running from one house to another, and never getting to know anyone?" Amy asked.

"That sounds good to me," Zoë said cheerfully.

"If I could paint, that's what I'd do," Faith said. "Escape. Get as far away from my mother-in-law as I can. Did I tell you that when I'm home she calls me three times a day?"

"Even after you put her in the hospital?" Zoë asked, then bit her tongue for having given that information away.

"I don't want to know how you found that out, but yes, even after I beat her up, she still calls me. I've changed my number so many times that I can't count them, but she pays people and Web sites to find it. Wherever I go, she finds me. She keeps three private detectives on retainers."

"What does she say when she calls?" Amy asked softly.

"She cries and wants me to talk to her about Eddie. He was her entire life. She had no friends, no relatives who she liked. She just had Eddie. And me."

"That's it," Amy said, standing up. "The more I hear from you two, the more upset I become. And to think that I thought I had problems because I like to stay in my safe little world. Let's go. You two have fifteen minutes, then we're out of here."

"Sometimes I think you actually believe that you're going to . . . I can't even say it out loud," Zoë said.

Amy leaned toward her. "I don't know what's going to happen, but I'm going to make an effort. I'm not going to sit here and whine about my life."

"But then, your life is wonderful, isn't it?"

"True, it is, but I think that maybe my husband's life isn't so great and if there is anything I can do to fix it I'm going to do it."

That made Faith and Zoë look at her in astonishment. "All this is about your hunk husband?" Zoë asked.

"Yes. At least I think it may be. I don't really know what's going on, but I want my baby to *want* to be born to us."

Faith and Zoë were still blinking at her.

"Get dressed," Amy said. "I'll tell you about it on the way."

"*You're sure about* this?" the woman called Madame Zoya said. She was as round as her sister, Primrose, but there was no coziness about her. She was as stern and unbending as her sister was sweet.

"Yes," Amy said firmly while the other two said nothing.

They were in a pretty sunroom of the Victorian house. When Amy had led them down Everlasting Street, Faith said that the street had not been there the day before. "I was right here. I went from that shop to that one." She pointed to opposite sides of the street. "There was nothing in between them."

"This town is magic," Amy said.

"Or it needs a good city planner," Zoë said, looking at the forest around them.

When they stood on the little porch and rang the bell, Amy said, "I hope Primrose's sister opens the door. I think that's the signal that she'll do it."

Faith and Zoë stayed behind her, both of them torn between nervousness and feeling ridiculous.

A short, stout woman opened the door and her frown had nearly made Faith and Zoë back down the stairs. But Amy smiled broadly and stepped into the house.

"I received your card and they're going with me," she said brightly as she surreptitiously slipped three one-hundred-dollar bills into the woman's hand. She hadn't told Faith and Zoë about the money for fear that they'd say that was proof the woman was a huckster.

She looked at the two women behind Amy. "They don't really want to do this. They don't even have my card."

"I know," Amy said, "but they promised and they have to honor that, don't they?"

The woman looked Amy up and down. "You usually get your way, don't you?"

"I think that may be part of the problem," Amy said.

There was a tiny bit of a smile from the woman, then she turned and they followed her to the back of the house, to a room with windows along one wall. She sat behind a big desk and looked at Amy as the three of them sat down.

"You know the rules?"

"I think I do," Amy said, "but maybe you'd better explain them again."

"You may go back in time to any three weeks that you want, and when you return, you may choose to remember or not remember."

"Remember?" Zoë asked, not understanding.

The woman looked at Zoë with a hard glare that seemed to go through her. "You were in a serious car wreck, were you not?"

Zoë just nodded and in her mind she begged the woman not to say more.

She didn't. "If you go back and manage to prevent the car accident, you may choose to remember that it happened or not. Your choice." She looked at all three women. "I must warn you that if you change the past, you will change the future, there is no question of that. If you choose a different . . ." Hesitating, she looked at Faith. "If you choose a different man back in, say,

1992, when you return here, you will have lived a new life."

"So we wouldn't really change just three weeks," Faith said, meeting the woman's eyes.

"No. It will be your entire life that you'll change. You'll make the decision during your three weeks in the past, but I can't control what happens in your new life."

"I'd like to do something that wouldn't make me end up in mandatory therapy," Faith said.

Zoë gave her a look that spoke of betrayal, that Faith was beginning to believe this absurd idea. "If we don't go to therapy, we won't be here visiting in Jeanne's summerhouse."

"That won't change," Madame Zoya said. "You will return here to now. You may each have lived different lives, but you'll still end up here in this room."

The penetrating eyes of the woman made Zoë slump down in her chair and she almost said, "Yes, ma'am."

Madame Zoya looked from one to the other of them. "Have I made myself understood?"

The three of them nodded.

"Did your sister tell you what I want to do?" Amy asked. "I don't want to go back into my own time. I want to go back to earlier. Your sister had never heard of that being done before."

"My sister doesn't know all that I do," the woman said dismissively. "Now, if you will join hands."

"I have a question," Faith said.

"And what is it?"

"Is this Amy's one time to go back and change things, or does it count as ours too?"

"This is hers," the woman said. "Now, will you join hands, and it would be better if you close your eyes."

"I think I'll keep mine open," Zoë said, and it was obvious that she wanted to see what the woman was up to. She had a little smile on her face that said she knew it was all just a joke and nothing was going to happen.

"Suit yourself," the woman said.

They reached across the chairs, took their hands, and Faith and Amy closed their eyes. There was a bright flash, then for a moment the three women couldn't get their breaths.

In the next moment they were sitting in darkness. "What's going on?" Zoë asked, blinking rapidly. Even if it hadn't been so dark, she wouldn't have been able to see anything as the bright light had nearly blinded her.

"Sssssh," Amy said. "Listen. I think I hear sheep."

"My foot is wet," Faith said.

"I think I know where we are," Amy whispered. "In fact, I think I know a lot of things that I didn't know ten minutes ago."

Gradually, the darkness receded and they saw that they were sitting on straw in a horse stall in a barn. A man wearing a dirty white jacket that reached to below his waist, tight trousers, and some sort of gaiters to his knees was staring down at them. His weathered face was nearly covered by a floppy leather hat, and he was holding an old-fashioned pitchfork. "What ye be doin' in there, Miss Amy?" the man said. "And who be your friends?"

Amy grinned. "This is Faith and this is Zoë. They've come from America to help me."

"Ah, more of your friends," he said, chuckling at some inner joke. "I brought you three bushels of beans. Think that will be enough?"

"Maybe," Amy said as she stood up, and walked to the far side of the barn with the man.

Faith and Zoë didn't move. They sat on the straw and looked at each other. They were wearing long cotton dresses that were high-waisted and low in the front.

Faith, with her ample breasts, was nearly spilling out over the top. She put her hand to her hair and found that it was again pulled back into a bun. She couldn't help feeling deflated. She'd like having the long, loose hair of her younger days.

"Your hair's still red if that's what you were wondering," Zoë said as she stood up, then tried to take a deep breath. "I think there's a corset under this thing."

Faith blinked at Zoë. "You're pretty." Zoë's face was free of makeup and her beautiful skin was rosy with youth.

"Yeah, well . . ." Zoë said, turning pink with a blush. She lifted the long dress to see her little leather slippers. "So where do you think our clothes are?"

Faith shrugged as she stood up. "I don't know, but Amy still has her ribbon."

Zoë looked at Amy, chatting with the man as though she'd known him all her life, and in her hair was the little braid and ribbon she'd had this morning.

Amy came back to them, the man behind her. He looked the two women up and down.

"He won't like this," he said, looking at the two women. "Ye know what he said about the last lot you took on."

"Yes, Jonathan," Amy said tiredly, "I know quite well what he'll say, but these women are different." When the man started to say something else, she said, "Don't worry, I'll make him something great for dinner and he'll survive. Go on, now, and see if Helen needs anything more in the kitchen. And get me some tarragon from the garden."

She waited until he'd left the barn, then she turned to the women.

"Look, I know you two have a thousand questions, but I don't have the answers, at least not yet anyway. I can't explain it, but I know this place, and I know that the dreams I had were true. It's 1797, and he bought me from a tavern from a man posing as my father.

"Since then I've . . ." Amy waved her hand. "I've more or less managed this place." She glanced toward the barn door. "They need me inside. If I don't oversee the kitchen they'll . . . I don't know what they'll do. Can you two look around for a while and I'll see you later?"

Zoë and Faith looked at her for a moment. "Sure," Faith said. "We'll be fine. Won't we, Zoë?"

It took Amy less than a second before she was running out the door.

Zoë looked at Faith. "Look at this place! Look at us! Am I asleep or dead? Or have I just fallen into a Jane Austen novel?"

"Don't ask me," she managed to say. "This is Amy's dream, not mine." She stepped around a pile of horse manure and left the barn, Zoë close on her heels.

Part Two

Twelve

❧

Zoë followed Amy into the house, but Faith didn't go. She didn't know if she'd just been transported into the past or if she was on the set of a BBC production, but she didn't care. What she wanted to do was look at everything, and she wanted to do it by herself, with no one bothering her.

She could tell that she was at the back of a large house. It looked to be only a few years old, and it was in a style that Faith had always loved: Georgian. Everything was symmetrical. The windows were huge and she knew the rooms inside would be large and beautifully proportioned.

The big area behind the house was graveled and there was an old wagon to one side. There were two men dressed like the man in the barn, and a woman wearing a long brown dress, a cloth bonnet on her head. They were all stealing curious looks at Faith, but none of them said anything.

She nodded to them, then put her hands behind her back, turned her face to the sun and kept walking. In the years that she'd stayed at home with Eddie, while he was wasting away, Faith had spent a lot of time reading. The books about the eighteenth century were always her favorite.

If by some chance she really was back in time, she knew what she most wanted to see. She took a left down a well-trod gravel road and there it was, that paragon of industry and efficiency: the kitchen garden. As soon as she stepped through the wide gate set in the tall, brick walls, she looked about her in wonder. It was at least four acres, and every inch of the space was being used in providing what was needed to feed the people of the main house and all the many employees.

There was a walkway wide enough for a horse-drawn wagon through the center of the garden and Faith strolled down it slowly, looking at everything.

She'd read that in the twentieth century many of the old varieties had been lost. If it couldn't be put in a truck and shipped, nobody wanted to grow it. The fruits and vegetables that were too soft, too tender, or rotted too quickly, were discarded as "useless." Flavor was not considered in choosing what would be offered for sale in the modern grocery store. But in a time when people ate what they could grow, enormous variety was encouraged—and flavor was the deciding factor.

Smiling, she walked on. She counted ten men working in the garden, but there were more in the seven greenhouses and six potting sheds. She stopped to look into one building at the magnificent compost pile. It was truly a work of art. Layers of household waste, grass cuttings, leaves, and manure were piled up and tended to as though they were beds of gold—which they almost were.

She looked up at the top of the brick walls and saw that there were troughs along the top. Her eyes followed the curved spaces down and saw that every bit of rainwater was caught and diverted into covered barrels.

Green, she thought. The twenty-first century made much ado about being "green" but here it was on a scale and intensity that modern people could only dream of.

She kept walking. There was an enormous bed of flowers and she knew it was to be used for cut flowers for the house. She paced it off and saw that the bed was nearly two hundred feet long. It would supply enough flowers for a palace, she thought. The heavenly smell of them almost made her dizzy.

Beyond the flowers were the fruits. She had never dreamed there could be this much variety as she looked at ripening raspberries, red, white, and black currants, gooseberries and strawberries. Some of the beds were edged with plants that she knew were wild strawberries. The plants made no runners and the tiny berries melted on your tongue.

At the end of the garden, she halted and her eyes opened in wonder. Before her was the herb garden and it was magnificent. It was divided into three sections, with one having a six-foot-high fence around it and a lock on the gate. She could guess what it contained.

When she'd been nursing Eddie she'd become interested in herbology. She read a lot and had even persuaded her mother-in-law to allow her to put in an herb garden. "If you hide the hideous thing," the woman said as though Faith had asked to plant tobacco in front of the house.

The herb garden was the thing she'd most enjoyed in her married life because she and Eddie had done it together. At first it had only been Faith's interest, but Eddie, in bed by then and horribly bored, had wanted to work with her. They'd ordered a lot of books, then they'd read and talked and planned a design for the garden. Faith knew some rudimentary drafting techniques and she'd used them as she drew what she and Eddie came up with. The garden was to be beautiful as well as useful.

In the end, they combined two gardens from France and one from England into one design. When they finally had what they wanted, they'd celebrated with sparkling apple juice in Waterford crystal glasses.

As soon as the weather warmed up, she helped Eddie into a deck chair, nearly drowned him in blankets, and he directed her as she used string and spikes to lay out the garden so they could see how it would look.

Eddie had been near her while she'd argued with the brick mason. "You want all them little paths just so you can plant what you can buy in jars at the grocery store?"

he'd asked. "Yes," Faith and Eddie said in unison. The man shrugged. "It's your nickel."

It had taken two weeks to level off the quarter acre perfectly flat, then restring the walkways. The men came and put in the bricks in the intricate design that Faith and Eddie had made. A few months after it was done, by accident, Faith overheard the brick mason bragging about the garden he'd put in. His hint was that *he* had designed it. She'd run home to tell the story to Eddie and they'd laughed so hard that he'd gone into spasms and the doctor'd had to be called.

Besides designing, during the winter, she and Eddie had spent long hours poring over herb catalogs and Internet sites as they planned what to plant.

Everything was timed perfectly and the huge boxes of moss-wrapped plants arrived just days before the brick was finished. Eddie sat in his deck chair with the plans on his lap as he told Faith where they were to be set.

The garden had flourished and she and Eddie had had six years with it before he died. They'd added and subtracted plants every spring, and during the winter they read about uses for the herbs. Since it was difficult for Eddie to get up and down stairs, against his mother's many protests, he backed Faith in converting one of the upstairs bathrooms into a sort of laboratory. He read recipes aloud while she made infusions and concoctions. They'd started with potpourris, but Eddie's mother hated the smell of them, so they'd gone on to concoct potions meant to soothe nerves and calm nervous stomachs. They'd laughed together at the hideous tastes they created and celebrated when they made something delicious. They made some great shampoos, and Faith's favorite, bath salts.

During all this planning, planting, tasting, and trying, Faith's mother-in-law refused to participate in any way. Even Eddie's attempts to draw her in had failed. When Faith was outside, she'd often seen the woman watching them from the upstairs window. Faith had waved, but the woman always turned away.

The day after Eddie's funeral, his mother had had a backhoe destroy the herb garden.

Now, Faith looked at the big herb garden and she felt at home. Even without checking, she knew what the three gardens were. One contained herbs for cooking, and the second area was for medicine. When Eddie's condition had worsened, Faith had delved deeper into finding out what herbs could do, and she'd tried some ancient remedies on him. They hadn't cured him, but they had helped relieve his pain and make his last days easier.

Faith knew the third area was for the poisonous plants. She crossed the first two gardens and looked through the locked gate. She saw henbane, foxglove, wormwood, and Bad Henry. Most of the poisonous plants were unfamiliar to her as she'd not grown them or used them. She knew them only from reading.

She was at the end of the huge walled garden and she looked back to see a big patch of open ground that had been temporarily fenced and inside it were geese. She knew that they'd be kept inside the fence for most of the day to do the weeding, and they'd turn the weeds into fertilizer. The geese also provided meat and eggs; they were used to weed the garden, and nobody kept watch better than geese. If a stranger came onto the land, they let out a ruckus that was louder than any alarm system. On this place, in this time, everyone worked; everything had a purpose.

Reluctantly, she left the beautiful walled kitchen garden and kept walking. She saw the barn with its dairy cattle. Two women were carrying pails of fresh milk toward the house.

There was a new stone stable and the stone-paved courtyard was as well kept as any house. Workmen tipped their hats to her, but no one questioned her.

Faith started walking through what she knew was a gentleman's parkland that was acres of what looked like an extraordinarily beautiful woodland. But Faith knew that this look of nature at its best had actually been designed by someone, perfectly laid out, and thoughtfully planted. There were huge rocks that she was willing to bet had been hauled in by a team of heavy horses. She could imagine Clydesdales, twenty of them harnessed together, and a man shouting as the giant horses hauled the boulder to where some human had decided it would look best.

She was musing on this thought, lost in it, and breathing deeply of air that had no car exhaust in it, and looking at a sky that had never seen an airplane, when she was almost run over by a horse. "Oh!" Faith cried as she put her arm up across her face and jumped back.

The horse, as surprised as Faith was, seemed to turn its head one way and its body the other, its front feet coming off the ground. The rider pulled hard on the reins to get the animal under control.

Faith, her hand still over her face, stepped farther back and tripped over the corner of one of the boulders she'd been admiring. At last the horse put its hooves on the ground and in the next second the rider slid off and ran toward Faith.

"Are you all right?" asked a small voice.

She moved her arm to look up at a pretty young woman, no more than sixteen, wearing a riding habit that was so tight it looked painted on. She had on a perky little hat that nearly obscured her right eye.

"I'm fine," Faith said, smiling and standing up. "I was more startled than hurt." When she stood she saw that the girl was shorter than she was, only about five feet. She was small and exquisitely beautiful.

"I think you must be one of Amy's Americans. Your accent . . . I've never heard such a way of speaking except for Amy. Do you also have wondrous stories about your country?"

Faith smiled. The girl had a sweetness about her that made Faith like her instantly. "I'm sure I do. How do you know Amy so well?"

"She's been here nearly a year. Did you not know that?"

"No," Faith said slowly. "Are you . . . ?" She didn't know what to call an earl. "His sister?"

"Oh yes," Beth said. "I'm Tristan's sister, but as he says, I am young enough to be his daughter. Oh my!" she said when the horse, which had been standing still, suddenly turned and galloped away through the trees. "Someone must have filled his food bin."

Faith laughed. "I was admiring your park."

"Oh, it is lovely, isn't it? Now that Sheba—that's my mare—has run home I'm afraid we'll have to walk back to the house. Do you mind?"

"No, I love it here." They started walking back toward the house, Faith feeling much taller and bigger than the tiny young woman. "Everything looks so new."

"It is. Did Amy not tell you about us?"

"Not much," Faith said. Except that her brother is very soon to be murdered in his sleep, she thought. "I'd love to hear everything."

"Amy does not tell us much about herself either," Beth said, looking at Faith as though she hoped she would elaborate. When Faith said nothing, Beth went on. "My brother built all this for his wife, Jane."

"I didn't know he was married."

Beth took a moment before answering. "She died less than a year after they were married."

"I'm so sorry," Faith said.

"My brother and she were deeply in love. They had been since they were children."

"Like Amy," Faith said under her breath.

"Yes," Beth said enthusiastically. "We do know that about her. She's told us about her husband, Stephen, and their two children."

"Did she tell you what happened to him?" Faith asked, curious to know what lies Amy had concocted.

"That he's waiting for her in America, but she can't go because of the war they're having there."

"I thought this was 1797. Isn't the American Revolutionary War over?"

Beth looked at Faith oddly. "Yes, but there is still great anger at us English," she said. "You should ask Amy what her friend Thomas Jefferson writes to her."

Faith had to cough to cover the choking sound she made at that lie. "Tell me more about your brother."

"When our father died, Tristan was just twenty-one and what he wanted most in the world was to marry Jane. But he didn't want to ask her to live in the house our family had lived in since . . . Well, my brother says we'd lived in it since the dawn of time but I think that's an exaggeration. He spent four years building this estate."

Dawn of time, Faith thought. That meant the house was at least medieval. "Where is this house?" she asked and tried to keep the excitement out of her voice.

"Back that way," Beth said, turning toward the stables. "I can take you to see it if you'd like, but I warn you that it's awful. Tristan keeps cows in it now."

Faith had to take a few deep breaths. A house that old being used for a barn! Horrible!

"He did a beautiful job," Faith said, getting herself back under control. "Who designed the park?"

"Mr. Brown. I cannot remember his first name, but then, he never used it."

"Did he go by 'Capability'?" Faith asked quietly.

"Yes! Do you know him?"

"I've heard of him," Faith said, her voice hardly above a whisper. She was walking in a new garden designed by the master, Capability Brown. She reached out and touched the bark of an elm tree in reverence.

Beth was looking at her in curiosity, so Faith quit caressing the tree and tried to straighten her face. "Did your sister-in-law get to live here?"

"Only for the year after they were married," Beth said. "She died in childbirth and the baby with her."

"How long ago was that?" Faith asked.

"Nearly five years. My brother—" She looked into the distance for a while before she turned back to Faith. "He was not the same after Jane died. They planned everything together. They thought they'd have a long life together and many children and . . ." Beth sighed. "It wasn't to be, I guess. We all thought Tristan was going to die after Jane did. My father's brother came to look after us, but now he is too ill to do much."

Faith remembered Amy telling about the gray-haired man who'd been so ill and that he'd been crying hard at Tristan's death.

"But Amy has put some life back in my brother."

"Ah," Faith said, and thought, twenty-first-century morals meet wounded hero. Fireworks!

"No," Beth said as she stopped walking and frowned at Faith. "It is not like that."

"I'm sorry, I didn't mean anything," Faith said, ashamed that what she was thinking had shown so clearly on her face.

"It's all right," Beth said as she started walking again. "Everyone who doesn't live here and hears Amy and Tristan together thinks that she and my brother are . . . Well, you know what I mean. I'm not supposed to know, but I grew up on a farm, so how can I not?"

"How indeed?" Faith said, smiling. "So Amy and your brother aren't . . . ?"

"They are friends. Do you know what she does for him?"

"I can't imagine."

"She makes him angry. Furious. She has a way about her that enrages him to the point where he throws things across the room. He shouts and he sputters and he tells her he's going to discharge her, but of course he never does."

"What does she do that makes him so angry?"

Beth smiled. "Amy tells my brother how to do everything. From food to washing, to horses and gardens, even to what my brother reads, Amy tells him that there's a better way to do it."

"Why doesn't he discharge her?"

"I like to think it's because most of the time Amy is right, but I suspect that the true reason is that she makes his blood flow. Since she has been here, he has started to do things again. He has had some people to dinner, and he's been to London twice because Amy refused to cook if he didn't go and get her something she wanted. The best part is that life is coming back into this place. The estate was so beautiful when it was built, but for years Tristan hasn't cared that it was falling into ruin."

"There!" Beth said, pointing toward the big house her brother had built for his doomed bride. "See it through the trees? Isn't it a pretty house?"

"I don't think I've ever seen a house more lovely. In fact, I think that in the twenty-first century people will still think that house is beautiful."

Beth laughed. "The twenty-first century! How absurd. The world will end before then. There's talk in London that the earth will end in just three more years when the century changes. But if it doesn't, it will most certainly end before the years go to two thousand." Laughing, she ran ahead toward the house.

Faith turned to look back at the parkland. Through the trees she could just see the walls of the kitchen garden. Had Capability Brown designed that too? She'd have to ask "him," the sad young man Amy had saved by making him furious.

"Been there, done that," Faith said aloud, laughing. A couple of times Amy had come close to putting her in a rage. But as Faith looked about her, she was certainly glad that Amy's determination had won out this time. Faith thought that if she never left this place, she would be content.

Thirteen

As *Zoë followed* Amy into the house, they went down some stone stairs, then Amy seemed to vanish into thin air. Zoë felt frantic as she tried to find her, wandering from one stone room to another, and getting in the way of more oddly dressed men and women.

After about thirty minutes, she found a kitchen that was so busy it looked like a food processing plant—old and without electricity, but still it was a place that could deal with enormous quantities of food. There were half a dozen women in long dresses, their hair covered by white caps, rushing around everywhere. A huge, old, scarred table stood in the middle of the room and it was loaded with baskets full of vegetables, big bowls of berries, and dishes of cooked food.

In the middle of this was Amy and she was quietly, but firmly, telling everyone what to do and answering their many questions.

Zoë moved to stand beside her. "What are you doing?"

"Running this place," Amy said. "It's a twenty-four-hour restaurant. Thinner," she said to a woman rolling out some dough on a marble slab. "It has to be thinner than that. Leave it that thick and it'll break a person's teeth."

When Amy moved to another part of the room, Zoë went with her. "How do you know all this? You came here when we did. That means you've been here, what? Ten minutes?"

"I don't understand it any more than you do," Amy said, "but I think I've been here since he bought me from my father."

When Zoë looked at her blankly, Amy said, "In my dream. Remember?"

"But wasn't that just a few days ago?"

"In our time, yes, but I know I've been here for over a year. Put it in there!" she yelled at a young man with a lamb carcass over his shoulder. "So help me, Jimmy, if you drip blood over my clean floor I'll make *you* clean it up!"

Amy looked back at Zoë. "I really can't explain it, but I know this place as well as I know my own house."

"What about the master?" Zoë asked, eyebrows arched.

Amy gave Zoë a look that made her stop smiling. "Wherever I live, I'm married to Stephen and I don't take my vows lightly. Why don't you go find something to do? I'm putting you and Faith in the yellow bedroom for tonight, and we can talk at supper. Until then, please find something to occupy yourself. I have masses of work to do." With that, she ran after a young woman who was entering with a basketful of eggs.

Zoë stared at Amy's back for a moment and thought of half a dozen scathing things to say. If she didn't want her and Faith to bother her while she worked, why the hell had Amy wanted them with her? It made no sense.

"Pardon, miss," said a young man with another dripping carcass over his shoulder.

"Yuck," Zoë said as she got out of his way. She had to move for a woman who was hurrying to the other side of the kitchen. Where was Faith? Zoë wondered. She must have run off as soon as they stepped out of the barn.

Zoë again moved out of the way of someone. Was she the only one who thought it was odd—not to mention impossible—to find herself back in time? Amy sure didn't seem to think it was strange to one minute be in a world with computers and automobiles, and the next minute to be yelling at people carrying dead animals across their shoulders.

When Zoë had to move yet again, she found herself near a staircase and went up it. At the top was a small hallway with several built-in cabinets. She looked around, saw no one, and opened a cabinet door. It was full of serving pieces, trays, and big platters.

When she heard a noise, she quickly closed the door and moved back. She could hear voices but they seemed a long way off. She feared that if she saw anyone, she might be ordered off the place. If Amy was just the housekeeper, what authority did she have? She couldn't order the owner to let her friends stay, could she?

Zoë walked quietly through the nearest doorway. She found herself in a dining room, a large area with a huge cherrywood table in the center. In the twenty-first century the table would be an antique, but here it looked brand-new. The chairs—all eighteen of them—were also new and the upholstery unworn.

Her artist's eye saw the sheer beauty of the room. Along one wall were huge windows that let in the sunlight. The ceiling was decorated with great ovals of plasterwork, truly beautiful. The furniture along the walls was new and looked to be made by the same person who had made the dining table and chairs. There were porcelain ornaments on the two sideboards.

Zoë was no historian and knew little about antiques, but she was sure she was looking at the finest that money could buy in the eighteenth century.

"Do you like it?" came a male voice, and she turned to see a tall man, dressed all in black except for his white shirt, standing in the doorway. She knew who he was since she'd drawn him several times. He looked like the picture of Nathaniel Hawthorne that Faith had found in one of Jeanne's books. In other words, he was divinely handsome.

More important, he had a manner about him that let her know he owned the house. If this man were wearing rags, he'd still be in command.

Zoë found that she was completely tongue-tied as she looked at him. Between his beauty and the fact that she was a stranger snooping in his house, she didn't know what to expect. When did they do away with drawing and quartering as a punishment for crimes?

He walked across the room to stand beside her. "This furniture is modern and some people do not like it, but I do."

When Zoë still didn't speak, he went on. "My mother always said that a true aristocrat sits on gold, but I never liked gold furniture. What do you think?"

"No gold," Zoë managed to say, then got hold of herself. "I didn't mean to trespass, but—"

"I am used to Amy's strays," he said, smiling and looking even more handsome. "She is going to bankrupt me." His words would have been offensive from someone else since they were referring to her, but from him, somehow, they put her at ease.

"Amy said she's been here for nearly a year," Zoë said, searching for conversation.

"Fourteen months," he said, and she had the idea that he could tell her how many days it had been. He's in love with her! Zoë thought. He is flat-out, no-holds-barred in love with her.

Zoë turned away from him, afraid that he would read her thoughts. If he was in love with Amy, how was he going to feel when she disappeared in just three weeks? On the other hand, someone who seemed to be Amy had been here for a year, so maybe that person would stay.

Zoë could feel him looking at her, as though he expected her to say something. She was searching for words when she saw a miniature portrait nestled in a white napkin lying on the top of the sideboard. It was no more than four inches tall, in oil and probably on ivory. She picked it up. "She's pretty."

When he said nothing, she looked back at him. He suddenly looked as though he might cry.

"I'm sorry," she said as she put the picture down. "I didn't mean to be rude." She stepped back from him.

"It is I who should apologize," he said as he picked up the little portrait and gazed at it. "Usually, this is in my room, but the frame has a crack in it, so it's to be repaired."

"I could do it," Zoë said.

"You? Do you have experience in this?"

"I've been working with framing for several years now," she said. She was watching him and figuring out who the woman in the picture was. Unfortunately, Zoë'd had quite a bit of experience with that look. Many of her clients had looked at photographs of deceased loved ones like that.

"Who was she?" Zoë whispered, letting the "was" tell him that she understood.

"My wife," he said, his eyes still on the portrait.

"I can make a larger picture from that," she said. "I can make copies for you."

He looked at her, blinking for a moment, then he smiled. "You are a painter?"

"Yes," Zoë answered and straightened her back. If she had a job here she wouldn't feel as though she were trespassing.

He put the picture back on the napkin. "I have a painter living here," he said, "and he will repair the frame. And he will make copies for me. He is painting my sister now. You will have to ask his permission if you are to work for him."

With that, he gave a little bow and left the room.

For a moment, Zoë stood there staring after him. He had dismissed her, and she had no doubt that it was because she was a woman. He'd said she was to work "for" the man. Didn't he think a woman could paint as well as a man?

While it was true that Zoë had never been to art school, had never had a lesson in her life, she had certainly read a great deal on her own. She knew what itinerant portrait painters in the eighteenth century did. Sure, there was a Stuart now and then, but mainly they painted on boards in a style that was stiff and, to Zoë's eye, ugly.

She went down the stairs to the kitchen where Amy was at the table kneading bread.

"I met your big, beautiful boss," she said from across the table. The people in the room didn't exactly stop what they were doing, but they did slow down, and the voices ceased.

"What's he done now?" Amy asked, not pausing in her kneading.

"I volunteered to paint some pictures of his wife, but he said he already has a painter. If I don't draw and paint, why am I here? What am I to do for three weeks? Play the pianoforte?"

"He told you about his wife?" Amy asked. If possible, it got quieter in the room.

"Not really," Zoë said, "but you remember that I've been living in other people's houses for years now, and I know what it means when their eyes look at a portrait in that way."

Amy quit kneading and wiped her hands on a damp cloth. After a glance at all the people in the kitchen who were staring at them, she put her hand under Zoë's arm and ushered her up the stairs.

"This place gossips more than any tabloid," she said when they were upstairs. "Zoë, I know that I brought you into this and I'll fix everything that I can, but it's true that he has a painter living here right now. If I'd known that when we were in Maine I wouldn't have asked you to come. I'm sorry. But couldn't you just enjoy what you see here? I can get him to buy you some paper and pens and you can sketch what you see. That would be nice, wouldn't it?"

"Why do you always call him 'he'? Doesn't he have a name?"

"Sure," Amy said. "It's Tristan, but it's also the eighteenth century. I can't call him by his first name because I'm a lowly housekeeper, and I'll be damned if I'm going to call him 'my lord.' " She gave Zoë a pleading look. "I really do have a lot of work to do. Feeding the people who live here is a major undertaking every day. If I run out of anything I can't just go to the supermarket. I have to wait for it to *grow!*"

"So you're telling me to entertain myself and get out of your hair."

"Pretty much," Amy said. "Why don't you find the painter and talk to him about his work? Maybe you two could . . ." Amy was looking at Zoë as though she'd never seen her before.

"Could what?" Zoë asked. "Paint by duet? Maybe I could set up a school and train some of these roving painters in modern techniques."

"I think that's a great idea," Amy said, still looking at Zoë in wonder.

"Why are you looking at me like that?"

"I was just thinking about something. You know that it's been said that there are no coincidences. Maybe you came back with me for a reason."

"And that reason was . . . ?"

Amy smiled brightly. "To let you give lessons to these bad painters who travel around and make rotten pictures. I think you should go talk to Russell."

"Russell being the painter?"

"Yes."

"And since you can say his name that means he's not of the upper classes."

"He certainly isn't."

"So how do I find him?"

"He's usually in the stables this time of day. Beth—that's Tristan's young sister and who he's painting—goes out riding now, so Russell hangs around the stableyard."

"Waiting for her?" Zoë asked. "Amy, what are you up to? Is he in love with his subject? The master's nubile sister?"

"Maybe," Amy said. "But I think you should make up your own mind."

"Okay, I'll go so you can get back to baking your four-and-twenty blackbirds or whatever. What does this Mr. Russell look like?"

"It's Mr. Johns. He's Russell Johns. You haven't heard of him, have you?"

"No. To my knowledge, his work didn't make the art history books."

"Maybe you can fix that," Amy said. "You could give him lessons." Her eyes were sparkling as though she were enjoying a great joke. "Russell is . . ." She hesitated.

"He's what?"

"Little," Amy said. "Little and scrawny and has terrible teeth. You can't miss him. He's probably with the head stableman now. If you can't find him, ask someone. I have to go," she said, and headed downstairs before Zoë could say another word.

"Why do I get the idea that a joke is being played on me?" Zoë said aloud. She hadn't been given much time to think about the bizarre idea of time travel, but if she had, she was sure she would have thought it would be different from this. She would have thought that they'd be three frightened, disoriented women who needed one another. Instead, Faith had disappeared as though she lived here and knew just where she wanted to go, and Amy! Zoë couldn't wrap her brain around the way Amy was acting, as though she were some freak of nature who lived comfortably in two time periods with hundreds of years between them.

"I think I'm the only sane one," Zoë said aloud as she left the dining room and turned left. She was in the huge central hall of the house. The floor was of black-and-white marble. There was a heavy table in the center that was probably medieval, and an enormous marble-encased fireplace in one wall. The ceiling was decorated in a geometric design comprising a large oval with curved-sided triangles around it.

The front door was open and she saw a couple of men walking past. She started to ask them where the stables were, but then she saw a wide gravel path that looked well used and she decided to follow it. She wasn't looking forward to a confrontation with the scrawny Mr. Johns. If his lordship, the master, was any indication of the state of women's rights around here, the little man would refuse to believe that a woman so much as knew which end of a paintbrush to use.

As she walked, she began to calm down. She was used to living in places that she didn't know, and over the years she'd perfected her ability to settle into someone else's home and make it her own for the time she would be staying with the family. She'd also learned how to say no. When the mistress of the house asked her if she'd "mind" putting in a load of clothes while they were out, she told her she did mind and wouldn't do it. Never once had she been fired for her refusal to do more than make portraits.

Some of the families she'd loved and some she had run from. She still sent postcards to a couple of them, always letting them know where she was and what she was doing. It was the closest thing she had to a family. In all the years since she'd been out of the hospital she had never once been tempted to marry some guy and have her own home. She'd never admitted it to Jeanne, but it haunted her every day to think what she could have done to make an entire town hate her.

When Zoë got to the stables, she stopped and looked at the beautiful stone buildings, with the horses sticking their heads out of the stalls to look at her. She thought what a shame it would be that someday these would probably be turned into tiny houses. She thought of the two world wars that were coming and she shivered.

"Too cold for you?" came a deep voice. "Or did someone walk over your grave?"

Zoë turned to see a tall man, with broad shoulders, and a muscular body. He looked like he'd worked out-doors all his life. He had strong features, with bright blue eyes. His black hair was a thick mane and there was a dimple in his chin. Zoë had seen more hand-some men, but she'd never seen one whom she was more drawn to. If she'd met him in her own time, she thought she just might have asked him to go home with her immediately.

He was staring at her, waiting for her to say something, but Zoë just kept looking at him and blinking. "Do you have a tongue, lass?"

There was a trace of a Scottish burr in his voice. She didn't know what got into her, but she stuck her tongue out at him.

He laughed in a way that made the horses prick up their ears. "Aye, you have a tongue. Are you one of the girls that came with Miss Amy?" he asked, then without waiting for her answer, he turned back toward the stables.

It seemed natural to follow him as he went into a big stall. Zoë didn't know much about horses, but she didn't think this one looked like a derby winner.

"Zoë," she said as the man picked up an iron tool and started for the horse.

"Is that your name?" He lifted the horse's leg between his and Zoë saw that the man's thighs were heavy, thick with muscle.

"Yes, that's my name," she said as she turned away to keep from staring at him. "I'm looking for Russell Johns."

"And what would you want with him?"

Zoë was trying to recover from her initial clumsiness. It wasn't often that she saw a man she was this attracted to. But how did one impress a man in the eighteenth century? she wondered. "I was told I'm to teach him how to paint."

The man paused with the horse's hoof in his hands. "Are you now?" he said coolly. "Are you sure he needs to learn his trade?"

From his tone, she could tell she wasn't saying the right thing. "I don't know. It's just what Amy told me to do."

"Miss Amy told you the man needed to learn to paint?"

"Not exactly." She was backtracking because she realized she seemed to have offended him. Whatever she was doing wrong, she was going to make sure Amy got the blame for it. She decided to tell him the truth. "Amy said he was a scrawny little man with bad teeth who hung around the stables waiting for the earl's young sister to return, and she—Amy, that is—suggested I give the man some art lessons. Amy didn't say so, but I don't think she believes he's very good at making portraits."

The man dropped the horse's hoof and gave her a dazzling smile that showed his even white teeth. It seemed that Zoë had done the right thing in telling him the truth. "Did she now?" he said. He looked Zoë up and down in a way that made a trickle of sweat run down between her breasts.

He wiped his hands with a cloth and said, "Can you really paint?"

"A bit," she said in a modest way that implied that she was actually very good.

"It's near dinnertime here and everyone is away, getting ready to eat. What say you that I get Miss Amy to put some food in a basket and we take it to the lake? Look what I have."

Her eyes widened as he held up a wooden box that was covered with runs of different colors of paint. "This is the painter's kit. He left it here." He turned it around in his hands as though he'd never seen it before. "Shall we take it with us and you can give *me* a lesson or two?"

Zoë smiled. "That's a great idea." She thought that if the man did have a rudimentary talent, maybe she could teach him enough to get him out of the stables.

"Can you ride a horse?"

Zoë looked at the big animal in front of her and gave a small smile. "I've been on a horse before," she said as she thought of pony rides at the fair.

The man sighed. "I was hoping you could not ride so you could get behind me." Again, he looked her up and down.

"I know nothing at all about horses," she said quickly. "Nothing whatever."

He smiled. "Wait here a moment and I'll get things ready. Why don't you look in that box and see if what you need is in there?"

Zoë sat down on the straw with the box full of art supplies. There was clean paper and pencils, charcoal, and a few pieces of chalk. There were watercolors too, but she had no water. "What's your name?" she asked as he left with the horse.

"MacKenzie," he said, then was gone.

Zoë looked down at the paper, picked up a pencil, and thought about nothing else.

"Miss Amy, I'd like a word with you."

She looked up from the bread she was thumping and met Russell's angry eyes. She had no doubt that Zoë had been to see him.

"I can explain," Amy said, moving so she was on the other side of the table from him.

"I would like to hear it." All of the women in the kitchen had stopped working and were staring at him. There wasn't a woman on the place—except Amy and Beth—who hadn't fluttered her eyelashes at Russell Johns.

"Zoë is a friend of mine and she's new here," Amy began, then picked up some carrots and started scraping them.

"And so you felt the need to lie to her about me?"

"She likes to paint and draw. She never stops. I thought you two might get on well together."

"So you told her I was a scrawny little thing with bad teeth and that I needed lessons? That she needed to *teach* me?"

The entire room stopped and listened, with a few of the younger women trying to suppress their giggles. They were used to Miss Amy going at the master, but she'd never done anything to Mr. Johns.

"I wanted her to feel at ease with you," Amy said. "I wanted her to meet you without knowing who you were at first. You know, Russell, you can be a bit intimidating to an innocent young girl."

"Innocent? She has the conceit of my old painting master. Has she even seen my work? Has she seen that I need no lessons?"

"No . . ." Amy said slowly. "I didn't let her see for fear that your great talent would make her put down her brush and never pick it up again."

Russell opened his mouth in astonishment. "Do you not fear for your soul when you tell such lies?"

"Only a bit," Amy said. Her head came up. "What have you done with her? So help me, if you threw one of your great rages and called her some name, I'll put sand in your meat pies."

When Russell said nothing, Amy looked at him hard. "You didn't do anything, did you? Who did you tell her you were?"

He turned to the women standing at the side. "I want a basket packed. Fill it with the best. And put some perry in there."

Amy walked around the table to him. "You didn't tell her who you were, did you?"

"I had no chance to tell her," he said. "She came to me with the idea that I was someone else. You told her that."

He was glaring down at her in a way that intimidated most people, but Amy didn't back away. "What did you tell her your name was?"

"I have many names," he said, not looking at her but watching the women pack a basket full of food.

"What are you up to?" Amy asked.

Russell took the basket a woman handed him, then smiled down at Amy. "Do not worry about us. I am going to let her give me drawing lessons." Turning, he walked toward the back door. "MacKenzie is my mother's name," he said over his shoulder.

Amy looked back at her kitchen staff. They were all standing still, doing nothing, but gazing at the place where Russell had been. She could practically see their hearts beating. "Work!" she said sharply as she clapped her hands twice. "Is that soup ready? Check that the oven isn't too hot. Agnes, tuck your hair up. I don't want any in the bread."

Amy turned away from them so they wouldn't see her smile. She knew that underneath his giant ego Russell was a good man. And she also knew that if she'd introduced Zoë and him as they actually were, they would have instantly taken a professional dislike to each other. Russell would have wanted to let her know that this was his commission and he wanted no competition. And Zoë would have been disdainful of his work even if it rivaled Michelangelo's. All she'd wanted to do was to get them to spend a few hours together before the truth was told. She had a feeling that if they got to know each other, they'd become friends, maybe even very good friends.

Amy refused to let herself think about what would

happen when they left in three short weeks, but she believed in taking love whenever and wherever it could be found.

So now Zoë and Russell were going off on a picnic with a box of art supplies. It couldn't get more romantic than that.

She took the smile off her face before she turned back to the army of people working in the kitchen.

Fourteen

"*It's beautiful here,*" Zoë said, her hand on a tree branch above her head, as she looked across the lake. Behind her MacKenzie was putting out the food on a cloth.

"Aye, it is," he said, glancing at the lake, but his eyes were spending more time on her. "Come and eat and show me what you did while I was away."

Turning, she smiled and went to sit on the cloth across from him. "What's this?" she asked as she picked up what looked to be a pewter mug.

"Perry," he said as he opened the art case. "Have you not had it before? It's made from perry pears."

She took a sip. It was delicious and she could feel that it was potent. She'd better not drink too much. She picked up a chicken leg, but stopped when she saw that he was looking at her sketches.

For a moment she waited for him to tell her they were fabulous, the best he'd ever seen. It was what most people did when they saw Zoë's drawings. But he didn't comment. Instead, he studied them, spending several minutes on each one, then he propped them against the tree, and looked at them from a distance.

Zoë swallowed. It was as though her work were being critiqued by a gallery owner, something that always made her nervous.

She got up and went to stand beside him to look at the drawings. She'd made three sketches of what she saw. First was the stableyard with the horses' heads turned toward her. After that was completed, she'd moved to the back of the stable and drawn the parkland, with a tall wall in the background. Last, she'd made a quick sketch of a wildflower she'd never seen before and had added a bit of color with the few chalks that were in the box.

"What do you think?" she asked. She wanted to sound cocky and sure of herself. After all, she was the artist and he was a stable lad, but her words came out sounding as though his opinion were important to her.

"Good," he said after a while.

"But what?" she asked.

"Nothing." He looked at her and smiled. "They are wonderful. I think you will be a good teacher. Now, what has Miss Amy given us to eat?"

"Hot dogs and Diet Coke," she said.

He looked at her with a twinkle in his eye. "You cannot befuddle me, Miss Zoë. I have been around Miss Amy for too long. When she first came here, the place was abuzz with all the odd things she had to say. Her language, even her ideas of what was right and wrong, were of great amusement to us. But now we are used to her. And she has changed us so much that I do not know what is hers and what is ours. Two months ago I went to London and I said to a shopkeeper, 'That's super.' He thought I was mad."

Zoë laughed. "She does have a way of making people do what she wants them to." She hesitated. "She seems to like the earl a lot."

"Poor man," he said. "Never the same after he lost his wife and wee babe." He picked up Zoë's cup and handed it to her. "Drink up. It's good for you."

"Some things are the same wherever you go. Men always want to get women drunk."

He put his head back and laughed so hard that she wanted to kiss his throat.

"Let's eat," she said, "then I'll give you a drawing lesson."

It took them nearly an hour to finish their meal. Zoë realized she hadn't eaten since . . . She didn't know what to call what had been done to them. The transfer? She'd managed to find the outhouse, but she'd had no food.

While they'd eaten, he asked her about herself, where she'd grown up and what she'd done as a child. It wasn't easy to answer his questions and not give away that she was from a different time. She didn't want him to think she was insane. She had grown up in Oregon, but in 1797, no one had heard of the place. She thought about her grandmother's stories. Their family had traveled to the new country of America in the early 1700s and had settled in Williamsburg. Her grandmother hinted that they may have lived in the governor's mansion. "More likely worked in his kitchen," her mother said.

Whatever they did, in the 1800s the family packed up and went by wagon train to Oregon and stayed there.

She told MacKenzie of her life as though her family still lived in Williamsburg. She knew that back then her family's name had been Prentiss.

"An old English name," he said. "Do you know where your family lived in England before you went off to the foreign country that doesn't want the interfering English telling them what to do?"

She laughed. "We did have some issues with them."

"More than a few," he said as he poured her more of the perry. "Now, shall we start the lessons?"

"Sure," she said, but she didn't really want to. For her part, she'd like to stay there for the rest of the afternoon and look out at the lake and they could . . . She put down the mug of perry. Enough of that!

Maybe it was the alcoholic beverage, or maybe it was the man so close to her, but Zoë had never felt less like giving an art lesson to anyone. She'd certainly done it often enough. In the houses where she'd stayed, one of the extra things she'd agreed to was to give art lessons to the children of the house. Zoë found that the rich loved to load their children down with lessons and having a professional painter teaching them had been a coup.

"What turns you on?" she asked as he picked up the pad of drawing paper.

"I beg your pardon?"

Zoë swallowed. "I mean, what would you like to draw? Landscapes? Flowers?" She pointed to the remnants of their picnic. "Maybe a still life."

"What about if I draw you?" he asked, looking at her.

"I won't be able to direct you if you're drawing me," she said. "How about the lake? We'll start with this angle. See the way the water shimmers? And see that little building on the far side? Look, like this." Reaching out, she lifted his hands in hers and moved his fingers so he formed a square with them. "Frame it, see what you like best, then draw that."

His face was close to hers and his eyes were looking at her, not at what he saw through his squared fingers.

"Cut it out!" she said, then moved away from him. Her face became serious. "We can't do this if you don't behave."

"All right," he said, smiling as he held up his hands and moved them about so he was framing different aspects of the landscape. "This one. I think I like the folly to the left of the picture and that tree in the foreground."

"Very good!" Zoë said, impressed. "That's a balanced composition. Okay, so the first thing you do is—"

"What does 'okay' mean?"

"If you've spent even ten minutes around Amy you've heard it before," she said, sounding like the stern teacher she was trying to be.

He just smiled and looked down at the paper on his lap. "Now what do I do?"

"You need to make a basic sketch to get your proportions right. This is the foundation of your drawing. If this is off, when you finish, no matter how good your technique is, the drawing will be bad."

He looked at the lake, then down at his paper, then up again. "You must show me," he said.

Zoë moved close to him, put her hand over his, and directed him in putting the curve of the lake on the paper. "See? Like this. Now where is the folly?"

His face was turned toward hers. "Here," he said, not bothering to look at the paper.

"That's—" She had meant to tell him that was wrong because he wasn't looking, but his finger was in exactly the right spot. "All right, so now we sketch in the little building."

Since the folly was on the far side of the paper, she had to reach across him to block it in.

"Would you look at the paper?" she snapped, then sat back on her heels. "You know, you really are throwing away the chance of a lifetime. I know about the class system in England and right now I'm giving you a way to get out of being just a stable boy all your life. Maybe you'll never be a real artist, but it's the eighteenth century. You could get away with making crude portraits and still make a living. Wouldn't you rather have that than shoveling horse manure for the rest of your life?"

He blinked at her a few times as he digested what

she'd said, then he took the pencil from her, looked up at the lake and made a few quick marks on the paper. He turned it around to show her. "Is this what you had in mind that I should do to get myself out of the stables?"

Zoë looked at the drawing, saw that it was perfectly in proportion, and that in just a few marks he'd captured the entire setting.

It seemed that a thousand thoughts went through her mind at once. Obviously, a trick had been played on her. This man was the painter, Russell Johns. She was going to kill Amy for lying to her, telling her he was a scrawny little man with bad teeth.

Besides Amy lying to her, so had he. He'd said his name was MacKenzie, and he'd worked at not letting her know the truth.

The first emotion she felt was anger. Two people had treated her like a moron. They'd lied, kept secrets, and made her the butt of a joke. But her second emotion was laughter. They'd got her a good one.

She saw that the man was looking at her with a fake expression of defiance, but underneath it she could see worry. He knew she'd figured out who he was and he was concerned that she was going to tell him she never wanted to see him again.

She wasn't going to do what he expected her to. "Your work is a bit primitive, totally unrefined," she said as loftily as she could manage, "but for a first attempt, I guess it is acceptable."

There was such relief in his eyes that she had to

work not to laugh. "Primitive, is it?" He turned the pad around and looked up at her then back down as he made quick marks on the paper. After only a minute, he turned the paper toward her. "Is that crude?"

Zoë had to prevent herself from gasping. His sketch of her was as good as a Boldini, the magnificent portrait painter from Edwardian England. However, he'd made her look as though she thought she was better than he was. "Mmmm," she said, as though it were nothing special.

He didn't say a word, just handed her the paper and pencil. His gesture said that if she thought she could do better, she was welcome to try.

This is it, she thought. If I don't do well at this, I'll lose his respect. She was glad she'd had a substantial amount of the perry because otherwise she would have been nervous. Instead, on the same paper as his drawing of her, she made a quick sketch of him, incorporating it with the one he'd done of her. She drew his face as quite a bit smaller than hers, and he had a look of almost fear, as though he were frightened of the woman above him. He was looking up at her in trepidation, seeming to be pleading with her.

She turned the pad toward him. For a moment his face registered shock, and Zoë thought he might get angry. In the next second, he began laughing so hard that he rolled over onto his side.

"You deserved it!" she said, laughing with him. "Of all the rotten tricks to play on me!"

"I did nothing," he said, laughing hard. "I was innocent, caught in a web of lies between you and that harridan in the kitchen. She rules the poor young master, but she's never ruled *me* before. She told the lies, not me."

"Oh yeah? So who was it that told me his name was MacKenzie?"

"It is. Russell MacKenzie Johns."

That made Zoë laugh harder. "It was a horrible joke and I shouldn't be laughing. You're as bad as that man."

"Which man?"

"Your boss. Or was that a lie too? Maybe you own this place and he just struts around."

"Lord Tristan?" Russell said, beginning to sober from his laughter. "You sound as though you don't like him."

"I told him I'd repair the frame on the miniature of his wife but he told me that only a *man* could do it."

"He said those exact words?"

"Well," Zoë said, "not in those words, but more or less."

"Ah, I see," Russell said. "Perhaps he didn't want to insult a man who has lived with him for nearly a year and who has been a friend to him. Could that have had something to do with it?"

"Maybe," Zoë said. "Women in my time tend to take things as being chauvinistic when maybe they aren't."

"Your time?" he asked.

She waved her hand in dismissal. "I mean, in my country. How about if you tell me everything about yourself?"

"My favorite thing to do," he said as he stretched out on the grass under the tree. "Where should I begin?"

"Where were you born? Where have you worked and have you had any training as an artist?"

This last question made him look at her with wide eyes. "Are you telling me that you do not?"

"I was in an accident," she said softly, "and when I woke up, I could draw."

"How old were you?"

"Nineteen."

"And you are now?"

"Twenty-five."

He looked at her for a moment. "That old and no husband? No children?"

"Never met a man I liked enough to want to keep. What about you? You're certainly older than me. You have a wife and children?"

"None," he said. "I have had offers. My mother has worked hard to find me a wife but I've liked none of them."

"Is your family from Scotland?"

He smiled. "My parents, not me, but I sound like them. Do ye hear the heather in my voice?"

"A little bit," Zoë answered, teasing. His accent was thick when he turned it on. "When did you know you wanted to be an artist?"

"All I ever wanted to do was draw or paint. When I had just turned three I nearly walked into the fireplace, but all I wanted was some charcoal. I drew the face of my mother on the wall."

"And what did she do?"

Russell smiled in memory. "I was told the story many times when I was growing up. We lived in London in one of the poorer sections. My father drove a big wagon and took kegs of beer to the public houses. He was as strong as his horses, and he was a sweet man, but he was not a scholar." He looked at Zoë as though she might condemn him for such a lowly father.

"But what about your mother?" she asked.

"She was no beauty, but she had the brains of a wizard." He chuckled. "And she had the gumption of twenty men. When she saw what I had drawn, she put on her best clothes and went to the house of Sir Markus Vanderstern." He glanced at Zoë to see if she'd heard of him, but she hadn't.

"In his day, he was a famous painter. There wasn't an earl or a duke whose portrait he hadn't done. It was said that his temper was as bad as his paintings were good. Everyone who sat for him feared him. He'd as soon rage at a duke as at the dustman."

"As mean as a six-year-old boy with a rubber band," she said, thinking of one house she'd lived in. "I bet your mother wasn't afraid of him."

"No," Russell said. "The day after I made the drawing on the wall, she went to his house, knocked on his door, and told the maid she wanted him to come to her home and see what her three-year-old son had drawn."

"I can just imagine how he responded to that."

"He ignored her for four days, but she set up house-keeping on his front stoop. Finally, he had the sheriff come to get her and she screamed that he was a coward, that he was afraid to see that her son was better at three years old than he was at a hundred."

Russell closed his eyes for a moment, then opened them. He was lying on the grass with his hands behind his head. "The old man heard her and he took her words as a challenge. Besides, by that time a crowd had gathered outside his house. They were watching this woman who wouldn't give up no matter what was said to her. He could see that the crowd believed her and thought that he was afraid to see a child who was a better artist than he was.

"He came out, told the sheriff to unhand the woman, then he followed her to our humble house."

"And he saw your drawing."

Russell laughed. "By that time I'd charcoaled all the walls that I could reach. There were faces everywhere."

"And what did he think when he saw them?"

"My father was at home taking care of me while his wife lived on the old master's doorstep, and he told me that the old man's jaw dropped down almost to his chest. He was that astonished at what I'd done."

"So?" Zoë asked when Russell paused. "What did he do?"

"He told my mother to bring me to him when I was seven. My mother said he'd probably be dead by then and she'd have to get someone else to teach me. My father said the old man sneered at her, said, 'Six,' then left their house."

"Wow," Zoë said. She was lying on the grass beside him, with an arm's length between them. "Wow, what a great story. You knew you could draw practically from the time you were born, while I didn't know it until I was an adult. Did you go to him when you were six?"

"Aye, I did. On my sixth birthday, my mother was there with me."

"She didn't leave you alone there with him, did she? You were just a child and with that bad-tempered old man!"

Again Russell laughed. "I told you my mother was clever. She'd had years to prepare for her only child going into apprenticeship. She'd found out that the old man could never keep servants. His rages, and the way he accused them of things they didn't do, made them leave. No one ever stayed more than a year."

"So what did your mother do?"

"She sent me to him with a box full of food."

Zoë looked at him in question.

"During the years that I'd been growing up and drawing so much that she said I was driving her mad, she set out to learn to cook. Custard pies. Meat pies. They were beautiful and tasted like heaven. I was given a cold bare room in the old man's house, but every morning she'd knock on his door and give me a box full of food. It was her plan for the old man to taste her cooking and hire her to work for him."

"Did she get it?"

"Oh yes, she did. She was his cook for two years, then she was his housekeeper. In my third year there, my father came to work for him too."

"So your whole family was there," Zoë said. "And you learned your art at the knee of a master."

"Hmph!" Russell said. "At the end of his boot was more like it. He was as mean as they come. He begrudged me everything I did, was jealous of me, and he fired my mother every three months."

"But she didn't leave?"

"Leave her only son?" Russell smiled. "She was a match for the master and when he told her to get out, she just laughed at him. And he knew that no one could replace her. She kept his house clean and filled his table with good food—even though he complained about every cent she spent."

Russell's voice lowered. "He died when I was sixteen and he left everything to my mother."

"That's wonderful," Zoë said. "He wasn't so bad after all."

"Yes he was," Russell said. "I'm sure that if he'd had even one relative he could abide, he'd have left everything to him, but he didn't. He'd done a lot of work for the church but they'd stolen half the money they owed him, so he couldn't leave it to them. My mother was the only person who'd ever come close to liking him."

Zoë looked up at the tree leaves for a while. "What happened to your parents?"

"They're still there," he said. "My mother lives in the master's house with my father. They're quite old now and my mother writes me every week with laments that I have not given her grandchildren."

At that, he turned and looked at Zoë. For a full minute, she thought of living with this man and staying here forever.

In the next minute, she got her mind under control. She'd only met him a few hours ago.

Russell reached across the space separating them and took her hand in his. "Sometimes a person knows when things are right," he said softly.

Zoë looked into his eyes and she wanted to roll over to him and put her arms around his neck. She wanted to kiss him, probably even make love with him, but she didn't. She knew she was going to leave soon and she didn't want to hurt him or herself.

Russell saw the change in her eyes and knew that the moment had passed. "So tell me the *truth* about your training. Did you spend three months on mixing the color that exactly matches the sun on a pond at noon?"

"Not quite," Zoë said, sitting up. "I never had a teacher. My talent is purely natural." She gave a great sigh. "Some of us have to learn to draw and some of us have a gift."

Russell sat up. "Is that so? What say you we have a bit of a competition?"

"You're on, baby!" she said, reaching for the sketch pad that was between them.

Russell touched the paper just as she did. He put his hand over hers and their heads were close together. Zoë sucked in her breath and held it. She was sure he was going to kiss her.

"I can wait," he said softly, and she could feel his breath on her lips. "But I warn you that I am as sure of what I want as I was the day I picked up my first piece of charcoal. You will give in to me."

Zoë wanted to give in to him right that moment, but she pulled back. "That's what you think," she said, and he laughed.

Fifteen

❧

It was nearly evening, and the beautiful room was glowing with the setting sun. It was a small, cozy room with cream-colored wallpaper that had been hand-painted with bamboo and luminescent birds.

Zoë, Amy, and Faith were sitting at a round pedestal table and before them was a feast of Amy's making: breads, early fruit, peas, parsnips, three kinds of meat. A huge pot of tea sat in the middle of the table. Amy had dismissed the servants, who tended to stand at attention and wait for someone to give them something to do.

"So, what have you two been up to today?" Amy asked as she put a slice of rare roast beef on Faith's plate.

The two women just stared at her. At last, Zoë said, "Should we kill her now or wait five minutes?"

"I vote for now," Faith said.

"Okay," Amy said, "so maybe I've been a little busy today and I haven't taken care of you two the way I should have, but—"

"Taken care of us!" Zoë said, then lowered her voice. "When did you become our *mother*?"

"Amy," Faith said, then took a breath. "All this," she waved her hand to include the house, even the world, "may seem normal to you, but Zoë and I realize that we have been transported back to another time. It's strange to us."

"It's more than strange," Zoë said.

Amy didn't seem in the least perturbed by their words or their attitudes. "More than strange, is it? Golly, Zoë, was that you riding on the back of that horse with Mr. Johns? You sure seemed to have your arms tightly wrapped around him. And you, Faith, didn't you return today with Beth and you two were laughing? I haven't known you very long, but I've never before seen such happiness on your face. And the gardeners said you spent over two hours in the kitchen garden and that you were practically wallowing in the herbs."

"What we did is beside the point," Zoë said, but she looked at her plate while she said it.

"Amy," Faith said, "I think we should take all of this a little more seriously than we have been. I'd really like a more complete explanation about how you know so much about this place when you only got here today."

"I don't know," Amy said. "I really and truly don't have an answer for you. It's as though there are two realities in my mind and each of them is as clear as the other. I remember my husband, Stephen, and my two sons. But I also remember growing up under the fists of my father and sister in that public house—even though I've told everyone that I grew up in America. Most of all, I remember him rescuing me, and—"

"Him. His lordship? Do you mean Tristan?" Zoë asked.

"Yes. Tristan," Amy said. "Part of me is horrified at the thought of calling him by his first name and another part thinks that's what I should call him."

"I heard how you've given the poor man a very hard time," Faith said.

Amy shook her head in wonder. "I know. I remember it. You'd think that if I . . . or my body, I guess, came here months ago, I would only remember the past I had here in this time. But I seem to have been cut in half ever since I first saw Tristan."

"You mean, since your first dream," Zoë said.

"A dream that was only a few days ago, but I seem to have been purchased by Tristan a year ago."

"Fourteen months," Zoë said.

Faith and Amy looked at her.

"He told me," Zoë said.

"You two certainly seem to have had a long, intimate talk today," Amy said, her eyes blazing. "You talked about his wife and about me."

"I did no such—"

"Are you two going to get into a catfight?" Faith asked. "If you are, I'm going to leave." She looked from one to the other, and when they were calm, she spoke again. "I think we need to figure out what we're to do here. Do you both agree?"

"Yes," Amy said. "But we know that. We're here to keep Tristan from being killed. That's the number one task, the only task, as far as I know."

"All right," Faith said. "Amy, what have you found out about who wants to kill him?"

She put down her fork. "No one. I've thought about it until my brain seems to have turned inside out."

"Did you think about it while you were yelling at boys about blood on the floor?" Zoë asked, an eyebrow raised.

"For your information, yes. I've been running that kitchen for so long that I could do it in my sleep."

"Then why were you so fierce about getting rid of me today?" Zoë asked.

"Tomorrow you can stay with me all day," Amy said sweetly. "I'll let you peel potatoes. How does that sound?"

Zoë mumbled something.

"What was that?" Amy asked.

Zoë narrowed her eyes. "I'm going to go out with Russell tomorrow. We're going to do some drawing."

"Oh," Amy said. "So maybe you liked that I sent you away from the kitchen. Maybe you liked that I got past your stubborn bullheadedness to meet a man you had decided you wanted nothing to do with before you even met him."

Zoë started to speak, but Faith looked at her. "I think you should give up. You're not going to win. And, besides, I don't think you want to win, do you?"

Zoë sighed. "Okay, let's go back to his lordship. You sure do like pretty boys, don't you?" she said to Amy, who immediately started to say something angry in return.

"So help me," Faith said, "if you two don't stop this—" She left her threat open.

"There's no one who wants to harm Tristan," Amy said.

"But there is," Faith said softly. "You and I know that someone kills him while he's sleeping. It may seem that everyone likes him, but at least one person doesn't. Who would benefit by his death?"

"His uncle and his sister would inherit the estates," Amy said.

"I can vouch that the sister is a lovely little thing," Faith said. "She adores her brother."

"Maybe she's in love with someone and her autocratic brother won't let her marry him," Zoë said.

Faith and Amy stared at her.

"It was just a thought," Zoë said. "Since both of you are so in love with her, maybe I should be the one to try to find out the truth about her."

"You can't interrogate her," Amy said. "It wouldn't be polite. And you're not—"

"Her class," Zoë said. "I know. Actually, I was thinking of getting chummy with her maid. Maids know everything their charges do. And I know that for a fact from all the rich houses I've lived in. Husbands rarely know anything about their wives, but the maids know it all."

"Good idea," Amy said, smiling at Zoë. "I knew I needed you on this trip. But don't just ask what Beth is doing, find out about everybody."

"What about the uncle?" Faith asked.

"He's too sick to care much about anything."

"What's wrong with him?"

"Who knows?" Amy said. "I'm sure that if I took him to our time a doctor could give him a bottle of pills and he'd be cured in three days. But he's not in our time, so the poor man is under the care of some old man who calls himself a doctor and—" She waved her hand. "This is one point where I've not been able to move Tristan. The doctor was a friend of his father's. He delivered both Tristan and Beth, and Tristan thinks the man can do no wrong. I've complained so much that I've been banned from the sickroom."

She took a breath. "I know it isn't right but I have so much to do I haven't had the time to tend to William. He's the sweetest man, but he's so sick that he does nothing but lie in bed all day. A horrible woman takes care of him. She empties his chamber pot, and watches over him, but *I* see to his food. Only the best of what we have is prepared for him. I'm sorry, but it is the best I can do."

Faith and Zoë blanched at the mention of a chamber

pot, but they didn't let Amy see it. Amy was so cool and blasé about living in the eighteenth century that they wanted to hide their own awkwardness.

"Let me look at him," Faith said. "I've had some dealings with illness."

Amy smiled at her. "I was hoping you'd say that. If I have to hold a gun on Tristan, I'll get you in that room. The head gardener told me he thought you might know something about herbs."

Faith frowned. All she'd done was walk through the big kitchen garden. She hadn't talked to anyone, hadn't picked a flower. So how had they seen her love of herbs?

Amy seemed to read her mind. "Don't let it worry you. You get used to it after a while. Everyone knows everything about everyone else." She turned to Zoë. "Is it true that today Russell asked you to marry him?"

Zoë choked on the wine she was drinking, and Faith patted her back.

"All *I* did was visit a garden," Faith said. "Have you really started a romance already?"

"You should see Russell," Amy said. "He could have invented the word 'stud.' Every female on this place has been after him and a couple have had him, but he doesn't give out marriage proposals."

"Look who's talking," Zoë said. "You and his lordship. He said you were going to bankrupt him with all the strays you bring into his house."

"He says that all the time," Amy said. "It means nothing. I told you that there's nothing between Tristan and me."

Both Faith and Zoë looked at her with eyes that said they didn't believe her, but Amy refused to comment.

"What happens when you leave here?" Faith asked. "It seems that your body was here before we visited Madame Zoya, so do you think that after we go back, your body will stay here?"

"And do what? Clean his floors?" Amy said bitterly. "I've learned enough here to know that Tristan and I could never marry. We're of different classes. No one would speak to either of us if we wed. That's too much of a burden on any marriage. That's why I—"

When she broke off, the other two women leaned forward. "That's why you did what?" Faith asked.

Amy took a while to answer. "You're going to think this is crazy, but I sent Tristan to London to hire a genealogist."

"He doesn't know who his ancestors are?" Faith asked. "But Beth said they'd lived on this land since 'the dawn of time.'"

"Not for him, for me," Amy said. She lowered her voice. "Yes, there is a, well, a closeness between Tristan and me, but I can't marry him. And, personally, I think that when the three weeks are up we're going to be sent back to our time and Amy the housekeeper won't exist anymore. If the memory of me is taken away, that would be okay, but I'm afraid that Tristan . . ." She looked down at her plate.

"He'll have lost two women," Faith said softly.

"Yes."

"So what does a genealogist have to do with anything?" Zoë asked.

"It's a long shot, but I'm trying to find my ancestors."

Both Faith and Zoë looked at her, considering what she was saying.

"You're trying to find one of your relatives in this time?" Zoë asked.

Amy nodded. "More or less. I don't know if it'll work, but it's the only thing I've been able to come up with."

"But what if—?" Faith began.

"They're housekeepers too?" Amy finished for her. "I don't know, but my great-grandmother was alive when I was little and she used to tell me stories about 'the old country,' meaning Scotland."

"Russell is from Scotland," Zoë said dreamily. The others looked at her. "Sorry. So what about you and Scotland?"

"My great-grandmother used to say that we came from a village in Scotland that was just north of Edinburgh."

"Doesn't that just about cover all of Scotland?" Faith asked.

"Probably, but the important thing is that she said there was a statue there for one of our ancestors. I don't know what he did, but they made a statue of him. I've always meant to go see it."

"What was your family name?" Faith asked.

"MacTarvit."

"Interesting," Faith said, leaning back in her chair and considering Amy. "You're playing matchmaker with the man you love."

"Love as a friend," Amy said, then when they said nothing, she grimaced. "Okay, so I like Tristan a lot. I've lived with him for over a year and we get along well."

"That's not what I heard," Faith said. "I heard the two of you fought all the time."

Amy smiled. "It's odd that we like each other. Stephen and I never fight, and Tristan and I rarely do now that . . . that . . ."

"You've established who runs the house?" Zoë asked.

Amy shrugged. "I guess so."

"So," Faith said, "you're looking for an ancestor of yours to marry poor, lonely Tristan."

Zoe's eyes widened. "You're counting on past lives, aren't you? You don't want a relative to marry him, *you* want to marry him. You in a different body, a different time, but it's still you."

"How about some dessert?" Amy said. "I make this dessert called 'floating island.' It's a bowl full of custard with toasted egg whites floating in it. Sometimes when my girls are beating egg whites by hand I'd give anything to have an electric mixer. Have you two missed anything like that?"

"We're not like you," Zoë said, her teeth clamped together. "We haven't been here for fourteen months. What I want to know is what you're doing besides fooling around with past lives. You haven't hired any witches, have you?"

"You're being ridiculous and I'm sorry I told you."

"I'm not," Faith said. "Look, you two, we only have one another and we need to stick together. We need to listen and learn and find out what we can to save Tristan's life. I guess it would be too much to ask that someone sleep in his room."

Zoë looked at Amy and started to say something.

"I paid a boy," Amy said quickly, "to sleep outside his door, but Tristan made him go away. And he won't let me sleep there either."

Both Faith and Zoë nodded at her.

"Lock him in?" Zoë asked.

"That makes him furious," Amy said.

"Move him to another bedroom?" Faith asked.

"He moves back," Amy said.

"A dog?"

"He says they snore and keep him awake."

"A guard at the bedroom window?"

"That makes him triple angry," Amy said.

"Well," Faith said, "it looks like you've tried quite a few things."

"If either of you have any new ideas, let me know."

"I'll bet you won't hesitate to try them," Zoë said.

"No, I won't," Amy said firmly. "He's my husband's ancestor and I want to help him."

"Your husband's ancestor?" Zoë asked.

"I think so," Amy answered. "Tristan is a lot like

Stephen. All right, that's it. I think we're done examining my motives for today. Do you two have plans for tomorrow?"

"I'd like to look in on the uncle," Faith said. "Is it William?"

Amy nodded. "I'll have to get rid of his nurse. She's like a bulldog standing over him."

Faith looked at Amy. "A touch of orris root?"

"My thoughts exactly." They smiled at each other.

"Oh great," Zoë said. "Herb bonding. If it's okay with you two, I think I'll go to bed. We don't have to sleep on a blanket on a stone floor, do we?"

"How about a feather bed? But you have to share it," Amy said.

Zoë looked at Faith.

"Sorry I'm not Mr. Johns," Faith said.

"Me, too," Zoë said, and the three of them laughed.

"Did he really ask you to marry him?" Faith asked as they followed Amy up the stairs.

Zoë only smiled, then gave a big yawn. "Tomorrow we're going to draw some of the people around this place. I wish I had a digital camera and fifty charged batteries. What I could take back to our time!"

"Who knows?" Amy said. "Maybe your drawings will survive the ages, and when we get back, they'll be in some museum."

"What I wonder is why Russell's paintings aren't in books."

They had reached the top of the stairs and they

looked at one another for a moment. It was likely, even probable, that Russell hadn't lived long enough to make enough paintings, or that his work had been destroyed.

"I think you should make sure that his name does live," Amy said, and Zoë smiled.

"Good idea. So where is this feather bed? I have to be up early to—"

"Go out with—" Amy looked at Faith and they said in unison, "Russell."

"Grow up!" Zoë said, but she was smiling.

Sixteen

❦

"Amy," *Tristan said* softly as he bent over her. It was night and the only light was from the moon outside his bedroom window. They were in the hallway, just outside his door. Amy was curled on the floor, a blanket over her, a small pillow under her head.

"Come on," he said gently. "Get up now."

When Amy didn't move, he picked her up in his arms. He took a step toward the stairs, as though he meant to carry her to her own room downstairs, but instead, he looked up and down the dark hall, then carried her into his room. He put her into his bed, where she snuggled down into the warm covers and kept sleeping.

But she didn't stay asleep. Within seconds, she awoke with a start and sat up. She was fully dressed. "You should have left me there," she said as she watched Tristan light a candle at the far end of the room.

"I cannot leave you out there in the hallway like a

piece of baggage. I have told you over and over not to sleep there."

"I know," she said. "I shouldn't but—"

"You had the dream again," he said.

Amy nodded as she flung back the covers and got out of bed. "Come on, get back in here. You must be freezing." He was wearing a long white nightshirt and his feet were bare.

"What about you?" he asked. "You were in the hall on the floor, with just a blanket over you. Do you know what woke me? Your shivering was making the door rattle."

Amy smiled as she held the covers back. "Better that than that you never wake up."

Tristan climbed back in the bed, then held out his hand to her in invitation.

"Please don't ask me again," she said, her voice low and near to tears.

"I hope that someday I will break you down and you'll come to me."

"I have—"

"Do not say it again!" he said loudly. "I know! You have a husband. You have two children. I know everything there is to know about them. I could pick your children out of a room full of brats."

She was standing at the side of the bed, smiling at him. "I can't," she said. "I really can't. It wouldn't be fair to Stephen. He wouldn't do this to me."

"You are mad if you think that a man would spend over a year with another woman and not bed her."

"Maybe," she said, "but I have to live with myself." She glanced out the window. "I think it's safe to leave you now."

Tristan threw back his head for a moment in despair. "Safe! What do I care about safe? I loved a woman who was taken from me, and now you . . ."

"Tristan," she whispered, "you don't love me."

"Do you think not?"

Amy could feel tears growing in her eyes. How could she love two men? She didn't know, but she did. And one of them was here with her now. He wanted her, had been begging her to join him in bed for months now, but she didn't because she was in love with—and being faithful to—a man who hadn't been born yet.

"I cannot," she said. "Please don't ask me."

"Ask you what?" he said. "Ask you to marry me and be my wife? Is that what I should not ask you? This man you say you love, where is he? Why is he not here with you?" He put up his hand when she started to speak. "I know. You say he is in your America. But I do not think he is. Sometimes I think he does not exist."

The truth of what he was saying showed on her face. "I can't marry you," she repeated for the hundredth time. "We've talked about this. I'm the kitchen help and you're an earl. We would have no friends, no society. You would give away everything if you were to marry me."

"What do I care for society?" he said. "I have hardly left this place for years. I need only Beth and my uncle. But Beth will leave me soon for some man who will not be worth her, as no man is, and God will soon take my uncle." He looked at her with great, pleading eyes. "I need you, Amy. You are the only woman who has made me feel life again. I have nothing else but you."

Amy felt herself being drawn to him. She tried to think of Stephen and the boys. She tried to remember happiness with them, but the months of this life with Tristan kept shoving the modern memories aside.

She hadn't told Faith and Zoë the truth about her and Tristan because she didn't want them to know how close she'd become to him. This morning, when Amy had opened her eyes and found herself in the barn, she knew that Faith and Zoë were confused, even dazed, but Amy wasn't. It was as though she'd arrived home after months away. She knew the man standing in front of them (second assistant gardener) and she knew the way to the house. The way to Tristan, is what she really thought.

When she'd run away from them, she hadn't given so much as a thought to what Faith and Zoë must be feeling. All Amy wanted to do was to see Tristan.

He had been sitting in the library, a book open before him. For a moment she just looked at him, this man she had only seen in a pictures, but, somehow, knew as well as she knew herself.

"I'm back," she said as she closed the library door behind her.

"I wasn't aware you'd been away," he said haughtily, and she knew what was wrong with him. Last night she had yet again turned down his marriage proposal.

After he'd paid her father for her, he'd dumped Amy at his house, the one he'd built for his deceased wife, and had not given her another thought. But after a day of looking about the place, she'd seen it as something that was in dire need of management. Tristan should have taken care of the estate, but he stayed in the library all day or went out riding. Other than that, he did little else. He ate sparsely and didn't seem to notice what was put before him. Whenever anyone from the estate was around him, they spoke in whispers. No one asked him questions. The employees just did the bare minimum of work they had to, then loafed for the rest of the day.

It had taken Amy three days to fully understand what was going on. Tristan's grief was hanging over the estate like a great dark tent. The workers were inside it with him and they couldn't get out. His young sister walked on tiptoe. His uncle lay in bed, slowly dying. The gardens that had once been so beautiful were overgrown and tangled.

Amy wanted to repair the damage, but she knew that she could do nothing without the master's backing.

On the fourth day, she went into the library and nearly attacked Tristan. "This place is horrible," she said to him.

"I beg your pardon." As an earl no one spoke to him

in that tone, certainly not a woman wearing the same raggedy clothes she'd worn at her father's pub.

"I want to put it right," she said. "I want your permission to put this place back together, to get all your lazy servants off their tails, and do some work. Will you back me?"

Tristan just stared at her. What did he care what she did? "Go. Do what you will," he said, then lifted his hand in dismissal.

It had taken Amy nearly a week to make the people on the estate know that she meant business, but her energy, her sharp tongue, and Tristan's support—which consisted of a mumbled, "Do what she says" now and then—all combined to begin to put life in the place.

When Amy had the estate somewhat in order, she took on Beth. She was a beautiful young woman who spent her days with the horses and the stable lads. She wore whatever clothes would let her ride with ease, and her long hair hung down her back and was usually filled with twigs and briars.

Amy confronted Tristan and told him she wanted to send Beth to London for some lessons on how to be a lady. That had started their first serious fight. They didn't know it, but at the sound of the raised voices, the outside workers had come running and squatted under the windows of the library, trying their best to hear every word.

When Tristan said he would not let Beth go, Amy accused him of caring only about himself and no one else. She called him selfish and self-centered. Tristan shouted at her that she was to get out, to leave his home and never come back. Amy hadn't moved. "You need me and Beth needs me. Are you going to let her go or not?"

"Not!" Tristan shouted.

"Then I'm going to get your father's sister to come here!" Amy shouted back.

At that, Tristan had turned pale and sat back down on his chair. "You do not know the woman. She is a shrew. She will—" He swallowed. "I cannot have the woman here."

"Then Beth is to go to her house in London and be fitted out with some decent clothes," Amy said. "She looks worse than I do. You cannot leave her here in this . . . this house of doom and gloom. She's young. She needs to meet people."

"Doom and gloom," he said as he turned away from her. "I guess it is."

She could easily handle his anger, but when he turned like this, with grief on his face, she couldn't stand it. She moved to kneel before him and took his hands in hers. She was no longer a lower-class person, but a liberated American woman. "Tristan," she said softly, "I know that you still grieve for your wife, but you have no right to take Beth with you. She is young and alive and she needs life."

Tristan looked at the young woman kneeling before him. Part of him was astonished that a lowly kitchen maid would dare to talk to him like this, to hold his hands as she was doing, but another part of him reached out to her. Since he was a child he'd had Jane. They'd grown up together. Then, when the happiest day of their life together was about to begin with the birth of their first child, she was gone. Within hours he'd gone from being wonderfully happy to wanting all life on earth to end. He still just wanted to be with her wherever she was.

"Yes," he found himself saying to this woman he hardly knew. He pulled his hands from hers. "Send Beth to my aunt, but let her come back to me soon."

"Of course," Amy said, standing up and looking at him. She'd wanted to touch his hair. She'd wanted to put her arms around him and comfort him, but she didn't.

After that day, things began to change around the estate. The workers had seen and heard that Amy could manage the master. And the truth was that they were tired of working at a place where they could take no pride in their jobs.

They soon learned that Amy was a hard taskmaster, but she was fair. If a person didn't work, he or she was discharged. And she expected a lot from everyone.

She'd had to hire a new head gardener and he'd taken over the outside, while Amy concentrated on the inside. She'd had the house cleaned from top to bottom and every piece of cloth washed, the sheets put into the sun to bleach.

When Beth returned from London after just six

months—all the time she could stand of her complaining old aunt—she came back to a house that smelled of lemon and beeswax. The garden was filled with vegetables that had been seeded in the greenhouse during the winter, and the fruit trees had been pruned. The kitchen garden that had once been acres of mostly weeds now hummed with honeybees, with butterflies darting about.

The parkland had been mowed and new flowers set out. Shrubs were blooming and rabbits were cavorting on the lawns.

But to Beth, the best thing was that her brother was no longer spending his days locked in the library. It was a bit disconcerting to see him and the housekeeper shouting at each other, but she soon got used to it. When it got too bad, she slipped into her uncle's bedroom.

Her uncle William's deteriorated health was the only bad part of her return. When she'd left he'd been able to sit up in bed and read, but now he was on his back in the darkened room. The windows were closed, the curtains drawn, and the room smelled of sickness.

"How are you?" Beth asked as she took the chair by his side.

"Much better now that I can look on your beauty," he said. His once handsome face was sunken, his eyes red, with deep hollows under them. He fell back onto the pillows. "Tell me every word of what you and my sister did." As he said it, he smiled a bit. "Is she as full of herself as she was when we were children?"

"More so," Beth said, "but she does know everyone."

"Knows them but I do not imagine that she is friends with any of them."

"No," Beth said, smiling, and reaching for his hand. It was hot and dry and didn't feel like skin at all. "I want to hear about you."

"There is nothing to say. I am just waiting to join my loved ones and see God. I have a few questions I want to ask Him."

Beth tried to smile, but, instead, tears came to her eyes.

He patted her hand. "Go and see everyone," he said. "I'll be here." The way he closed his eyes made her think he was too tired to talk more.

"Yes," she said, then tiptoed from the room.

Beth's thoughts about Amy were that anything that made her brother want to live again were all right with her. But as the months went by, she saw that her brother was falling in love with Amy, and that Amy was refusing him.

"I don't know what to do about it," she told her uncle on her daily visits to him.

"I think that Amy is a wise woman," William said gently. "You are like me and a romantic. I would like nothing better than to see the earl marry the kitchen maid, but Amy sees the truth of what that would bring them. They'd not fit into his world or hers."

"I think it's something else," Beth said. "I don't know what it is, but there is something more."

"It is between them," William said, closing his eyes and letting Beth know that he'd had enough excitement for the day.

Now, Amy and Tristan were alone in his bedroom, the moon was shining through the window, and she was again turning him down. "I cannot, I will not," she said.

He dropped his hand to his side. "As you will," he said.

"Don't look at me like that. Your sadness will not get me in bed with you."

He smiled. "What will?"

"If you turn into Stephen."

Tristan smiled broader. "I will do my best to do that. I mean to try tomorrow and the day after that."

Amy's face turned serious. "If there is time," she said.

"You cannot mean to tell me your dream again!" he said. "I have heard it until I know every second of it. We have identified the men in the room."

"Yes," Amy said, "and how could I have dreamed of men I didn't know if the dream wasn't real?"

"I do not know," he said, "but I do know that you cannot sleep outside my door." Bending, he opened a drawer in the bedside table and pulled out a pistol. "See this? I do take your dream seriously."

"That won't help," Amy said. "You were sleeping when he stabbed you. And you had on your clothes. I've wondered if he stabbed you somewhere else and carried you to your bed."

"That is absurd. How could he do that and not be seen?"

"What makes you think he wasn't seen? Maybe you . . . I don't know, maybe you got drunk and someone helped you to your bed in your clothes and later someone stabbed you to death."

"I will put away the port in the morning," Tristan said.

"Stop laughing at me. We only have three weeks to stop this, then—" She cut herself off because she hadn't meant to tell him about the three weeks.

He jumped on her words. "What does that mean, that we have only three weeks? What are you planning? Does it have to do with these two women you brought here with you? And where do they come from? They have no baggage, not so much as a hairpin, and they talk even more strangely than you do. And they know so little about our lives! The young one asked how we got water out of the ground. Who are they and what are you planning with them?"

"Their luggage was lost," Amy said, thinking that she would have to talk to Zoë about keeping her mouth shut. If she were to tell someone they weren't just from a different country but a different *time*, Amy didn't know what would be done to them. These people still believed in witches. "They're friends of mine, isn't that enough? Faith is a widow and she spent years nursing her sick husband. I thought she could help with your uncle William. Wouldn't you like to get rid of that sour-faced woman who hovers over him now? Faith is a master herbalist."

She tucked the covers around him. "And Zoë is a painter and I think she's going to apprentice to Russell."

"A woman painter?" Tristan said.

"You say things like that around Zoë and she'll take your ears off."

"I am sure I will be shocked as I am not used to having a woman tell me what she thinks," he said with great sarcasm.

She straightened up and looked at him. He was so very handsome and more than anything in the world she wanted to climb into bed with him. Maybe not for sex, but she'd like to feel a man's arms around her, like to again feel protected and loved.

"Amy," Tristan whispered.

She quickly stepped back from the bed. "I have to go. Listen, tomorrow, if you could . . . I mean, if we could . . . Uh, my friends." She looked at him imploringly.

"Yes, I understand. Your friends know you are married and I am not to look at you with eyes that hunger for you. I can restrain myself, but can you?"

Amy smiled. "Easily," she said, then slipped out the door and closed it behind her. No, it was never easy to hold herself back when she was with Tristan.

"Stayed in there long enough, didn't you?"

Amy looked up to see Zoë standing in the hallway in her borrowed nightgown, her arms crossed over her chest against the cool night. Amy's first thought was to defend herself, but she didn't. "Didn't I tell you that Tristan and I have mad, passionate sex every night?

Some nights we're so loud we scare the pigeons off the roof. So, did you just come back from Russell's bed?"

"I wish," Zoë said. "No, it's just the newness of the place. I couldn't sleep."

"You'll get used to it." She started walking Zoë back to her room.

"Amy," she said outside the door, "have you ever thought about what will happen to us if we don't go back? What if the three weeks end and we stay here forever?"

Amy took a deep breath. "I think about it every day, and what I come up with is that I'll worry about that when it's the end of the twenty-second day."

"You'll marry him, won't you?" Zoë nodded toward Tristan's door.

"I don't know. I don't know anything except that I need to keep him from being killed."

"What if you prevent it tomorrow? Will we be sent back then or will we get the whole three weeks?"

Amy looked at Zoë, trying to read what was in her eyes. "You like it here, don't you?"

"It's not bad," Zoë said, as usual trying to tell as little about herself as possible.

"You're more free here, aren't you? There isn't anyone in this world who hates you for whatever you did."

"True," Zoë said. "I don't think I knew how much my lack of memory bothered me until I came here. I think that in my real life I lived in constant fear that someone from my past would show up and spit at me. One time some workmen dropped a big metal frame with a crash and I threw my arms over my head and ducked. It made everyone laugh, but later I realized that I've always thought that at any time someone could come at me with a gun."

"That's awful," Amy said. "No one should live like that. I think that when we go back you really need to find out what happened to make all those people dislike you."

"I'd rather know anything than whatever I did," Zoë said. "You know what I'd do if I went back to when I crashed my car? I'd leave town. I don't know what happened to make everyone hate me and I don't need to know. I'd just throw things in a bag, get on a bus, and never look back."

"That's not a bad idea," Amy said. "You'd miss out on being in the wreck and that's what really matters."

"Yes, that's what's important. As long as I can still draw. If I go back and find I can't draw . . . Anyway, on the day I was in the crash, I wouldn't get in any moving vehicle." Zoë yawned. "I think I can sleep now." She put her hand on the bedroom door, then turned back to Amy. "What were you doing in his bedroom?"

"Sex and lots of it." Amy tensed again.

"Okay, have it your way, but if you want to talk, I'd listen."

"Thanks," Amy said, then pushed Zoë into the bedroom and shut the door. She looked out the window at the end of the hall. By her calculations it was only about two hours before she had to get up and start making bread. Oh, for an electric bread machine, she thought as she went down the stairs. And flush toilets and automatic washers, and great big grocery stores and trucks to carry things home.

Seventeen

❦

When Faith awoke the next morning, she knew exactly where she was and a wave of excitement ran through her. She was not in her apartment in New York. She did not have an appointment with a therapist where she'd yet again have to try to make her believe she wasn't going to kill herself. And the best, she wouldn't have to talk to Eddie's mother about how wonderful a man he'd been, and how he was now with the angels. She wasn't going to have another long, lonely day with little to do and no one to do it with.

Turning, she saw Zoë asleep beside her and heard the girl's soft breathing. Without her makeup and her air of being tougher than the rest of the world, Zoë looked like a teenager. Faith really hoped that she would find love with this painter whom she'd talked of the day before. She didn't care if Zoë had the man for only three weeks; it would be worth it just to see Zoë smile as though she meant it.

Faith gently pushed the covers back, got out of bed, and reached for the gray cotton dress she'd been wearing when she'd tumbled into the barn with Amy and Zoë. It took her twenty minutes to tie the strings on her corset and pull on her petticoat and long underdrawers. She would have liked to take a shower and put on clean clothes, but she couldn't do that.

Her mind was whirling with all there was to do this day. She planned to spend more time in the kitchen garden, learning what she could from their methods of gardening. What had been lost in our modern world of pesticides and fertilizers that were polluting our waterways?

She also wanted to look in on Beth's uncle William and see what medicines he was taking. What herbal concoctions were they using that she could take back to the modern world? Yesterday, she and Amy had joked about using orris root on the man's nurse. She'd realized it even at the moment that they were trying to impress Zoë with their knowledge of herbs. Orris root was poisonous in large quantities, but in small amounts it made a person sick with vomiting and diarrhea.

She looked out the window. The sun was just beginning to rise, and she saw several of the workers walking about, already starting their jobs. For the first time since Eddie died, Faith knew that she wanted to start the day as soon as possible.

Smiling, she left the bedroom, silently closing the door behind her. When she turned, she saw the woman

Amy had told her about going into Uncle William's room. As Amy had said, she was fierce-looking. Tall and thin, her iron-gray hair was pulled back on her head tightly. Her face was long and looked as though she'd never smiled in her life. She reminded Faith of those portraits of American Puritans: stiff and unbending, and judging everyone they met.

The woman looked Faith up and down and obviously found her unsatisfactory. Faith hadn't yet pulled her hair back so it was hanging loose about her shoulders, and the front of her dress was not fully buttoned.

The woman was holding a tray with a napkin draped over it, food for the sick man.

"May I take that in?" Faith asked politely. "Amy asked me to look in on the patient and—"

She broke off because the woman ignored her. She opened the bedroom door, went into the room, and shut the door behind her in Faith's face.

For a full minute, Faith stood outside the door with her fists clenched and felt a strong sense of déjà vu. It was exactly what she'd been through so very many times with her mother-in-law. The woman loved to make a contest about who was more needed by Eddie, her or Faith. She'd heard the woman say that only she could do so-and-so, and that Eddie liked her way of doing something better than what Faith did.

Through all those years, Faith had given in to the woman. After all, it was her son and he was dying. How could she fight that?

But now was different. Now she had people on her side. Faith could go to the kitchen, tell Amy what was happening, then she'd go to the earl and Faith would be allowed in the room with the sick man. Or she could go to the kitchen and mix up a batch of orris root and make the woman so sick that she'd have to leave the patient's side.

Faith didn't like either of those ideas. She thought of how Amy had come to another time period, all alone, and she'd managed to put herself in a position of command.

"If Amy can do it, so can I," Faith said as she opened the door and went into the room.

Her first impression was of the musty, airless smell. The windows were shut, and the curtains were drawn so that there was no light in the room. It took a moment for her eyes to adjust before she saw the woman sitting on the far side of the room. She seemed to be knitting.

"Get out," the woman said in a rough voice. "He is not to have visitors who are not family."

Involuntarily, Faith took a step backward, then she stopped. Ever since she was a child, she'd been intimidated by women like this one. They had an air of authority about them that had always made Faith want to run and hide. Her mother and Eddie's had both terrified Faith all her life.

Faith drew herself up, put her shoulders back, and said, "You're wanted downstairs immediately." To her astonishment, the voice that had come out of her was her mother's, and there was some of Eddie's mother in there too.

When the woman put her knitting down, got up, and walked past Faith as though she weren't there, she wanted to give a whoop of joy. At the door, she said, "Do not touch him," in a threatening voice that didn't scare Faith at all. As soon as she was gone, Faith went to the big windows at the far end of the room and pulled back the heavy curtains. The dust that came off them made her cough.

When they were open and light was coming into the room, Faith turned back to look at the bed. There was so much dust in the air that for a moment she couldn't see anything or anyone.

She coughed some more, waved her arms about through the dust, and stepped closer to the bed. As her eyes adjusted, she was at last able to see a face barely visible on a pillow. It was long and pale and had scraggly gray whiskers.

If he hadn't had his eyes open, she would never have believed the man was alive. He blinked at her, but it was like looking at a cadaver come to life.

"Who are you?" the man managed to rasp out, his voice hoarse and weak.

"Faith," she said, staring at him in disbelief while trying not to show her revulsion. "I'm a nurse, I'm a friend of Amy's, and I've come to look after you."

"Faith," he said, and his thin face seemed to give a bit of a smile. "That is a good name for you. You look like an angel. Perhaps you are and you have come to take me from this earthly place."

She didn't smile at his words. "I want to examine you," she said softly as she sat down on the bed beside him. She saw that his body under the covers barely lifted them. Slowly, she rolled back the coverlet, then a dingy sheet. At last she came to the man underneath. He was the thinnest person she'd ever seen, his body wasted away to less than a hundred pounds, but by the length of him, he was at least six feet tall.

And he was filthy. His body reeked of old sweat, as though he hadn't had a bath in a very long time. Worse, there were bedsores all over him.

"I apologize for my appearance," he said. "I am taking a long time to leave this earth. I seem to be going by ounces every day."

She could tell he was embarrassed by his condition and didn't want her or anyone else to see him as he was.

"Don't talk," she said softly. "I'm going to turn you over now. Just be still."

"I will do what you wish," he said gallantly, but she could tell he was feeling deep shame at the circumstances.

In the last years of Eddie's life, Faith had turned him in bed, lifted him onto bedpans, and emptied and cleaned them afterward. She was used to what needed to be done with patients in their last months alive. With expertise and great gentleness, she put her arms around his bony shoulders and turned him so she could see the back of him. She didn't let her horror show at what she saw under his nightshirt. There were deep sores over skin that barely covered his bones. Instead, she smiled as she put him back onto the pillow.

"You are truly an angel," he said. "Your touch is gentle."

Faith was working to keep her true feelings from showing on her face. She covered him with the sheet, then stood over the bed, looking down at him for a moment.

"You can see that there is not much to be done," he said, smiling.

"Do your teeth hurt?" she asked.

"There are not many of them left to hurt," he said, still smiling. "I lose one about every month now." It was the closest he'd come to making a complaint.

Faith nodded, then went to the tray of food set on the bedside table, and lifted the napkin. There was a glass of milk and a bowl of something white. "What is this?" she asked as she picked up a spoon and poked at it.

"It is the invalid's last meal. What a child eats. We come into the world with that and leave with the same thing."

"What do you have for lunch and dinner?" She looked at him. "Please don't make any jokes. Just tell me the truth."

His smile left him. "It is the same, but sometimes I am allowed beef broth for dinner. I do not have much of an appetite. It does not matter what I eat. I am just waiting to leave this earth now. Dr. Gallagher assures me that I haven't much longer to wait."

Faith turned away from him for a moment and stared out the window. She had to get herself under control. She took a deep breath and looked back at him.

"William," she said, "I don't know what's wrong with you and I don't know how much longer you have to live, but I can assure you—no, I promise you—that I will make what time you have left more comfortable than it is now."

He looked at her with wide eyes, not knowing what to say in response to her heartfelt declaration. Bending, she tucked the sheet around him, and tried to smile.

In the next second the door opened and in walked the gray-haired woman, his nurse. "What have you done?" she cried. "The light hurts him." She hurried across the room to draw the curtains over the windows. When the room was again dark and the dust was flying about, she turned to Faith. "I will tell the doctor of this and he will see that you are kept away from this room."

Faith gave her a cold little smile. "You think so, do you?" She walked past the woman and left the room. When she was outside, she leaned against the door and took a few deep breaths of air, and for a moment she looked heavenward. "Did you see that, Eddie?" she whispered. "Did you ever see anything more horrible? But I'm going to fix it." She raised her fists. "Whatever I have to do, I'm going to make that man's last days comfortable."

She hurried down the stairs and went straight into the kitchen. Amy was in the middle of the room, directing some women at their cooking. Faith meant to tell Amy what she'd seen, then demand that she be given free rein over him. She meant to be adult and professional. Instead, Faith took one look at Amy and all that she'd just seen came into her mind—and her stomach rebelled. She put her hand over her mouth and started running for the back door and the stairs outside. Amy was right behind her.

Faith threw up in the courtyard. She put her arms against the stone wall of the house and heaved up what little was in her stomach. It all seemed to go through her in great waves even after she was empty. She was aware that people were near and that Amy was saying things to them, but she didn't know what they were doing. All that was in her mind was what she'd seen in that room.

"Better?" Amy asked as she handed Faith a damp cloth to wipe her mouth.

Faith nodded as Amy led her to a stone seat along the wall. They were alone so Amy must have sent the other people away.

"Tell me what happened," Amy said, her arm around Faith's shoulders.

"Have you seen him?" Faith managed to ask. Her stomach was still lurching.

"Not for months. I told you that Tristan left everything in the care of the family doctor."

"A doctor?" Faith said, her voice rising. "How does he call himself that?"

"He's the best the eighteenth century has," Amy said calmly. "Faith, I know what it is to have culture shock. I've been here for over a year and some of the things that go on still stun me, but you have to remember that you and I and Zoë have the benefit of a couple hundred years of learning. Not that we're better than they are. I like their fresh food and handmade items."

She quit talking and pulled Faith closer to her. "Tell me what you saw."

"I don't know what's wrong with him, whether he has cancer or TB or maybe just a food allergy, but I know that no matter what his illness is, no human being should be treated like that." She took a deep breath, then let it out slowly. "The entire backside of him is covered in bedsores, and he has bug bites all over him."

"Bedbugs and fleas," Amy said, taking her arm down from around Faith. "I know them well. When I got here I made them burn all the feathers in the mattresses and wash all the linens in lye soap. I made them take scrub brushes and scour the bedrooms. The bugs and fleas are still a problem but much less of one now."

"You didn't touch *his* room," Faith said and there was accusation in her voice.

Amy didn't take offense. "No. I was told by Tristan and Beth that their uncle was under the care of the doctor and I wasn't to do anything to him or his room. All I do is prepare his food."

"Do you know what she feeds him?"

"What we eat," Amy said. "I oversee the trays she takes to him. He gets the best that my kitchen makes."

"Then she eats it herself," Faith snapped. "William is given only milk, and a bowl of bread mixed with milk. Sometimes he gets beef broth."

"But I have made special, soft things for him," Amy said. "Dr. Gallagher told me that William's teeth are bad and that I should give him only soft food. I have personally mashed peas and made him soups with every vegetable ground up."

"He doesn't get the food," Faith said. She put her hands over her face. "Amy, he is a skeleton. I don't know how he's alive. He's malnourished, and I'm not sure, but I think he's losing his teeth due to scurvy."

"Scurvy!" Amy said in disbelief. It was a disease caused by the lack of vitamin C.

They were silent for a moment, then Amy said, "What do you need to take care of him properly? Other than to get rid of that woman, that is?"

Faith took a breath. "He must be removed from that room. If there were a way to do it, I'd say burn the place down. It's riddled with fleas and bedbugs."

"Trust me on this, but lye soap is as harsh as a fire. My kingdom for rubber gloves!"

"I need to take him someplace where there is sunlight and warmth. He's a modest man and I don't think he'll want people to see him as he is, but he needs to get outside."

"I'll have no trouble getting you anything you want. Tristan loves his uncle very much. The stories he tells about how his uncle used to ride with him and go fishing! I think he was more of a father to Tristan than his own father was."

"Yet Tristan leaves the man in the hands of a quack like that doctor."

"I'm glad that in our modern world we no longer trust doctors so completely that we allow bad things to happen to our loved ones."

"Point taken," Faith said. "Sorry."

"I feel this is my fault," Amy said. "If I'd—"

"What?" Faith said. "Taken on more responsibility than a morose, brooding earl and his neglected sister? Not to mention this whole estate. When would you have had time to take care of an ailing man?"

"True," Amy said, "but I should have done something."

Faith looked at her. "If this so-called doctor has been with the family for a long time, then I guess he's the one who delivered Tristan's wife of her first child."

"Yes," Amy said, blinking. "He did."

"And she died," Faith said, her jaw clenched. "And no doubt she died of childbirth fever, which is caused by filthy hands and going from one delivery to the next without so much as washing."

Amy put her hand to her mouth. "Tristan told me that he thought his wife died because the doctor came so late. He'd been in the village delivering some woman of twins."

"Did *they* live?"

"No," Amy said, looking at Faith. "All three of them died, plus Tristan's wife and child. He calls it the Night of Death."

"More likely it was a night when the doctor didn't wash his hands before delivering the babies. Why should he when birthing is such a messy, dirty job anyway? Why bother washing your hands when you're just going to get them dirty again?"

"Okay," Amy said slowly, "tell me what you need for William. I'll take care of the doctor and that nurse. I've always disliked her anyway, but she's supposed to be the best in the county."

"Where can I take him?" Faith asked. "It needs to be warm, sunny, and private."

"I don't know," Amy began, then her eyes brightened. "The old orangery."

"An orangery?" Faith asked. "I didn't see one in the kitchen garden."

"It's not there. The largest greenhouse has some orange trees, but the old orangery is intact. It had some glass panes missing, but I had them replaced with boards to keep out the rain and animals. It has a wood-stove at each end. The problem is that the place hasn't been used in a while and it's dirty."

"It's at the old house, isn't it?" Faith said as she stood up. "Beth told me about the place. Is the house medieval?"

"Shakespeare could have lived in it. It's all half-timbered and plastered."

"But Tristan has cows in it," Faith said in disgust.

"I'll have you know that that house is number one hundred and thirty-seven on my list of things to take care of around here." She was smiling.

"I'll need a bathtub," Faith said, her eyes with a far-away look. "Please tell me that you have such a thing."

"Yup. A nice big one made of tin. The only problem is that it has to be filled and emptied by hand."

"Can I get some help?"

"Sure. Tristan owns every house in the village. They all work for him in one capacity or another."

Faith smiled. "There were men before machines. I'll need towels, clean sheets, and personal cleaning materials. Please tell me that you have soap and shampoo that aren't made with lye."

"Wait until you see this stuff that Beth makes. She has recipes from her great-great-et-cetera-grandmother and it's heavenly. I'll get her to send some over."

"Yes, please send it. But don't let Beth come until I've had a few days alone with him. And speaking of an orangery, do you have any citrus fruit?"

"Lemons and limes, and I'll get Tristan to send someone to Southampton to get some oranges. They come in on the ships that dock there, then they're sent to London. But I like to cut out the middleman."

Faith laughed. "How did that man survive before you came along?"

"I really don't know."

"I'll need some straws too," Faith said. "You don't

by chance have any nice, clean plastic straws, do you?"
When Amy didn't answer, just gave her an odd look, she
said, "What?"

"Straws?" Amy said. "I'm not a historian, but I would
imagine that the original straws came from the barn."

"Barn?" Faith said. "Straw. I get it." She laughed.

Amy put her arm through Faith's. "Feel better now?"

"Much. How far away is this orangery? Is it possible
that William could be carried there? I'm afraid that
horses or a wagon might be too rough and will take his
fragile skin off."

"Yes, there's someone here who will be glad to carry
William anywhere. And I'll see that you have as much
help as you need," Amy said. "Now I better get back to
the kitchen or we'll have no dinner. The orangery is
right down that path. Why don't you go on ahead and
I'll send some women to start cleaning?"

"And when it's done, you'll send William?" Faith
asked.

"Yes," Amy said, studying her. "You know, you look
younger than you did yesterday."

"I have a purpose here," she said. "I was afraid
that—"

"That I'd dragged you and Zoë here for my own selfish reasons and that you'd have nothing to do?"

"More or less," Faith said as she started walking backward. "Don't forget the bathtub and I'll need lots of hot
water. And soft soap," she said louder as she got farther
away.

"I won't forget anything," Amy called back.

"I will," Faith shouted. "I'm going to try to forget a lot of things." Turning, she started running down the path. She made a detour to run through the kitchen garden. Based on what she'd heard so far, she was sure that everyone in the garden knew what she was doing. Yesterday she hadn't liked that idea, but today their nosiness made her feel as though she were part of an extended family. She ran straight through to the herb area and grabbed an armful of mallow, and another of lemon verbena. She'd put the mallow in the tub as it was good for rashes and boils. The lemon verbena was just to make the room smell good.

As she left, a stout man with gray at his temples raised his hand to her. She guessed he was the head gardener and he was letting her know that what she had picked were good choices.

By the time she saw the chimney stacks of the old house, she was out of breath but feeling wonderful. The house was just as Amy had described, as though William Shakespeare had lived in it, with its half-timbered upstairs and its plastered lower floor. She could imagine Queen Elizabeth walking in front of the house, a half-dozen beautifully dressed courtiers behind her.

Her illusion was ruined when she saw a cow saunter out the front door. "I don't have time to worry about that now," she said as she looked for the orangery.

She found the beautiful old glasshouse in what had once been the walled kitchen garden. It was half the size of the new garden, barely over an acre, but Faith could imagine what it had once been. She could see the remnants of brick pathways, could see untrimmed box hedges, and there were herbs along one wall. They were so old that their centers had died out. A few fruit trees, unpruned, but still alive, were espaliered against the walls.

At the far end was the orangery, where the precious orange trees had once grown. Now it stood forlorn and unused, some of the glass on the end wall replaced with slabs of wood.

The door was ajar and she had to pull hard to get it open. Inside, it was dusty and dirty, but the stone floor was good and there was a woodstove at each end of the long, shallow building. Old, dry vines were at one end of the room. Grapevines, she thought, but they looked as though they'd been dead for a long time. Outside, at the other end, fruit trees that had once been kept pruned were now wild, with their branches spreading out over the glass of the orangery, filtering the sunlight inside. The branches let in the warmth and light but not the glare.

She would put a bed for William at one end, close to the stove, and a bed for herself at the other end, under the old vine. The truth was that she'd like to get away from the main house, which had so many people in it that a person was never alone. And she'd like to have her own bed.

"You plannin' to live in here?" came a woman's voice,

and Faith turned to see three women with buckets in their hands.

"I'm going to look after Mr. William in here," she said.

The women looked at her as though she were daft. "But, miss, he's dyin.'"

"Maybe so, but he'll die clean. Can you tell me where there's a water supply near here? And where's the . . . The . . . uh?"

They understood her well enough, and showed her where the rain barrels were. The water collected from the walls was funneled into big barrels and Faith saw that she had an abundant supply. True, she had to carry it in buckets, but it was better than nothing.

There was an outhouse nearby. She was learning what she'd seen when she'd visited Monticello, that there were outhouses placed at frequent intervals throughout the garden. "Easier than putting in a septic tank," she mumbled.

It took nearly four hours to get the orangery in shape. Amy had been as good as her word and she'd sent eight people to help Faith get the place ready. After the women spent two hours scrubbing, men arrived with a wagonload of furniture and clean bedding. As Faith told the men where to put the beds and four cabinets, she couldn't help asking about the nurse.

"Did Amy let Mr. William's nurse go?" she asked as casually as she could manage.

When all the women stopped cleaning the glass and

looked at the men expectantly, she knew they were as eager to hear what had happened as she was. One of the men turned out to be a good storyteller and he reveled in telling the juicy gossip about the way Amy had thrown the woman out.

"His lordship heard the ruckus," the man said, "and he went running. He thought the house was on fire. When he saw it was just Miss Amy he tried to tiptoe out of the place. He didn't want to get caught in the middle of it."

The man took a breath for emphasis. He liked having an audience. "But the nurse was having none of it. She saw him and demanded that he tell Miss Amy that she was to stay. She said that the woman with the red hair—beggin' your pardon, ma'am—was a hussy and not fit to take care of a gentleman like Mr. William. She said you had other plans for the man than just gettin' him well."

"What other plans could I have?" Faith asked.

"Marriage," the man said, and the women nodded.

Faith laughed, but the others kept looking at her in question. "I just want to make the man comfortable," she said. "So what happened next?"

"His lordship took Miss Amy's side and the nurse was sent back to town in a wagon. Now Miss Amy is tearin' out Mr. William's room."

"And what has she done with Mr. William?"

"Thomas is carryin' him here now," the man said.

"Then let's get this finished," Faith said. "Come on,

we don't have much time. When you get the furniture in I need enough hot water to fill that tub."

"It's on the wagon," the man said. "You plannin' to take a bath?"

"No, I'm going to bathe Mr. William."

She ignored the stares and the mumbles of "It'll kill him for sure to put him in a bath," and went about telling the men where they were to put the beds. She guessed it was odd that she was moving a sick man out of the house and into a dilapidated old greenhouse, but she wanted William to have fresh air and sunshine.

She hustled the workers so much that when a huge man arrived, a frail, emaciated William in his arms, Faith was ready for him. "You may leave now," she said to the workers. When they hesitated, she repeated herself. "I think Amy has dinner ready." She didn't know if it was the mention of Amy or the food, but they went scurrying.

As they went out the door, she stepped aside so the enormous man could enter. He was holding William as though he weighed no more than a dishcloth.

"William," Faith said softly to the man. His eyes were closed and she could hardly see his breath move his chest under the sheet thrown over him.

He opened his eyes a bit. "It is my angel," he said, but she could see that the effort to speak was almost too much for him.

"I want you to listen to me. You're too dirty to put in the bed, so I'm going to put you in a tub of warm water and give you a bath. Do you think you can handle that?"

William opened his eyes and looked up at the man holding him. "A woman to bathe me," he said. "Do such pleasures exist?"

"I think it will not be the first time," the man said, and Faith saw that the two men knew each other well.

"Can you help me undress him?" she asked the big man.

"He has done it often enough," William whispered. "Thomas has been my companion since I was a child."

"Come on, then," Faith said, as she walked toward the filled tub. "Before the water gets cold." She put her hand in it to test it, then twisted the mallow to release its oils and tossed the cuttings into the water.

She watched as Thomas dropped the sheet off William's thin body and exposed him in his nightshirt. She could see the sores on his legs.

There was a moment of embarrassment when Thomas removed the nightshirt and William was naked, but that was gone when Faith saw the state of his body in the daylight.

When William's body first touched the water, he cried out in pain, but he bit on his lip to suppress his cries. Faith's already high estimation of the man rose even more.

It took a few minutes, but the water stopped hurting William's raw skin and began to soothe it. Faith started to tell Thomas that he could leave but she didn't. She didn't know the story, but she had an idea that the man loved William but had been turned away by the doctor. Now that they were in contact again, Thomas wasn't going to let William out of his sight.

While she'd been cleaning and directing the others, Faith had tried to get her revulsion of William's body under control. But as she looked at his arms and face, and in the clear water of the tub she could see the full extent of the damage, her stomach again lurched. She could see his heart beat under ribs that she could count.

"I fear I am not a manly figure," William said, looking up at her.

"Tell me about when you first got ill," she said. She picked up a paper-wrapped bar of soap that Amy had sent and smelled of it.

"Is that from Beth?" he asked.

"It is and it smells wonderful." Faith held the soap under his nose and he closed his eyes at the fragrance.

"It's from the women in my family and we do not know how old it is," he said. "Beth has the book of receipts. Tristan's mother never made the soap, but then she hated my mother."

"Her mother-in-law," Faith said through her teeth. "I can understand that."

"Do you have a mother-in-law?"

"Yes and no," she said. She dipped the soap in the water, sat down on a little stool by the tub, and began to gently wash him. After just one arm, the water turned dark. "I'm a widow."

"Ah," he said, leaning his head back against the tub. "You have lost the husband but kept the mother."

"And you thought *you* lived in hell," Faith said.

William laughed and, in spite of his weakness, it was a good sound.

She knew he was embarrassed by her washing of him, but she wasn't. She had bathed Eddie hundreds of times. "Will you get me some more hot water?" she asked Thomas. That he left her alone with William seemed to be a sign that he trusted her.

"Tell me about your illness," Faith said.

"Must I?" he asked, his eyes closed. "I have not been bathed so since I was a child."

She stood up and got a bottle off the cabinet at the foot of the tub. "Is this the shampoo?"

"Does it smell like sunlight in a bottle?"

"Yes, it does." She could hardly bear to take it away from her nose. "What is in this stuff?"

"Great secrets," William said. "No man in my family has ever seen inside Beth's book. That book of receipts is passed from one woman to the next and no man is allowed to see it. I think the women fear that we men will find out that they are using black magic to ensnare us."

"I think this came directly from heaven." She poured a bit out into her hand and began to shampoo his hair. It was matted and she could feel sores on his scalp. Lice, she thought.

"You have the hands of a goddess," he said, his eyes

closed. "Did you step off Mount Olympus to attend to this lowly human?"

"And were you born with a silver tongue?"

"Enough to get me in more trouble than I should have been," he said.

There was half a bucket of warm water on the floor and she used it to rinse his hair.

He had been in the tub for nearly an hour and Faith thought that was quite long enough, but Thomas wasn't back yet with the fresh water.

"Is there some reason you don't want to tell me about your illness?" she asked. "Was it caused by your visiting places you shouldn't have?" She thought that if he had a venereal disease all the washing in the world wasn't going to cure him.

"I broke my leg," he said.

Faith heard a sound and saw that Thomas was arriving with a wagon. "Then what happened?"

"I had the leg set but I developed a fever that would not go away." He shrugged his thin shoulders.

"I don't understand. You obviously didn't die from the fever, so what happened?"

"I could not get well. Dr. Gallagher did all that he could. He isolated me in my nephew's house when I was the most sick, and he gave me a nurse, but I did not recover. I was out of my head for nearly a month, and when I awoke, I was as you see me, only not so bad as I am now."

Thomas came into the orangery carrying two big

buckets of hot water. Faith got him to pull William upright, then hold him so she could rinse the back of him. The big man held his arms straight out, under William's frail arms, so his rough hands wouldn't hurt the sores on William's back. Faith washed more of William as he hung in Thomas's strong arms, then she poured warm water from a dipper over him.

Thomas and she carefully turned him, then she did the same to the front of him.

When he was as clean as she could get him, Thomas held him while she gently pulled a clean nightshirt over his head.

"I beg you," William whispered. "I must sleep now. I have no more strength."

"Not yet," Faith said. "First, you're going to eat."

"I cannot," William said as Thomas carried him to the bed and gently put him on clean sheets, a big feather pillow behind his head.

"Yes you can," Faith said. "You eat and I'll let you sleep."

"My teeth . . ." William began, his eyes closed.

"I'm going to work on them when they're strong enough to handle a good brushing. But right now you're to drink this."

She glanced at Thomas and saw that he was smiling. She knew he must be as horrified by William's skeletal form as she was, so he was glad she was making him eat. He dipped the buckets in the dirty water in the tub and took them outside to empty.

By the time the tub had been emptied, wiped out, and leaned against the wall, Faith had managed to get most of a glass of lemonade and half a cup of warm spinach soup down William. When she finished, he was so tired that he was barely conscious, but she knew that what she was doing to him was what he needed.

When she finally let him sleep, his head fell to one side in complete exhaustion.

"Good," Thomas said. "Good."

Thomas didn't look as though he were going to win any awards for scholarship, but she could see the love he had for William. His words of praise made Faith feel the best she had in a long time. "Thank you," she said. "Will you stay with him while I see to some things?"

"Aye, I will," Thomas said, and sat down on the chair he'd brought with him in the last wagonload.

Eighteen

❧

"Good morning," Faith said to William when he finally woke up. He'd slept for nearly eighteen hours. Maybe the way he found himself upon waking was a bit disconcerting, but not to Faith. He was lying on his stomach, his nightshirt up to his neck, the whole back of him naked, and Faith was dabbing at his sores with a soothing herbal ointment.

The sun was coming in through the overhead glass so the room was pleasantly warm. Yesterday, while William slept, Faith had gathered equipment and cut herbs, then worked into the night brewing potions to use on William. Thomas had made a pallet on the floor for himself, and his even, quiet snoring was calming as she worked. She'd gone to bed only when it was too dark to see what she was doing.

When the sun came up, Faith was at work again, and by mid-morning, she was ready to start on the sores on William's body. Thomas had walked to the main house and brought back a box of food and more things that Amy thought they'd need. He produced a box of oranges with a smile of triumph. There was a note from Amy in the box, written on heavy paper with what looked to be a quill. Yet another use of the geese, she thought.

Tristan went to Southampton yesterday as he said he could ride the fastest. He rode all night, got the oranges, and came back immediately afterward. He didn't sleep. I told you William is a well-loved man. Tell Thomas whatever you need. If it can be had, we will get it.

Faith read the note to Thomas and he smiled. "Aye, he is well loved."

She wanted to say, Then why the hell was he allowed to rot in a bed? But she said nothing as she sat down at the table he'd brought with him and ate breakfast.

She couldn't help admiring the change in the old orangery. The surfaces were covered with objects that, to Faith's eye, were beautiful. There was no plastic, nothing that hadn't been painstakingly made by hand. The herbs she had placed about the room smelled divine. She'd even put sprigs of wormwood around the edges to repel bugs.

Yesterday she'd started to tell the men to cut down the old grapevine, but on impulse she'd watered it. The vine grew out of a cleverly designed trough into which water was poured at one end and flowed out across the whole root system. Time would tell if there was life in the vine.

The room was filled with steam from the pots of water she'd boiled on the fire that Thomas had built for her outside. The tops of the cabinets were covered with pots and bowls and a couple of big marble mortars and pestles.

After she and Thomas had eaten breakfast, she'd asked him to turn William over onto his stomach so she could get to the sores.

Faith gently lifted William's nightshirt off his sleeping body and began to apply the ointment she'd made of self-heal and soapwort. It was something that she'd used on Eddie when a bandage had made a blister on his skin.

William wasn't embarrassed by his nudity or Faith's touch. "Ah, at last," he said when he woke up to feel her warm hands on his skin. The sun was shining through the tree leaves and into the building. "I have at last died and I am in heaven."

Thomas gave a guffaw of laughter.

"Dear Thomas," William said. "He always laughs at my jests."

"I don't think your death wish is a reason to laugh," Faith said.

"I have never wanted to die," he said. "I just thought it was God's plan for me."

"All right," Faith said, "you win. Sorry." He'd flinched

when she touched one of the many sores on his back. Now that he was clean, and he was in a bright room, she could see the extent of his wounds. She didn't know what had started his illness, and without a modern doctor and equipment, she'd never know, but from what she could see, his real problems were lack of food and care.

When she'd covered the back of his body with ointment, she pulled his gown down. William asked Thomas to take him to the outhouse, and Faith was pleased. Now William had the energy to want to get out of bed.

While they were gone, Faith glanced at the mirror that Amy had sent and tidied her hair. It was pulled off her face but not too tightly. And Amy had sent Faith a clean dress. Last night she'd managed to give herself a sponge bath and today she hoped to use some of Beth's shampoo to wash her hair.

"Hungry?" she asked William when Thomas brought him back inside.

"I am," William said as though it were the strangest thing he'd ever felt. He winced when Thomas put him in the bed, and he lay back against the pillow wearily, but there seemed to be some color in his face.

First, there was fresh-squeezed orange juice that Faith had made that morning. She got an entire glass of it down William, who used a real straw to sip from the glass that Amy had sent to her. Hand-blown, hand-etched, eighteenth-century glass, Faith thought as she looked at the beautiful object.

Thomas went outside with a skillet and a big pat of hand-churned butter and fried an egg that was laid that morning. Faith dipped bread that was still warm from the oven in the egg and mashed it up for William to eat with his loose teeth. He couldn't really chew but he could dissolve the food in his mouth.

With every bite, he closed his eyes and gave himself over to the flavor. For Faith, watching him eat was close to a sensual experience. He was thin and gaunt, but she could see a bit of the man he'd once been.

"Can Thomas shave you?" she asked.

"Perhaps he should shave my head as well," William said as Faith fed him another bite.

She knew he was referring to the head lice. "I have parsley seeds," she said. "I could wrap your head in them, but if you'd rather have Thomas shave your hair off, I'll understand."

"Thomas or a beautiful woman?" William said. "I will have to think on that."

Faith laughed. "Maybe I shouldn't help you get well. You might be dangerous."

"And since when did a woman dislike danger in a man?"

"You, Mr. William, are going to be a problem," she said as she took his empty plate to the cabinet where she had a big porcelain bowl of water.

She tidied up while Thomas took the bowl of hot water Faith handed him and the straight razor and a bar of Beth's soap. For a moment Faith held her breath, but from the way Thomas wielded the razor and the way William moved his face, this was something they'd done many times before.

Thomas gently cleaned William's face of excess soap.

"I hope I—"

William broke off because they heard the sound of a horse approaching. Faith went to the door and saw a tall, dark man sitting atop a black horse as if he'd been born on the animal. She knew without a doubt that this was Tristan. Even though she'd been his guest for a few days now, she'd seen him only from a distance.

"I believe this is your nephew," Faith said, turning to look at William. He was watching her intently.

"Tristan," he said, and tried to sit up straighter. Faith ran to help him.

"He is beautiful, is he not?" William said when her face was close to his.

It was probably her imagination but she thought she heard jealousy in his voice. "If you like boys," she said under her breath.

William gave a sound like a laugh and he seemed to sit up straighter in the bed.

When Tristan Hawthorne walked into the orangery, it was as though the room filled with him. It was a big area, at least sixty feet long, but Tristan seemed to take up all of it. When Faith had first seen the drawing of him that Zoë did, she'd thought he looked like Tyler, but now she knew he didn't. Tyler was a good-looking, hometown boy, and wasn't in the same league as this man.

"Tristan," William whispered and lifted his arms. Faith could see his thin arms shake with fatigue, but he held them aloft to welcome his nephew.

Tristan took his uncle's hands in his, then bent forward to kiss his cheek. "You look . . ." He couldn't say anything else as he stared at William, his eyes drinking him in.

"I was saved by an angel," William said. "I was praying for death, when this angel came and saved me."

Faith could feel her whole body turning red. "I only did what anyone would do," she managed to say.

Tristan turned to look at her, an intense gaze that made her uncomfortable. In that moment she had even more admiration for Amy. How in the world had she been able to take on this man? Faith knew that she would never have had the courage to stand up against his intense glare.

"No," Tristan said, "you have done more than what we did. I thought that the doctor . . ."

He couldn't seem to say more, but she couldn't let him carry his guilt. She knew how it felt to think that if only she'd done something different, the bad wouldn't have happened.

"You did the best you could, and it's to your credit that you trusted me, a woman you'd never met, to take care of your uncle. For all you knew I could have been a charlatan."

"No," he said. "I trusted Amy. I have trusted her from the beginning."

And loved her, Faith thought. Tristan was as in love with her as much as she'd ever seen anyone in love. Amy, Amy, Amy, she thought. What are you doing to this poor man? His beloved wife had died and now he was in love with Amy—and she was going to leave him in less than three weeks.

Faith smiled modestly and stepped away from the two men, giving them time alone. She didn't know what was going to happen with William. She could clean him all she wanted, but if there was something wrong with the inside of him, he still wouldn't be well. She would just have to wait and see.

She left the walled garden and walked toward the old house. The front of it was trampled by cows and thick with manure, but she could see how beautiful it had once been. But the house had been abandoned when Tristan had built the new one for his doomed wife.

As Faith walked around the house and even got close enough to look in some of the windows, she knew that to these people the old house was nothing special, but to her modern mind it needed to be preserved and treasured.

She picked some wildflowers from the fields and when she got back to the orangery, Tristan was gone and William was asleep. But he woke up an hour later and said he was a bit "peckish." Faith knew this meant he was hungry.

Three days later, William's mouth had healed enough

that he could chew food, and with Faith's help, he had taken a few steps. At first Thomas had tried to support him, but William said he was a clumsy oaf and not good as a crutch.

"But I guess I'm the right size," Faith said.

"Exactly the right size," William said as he put his thin arm around her shoulders and took his first hobbling steps. His legs had been unused for nearly a year and the muscles had come close to atrophy.

After the first attempt at walking, Faith had to rub his legs to relieve the pain of cramping.

At the end of the first week, William was walking on his own with the help of two canes—and that's how Beth saw him. Faith knew that Tristan had ordered her to stay away from her uncle, but it looked like he had at last rescinded his order.

Beth rode her horse into the walled garden and when she saw her beloved uncle, she slid off before it stopped. When Thomas and Faith saw the way the girl was running toward her uncle, as though she meant to launch her strong, young body onto his, they took off to intercept her. But Beth reached him before they did. William was smiling, not in the least worried that his healthy young niece was going to tackle him.

Beth stopped just short of leaping on her uncle, took his hands in hers and pressed them to her face. Behind her Thomas and Faith stopped, out of breath and panting. William looked at them in amusement over Beth's bowed head.

"You look wonderful," Beth breathed. "You have doubled your weight, and you are walking."

"Not quite double," William said as he put his hand on her hair that was warm from the sun.

"Not from lack of trying," Faith said. "He eats his weight in food every day. Amy says she's going to have to hire a new cook just for him."

"Tristan will hire a dozen cooks," Beth said. "A hundred of them." She still held her uncle's hands and couldn't take her eyes off his face. "Come and tell me everything that you have done," she said. "I want to hear it all."

William tucked Beth's arm in his and started to walk toward a bench. When Faith saw that he'd left his canes behind, she picked them up and didn't remind him of them. He wanted to make his beautiful young niece think he was more well than he was.

Faith went into the orangery and began clearing up from their last meal. As she looked around she thought that soon there'd be no need for her to stay here alone with William and Thomas in their own little world. But she knew that the last week had been the happiest of her life. She'd had her own house, her own kitchen of sorts, even her own garden. Every afternoon in the last week William had sat on a chair while Faith had taken a shovel to the plants. He'd told her that she could get someone to do the work for her, but Faith had wanted to dig for herself.

As with everything else on the estate, everyone knew

what she was doing. Three times she'd awakened in the morning to find pots of herbs and flowers on the doorstep. During the night someone had delivered them to her and, the next morning, she'd happily planted them.

"This suits you," William said. "This garden, this place, it all suits you."

She knew what he was actually saying. She had saved him and sometimes he seemed to believe himself to be in love with her. But she knew he wasn't, and she wasn't in love with him either. For all his teasing and laughing, she understood why William Hawthorne had never married. He wasn't a man who'd likely be faithful to any woman.

"Yes, it suits me," she said. "I'm really just a class above a farmer."

He hadn't said anything to that, and she thought he agreed with her. His class system, which was ingrained in him, only made her laugh.

Now, she left him alone with his niece, to spend time together. It was two hours later that Beth came inside the orangery. "You have made it very nice in here," she said, looking around. "Is that old vine growing?"

"Yes. It's just showing the pink tip of the leaves. I think it got just enough water through the broken glass to keep it alive."

Beth touched the vine for a moment, then turned to look back at her. "My brother, Tristan, and I have talked about what we can do to repay you for what you have done for our uncle."

"It was nothing," Faith said. "You've taken me in, fed me, clothed me. I couldn't ask for more."

"But Tristan takes care of a hundred people, but they did not save our uncle. We want to give you something."

"No, please," Faith said. "I don't need payment." She thought that the truth was that if she was going to stay there, a nice fat pot of gold might prove useful. But she was going to leave in less than two weeks, so what good would gold be to her? "Really, I can't take anything."

"We talked to Amy and she suggested that you might like this for a reward." Beth held out a little packet wrapped in paper with a pretty block-printed design.

Faith had an idea that it was some wonderful book, but of what use would it be to her? When they'd been sent back in time, they'd arrived wearing different clothes. Faith was sure that whatever they had here would be taken away from them.

She took the book and thanked Beth for it. "How very sweet of you to think of this," she said. "It was most kind."

"Will you open it?" Beth asked.

Smiling in a set way because she was sure she knew what was in the package, Faith opened it—and her mouth dropped open. It was a book of hand-copied recipes for the fabulous soap and shampoo and four other products. Faith's first thought was that she could memorize the recipes. If she put them to memory, she could take them back to her time.

She looked at Beth with wonder in her eyes. "These are . . ." She didn't know what to say. "Thank you."

"They are worthless as they are."

"I beg your pardon?" Faith said.

"Read one."

Faith looked at a recipe for face cream. It was simple enough: oil, water, a bit of beeswax, a few herbs. Then at the bottom she saw that it called for something called "balm." "What is this last thing?" she asked. "A Balm of Gilead?" She looked at Beth's eyes and saw that she thought this Biblical herb was not attainable. "We have this in my country," Faith said, and wanted to add, "In my time."

"Would you like to take a walk?" Beth asked.

"Certainly." Faith slipped the book into the pocket of the apron she was wearing and followed her outside. She stopped to tell Thomas to look after William while she was gone.

William looked at his niece in surprise. "Do not tell me, Beth, that you are going to show her the secret of the women of this family?" His voice was teasing, but Faith could hear a deeper note under it. "Do you say that my life is worth that much to you?"

Beth, who had just a short while before been in tears to see her uncle, now gave him a look of dismissal. "You will never know," she said to him over her shoulder.

Faith looked at William in question.

"Do not ask me to tell you," William said loudly as the women left the garden. With the weight he'd gained his voice had improved. "Only once did I try to invade their secret. My father made sure I did not sit down for a week."

"Beth," Faith said when they were outside the walls, "what's he talking about?"

They were walking past the old house, but Beth didn't so much as glance at it. "Do you remember that I told you my family has lived here for a long time?"

"You said 'since the dawn of time.'"

"Yes. That old house that you love so much—no, don't deny it, I've heard how you shoo the cows out and wander through it every day—was the third house my family has had on this land."

"Third?" Faith asked, thinking about how long they must have lived here.

"Come, and I will show you something that will interest you."

Faith had to hurry to keep up with young Beth as she walked quickly across the pasture, then through a gate and into the woods. There was a narrow path, meant for one person only, that snaked through the dark woods. She looked up at the trees, growing so close together that no sunlight came through, and she wondered if she was seeing virgin forest: uncut since the creation of the world.

"No one is allowed in here," Beth said. "There have been signs of wolves so sometimes I've taken Thomas with me, but never Tristan or my uncle. My mother hated it in here and refused to go, but then she was not of Hawthorne blood. I learned what I know from my grandmother and she from her mother."

Faith had no idea what Beth was talking about, but the hairs on the back of her neck were beginning to stand up. The woods were dark and a bit creepy, and Beth's words made it seem as though they were going to come upon a house full of witches.

"Beth, are you sure it's all right for us to be back here alone?"

"Of course. There!" she said at last. "Look at that."

Faith saw a clearing in the woods just ahead of them. There was a little hill and unless she missed her guess it was man-made, and looked to have been built a very long time ago. On the top of it was a short, round tower of stone, with a door in it, but no roof that she could see.

"What in the world is that?" Faith asked. "And how old is that thing?"

"It was there when one of my ancestors went on the Fourth Crusade," Beth said.

"Crusade? So we're talking about the year one thousand?"

"The Fourth Crusade was from 1201 to 1204," she said, looking at Faith oddly, as though wondering if she'd ever been to school. "The tower is older than that. My grandmother told me that all the stones from the fields were piled here, then the stones were covered with dirt. More stones were used to build the tower."

"I wonder if it could be Roman," Faith said, looking up at it. It couldn't have been more plain. The trees had been cut back from around it and from the look of the place, some trimming had been done recently. "Do you take care of it now?"

"Yes. I will pass it on to my daughter."

There wasn't a weed around the base of the building. If Beth was taking care of the tower, she was doing a good job. With the trees cut back, it was bright on the little hill and the sun fell onto the top of the stone building.

Beth reached into her pocket and withdrew a big iron key. "I am going to show you what is inside."

Faith's first thought was to say no, thanks, and run back to the orangery. What in the world was inside that could be such a mystery that it was protected by the women of the family, with no men allowed to see it?

Beth led the way up a narrow stone staircase that was embedded in the hillside, and every fairy tale Faith had ever heard went through her head. Maybe some monster was chained inside the building. Maybe—

She held her breath as Beth put the key in the lock and opened the door. The hinges were so well oiled that they made not a sound.

When the heavy oak door with its giant iron hinges swung open, Faith drew in her breath. But when she looked inside, she let it out. The ceiling was a pointed greenhouse roof, set several feet down from the top of the tower so it couldn't be seen from the outside. Inside was a circular room, no more than twenty feet in diameter. In the center was a circular stone bench and around the edges were tall shrubs. It was quite hot in the tower and dry.

Faith looked at Beth in question but the girl said nothing. Curious, Faith went to look at the plants. The smell was heavenly and she recognized it immediately. "It's the smell of the soap and the shampoo."

Beth nodded but said nothing. Faith knew there was some secret that she was being told, but she didn't know what it was. She looked at the leaves of the plant, but it didn't seem familiar.

Then, all of a sudden, it came to her. She looked at Beth. "Balm?" she said. "The *real* balm?"

Beth nodded.

Faith looked back at the plants in wonder. There was a story that the Queen of Sheba had given King Solomon a balm of Gilead. And the same balm was mentioned in the Bible. For centuries scholars had argued about exactly what plant it was. In modern times there was one plant called the Balm of Gilead that grew in the Holy Lands and it was rare and protected. But there were many who believed that the real balm was an extinct plant called *Balsamodendron opobalsamum.*

"Where did this come from?" Faith asked, staring at the plant. If this was the true balm, then its oil had been used to anoint kings, and it smelled so good that there was a belief that in heaven there would be streams of opobalsam oil.

"Some of my ancestors were Knights Templars and they brought seeds back from . . ."

"The Holy Lands," Faith finished for her as she touched the plants with reverence. "No one else has these plants, do they?"

"I don't think so. I've never seen it in anyone's garden. It has to be protected from the rain because it doesn't like water."

"But it likes sun," Faith said as she put her hand on the sun-warmed stone wall. The tower with its stone walls and glass roof was all solar power. The sun came in through the glass roof and the stones stored the heat. Even when it rained, there would still be warmth in the stones. All in all, it was as good an environment as England could give the Mediterranean plants.

"I'm impressed," Faith said. "This is . . ." There weren't any words to describe how wonderful she thought it was that this family had been able to preserve this precious plant for hundreds of years. "What you've done is truly magnificent."

Beth went to a part of the wall near the door, twisted a stone, and removed it. Inside was a hollow space that seemed to be full of envelopes. She removed one and handed it to Faith. "These are for you."

Faith knew what was in the envelope: seeds. Seeds from a precious plant that had been extinct for a very long time. She very much wanted them, but how was she to get them back to her own time?

"Amy has hinted that she will leave soon," Beth said.

"Tristan refuses to listen to her, but I know she means it. I assume that you and Zoë will go with her. When you leave you may take the seeds with you, and you can plant them in your country. Do you have dry parts in your country?"

Faith thought of Arizona and southern New Mexico. "Oh yes, there are lots of dry areas." They had no English-speaking people there in 1797, but they would. Even as Faith's hands tightened possessively over the envelope, she kept thinking that she'd never be able to take the seeds with her.

"Thank you," she said. "Thank you very, very much."

"I will probably be haunted by the ghosts of my ancestors," Beth said. "My grandmother made me take a vow not to share the seeds with anyone. Only we can make the products that use this holy plant."

"Have you ever thought of going commercial?" Faith asked tentatively. The look Beth gave her was all the answer she needed. Beth was Lady Elizabeth and, no, she did not make things to sell to the public.

Faith had to turn away to hide her smile. It was hundreds of years away, but she knew there would come a time when all classes went into business. She looked about the round tower and wondered what would happen to it. If there was even one break in the female-to-female lineage in the family, no one would know what the plants were or how to take care of them. She could imagine the land being sold and a dozen ugly little houses being built where this forest was now.

"Is something wrong?" Beth asked.

"No, of course not," Faith said, holding the seeds close to her breast. "It's just that I'm amazed at all this. It's wonderful. Extraordinary. And beautiful. That you've been able to preserve it for so long is truly . . ." She couldn't think of the right words. "I promise that I'll do what I can to see that this plant lives on."

"I think we should get back to my uncle now," Beth said and stepped toward the door, but she turned back and looked at the floor. Bending, she picked up something blue.

"What's that?" Faith asked.

"It's a bit of indigo ribbon," Beth said, frowning. "I think someone has been in here."

"How could they?" Faith said quickly. "The door is heavy and kept locked. No one can get in. I bet the ribbon blew in through there." She pointed upward to a pane of glass in the roof that had a hole in it. It was only about two inches wide, but something like a ribbon could have blown through it.

Beth's frown left her. "I'm sure you are right. I will have Thomas repair that."

"Good idea," Faith said as she held the door open for Beth. As she left, Faith stuck out her foot and rubbed out a little patch of pink chalk on the floor. Yesterday she'd seen Zoë wearing a ribbon in her hair just like the one that Beth had found in the tower room. That, combined with the chalk, told her that Zoë had been in there. But how? she wondered. She wouldn't put it past that painter who was never out of Zoë's sight to have stolen the key from Beth and used it. And what did they do once they were inside the tower? That didn't take much guesswork.

As Faith followed Beth down the stairs, she vowed that as soon as they got back to the orangery, Faith was going to find Zoë and tell her to stay out of things that didn't concern her.

She stuck the envelope of seeds inside her dress and went back through the forest behind Beth. This time, she thought the woods were the most beautiful place she'd ever seen, and she looked at the lush growth with new eyes. Was there anything in it that she could use?

They were almost to the gate when she stopped. "Beth, wait a minute."

Faith had seen something in the forest that she didn't like. She lifted her skirt to above her ankles and made her way through the damp undergrowth. She had seen a glimpse of red.

She stopped near a big oak tree and turned to see Beth just behind her. She nodded toward a stand of red-topped mushrooms. "Those are deadly," she said. "And hallucinogenic, as well."

"Halluci . . . ?"

Faith wasn't going to explain a drug trip to someone of Beth's age. Who knew what she'd start? The drug age hundreds of years early? "I think they should be destroyed."

"No one is allowed in here, but go ahead. It does not matter."

Faith used her feet to knock over the big mushrooms, then grind them down. In her own time she wouldn't have done it, but in this age she knew that people ate whatever grew. She had seen that they ate puffballs, something that modern people thought were poisonous.

"All right?" Beth asked.

She nodded and they started to walk out of the forest, but as they got to the gate, Beth stopped her. "I have something to ask you."

Faith could tell that Beth was nervous about whatever she wanted to say.

"I greatly admire what you have done," Beth said.

"It's only what anyone would do," Faith began.

"You know more than the doctor!"

Faith refrained from making a sarcastic remark at that. Amy had sent her a note saying that Tristan had taken care of the doctor and he wouldn't be bothering her. "I know some different ways of working, that's all," Faith said at last.

"I want to learn from you," Beth said. "I want you to teach me what you know. I know I have no true experience, but I have taken care of the tower since I was twelve. The only thing I have to do now is to sit for a portrait with Mr. Johns and he is . . ."

"Teaching Zoë," Faith said diplomatically.

"That is just what Tristan said." They looked at each other and burst into laughter.

"Of course you may come to me," Faith said. "You

may stay all day and all night. I'll teach you the tiny bit that I know and I'll be glad for your company."

"I am glad you came here," Beth said. "Very, very glad."

"So am I." Faith slipped Beth's arm through hers and they walked back to the orangery.

Nineteen

"*If they find* us in here," Zoë said, "they'll . . . What *do* they do for punishment in the eighteenth century?"

Russell didn't look up from the canvas on his easel. "Sometimes you sound like you know nothing about your own century."

"Didn't I tell you that I come from the future? We have spaceships and lots of little green men."

"Hmph!" he said, glancing up at her nude body as it was stretched out on the silk coverlet, the bushes in the tower behind her. "I can believe it. Would you please stop talking so I can paint?"

"I didn't think you cared what my face was doing."

"Only sometimes," he said, glancing up at her in a way that made her body feel warmer than it already was.

"Shouldn't we take a break soon?"

"Your breaks are more tiring than work," he said, his eyes on the canvas.

Zoë put her head back into the position that Russell

had placed her in and looked up at the glass roof. He'd shown her the stone tower only after they'd been lovers for an entire week, and from the way he acted, she knew he'd been saving it for someone special.

"What in the world is this place?" Zoë asked when he led her to it the first time.

"Be quiet," he said. "I don't want anyone to hear us."

"Who could hear us? Nobody's been here in years. Well, except for whoever cuts the weeds. It doesn't even have a roof."

"That's what I thought," Russell said as he went up some narrow stone steps that were nearly hidden in the hill that the tower stood on. When they were at the top, she watched him pull a huge iron key from his pocket and slip it into the lock. She figured it would be rusted shut but the key turned easily.

"Where did you get that key?"

"Borrowed it," he said, glancing around as he opened the door.

"From whom?"

Russell just smiled as he pulled her inside the tower, then closed the door behind her.

It was very warm inside the stone circle and there was indeed a roof, but it was made of glass. In the center was a round stone bench, and along the edges were big shrubs with pale green leaves. They smelled wonderful. She looked back at him. "Okay, I'll bite. What is this?"

"It's the family secret," Russell said, his voice low.

"Some secret. Plants have to be taken care of so

somebody looks after this place. And they cut the grass outside. So who takes care of it?"

"Beth."

"What?" Zoë said, running her hand over the leaves of the plants, then she drew back. "These aren't poisonous, are they?"

"I have no idea what they are. All I know is that young Beth takes care of this tower by herself with only a little bit of help from Thomas."

"Thomas? Is that another brother?"

"Not quite. He's the big guy. The giant? He stays near William, waiting to be needed."

"Oh yes, I saw him at Faith's."

Russell shook his head at her. "And when did you see her?"

"For the ten minutes when I wasn't with you," she said, then looked at him from the corner of her eye. "You haven't seemed to mind that I've given you all my attention."

"No," he said, "I've not minded at all."

She glanced about the tower. "Tell me about this place." They'd been lovers since the second day after they met. Zoë thought that she'd teach him a few tricks she'd learned in her years of living in the houses of the rich, in her century. But if Russell was an example of his century, there wasn't anything they needed to learn.

They spent three days doing nothing but making love. Russell knew the estate well and knew lots of interesting places they could go and not be discovered. Although one day Faith had nearly seen them when she'd gone into the old house that was near the orangery where she was staying with Tristan's sick uncle. Zoë and Russell grabbed their clothes and hid in a little anteroom until they heard Faith leave.

"That was a close one," Zoë said.

"And what would she have done if she had found us?" Russell asked as he took her clothes out of her hands and began to kiss her neck.

"Faith? She'd probably die of embarrassment on the spot. From the story she told us, she got married and became a virgin. Or at least a saint."

"And what about Amy?" Russell was kissing his way down her chest as he pushed her against the old bed that was still in the house. It was too big to remove. He ignored the squeaks of whatever creatures they disturbed when he pushed her onto the bed.

"Amy?" Zoë asked, as she arched her back. "She's a dark horse. I can't figure her out. I could believe that she doesn't touch that hunk Tristan or she's in the bed with him half of every day. She could go either way."

"What's a 'hunk'?" he asked.

"You," she said, then kissed him back.

After three days of lovemaking, their second love took over and they began to draw and paint. It was Russell who started it. "Lie there," he said as he picked up his pad and pencil. "Just like that. I want to capture you in that exact position."

It had taken only half a day before they were in competition as to who was going to pose and who was going to draw.

It was on the fifth day that Russell had grown serious and pulled out the oil paints. Zoë had used oils before but she didn't favor them. She preferred watercolors, and pencils and chalk. Her portraits were done in these media and her clients had loved the sweetness of them.

"I want to have something of you," Russell said.

Zoë started to reply, but she didn't. Somehow, he knew that she was going to leave. And she knew he sensed that she was going to leave as abruptly as she'd appeared, and he wanted some piece of her to keep forever.

Zoë had done her best to keep it light between the two of them. She felt that not going to bed with him for a full twenty-four hours after they met had been a giant strength of will. She'd never been a promiscuous woman. She'd had two intense flings with men her age while living in the houses of her clients, but when the job was over, she'd had no problem leaving them.

She liked to tell herself she was going to feel the same about Russell, but she knew it was a lie. She liked him. She liked his sense of humor, the earthiness of him, and she loved his talent. She especially loved that his life was driven by a passion for art. He was a kindred soul.

One of the things she liked most about him was where his passion took him. While he stayed with a family for at least a year, ostensibly to make portraits of all of the family members—just as Zoë did—the truth was that he spent several hours each day drawing the people who worked in the fields and in the house. The ordinary people. "The people who make the world function," he said.

She was impressed at how fast he could draw. He told her he'd had to learn speed to keep his old master from whacking him on the knuckles with a sanding board. Whatever the reason, Zoë said he was the original camera—then she'd had to make up an explanation of what she meant. He'd never shown his quick sketches to anyone before Zoë. "People would not like them," he mumbled, and she saw that he was pretending that her opinion didn't matter to him—but it did.

As she looked at his drawings she could understand why people in his time didn't care for them. They were the forerunners of Impressionist paintings and she loved them. She took the paintbrush away from him and did her best to show him how, in a hundred years, Monet would paint a pond.

"But it's not finished," he said. "It's not clear what you're seeing."

"That's the point," she said. "It's an impression of what you're seeing. You have the real thing to look at, but this is paint. It's not a real pond, not real lily pads, so you have a lot of freedom with how you reproduce it in paint."

It was a simple concept and easily understandable to her twenty-first-century brain, but it was revolutionary to him. "A good likeness" was paramount to him. But then, he didn't have photographs to compare with.

After Russell started with oils, Zoë quit competing with him. She knew she'd not be able to take anything back with her when she left, so she rather liked the idea that maybe she'd someday see a portrait of herself on the wall of a museum. For days now, she'd posed while he painted. It had taken only his asking to get her to pose nude.

Each day they went somewhere different and Russell began a new painting of her. They didn't speak of it but she knew that his idea was to get as much on canvas as he could before she left him forever. She wondered when he slept because each morning he'd show her what he'd done during the night.

"Faith was here yesterday, with Beth," Russell said.

"Did she give you the key?"

"Faith? No."

"Very funny," Zoë said. "If you want me to stay still, tell me what you know."

"Every family has secrets and this one is no exception," he said.

Zoë looked at the plants. "What are these plants?" If they were marijuana she'd understand, or maybe not as they weren't outlawed yet.

Russell glanced up at her. "I do not know what they are. Beth takes care of them. Her brother never comes here and her uncle has been too ill."

"Faith did a good job on the uncle, didn't she?"

"More of your enlightened practices from your young country? For a people so young, you have certainly learned a lot in a short time."

She started to reply, but instead just looked at him. He was a good listener and, more than that, he was intelligent. He seemed to take tiny pieces of whatever she said and put them together to make a whole.

"I have finished with your mouth, so why do you not tell me more about yourself?"

She laughed because he made it sound as though they'd just met this morning. "I'm boring," she said, but in the next second she found herself telling him more of her life story. She had to adjust it to sound as though it happened in the eighteenth century, but it was the same tale. Wherever she lived, she still didn't remember what happened.

"Love," Russell said when she'd finished. "Whatever happened, it had to do with love. Only love can produce such hatred."

"You sound as though you know all about true love," Zoë said.

"More than I want to, but, no, before you ask, I have never been in love. Not in what I consider love, something that takes over my entire being. I've seen it in others and I want no part of it."

"Me either," Zoë whispered, then her eyes met Russell's and for a moment the earth seemed to stand still. In the next second, the painting was abandoned and they were making love among the fragrant plants, on the sun-warmed stones.

Afterward, she lay in his arms. Their nude bodies were coated with sweat and they had quite a few leaves stuck to them.

"How long do we have before you leave?" he asked, his voice barely a whisper.

"I don't . . ." she began, but then drew in her breath. "I have three weeks, from beginning to end."

"Half the time is gone," he said. "Can you not stay?"

"I don't think I'll be given a choice. I think I'll just leave."

"Then it is sorcery."

"Perhaps," Zoë said. She put her head on her hand and looked at him. He had become so familiar to her in the last few days that she couldn't imagine being without him. "You will find someone else as soon as—"

He put his fingertips over her lips. "Do not say that I will find someone else quickly. I will never find someone to share my heart and my work with. It would take three people to fulfill all that you and I have together."

"Don't say that," she whispered, and tried to move away from him, but he wouldn't let her. His arm held her, close to his big body.

"Are you saying I am not to tell you the truth about how I feel about you?" he said. "I have bedded many women, but I have never told any woman that I love her."

"Russell," she said as she tried to keep the tears from coming, "I can't love you or anyone. I'm not—"

"Not what? Worthy of love?"

"I don't know," Zoë said. "I don't know what I did that made people hate me and you've said it had something to do with love. I have dreams of seeing a man shoot himself in the head. Did I do that? Did I make a man take his own life?"

He moved her head to rest on his shoulder. "You say that you do not know what you did. The truth is that you do not know what happened. It is a very different concept. I think you should find out the truth."

"Yes," she said. "I know. I should find out the truth about what I did—Sorry, I should find out what happened."

He stroked her hair. "And when will you do this?"

"I guess I'll do it when I return," she said.

"You cannot stay here? With me?"

"And spend our lives together? Painting and learning and making love? I'm not sure I deserve such happiness."

"Nor do I," Russell said. "I think that all I can hope for in this life is what I was given when my mother got me a good teacher."

She looked at him. "Russell, your talent is monumental. You aren't just some hack itinerant portrait painter like I am. You have talent and training, and I want you to promise me to use it. I think you should continue your work of drawing the common people. There will be lots of portraits of the upper classes, but without you to record them, the ordinary people will be lost."

"And you know this, do you?"

He was trying to lighten the mood, but Zoë didn't want to. "Promise me," she said. "Swear to me that you'll continue with your drawings of the people in the fields and in the kitchens."

"All right," he said, but she could tell that he thought her words were silly.

She persisted. "Swear to me."

"I swear on my mother's life," he said at last, then gave her a quick kiss and rolled away. "Go back to your pose so I can work on this painting enough to be able to finish it . . ."

The words of "after you are gone" hung in the air.

She wrapped the silk coverlet they'd brought with them around her and watched him dress. This is just a fling, she told herself. It meant no more to her than the other two times she'd had affairs, but she couldn't make herself believe the lie.

She looked about the stone walls at the plants at the edges and wished she could stay here with him. Stay in this century, stay with this man. She even wanted to stay with the other people, with Faith and Amy. The whole household was abuzz with how Faith had miraculously "saved" Tristan's uncle. Zoë had stopped by the orangery two days ago to see her.

"All I did was give him a bath and some food," she said. "They were letting him starve to death."

Zoë stared at her in disbelief.

"Yeah," Faith said. "Who can understand it? But I'd read about things like this in books. There have been kings who have been starved to death under the orders of some so-called doctor."

As Faith talked, Zoë walked around the big building, looking at it. "You've set this up like a home." She motioned to the vines that grew at one end of the big greenhouse, and nodded toward the cabinets that were along the walls. "This looks like a set for a movie about Merlin." The cabinet tops were covered with mortars and pestles, and copper pans; herbs were hanging from the ceiling and spilling out of the drawers.

"My laboratory," Faith said. "Here, smell this." She opened a glass jar and held it out to Zoë.

"Wonderful. What is it?"

"I have soap, shampoo, and face cream. They're all made by Beth from secret recipes handed down from the women in her family. The products work beautifully and the smell is heaven. I've never encountered anything like it in all my years of working with herbs."

"I had no idea you knew so much about these old herbs."

"I wasn't aware that I did either," she said, looking out the window to where William sat in a chair in the sun, Thomas hovering nearby. "You know something, Zoë? I'm finding out that I know a lot more about everything than I thought I did."

"Me, too," Zoë said.

Now, holding the cloth about her nude body, Zoë looked at the plants in the tower. "I know what these plants are and what they're used for."

"And what is that?" Russell asked as he walked toward her. He took the cloth off her, spread it out on the floor in front of the bushes, and got her back into position as she told him what Faith had told her. When she'd finished, she said, "I knew I'd smelled something like these bushes before, and it was in the jars that Faith had."

"The family secret," Russell said as he went back to his easel. "A weak one as secrets go."

"So tell me what other secrets you've found out in your travels."

"They mostly seem to involve mistresses."

"Ah," Zoë said. "Men who love the kitchen maid but marry the heiress."

"Exactly," he said.

They looked at each other and smiled, letting themselves believe that if they were in the same situation they wouldn't be that stupid.

Twenty

❧

"*Tristan,*" *Amy said,* "I can't stay here all day. I have too many things to do. I—"

He pulled her back to the blanket spread on the ground in the center of the secluded grove of trees by the lake. "My great-grandfather planted these trees and the shrubs," he said, ignoring her words. "See how they make a perfect circle? And no one can see in here except from the lake. Every man who has seen this thinks he is the only one to think of its use as a trysting place. I thought I was going to have to wrestle Russell for this space. He and that girl of his have spent whole days in here."

"Zoë?" Amy asked, sitting on the far edge of the blanket. After dinner, he had come to her in the kitchen and said that there was something that he needed her for. From his expression she thought that there'd been a disaster. She didn't say a word, just followed him out of the house, and didn't protest when he lifted her onto his horse, then got on behind her.

When she saw the picnic he'd had laid out for them in the seclusion of the little grove of trees and aromatic shrubs, she tried to protest, but she couldn't. "Tristan, please," was all she could say as he stood on the ground and looked up at her on the horse.

"Come, sit with me. I have wine from France." He held up his arms to her and she nearly fell into them. He carried her to the blanket. As he poured her some wine, he said, "How long has it been since you had a full night's sleep?"

"Since I came here," she said quickly, but she knew that wasn't true. She had memories of living and working in his house for much longer than just the two weeks since she'd sat in Madame Zoya's sunroom. That seemed like a hundred years ago.

"Now you can relax. I am here with you and we can see if anyone approaches. I am safe."

Amy couldn't help looking at the trees around her. For about six feet up their trunks were thick shrubs, but she could see spaces between them. Someone with determination could make a way through to him.

"Amy, please," he said. "I am safe. I think your dream is just that, a dream and nothing more. It is something you think could happen, certainly not what will happen."

She couldn't tell him that she'd read of his death in a book in the twenty-first century. All it said was that Tristan had been stabbed to death by an unknown assailant in 1797. There were no details. When Amy wished to return to the past she'd said she wanted to go back "three weeks before Tristan was killed." She'd thought that would give her time to find out who wanted him dead. But so far, she'd found no one who even disliked him.

She drank more of the wine. That and the warm day, the bees buzzing about them, the beautiful lake before them, and most of all, Tristan near her, were making her relax.

"Come to me," he said, and held out his arms to her.

Amy did the best she could to stiffen her back. She had made it this far in turning down his advances; she couldn't let fear and exhaustion weaken her.

"I will not make advances toward you," he said. "But put your head on my lap and close your eyes. In your dream, you did not see yourself with me, did you? No? Then I am safe when I am with you. Perhaps you should stay with me every second."

She couldn't help smiling, and when he kept his arms extended, she went to him. She put her head on his lap and closed her eyes. Within minutes she was asleep.

When she awoke, she was lying on the blanket with another one over her. It was near sunset and Tristan was nowhere to be seen. Immediately she sat up, fear in her throat.

"Ssssh," he said as he came into view. "I am here."

She rubbed her eyes. "How long have I been asleep?"

"Hours. You needed it. Amy, if you'd—"

She gave him a hard look that made him laugh.

"I was about to say that if you stayed in your bed at night you would not need so much sleep in the daytime."

"When I know you are safe, then I will sleep."

"And when will that be, Amy?" He sat down by her.

"I don't know," she said, but even to her ears, she sounded as though she were lying. When he was safe she'd be taken away from here, away from him.

"I do not understand any of this," he said.

It was warm outside and his coat lay on the edge of the blanket. He had on tight black trousers and a big white shirt. Amy was afraid to look at him. Between the setting and the beauty of the man, she was having trouble concentrating on her being in this time for a reason. The smell of flowers, the setting sun on a blue lake, and warm breezes, did not help her to remember another time and place, another man.

"Your friends are enjoying themselves," Tristan said in his deep, beautiful voice. "They have lives here. Your friend Faith has set up an apothecary shop in the old orangery. She tends to a dozen people a day and they have nothing but good to say about her. And Beth has started to spend part of each day with her."

He looked at the lake. "And your Zoë . . ."

"Don't tell me," Amy said. "I hear the whispers in the kitchen. Two of the youngest women want to pull Zoë's hair out. They wanted Russell for themselves."

"Your friend and my painter work together," Tristan

said in a faraway voice. "How I envy them. He was to work on Beth's portrait, but he has set it aside. I do not have the heart to tell him to get back to work." He leaned back on his arm, just a few feet from where Amy was sitting upright.

"Do you know what I did?"

"What?" she asked, turning toward him, then was intrigued by his half smile.

"I sneaked into his room to see what he has been doing."

"And what did you find out?"

Tristan drank some wine, then lay back on the blanket, his arms behind his head. "He has been drawing the workmen."

"He's always done that," Amy said. "I've seen him when he thinks no one's looking."

"Ah, but there was something else."

"Will you stop teasing me and tell me what you saw?"

"I think not. It would shock you too much."

"Shock me?" Amy said. "Tristan, if you know something bad about Russell, I think you should tell me. Zoë is just a girl and she's been through some really bad things in her life. I need to protect her."

"From Russell?" he asked. "He is a good man."

She bent toward him. "You don't know about these things like I do. I watch *Law & Order SVU* all the time and people—"

He was looking at her with curiosity. "You say the

most unusual things. Why don't you tell me what you
have seen?"

"I'm not going to indulge your prurient interests.
Now tell me what you know that Russell is doing to
Zoë."

"What the man is doing to her?"

"Tristan!" she said.

"Look in my coat pocket and you will see."

She picked up his coat and looked in the two outside
pockets but found nothing. In the inside pocket was
what felt like a piece of single-ply cardboard. She pulled
it out and looked at it. It was a sketch of a muscular
man, bending slightly, one leg forward. It was Russell
and he was nude and smiling at the artist in a way that
left no doubt as to what was in his mind.

After a moment's shock, Amy laughed. When Tristan
reached for the card, she pulled back. "Oh no you don't.
This is mine!" She set the card on the far side of the
blanket, then stretched out beside him, two feet of space
between them. "And here I've been worried about *her.*"

"There were other pictures in his room."

"Let me guess. Pictures of Zoë. Starkers."

"If you mean nude, yes. She certainly is an attractive
young woman."

Amy looked up at the sky that was fading in light.
"So Faith has William, and Zoë has Russell."

"I do hope your Faith does not think she has my
uncle. He has always had a wandering eye. He could
have had any of many women for a wife, but he could

not bear to think that he would have to stay with just one woman."

"Like you," Amy said.

"Me? I—!"

"I didn't mean to imply that you're not faithful. I meant that you could have any number of women for a wife."

He moved his hand out to take hers. "Amy, I do not want other women. I want—"

"Tristan, I can't," she said, turning her head toward him, but she didn't move her body closer.

His hand went up to her wrist.

"Please don't," she said, her eyes beseeching. "There are things about me that you don't know."

"Then tell me!" he said as he sat up abruptly. "Tell me and I will listen to everything you have to say."

Amy didn't sit up, nor did she let his anger upset her. "You wouldn't believe me. You couldn't believe me."

"Try me."

Amy lifted up on her elbows. She was very tired. She couldn't help it but she felt as though she were alone. Faith and Zoë had come with her, true, but it was as though they had abandoned her. She'd wanted them to help her guard Tristan, but they hadn't. Faith had moved out of the house after only one night. It was true that Tristan's uncle would probably have died without Faith's interference, but there was a part of Amy that wanted to scream that they'd been returned to the past to save Tristan. They hadn't been sent back in time to help an affable, philandering uncle who would probably never marry, never leave any mark on the world. Amy felt sure that Tristan's life would mean something to her family, especially to Stephen, and maybe even to the world.

But Amy was absolutely alone in trying to save Tristan. Zoë spent every day with her clothes off, drawing nude pictures of her boyfriend, and Faith was the local healer.

"Tell me what secrets are eating at you," Tristan said as he sat down by her and took her hand in his.

"I can't—"

"Yes!" he said. "Amy, you cannot keep this up." He put his hands on her shoulders and turned her to look at him. "I know I am not your husband—would to God that I were—but I am not. But I am here and he is not and I am taking his place."

When she moved back from him a bit, his fingers sank into her shoulders. "Do not look at me like that. I think I have shown you that I will not force myself on you. If nothing else, I have too much pride for that. Amy, do you think that I do not see what is happening to you? Have you looked at yourself in a mirror?"

He didn't wait for her to answer. "You have lost over a stone of weight and your face is drawn. Your clothes hang on you. Your eyes are sunken into your face and you look twenty years older than you did just a week ago."

He moved his face closer to hers. "I admit that I want you for my lover, but if I cannot have that, then I want you for my friend. You tell me that you have a recurring dream that I will be found dead, but I think it is more than that. Dreams fade with the daylight. I want you to tell me what is making you so ill."

"Or what?" she said, her face just inches from his.

"Or nothing," he said. "There is no threat between friends. I care about you and I want to know what is wearing you down."

She wanted to talk to someone. She wanted help from someone. She'd tried to get that help by bringing two women with her, but she may as well have come alone for all they were interested in Tristan.

"Everyone thinks I'm so strong," she said. "My husband, Stephen, and now Zoë and Faith, think I'm a bulwark of strength, but I'm not. I lost a baby and . . ."

When she trailed off, he moved back on the blanket until his back was against a tree, then he extended his arm to her. "Come and let me hold you while you tell me all of it. I know what it is like to lose a child."

She told him. The sun set, the stars came out, they finished the wine and the food, but still, they stayed there and Amy talked. She told him about losing the baby, then how her husband arranged for her to go to a cabin in Maine to stay with strangers.

Tristan said nothing. For a long while he didn't ask a question. She told him about the bookstore and the book that said he'd been killed.

"It was not a dream," he said, as though reassuring himself that he'd been right all along.

When she got to the part where she found herself in a barn and she was in another time, his arm tightened around her, but he said nothing.

When she finished, she turned to look up at him. The moon was out and it bathed his face with a silvery light.

"If all that I know did not fit with what you have told me, I would not believe you. But I have noticed more than you think and I believe that what you tell me, impossible as it is, is true."

He moved so he was facing her. "I want to hear every word about your world. What is different in your time?" His eyes were bright with excitement.

"Oh no, you don't," Amy said. "If I tell you about my world you'll write it all down and it'll mess up the future."

"Is the future so perfect that it could not stand a little of what you call 'messing up'?"

"Actually, I think it could stand a lot of changing, but I don't think I'm supposed to do it."

"What makes you think that? Did the witch who sent you here warn you of doing anything to hurt the future?"

"No," she said. "We were given three weeks to change the future. My future, that is, and I truly believe that you're somehow connected to my future. Faith and Zoë get to go on their own trips back to whenever they want. From the way things are going, maybe they'll want to come back here for three more weeks."

"Perhaps I'm to go to the future with you."

Amy looked at him in horror. "And do what? Sleep in my guest room? I don't think so."

Tristan got up to stand on the grass. He put his hands behind his back and began to pace. "If what you say is true—"

"As opposed to my being a lunatic."

"Exactly," Tristan said. "If this is true, then you are to change something here. To that end, you already have."

"What have I changed?"

"My uncle will live."

"That was Faith, not me. Tristan, no matter what you say, or how you put this under a microscope, I think I was sent here to keep *you* from getting killed. And that's what I've tried to do."

"I think there is something more here. I wish—" He looked at her with such pain in his eyes that she gasped.

"What is it?"

"I wish you had come back before my wife died. I wish Faith had been here to save her and the baby."

"Cleanliness," Amy said. "That's all that was needed. Your horrible old doctor delivered some twins in the village and didn't bother to wash his hands before or after. Then he went to your wife and delivered her with his filthy hands. It's called childbirth fever and no one will find the cause of it until Victorian times, about a hundred years from now."

"It could be that simple?" Tristan said.

"Yes, it could. Tristan, I'm sorry. It's not as though

my world has found cures for everything, but we have found out about washing our hands. I've seen old paintings of men wearing suits while they operate on someone."

"And what do the men in your time wear?"

"The men *and women* who operate wear specially made sterile gowns and thin rubber gloves on their hands. They work in a sterile environment."

Tristan put out his hand to pull her up to stand beside him. "I want you to tell me everything about this." His voice lowered. "I want to prevent what was done to my wife and my uncle from happening again."

"You want to be a doctor?"

"No, I just want to take care of my family."

"Will you keep a guard with you?" she asked. "At all times? I want to keep you alive until . . ."

"Until you leave?"

He looked at her, then pulled her into his arms and kissed her. For a moment he held her in his arms, her head against his chest, his heart beating against her cheek. "Do not tell me that I cannot touch you. He will have you for the rest of your life. You will go back to him and it will be his children that you have. I have only now, these few days with you."

"Tristan . . ." she said, but she didn't push away from him.

It was he who put her at arms' length. "You and I are going to do what the others are doing. We are going to learn. You are going to tell me what you can that will help me in my world. Never again do I want to have a woman die in my arms, her blood flowing out of her like a stream of death. Never again do I want to see someone I love lie in a bed and waste away when all he needed was a bath and some good food. Will you help me?"

"Yes, of course. I'll do what I can, but I still must save your life. Someone here hates you and wants you dead."

He smiled at her. "I will find him even if I have to sit up all night and watch for him. Come! We must go to the house and get food, then you must tell me everything."

Twenty-one

❧

"*You look horrible,*" Zoë said.

"Thanks," Amy said. "You've made my day."

"If you're having trouble sleeping I could give you something," Faith said.

They were in the main house, sitting at the round table in the south parlor, a full tea in front of them. It was the first time they'd all three been together in nearly a week.

"Do you know that you're beginning to sound like a drug dealer," Amy said to Faith. "Are those things you're giving people legal?"

Zoë and Faith looked at each other.

"Don't look at me like that. Yes, I know where I am. I haven't forgotten. A few days ago I told Tristan everything."

For a moment neither Zoë nor Faith could speak.

"You did what?" Zoë said at last. "What do you mean by 'everything'?"

"Time travel, the works."

Both Zoë and Faith fell back against their chairs and stared at her.

"I had to explain why he and I couldn't . . ." She looked down at her plate, then up at Zoë defiantly. "Why we couldn't do what you and Russell are doing all over this estate."

Instead of being embarrassed, Zoë smiled. "Lusty man is my Russell. Think I could take him back with me?"

"You don't fool me," Amy said, her eyes narrowed. "When we leave here you're going to leave your heart behind."

"And you aren't?" Zoë shot back. "The way you and that gorgeous babe look at each other could melt the silver. I hope you aren't trying to make us believe that you aren't bouncing around in his bed every night."

For a second Amy's eyes blazed with anger, then she let out her breath, put her elbows on the table, and her head in her hands. "I should be so lucky. It was easy when all he wanted from me was sex. I could get away in ten minutes, then go cry myself to sleep. But now he wants information about the future."

"What kind of information?" Faith asked. "About cell phones and that sort of thing? Or who's going to win the next election?"

"The stock market?" Zoë asked.

"No," Amy said tiredly. "He wants to know all I can dredge out of my tired brain about modern medicine."

"Good thing he didn't ask me," Zoë said, "or he'd be out the door in five minutes. Why don't you send him to Faith?"

"He's already sent the village to me," Faith said. "How can I take on more? Most of what I do is tell them to take a bath and brush their teeth. If I stayed here . . ." She looked at them. "I think I might end up being burned as a witch."

"Wrong time period," Zoë said. "I think. When did that happen in Salem?"

"Could we get back to the problem at hand?" Amy said. "We only have three more days."

"Yes," Zoë said, and there were tears in her voice. "Three more days. How will I live without him?"

Faith put her arms around Zoë and hugged her. "And I don't know how I'll be able to return to a life of uselessness."

"You both have your times to go back and change your futures," Amy said. "Remember Madame Zoya whom neither of you believed in? She said you will have your own lives to fix."

"What good will that do?" Zoë asked, sitting upright and out of Faith's embrace. "Russell is here, not there. Even if I take another three weeks with him, that's all I'll get."

"I think you need to find out what happened to you in our time," Faith said in a motherly way.

"Look who's talking. I think you should find out who killed your boyfriend."

As soon as she said it, Zoë clamped her lips shut. "Sorry, I didn't mean to say that."

Faith looked at Zoë, then Amy. "What is it that you two know that I don't?"

"I don't think now is the time to go into this," Amy said. "I called you two here to talk about Tristan."

Faith stared at Zoë. "I want you to tell me what you know."

"Go ahead and tell her," Amy said, frustrated that she could never seem to get the women to talk about what she thought was their reason for being there.

Zoë took a breath. "I saw it on the Internet. Six months ago a skeleton was found at the bottom of a cliff in your hometown. He was identified as Tyler Parks."

Faith looked as though she'd been slapped. "Ty is dead?" she whispered. "When did it happen?"

Zoë looked at Amy as though asking her for help.

"Tell her all of it," Amy said.

"He didn't just die," Zoë said as she reached for Faith's hand. "He was murdered about fifteen years ago."

"How?" Faith whispered.

"A blunt instrument," Zoë said. "Maybe a . . . a rock."

Faith got up from the chair and walked to the far end of the room. "That's why Ty never came back," she said. "After we had our fight I never saw him again. We all thought he left town. The money he made from the sale of the land was given to his mother. I talked to her once and she also thought he'd run off. I always thought it was because of me, because of our argument. And because I married Eddie soon afterward."

When Faith looked back at them there were tears in her eyes. She put her hand to her mouth. "But he didn't leave me."

"Is that better than death?" Zoë asked.

"Yes. I mean, no." Faith sat back down. "I . . . He didn't leave me."

Zoë looked at Amy.

"Someone murdered him," Amy said. "It was a long time ago, so I doubt if they'll ever find out who did it, but—"

"My mother," Faith said. "She killed Ty."

"What?"

"I didn't understand it until now, but on her death-bed she told me she'd killed him. I thought she meant she'd killed the love that Ty and I had. It looks like she meant she actually killed Ty. She so wanted me to marry Eddie that she killed to attain it."

Amy raised her eyebrows to Zoë.

"I can go back," Faith said. "Just like you went back to change your past, I can go back and change my life with Ty. When he climbs in my window, I'm going to be packed and ready to leave with him. We're going to live in that old farmhouse and I'm going to have a ten-acre herb garden. If I could figure out a way to take Beth's seeds back with me, I might make some of her products."

"Put them in your hair like Amy's ribbon," Zoë said,

and Faith's eyes widened as she remembered that the ribbon Amy had been wearing was still in her hair when they arrived in the eighteenth century.

"What a great idea," Faith said. "I could—"

"Would you two mind if we talked about why we're here?" Amy said. "We have three days left and I'm worried about Tristan being killed."

"I'm sorry, Amy," Faith said, "but I have to leave now and think about all this. This is a big change in my life and . . ." She didn't say anything else as she seemed to float out of the room.

"Wow," Zoë said. "I thought she'd be angry to hear that her old boyfriend had been murdered."

"Better dead than to have dumped her," Amy said. "I think we just released the source of Faith's lifelong depression."

"Let's send Jeanne a whopping great bill," Zoë said.

"Let's talk about what we need to do to keep Tristan alive."

"When you saw him dead in your dream wasn't he in his bedroom in this house?"

"Yes," Amy said.

"So why don't you move him to that greenhouse Faith lives in and let lots of people sleep around him?"

"I don't think Tristan would agree to that. He has a real stubborn streak in him."

"Then get Faith to drug him. Or tell him you'll sleep with him if he'll do it." She raised her eyebrows at Amy's look. "We all have to make sacrifices."

For the first time, Amy smiled. "This meeting has not gone as well as I hoped it would, but it has certainly been interesting. I think you're right and I'll do everything short of sex or murder to get Tristan out of this house."

"Good," Zoë said, standing up. "Then we're done. I'm—"

"Everyone in this village, and probably for about three over, know what you're going to do today and have been doing since you arrived here."

"Celibacy can sure put a woman in a bad mood," Zoë said.

Amy ignored that remark. "Is it too much to ask if you did what you said you were going to do and talk to the maids about anyone who might be harboring a grudge against Tristan?"

"I did better than that, I asked Russell. He put the word out to the women and they're to tell him anything they hear. So far, there's been nothing. Now, if you don't mind, I have something else to do." She left the room.

Amy put her head in her hands. "Oh, Stephen," she moaned. Just three more days, and she'd be back with him. Just three more days.

Twenty-two

❦

"Are you *feeling* all right?" Faith asked Amy. "You look—"

"I don't need another person to tell me how bad I look." They were standing in front of the orangery and Amy was studying the glass walls. "I don't think this place is safe."

"If it were a prison it wouldn't look safe to you." Faith took her hands. "Amy, everything that can be done is being done. Tristan will have Thomas to look after him. He's going to sleep in a dormitory with lots of other people." It was all Faith could do not to let her displeasure show. In these past weeks her life had become very comfortable. True, it had been hard on her to see the line of people who came to her with diseases that she couldn't cure, but aside from that, she and William and Thomas had formed a nice life. William was very easy to live with. His constant good humor had kept a smile on her face, and as he healed, he began to help her with the herbs. One morning, in a moment of honesty, he'd told her that his life had never been useful.

"I am sure my nephew has told you that I have never achieved much. I was much younger than my ambitious older brothers, and I was my mother's favorite. I stayed with her until she died, but by that time I had no inclination to marry and burden myself with children. She left her money to me and I spent years traveling about the world. I even went to that America of yours."

"You didn't tell me that."

"If I had, I might have missed out on the stories that you have told me. I did not see it as a place of great advancement that you seem to know it as."

Faith had to turn away to hide her red face. She'd joined Zoë in coming down hard on Amy for telling Tristan the truth, but she realized she'd told William a great deal more than she thought she had.

"I know you plan to leave here," he said, then held up his hand when she started to speak. "I listen more than you think and I hear you whispering with the other two women. I know that the time is coming soon. I was wondering . . ."

Turning, Faith looked at him.

"If you feel that you need to leave because you have no real place in this world, I would like to make you an offer. The old house, the one you have ranted about having cows in it, is mine."

She smiled at his use of the word "ranting." She wanted to protest that she'd done no such thing, but she had. Good! she thought. Maybe she'd made enough of an impression on him that after she was gone they'd take care of the house and not let it fall into ruin.

"I can offer you the house," William said softly. "And me."

She realized that he was offering her marriage and a comfortable life with him. It would be nice, she thought, to live here. She would love to oversee the remodeling of that wonderful old medieval house, and she'd like to continue working with the herbs and applying what she knew while learning more.

She looked at William. He had gained a lot of weight in the last weeks and she was beginning to see the man he once was. He was handsome, intelligent, and wonderfully good company. He would make fine husband.

She looked down at the big white marble mortar and pestle that was filled with ajuga leaves. She was pounding them to make an infusion to use on mouth ulcers. No, she thought, she'd had a life of comfort with a "fine husband." Eddie had been good company and he'd had more money than they could spend. If he hadn't been ill and had a mother from hell, he would have made a great husband.

Except for one thing, she thought: passion. She and Eddie had never once had passion. When she looked at Tyler, her knees had weakened. She'd never felt that with Eddie.

"I'm going to hold out for passion," she said aloud,

then looked at William in horror. What an awful thing to say to a man who'd just proposed to her!

William surprised her by letting out a loud laugh. "You are a wise, wise woman," he said, then he looked at her in a way that he never had before. "Give me a bit more time and I think I can fulfill your wish."

Faith returned his smile. She wanted love with her passion. Not a one-night stand, but true love and passion that made her knees weak. "It would take you more than a bit of time to take *me* on," she said to William.

He laughed again and reached for her, but Faith eluded his hand. "Sit down and eat," she said in the motherly voice she usually used with him.

Since that day there had been an easy, teasing camaraderie between her and William that she'd enjoyed immensely. But now Amy was moving into their cozy glass house with Tristan and probably half a dozen retainers.

"Do not look so down," William said. "My nephew is a man of humor."

"Yeah, but does he pick up his socks?"

William smiled at her ill humor and went back to taking the flower heads off the chamomile that Faith had given him to work on.

Since Zoë had told her about what happened to Tyler, Faith had not been the same. She was restless now. There were only two days left, then what would happen? Would the three women disappear in a puff of smoke? And if they did, would they end up back in Madame

Zoya's sunroom? Would Faith and Zoë be given second chances at their lives?

Turning, Faith left the walled garden and headed for the tower. Yesterday she'd confronted Zoë about her and Russell being in there.

"Keep your shirt on," Zoë said. "We didn't hurt anything."

"It's a matter of privacy," Faith said. "And where did you get a key?"

"Russell said he borrowed it."

"Stole it, more likely," Faith said. "I want that key." She had an idea that Russell had had a duplicate made from Beth's key, and he'd probably done it while she was in London. She didn't blame him. The tower would be an excellent place to paint when it rained. And a place to escape the girls who made eyes at him every minute of the day.

The truth was that Faith wanted to use the tower as her own private sanctuary, a place where she could go to be alone. It seemed that soon she was going to be faced with a great many decisions in her life and, this time, she wanted to do what was right for her. Not for Ty, Eddie, her murderous mother, or even for Eddie's battle-axe of a mother. Faith needed to figure out what was right for *her*.

As she went through the quiet forest, she stopped once because she thought she saw a shadow move. She waited, but saw no one, then went on to the tower quickly. Beth had told her about wolves in the forest and she didn't want to meet one of them.

In the days since Beth had shown her the plants in the tower, Faith had asked every question she could think of about them and the recipes, the "receipts" that Beth had written out for her. Beth had shown Faith how to cut the bark of the shrubs to get the sap out, then how to use it to make the ingredient in the face cream, the shampoo, and the soap. They were simple recipes with one, single, extraordinary ingredient.

Since working with the balsam plants, Faith felt as though they'd become her friends. She felt honored to be near something so old as they were, plants that had had so much written about them. Even in the ancient world it was said that they grew in only one place on earth: Jericho. She would spend hours in the tower looking at the plants, inhaling their divine fragrance, and wondering what catastrophic events had caused the plant to become extinct.

Faith went to the stone where she knew Beth kept seeds hidden. She'd said that her ancestors had done everything they could to get the plant to grow in their gardens but it wouldn't. It had taken years to find out that it liked the dryness inside the tower, the heat reflected off the stones, and the small amount of water poured onto its roots.

Faith had written down every word that Beth told her about the plants themselves and her family's history with them, then Faith had memorized it all. She knew that since the plant was extinct in her time, that meant the Hawthorne women's preservation of it had not survived. One lightning strike to the glass roof, one flood, and the plants would die, Faith thought. If it was at all possible, she was going to preserve the precious plants. She had spent hours sewing tiny tubes that would hold the seeds. On the last day she planned to tie them in the hair of the three women.

When she left the tower it was nearly nightfall and the woods were growing dark. As she walked quickly down the path, Faith looked from right to left, remembering the shadow she'd seen on the way in. She was almost to the gate when she stopped. Hadn't that shadow been where she'd seen the poisonous mushrooms? When Eddie was alive and they'd spent their days reading about herbs, he'd made jokes about that brilliant red mushroom. In the sixties and seventies, the hippies made psychedelic drugs from it.

She was musing on this when it occurred to her that wanting to get high was not just a modern desire. She overcame her fears of whatever was lurking in the woods, turned off the trail, and went into the darkening forest to look for the mushrooms. She'd knocked down all of them she'd seen but she could have missed some.

Within minutes, she saw that she'd missed several of them and that someone had taken the trouble to hide them under leaves. There was one freshly broken stem in the earth, showing that within the last hour or so, someone had broken off one of the poisonous mushrooms.

Annoyed, Faith stood up and destroyed the rest

of them, but it looked as though someone were using them. For what? A trip?

Her head came up as she looked back toward the trail. People did things on drug trips that they didn't usually do in life. Sometimes it was silly; sometimes it was violent.

"Tristan," Faith said out loud. In the last weeks Amy had lost weight, had pretty much given up sleep, as she tried to figure out who hated Tristan enough to kill him. What if no one hated him? What if someone on a drug trip went berserk and stabbed him?

For a full minute, Faith's mind's eye could see the inside of the orangery. Tristan's big bed had been moved in there that morning. Amy had posted guards at the entrances to the walled garden, but their instructions were to allow no strangers in. She'd even shown them how to search people to make sure they carried no knives.

Zoë had laughed at Amy for her paranoia, but now Faith seemed able to see it all. It wouldn't be an enemy who killed Tristan, it was someone he knew, someone who thought it was fun to eat a bit of a poisonous mushroom and feel like he was flying or . . .

Faith didn't take time to think any more. She'd left her big knife on top of the cabinet nearest Tristan's bed. She grabbed her skirt up to her knees and took off running as fast as she could. As she ran, cursing her out-of-shape body, she wanted to hit herself for not listening to Amy, not paying attention to her. Faith had been so wrapped up in her own problems that she'd left Amy alone. She and Zoë might as well not have come to the eighteenth century for all that they'd helped Amy.

When Faith could see the walled garden, she ran even faster. Her lungs were about to burst, but she didn't slow down. When she was still a hundred yards from the gate, she saw William saunter outside the wall.

Faith didn't know how else to get his attention but to scream at the top of her lungs.

William turned and started toward her. Faith didn't slow down but dropped her skirt and waved at William to go back. "Tristan!" she yelled, then tripped on her skirt and fell flat on her face. As she was trying to get up, she looked up at William and saw that he understood.

With all the energy he had, he hobbled back between the gates on his canes and out of sight. Faith got off the ground and started running again.

There were three people in the walled garden when she ran through. They were all trusted employees and were resting from having moved furniture for Tristan into the orangery. He's not here, Faith thought. Tristan isn't here yet. She was relieved, but she didn't slow down. The people in the garden stopped to look at her as she sped past them and into the orangery.

What she saw inside made her halt in terror. She could see the bottom half of Tristan lying on the bed. In front of him was the young woman who brought Faith herbs twice a day. William's frail body was behind her, his thin arms around her shoulders. When he heard Faith enter, he turned the girl. Faith's largest knife was dangling from the fingertips of her right hand, and her eyes had the wild look of someone who had just taken a hallucinogenic.

Behind them Tristan, eyes open, was lying on the bed in absolute stillness.

Faith put her hand to her mouth. "He—"

William, still tightly holding the girl to him, moved aside and Faith saw Tristan. His eyes were open and, best of all, there was no blood on him.

Faith ran to him. "Are you all right?" Her hands were running over his chest, down his legs. "Did she hurt you?"

"I am fine," he said, looking a bit dazed. "I fell asleep. The sun and . . ." He waved his hand about the beautiful room, then looked at his uncle. "What is wrong with her? She looks mad."

Faith stood up and looked at the girl William was holding, his face white from the exertion. She took the knife out of the girl's hand.

"I think someone has fed her a mushroom that's made her temporarily crazy," she said as she pulled the girl out of William's arms.

"But why?" Tristan asked.

"My guess is sex," Faith said. "Someone found out about a certain mushroom's ability to get rid of a girl's inhibitions."

William and Tristan were looking at her in puzzlement. "You know," Faith said, "candy is dandy, but liquor is quicker?"

That made the men nod in understanding. Faith led the girl to the door and called to Thomas to come and get her.

"Take her into the house and keep her in a room until her reason returns," she told him. "Don't hurt her and don't let her hurt herself."

In the next minute Amy came up on Tristan's big black horse, jumped to the ground, and pushed past Faith to get to Tristan. As soon as she saw him as he had been in her dream, wearing the same clothes, on the same bed, with the windows behind him, she burst into loud tears.

"I knew it all. It was all in my head," she said, crying copiously and holding on to Tristan's hands as he sat on the edge of the bed. "I didn't put it together. In the dream I saw you and I saw the men around you. I even saw Beth. This place is so different from my dream that I thought you'd be safe. And you were so well guarded. You —"

"Amy," Tristan said as he pulled her up from the floor.

William put his arm around Faith's shoulders and led her outside. "How did you know?"

"The mushrooms," Faith said. "I saw them by the tower, but in my vanity I thought no one but I knew what they could do. Amy begged us to help her with Tristan, but I paid no attention to her. But if I hadn't come back with her, and if I hadn't taken you from that room, Tristan would have died."

"Sssssh," William said and pulled her into his arms so she could cry on his shoulder. "It has worked out as it should. It is his destiny to live."

"Yes," Faith said against his shoulder. "Maybe Tristan's destiny is back on its rails again." She smiled when William looked at her in question. "It doesn't matter. Tristan is safe now." Behind them, they could hear Amy and Tristan talking quietly inside the orangery.

"What say you that we spend tonight in the house?" William said.

"Yes," Faith said. "I think we should. Let them have their time alone. But I'm going to send them a huge supper. Amy needs to eat."

William laughed. "I think you would like to feed the world. Tell me, in your time, do they still have poverty?"

"I have no idea what you mean by 'my time,'" she said with all the innocence she could muster. "I grew up in . . ."

"Quick!" William said. "Give me the name of an English county."

"California," Faith said. She looked around them and they were in the parkland that had been designed by Capability Brown. In just a very short time, she'd never again see this place, this time, or these people.

She looked at William. He was still many pounds under what he should weigh and there were still circles under his eyes, but he was freshly shaven and his shirt was so white it sparkled.

"Ah," he said, "I have seen that look before, but thought never to see it again."

"Do stop talking," she said.

He put his arms around her and kissed her, then held her against him. "I might not have the strength to . . ."

"That's okay, Faith said. "I'm good on top."

He laughed and they walked to the house hand in hand.

Twenty-three

❦

Just as they had dreaded, one moment they were in the eighteenth century and the next they were in Madame Zoya's sunroom. Instantly, Zoë started crying.

"I was afraid of that," the woman said. "It often happens when people want to go far back in time."

"I'll never see him again," Zoë said. "He's dead. Dead hundreds of years ago."

Madame Zoya looked at Faith and Amy. "Was it a success for you two?"

Faith's hands went to her hair and her face lit up. "Oh yes!" she said. "A great, overwhelming success. Nothing in my life has happened to equal what I learned and saw in these last weeks."

"You didn't have to leave anyone behind," Zoë said. She pulled two tissues out of the box on Madame Zoya's desk and blew her nose.

"Have you two decided when you want to go back to?"

"I have a question," Faith said. "When we went back in time we arrived there wearing clothes of that time. I want to know if we can go back in our own time and keep these clothes on."

"What does that matter?" Zoë asked, tears on her cheeks.

"Pockets," Amy said dully. "She wants to return with her pockets full." She wasn't crying, but the thought of never again seeing Tristan and Beth and the whole estate was weighing her down.

"You want to take money back with you?" Madame Zoya asked, her tone letting them know what she thought about that. "I don't think that—"

"I want to take seeds," Faith said as she ran her fingers through her hair and pulled out long, thin tubes of cloth. Her precious seeds were inside. "I want to take some very special seeds back with me."

"Ah," Madame Zoya said. "Seeds. And how special are these seeds?"

"They are from a plant that is extinct today."

"It's a plant that's in the Bible," Amy said, pulling tubes from her hair. Faith had intertwined them in her and Zoë's hair on their twenty-first day in the eighteenth century.

"Interesting," Madame Zoya said. "Would you two like to go back now or would you like twenty-four hours to recover?" She glanced at Zoë who was still crying.

"I'd like some time to think," Faith said as she put her hand over Zoë's.

"All right," Madame Zoya said. "I will see you two tomorrow at two o'clock."

They left Madame Zoya's house, went outside and walked to the main street. For several long minutes they stood there looking about them at the paved road, at the cars whizzing by, at the women wearing trousers and makeup, and the buildings with their big glass windows.

"It's another world," Faith said. "I—" She didn't know how to tell the others that she wanted to be alone. She needed some time to think about where she'd been and what she'd done. And she wanted to think about where she was going tomorrow. Did she really want to do her life over? She had some decisions to make, and she wanted to make them without hearing the opinions of others.

"I'll see you two back at the house at about seven," Amy said, then she turned down the street, away from them.

"She wants to see what the books say her lover boy did after she left," Zoë said, as she blew her nose.

"And wouldn't you like to know what Russell did?" Faith asked. "Maybe you can't have him in the flesh, but you can read about him."

Zoë looked at her suspiciously. "What I want to know is where you disappeared to for those last two days."

"Zoë, darling, I've heard that every generation thinks it created sex, but it's not true. Now dry your eyes, dear, and go find out about your boyfriend."

With that, Faith turned and went down the street in the opposite direction of Amy.

❧❧

Faith didn't get back to Jeanne's summerhouse until nearly nine. She'd spent a lot of time walking and thinking about what her life had been and what she'd been through in the last three weeks. She kept thinking about what Amy had told them that Primrose had said about destiny. If destiny was like a train and it could be derailed, then Faith's train had been pushed into the mud a long time ago.

She tried to boil it down, but it seemed that what she'd learned in the eighteenth century was how important it was to be useful. In a mere three weeks she'd become a person who was needed by others and it had fulfilled some need in her that she hadn't even known was empty.

Zoë had teased Faith about having come out of her depression because she found out that Ty hadn't jilted her, but Faith knew there was more to it than that. All her adult life she'd felt that she'd had a choice between two men and that she'd chosen the wrong one.

What she'd asked herself today was whether either man was right for her. It was easy to say that her mother had forced her into marrying Eddie. And it was easy to blame her mother-in-law for all the misery in her marriage, but what part had Faith played in it all? She liked to think of herself as an innocent bystander, but she hadn't been.

By the time she got back to the summerhouse, she was glad to see that the lights were off. She was afraid that Amy and Zoë would be up with a bottle of wine and wanting to spend the night talking.

Instead, there was a note from Amy on the breakfast table saying that she and Zoë had gone to bed, hope she didn't mind.

"*Ready?*" *Madame Zoya* asked Faith and Zoë the next afternoon.

"Yes," Faith said. Her hand was on the seed capsules in her pocket, and she'd given Madame Zoya three capsules. It was the least she could do.

"I'll see you two tomorrow," Amy said when they left the house. "I'll make us a nice dinner and you'll tell me everything that happened in your new lives."

All morning they'd talked about the idea that if they went years back into their pasts then when they returned their entire lives would be different. Amy said that if Faith went back and married Tyler, then lived a new life, maybe when she returned she'd have children at home waiting for her.

Faith hadn't replied because she had some other ideas about what she'd like to do with her life.

As for Zoë, she made it clear she didn't have much

hope. She said she'd run away from her hometown and avoid the car crash, but then what? Whatever she'd done would still be there. "And Russell wouldn't be," she said.

Amy didn't say anything. She'd been so tired yesterday that she'd slept all afternoon and through the night. For the first time in weeks she'd been able to relax because Tristan was safe. As far as she could tell, saving him hadn't changed her life at all. She'd called home, listened to the same message in Stephen's voice saying that Amy and their two sons were out, please leave a message. It was all exactly the same now, but today she hoped to search the Internet to find that Tristan or his descendants had done something great.

Whatever she found out, she was determined to be cheerful and not let Faith and Zoë see her true feelings.

"And when we return, you can tell us about Tristan," Faith said.

"I will," Amy said, but she had volunteered no other information. She closed the door behind them.

"Is it me or do you think that under her fake cheeriness she looked disappointed?" Zoë asked.

"I think she has to be going through a bad time. She was in love with Tristan and she had to leave him. That must have hurt."

"What I want to know is what the two of them did those last two days. I know you were in bed with William. I just hope you didn't kill him."

"He managed to live," Faith said dryly. She was glad to see that Zoë hadn't put on her dark makeup again.

Now she looked like a pretty young woman who wanted to live.

"And I—" Zoë looked into the distance.

"Zoë," Faith said as she put her hand on her arm.

"I'm okay," Zoë said. "Really I am. I spent some time on the Internet last night."

"And?"

"Let's just say that I memorized some things too."

"What does that mean?" Faith asked.

"I'll tell you later—if it works out, that is," Zoë said. "So tell me, was William good in bed? As good as Tyler?"

"Different," Faith said, smiling. "All three of my men were different from one another."

"You're the one who's different," Zoë said. "I wouldn't recognize you from the woman I first met here."

"Really?" Faith said. "And what about you? Did they run out of industrial-strength eyeliner?"

They had reached the road to Madame Zoya's house. Zoë turned down it and started walking backward. "Since my portrait is hanging in the Louvre, I thought I ought to have a face that matches it."

Faith stopped walking and stared at her. "Zoë! Is that true?"

Zoë just shrugged, laughed, and raced ahead to Madame Zoya's house.

Part Three

Twenty-four

❧

"*Okay,*" Amy *said* after she'd poured the wine. "I want to hear every word of it." She'd spent the morning in the library and the afternoon making a dinner for the two returning women.

It had taken all she had to overcome what she feared could become a deep depression. She had saved Tristan, yes, but she'd also lost him. That emotion was understandable, but the one she didn't like in herself was a feeling of disappointment in the fact that, as far as she could tell, nothing had changed in her life. But hadn't she said that her life was perfect? So she should be glad that she'd not changed any of it.

She'd called home, talked to her father-in-law, and he was the same gruff man she'd always known. What had she expected? That if she kept his ancestor alive, Lewis Hanford would turn into a gentleman? It hadn't happened.

Stephen and the boys were still camping, but they'd

be back in time to meet Amy's plane tomorrow. She was looking forward to seeing them again, although she knew she'd never tell Stephen or anyone else what had happened to her. Stephen would tell her she'd been reading too many romance novels, then he'd laugh at her.

As Amy had been cooking today, she realized that the only people she could talk to about what had happened were Zoë and Faith. It was ironic that these two women whom she'd feared for being strangers might be her friends for life.

Amy left the women at the table and went into the kitchen to get the bread she'd baked. No jealousy! she told herself. Whatever had happened to Zoë and Faith in their three weeks in the past—but just minutes in this time—had certainly changed them a great deal.

Amy remembered the Faith she'd first met, a stooped-over old woman who looked as though she expected people to be mean to her. The woman who was in the summerhouse now stood up straight and looked like she owned the earth. What in the world had happened to her?

As for Zoë, she looked great. She was wearing some New York–type outfit that could have come off a runway. Her eyes were alight and she laughed at everything.

Both women were wearing wedding bands.

Amy took a deep breath and went back into the dining room. "Tell me!" Amy said as she sliced the bread. "I want to hear it all." The only thing they'd told her so far was that they had both wanted to remember everything in both lives, the new one as well as the old one.

"It all seems so long ago," Zoë said, turning to Faith. "Doesn't it?"

"A lifetime. Whereas we were only gone three weeks to the eighteenth century, and when we returned, our lives were the same, this time my life has been totally different," Faith said. "What about you?"

"Completely different," Zoë said.

They looked at Amy.

"The same," she said. "Not one change that I can tell."

Faith and Zoë looked at her in sympathy.

"What happened to Tristan?" Faith asked.

"He lived. Remember that I told you I had him go to London and hire a genealogist? Well, it seems that he did find relatives of mine, and he married a young woman who was an ancestor of mine and they had four children. And guess what?"

"What?" Faith asked politely.

"His two sons became doctors, and his two daughters married doctors."

"Goodness," Faith said. "A whole family of them. That's wonderful."

"But the bad news is that the title was dissolved right after World War I, and the estate was sold. We didn't save his family forever, but it lasted longer thanks to us."

They were silent for a moment.

"This looks great," Zoë said, staring at the food. "I'm starving."

"So?" Amy said. "Are you two married? Kids?"

Faith and Zoë nodded, their heads bent down in silence.

Amy slammed the wooden cutting board down on the table. "That's it! I'm not going to have you two feeling sorry for me. Do you remember what my husband looks like? And my kids? Just a day ago, that's right, just one day ago in real time, you two were feeling sorry for yourselves because I had it all. Now here you are feeling sorry for *me* because you two have it all. You cannot have it both ways!"

Faith and Zoë looked at each other and began to laugh.

"She's right," Faith said.

"Perfectly right. So who goes first?"

"Zoë," Faith said. "I want to know why that town hated you."

"They didn't," Zoë said, then paused to hold the suspense. "They did hate the person who made a man kill himself, but they just *blamed* me." She put her hand on Faith's arm. "You'll love this: The whole thing was caused by my sister."

"Damn my waistline, give me more pasta!" Faith said. "I want to hear everything. Don't leave out a word."

"You have to understand," Zoë said, "that when I went back, I didn't know anything more than I did when I arrived here. My memory didn't come back until—"

"The night of the car wreck," Amy said.

"That's right. How did you know?"

"That's what would make the story good," she said, then waved her hand. "Go on. Sorry for interrupting."

"I went back to two weeks before the crash," Zoë said, "and everything was fine. No one hated me. No one paid much attention to me. I was just an ordinary girl in an ordinary town where nothing much happened. I'd graduated from high school but I had no plans to go to college."

"With your talent?" Faith asked. "Were you crazy?"

"That's the odd thing," Zoë said. "I was so ordinary that I didn't know I had any talent. You guys may be too old to remember this, but funding has been cut in schools so much that we don't have art classes anymore. My teachers used to tell us to draw a farm and we did. No one ever told me to draw the faces of my classmates, so I never tried. And at home I wasn't exactly surrounded by creative people."

She ate a bite of food. "I have to backtrack a bit. When my parents died, I was just thirteen, so I was sent to live with my sister. She was ten years older than me, married and had two kids, so she didn't exactly welcome me. All she talked about my last year of school was how glad she was going to be when I could get a job and help with the expenses."

"Nice woman," Amy said.

Zoë said nothing for a while. "Back then, while I was in it, I didn't see how bad it was. When I went back, knowing what I do now, I saw how truly horrible it was. My sister had been the prettiest girl in the school. She was on the local floats and she won every beauty contest there was. The whole town celebrated when she married her male counterpart, the best-looking guy, captain of the football team, all that."

"The golden couple," Amy said, and looked away. It sounded like her and Stephen. "But the real world is different, isn't it?"

"Right," Zoë said. "She was pregnant when she got married and he got a job selling used cars. It's amazing how soon that high school glory can disappear. When I went back, my sister looked old and haggard."

She looked down at her plate. "Well, maybe she didn't look too old or too haggard."

"What did you do about the car crash?" Faith asked.

"You once told me that if you had it to do over again, you'd just leave town," Amy said.

"That's what I did," Zoë said. "I figured that whatever was going to happen would happen whether I was there or not, and I wanted no part of it. I had access to a hundred and fifty dollars, so I took it, a few pieces of clothing, and I left town without saying a word to anyone. I went to New York."

"And it's my guess that you looked up someone you'd found on the Internet," Amy said softly.

"I did," Zoë said, grinning at her.

"You two are leaving me out," Faith said. "What man did you find on the Internet?"

"Who said it was a man?" Zoë asked.

"Oh, sorry," Faith said. "I'm sure you found out you had a half sister whom you'd never met, so you looked her up, and she's the one who's made you smile like that."

Amy looked at Zoë. "You stole my idea, didn't you?"

"Yes," Zoë said. "I ripped off your idea completely. That night when we came back from the eighteenth century, I looked for Russell Johns on the Internet. I'd read a lot of art history books but I didn't remember hearing his name. But after we came back here, he was all over the 'Net. You know what for?"

"His paintings of common people," Amy said. "In Tristan's time, he was always sketching us as we pulled bread out of the oven. He loved the washerwomen. Hey! Do you think we're in any of his pictures?"

"I don't know about you two, but I saw several nudes of me," Zoë said, and the three of them laughed.

"In the Louvre," Faith said, and that made them laugh more.

"So what happened to him?" Amy asked as she buttered a slice of bread. "He was such a talented man."

"He married and had some children," Zoë said softly. "I cried in jealousy when I read that."

"But not now," Amy said as she nodded toward Zoë's wedding ring.

Zoë turned the ring on her finger. "No, not anymore. You see, I took Amy's idea about descendants and I searched until I found Russell's family tree."

"Don't tell me!" Amy said. "You found out that one of his descendants lives in New York, you memorized the address, and when you left your sister's you went to him. Is he a painter?"

Faith and Zoë were looking at her in astonishment.

"When did you get so good at stories?" Faith asked.

"I think I'm like Zoë and her art. I think maybe I've always been good at stories, but I didn't know it. So, am I right?"

"Yeah," Zoë said, "but he's not a painter, he's—"

"A photographer," Amy said, then when she looked at their faces, she said, "Okay, I'll shut up. You tell your story, Zoë."

"Thank you. But, yes, he's a photographer. He does some commercial work but he's made his name by . . ." She looked at Amy as though daring her to say a word.

Amy made a zipper sign over her lips.

"Russ photographs people in ordinary situations doing ordinary things. He's won a lot of awards."

"Russ?" Faith asked.

Zoë shrugged. "Last name is Andrews, but the first is the same."

"And you are madly in love with him," Amy said, then looked at them. "Am I allowed to say that?"

Zoë laughed. "Of course. You want to hear something weird?"

"I don't know if I can stand weird," Faith said. "I shock easily."

"When Russell and I were together, back in his time,

he asked me a lot of questions about my life. I couldn't tell him about Oregon because, well, it didn't exist back then, so I told him as much as I knew about my early family history."

She looked at Amy as though challenging her to finish the story. Amy frowned in concentration for a moment, then her face lightened. "You didn't! He didn't!"

"I'm lost," Faith said.

Zoë smiled. "It seems that the great painter, Russell Johns, sailed to the American colonies in the fall of 1797. He settled in Williamsburg, and today you can see his portraits of some of our forefathers."

"I hope he got Amy's friend Thomas Jefferson," Faith said, deadpan.

"Who told you that?" Amy said. She looked at Zoë. "Who did he marry?"

"A young woman with the last name of Prentiss."

"Your family's name, I take it," Amy said.

Faith frowned for a moment. "If you're related to Russell's wife and your husband is descended from their children, does that make you and your husband cousins?"

"Just like royalty," Zoë said, and they laughed.

"Okay, so now tell us what made the town hate you," Faith said.

"Ah, that," Zoë said. "The entire memory of that came to me at what I think was exactly the time that my accident happened. I'd meant to pay attention to the date and take care of myself, but when I got to New York, I went to Russ's that first day, and we hit it off rather well, so, uh . . ."

"You were in bed with him when the wreck was to happen, weren't you?" Amy said.

When Zoë nodded, Faith said, "How are you doing this?"

"I don't know, but it's like I can see it in print. I just seem to know. But I'll stop talking. Zoë, tell us what you remembered."

"I don't like to remember it even if I know it didn't really happen. At least not my part in it."

"What did your sister do to you?" Faith asked, making the others smile.

"Now you're the storyteller," Zoë said. "And you're completely accurate. It was all my sister's fault."

"*I don't want* to hear another word," Zoë said to her sister, Karen. She put her hands over her ears. She was sitting in Karen's living room, on the old, worn-out couch, and her sister was pacing.

"You have to help me. You're the only one I can trust." Karen put her hands on Zoë's wrists and uncovered her sister's ears.

"What about Bob?" Zoë asked. "How could you do this to him?"

"Bob?" Karen said in disgust. "What does he care?

The highlight of his life was when he made three touch-downs in one game. It's been downhill since then. Please, Zoë, this is for my whole life."

Zoë looked up at her sister and wondered how she'd been able to pull off an affair with the most important man in town. Alan Johnson was the oldest son of the richest man in town and he'd done nothing in his life that hadn't flourished. He was on every charity commit-tee. He was married and had two children, a boy and a girl, who were polite and sweet-tempered. His wife was beautiful and spent the time her children were in school volunteering at hospitals and old-age homes.

"I don't understand why he was having an affair with you," Zoë said.

Karen whirled on her in a flash of rage. "For your information, underneath all of this—" She waved her hand to include the house with its aluminum win-dows, its stained carpets that were littered with kids' bright plastic toys, and herself in her often-washed sleeveless dress. "Underneath this I'm a very desirable woman."

Zoë was really trying to understand, but she couldn't see it. Yes, her sister used to be quite pretty, but not in a movie star way. She was more hometown-girl pretty. And the years since she'd married had not been kind to her. The fact that she smoked two packs a day and drank Coke that was half bourbon with dinner didn't help.

"He really loves you?" Zoë asked.

"Do you find that so impossible to believe? Alan does love me, and he's going to divorce that cold bitch of a wife of his and marry me."

Zoë just sat on the old sofa and stared at her sister. Karen was always telling Zoë that she knew nothing about life, but even she knew that this was a story so old that comedians used it in their stand-up acts. But Zoë also knew that she couldn't reason with her sister. When she was like this, smoking one cigarette after another, and saying she *had* to do this and *had* to do that, she was impossible to talk to.

"I want you to go with me," Karen said.

"Where?" Zoë said and hid her crossed fingers. Please don't let it be to go see Mr. Johnson. One year he'd dressed up as an Easter bunny and had given Zoë the prize for the most eggs found. She didn't want to have to face him in this ugly affair. And, too, there was Bob, Karen's husband. Maybe he wasn't the most exciting man in the world, but he loved their children and he was totally devoted to them. Last year he'd been passed over for a promotion because he'd missed so many days at work when he stayed home with the kids because Karen couldn't "get herself together."

"To see Alan."

"Karen," Zoë said, her voice a whine. "I don't want to do that. Please don't make me do that."

"After all I've done for you!" she started, saying all the things that she'd said a million times before. It seemed that Zoë was to give her life to Karen in eter-

nal gratitude for taking her in when she was orphaned.
Never mind that Karen got a free live-in babysitter.

"I'll stay with the kids and you go. You should be
alone with him," Zoë said.

"No. I want Bob to stay with the kids. That'll keep
him from snooping into my life."

"He knows about you and Mr. Johnson?" Zoë asked
in horror.

"Will you stop calling him that? You make him
sound like a . . . a pillar of the community and I'm the
slutty secretary. It's demeaning to me."

Zoë looked down at her hands and avoided her sister's eyes.

"Look, Zoë," Karen said, her tone changing. "It's just
that I need to see him. I got a weird phone call from
him today, and—"

"What did he say?"

"Nothing that would concern you, but if you must
know, I think he's having doubts about us." She waved
her hand in dismissal. "It's nothing. I told him I might
tell his wife, but of course I wouldn't. Anybody who
knows me knows I wouldn't do something like that. No,
Alan is going to have to stand up in front of the entire
town and tell them that he loves me and only me."

"What about the children?" Zoë asked.

"Don't you dare get that holier-than-thou look on
your face. *You* have never been trapped like I am. Do
you know that I could have gone to college? I could
have had a full scholarship, but I turned it down to

marry Bob. I thought he was going places, doing things. What a fool I was."

Zoë didn't dare look up. Her sister had barely kept a C average at school. Who was going to give her a scholarship? For what? And Zoë too well remembered that Bob had tried to break up with her before they graduated. *He* had been offered a four-year football scholarship at the state university, but when Karen became pregnant and insisted on keeping the baby, he'd given it up to marry her.

Karen glared at her sister. "I've done everything for you and Bob and the kids. Now it's time for you to do something for *me*. You're going to go with me tonight and that's it. I don't want to hear anything else about it. Now go get dressed. We'll leave as soon as Bob gets home."

Which means that *he* has to make dinner for the kids, Zoë thought.

An hour and a half later, she was in the car with Karen. Her sister was wearing a short, red cocktail dress with a fake diamond necklace.

"Should you be wearing that?" Zoë asked, looking at her sister as she inhaled deeply on her cigarette. Once again, she'd forgotten to put the window down.

"I want to look my best," Karen said. "Someday when you have a real boyfriend, not that geek you pal around with now, you'll understand a woman's need to sometimes wear something other than jeans." She gave a little smile at Zoë's Levi's.

When they got to Mr. Johnson's house, Karen turned off the headlights at the top of the drive. "This is just one of the little things we've had to do," she said, smiling at Zoë as though they were in a conspiracy together. She maneuvered the car by the landscaping lights along the drive, hiding it way in the back, behind the garbage bins.

There was only one light on in the house. "That's his study," Karen said. "It's where we meet when we need to be alone." She gave Zoë a look to let her know what she meant by that.

"I'm not going in," Zoë said.

"Of course you aren't," Karen said. "I just needed you to come with me so Bob would have to stay with the kids. I didn't want him free tonight."

Karen pulled the sun visor down and reapplied her lipstick in the little lighted mirror. "Just wait here. I shouldn't be too long. Well, maybe I'll be a long time."

Zoë knew that if she said anything to that, Karen would blast her, and she didn't want to hear it. She watched her sister walk into Mr. Johnson's house, her hips swaying, her high heels tapping on the pavement.

I have to leave this town, Zoë thought as she sat in the car and waited for her sister. Karen had said Zoë owed her for all the years she'd taken care of her "for free," but Zoë was now old enough to see that she'd more than carried her weight. It occurred to Zoë that if it weren't for her taking care of the children, Karen wouldn't have had time to have an affair.

When the car door was jerked open, Zoë almost fell out. Karen had a frantic look about her and her eye makeup was running down her cheeks.

"You have to talk to him," Karen said. "He's crazy."

"Me? What can I say to him?"

"I don't know," Karen said, "but he won't listen to me. He keeps talking about money, but what does that have to do with me? He's bought me a few measly presents, but not much. Zoë, he's always liked you, so maybe he'll listen to you."

"I can't—" Zoë said, but Karen grabbed her arm and pulled her out of the car. "I'm not going in there! I can't." For once Zoë felt strong. It seemed that all her life she'd been intimidated by her older sister. Karen was the pretty one, the social one, the one who was going to make it in the world. Her parents had never said it, but they thought Zoë was "the weird one." The girl who stayed to herself and rarely talked to anyone. The loner.

"I'm not going in there," Zoë said again. "This is your problem, you made it, and I'm not getting involved in it."

"It's not me," Karen said, and put her hands over her face. "It's something else. I don't know what it is, but he's . . ." She looked at her sister with pleading eyes. "I think he's going to kill himself."

"Call the police," Zoë said, and reached inside the car for her cell phone.

"No!" Karen said. "Listen, Zoë, I'll do whatever you want if you'll help me on this. I can't let the town know about this. I can't let Bob find out. Or the kids. Did you think about them?"

"You're not going to turn this around on *me!*" Zoë said. "You—"

"Please?" Karen begged. "Please. Just go talk to him."

"If I do this, then I'm going to leave," Zoë said. "You're always saying I owe you my whole life, but this will pay it off."

"Of course," Karen said. "I'll give you anything you want. I'll help you find an apartment and I'll help you decorate it. And Bob will get you a car. How about a nice BMW convertible? You'd like that, wouldn't you?"

Zoë wasn't so naïve that she thought Karen would actually help her, and when she said "leave" she hadn't meant an apartment two miles away from Karen. No, helping her sister in this crisis would get rid of the burden of gratitude that Zoë lived under.

Karen stepped aside so Zoë could go into the house. Her heart was beating hard as she went inside. She left the door open in case she wanted to run out. The house was dark except for a light shining around a half-closed door to her left, and it seemed eerily quiet.

"Mr. Johnson?" she called out, but he didn't answer. She went to the door and pushed it open. The room was his study, with bookshelves around two walls and big glass doors leading out to a patio. There was a blond oak desk and behind it sat Mr. Johnson. He was holding a gun to his head.

"Please," Zoë said. "Mr. Johnson, please don't do this."

"Zoë, I can't live like this anymore," he said, then he shot himself through the temple.

For a moment she couldn't move. She just stood there staring at him.

In the next second, his wife ran into the room. She looked from her husband, his bloody head slumped on the desk, then she looked at Zoë. She raised her hands in fists as she ran toward her.

"You killed him!" she shouted. "You killed my husband."

"I . . . I didn't," Zoë stammered, backing up toward a wall of bookcases, her arms across her face to protect herself. When Karen appeared behind the woman, Zoë had never been so glad to see anyone in her life. Karen ran to Zoë, put her arm around her shoulders in a protective way, and led her out of the house while the wife ran to the phone.

"He shot himself," Zoë said, her whole body shivering. "I saw it."

"That's what I was afraid would happen. Look, I have to do something, so you take the car, and—"

"Karen, you can't go back in there. There's a loaded gun in there. She'll kill you."

"I have to get some things. Look, Zoë, you take the car and go. Meet me at that drive-in on Fourth. I'll be there as soon I can get there. All I ask is that if the police question you, you say I was with you."

"You can't—" Zoë began, but all she could see in her mind was that man shooting himself.

"Trust me," Karen said as she led Zoë back to the hidden car. "I know I've not always been the easiest sister in the world, but you don't want to see me in jail, do you?"

"Jail?"

"There are some things of mine in that house that could make people think I had something to do with his death."

"Things?" Zoë asked. She couldn't seem to think very well.

"Letters. I have to find them and get rid of them, and I have to have an alibi. Remember! I was with you all night. Now go." She shoved Zoë behind the steering wheel and put her hand on the key. When Zoë didn't react, Karen started the engine for her, then closed the door. She didn't stay to wave goodbye, just ran back into the house.

"*So I left,*" Zoë said to Faith and Amy, "and about a mile away, I drove into a tree. When I woke up, I was slathered in bandages, I couldn't remember anything, and the whole town hated me."

"She put you behind the wheel of a car after you'd seen something like that," Faith said in wonder.

"Your sister told the town the man was having an affair with *you,* didn't she?" Amy said.

Zoë shrugged. "When all that was going on, I was in a hospital bed unconscious, and when I rewrote history, my accident hadn't happened, but, yes, I think that's what she did."

"An all-time low," Faith said. "Even for a sister."

Zoë nodded. "As you pointed out, on the night I was supposed to be in the car wreck, I was in bed with the man I was to marry."

"So what happened this time around?" Faith asked.

"After I left Russ's apartment the next morning, I realized what day it was and I wondered if Mr. Johnson had still shot himself. Or had I changed things so much that he didn't do it? I checked the Internet and he had, indeed, killed himself."

"Was your sister there?" Amy asked.

"Yes," Zoë said. "She told me she hadn't really needed me that night, that I was just her cover, so when I wasn't there, she went alone. She left Bob with the kids, put on her red dress, and went to see Alan Johnson."

Zoë looked down at her empty plate. "I found out some things later, but I knew nothing that day in New York. When I got back to my apartment, I had four frantic messages on my phone from Karen. She said I had to call her, that I had to come home, that she needed me. She said I couldn't abandon her after all she'd done for me."

Faith put her hand over Zoë's wrist to calm her.

"It took me a while to piece together the story of what happened the first time, but . . ." She looked at Amy.

"I don't think it would have taken much on your sister's part to make the woman believe that her husband was having an affair with you rather than the worn-out mother of two kids," Amy said.

"I don't think it did," Zoë said, "and when I had the wreck and was conveniently in a coma for a while, I think my sister did everything she could to sully my name, and save her own skin."

She smiled. "But the second time around, things happened in a very different way. When Mrs. Johnson came home, there was her husband dead, and my sister was tearing through the study trying to find the letters. Mrs. Johnson immediately called the police, and they . . ."

"They what?" Faith asked.

"Put my sister in jail for a few days."

"Serves her right!" Amy said.

"I guess so," Zoë said, "but she begged me to come back and be with her, but I wouldn't. Thank heaven, this time around I'd had time away from her, not to mention three weeks in the eighteenth century, so I could tell her no. If it had happened right after I left—"

"You would have been stuck there for the rest of your life," Amy said.

"Probably."

"So what happened this time around?" Faith asked.

"They let my sister out of jail when they saw it was a suicide, but of course everyone wanted to know why such a great man had killed himself."

"And of course they blamed a woman," Faith said.

"Completely. The police found the letters my sister had written him, so everyone knew about the affair."

"Why did he really kill himself?" Amy asked. "I don't think that men of this century kill themselves over love."

Zoë couldn't help smiling. "How diplomatic of you. They certainly don't kill themselves over trashy women like my sister." She took a sip of wine. "It seems that the man had a gambling problem and was up to his ears in debt. It took a year for all the ugly details to come out, but everything he was involved in was a fake. He had no money, nothing. His wife lost everything and had to get a job."

"And your sister?" Faith asked.

"Bob divorced her and kept the kids. Karen moved away and the last time I saw her . . ."

"What?" Faith asked.

"She visited me in New York and she thought I'd be the same little girl she'd bullied all her life. But I'd changed. When she said something nasty, I just laughed at her. I kept remembering that while I was lying in a hospital fighting for my life, my sister had been letting the town believe that Mr. Johnson and I had been having an affair."

"It makes more sense that he'd want a gorgeous dame like you than a Tobacco Road girl," Faith said.

Zoë laughed. "You two are good for my ego."

"And what about Russ?" Amy asked. "Did she make a pass at him?"

"She's doing it again," Zoë said to Faith. "Yes, my sister in her polyester dress, with her four-pack-a-day habit, made a pass at my boyfriend. And when he pushed her away, she got so angry she tried to make me believe he'd come on to her."

"Classic," Amy said. "I bet she went away in a rage."

"Oh, yeah," Zoë said. "In a fury. But it didn't bother me. In my head were the years of hurt I'd suffered at her hands. I didn't realize it then, but I was really beaten down by what that town had done to me. There I was in a hospital with my cracked skull and they hated me without even trying to find out the truth."

"Do you think she felt any guilt? I mean the first time," Faith asked.

"Some. I remember her face when I saw her when I burned the car on the town square. She couldn't get away from me fast enough. The truth is that I'm ashamed of myself because I can't forgive her."

Amy looked at Zoë. "Primrose said that there was always true love involved in anything Madame Zoya did. Where was your true love?"

"I'm not sure," Zoë said. "I know I had a boyfriend of sorts. We'd gone together all during high school, but he turned on me as soon as there was a hint of scandal. I didn't miss him."

"I think your true love is that art of yours," Faith said. "When you thought you'd lose your talent, you were willing to keep the hatred of an entire town and the damage to your body. If that isn't true love, I don't know what is."

"I never thought of that," Zoë said, "but it makes

sense. I think my true love has now expanded to my husband and daughter, but, yes, if I had a true love back then, it was the talent I'd been given. And art led me to the two men in my life."

"So how much like Russell is the new guy?" Faith asked.

Zoë laughed. "Wait till we get to you. I'm going to ask you nothing but personal questions."

"Like who's the better lover of all my three men?" Faith asked.

Zoë laughed.

"What did you answer?" Amy asked Faith.

"I didn't," Faith said, and the women laughed together.

"I have a blueberry cobbler," Amy said. "How about if we have it in the living room?"

"And hear Faith's story," Zoë said.

"My thoughts exactly," Amy said.

Twenty-five

꧁

In record time, the three women had cleaned up the dishes, put everything away, and were ensconced in the living room, ready to hear Faith's story.

"I think that you should guess," Faith said.

"That's not fair," Zoë said. "I'm no good at stories."

"I like the idea," Amy said. "Let me see." She stared hard at Faith. "I'm not sure that what we think happened, did."

"You didn't marry Eddie," Zoë said. "That's for sure. And I don't think you were in love with William enough to want to find his descendants, so that means you married Tyler."

Faith just smiled and looked at them over her wineglass.

"I don't think so," Amy said. "I think that your time in Tristan's world changed you. I think that if you'd gone back in your time before that, you would have married Tyler, but . . ."

Zoë was looking from one to the other of them, then she got up, went to Jeanne's cabinet and withdrew drawing supplies. "I'm glad to see that some things haven't changed. Did I tell you two that some of *my* drawings have survived from the eighteenth century? They say they were done by a student of Russell Johns."

"Any of the nudes of him?" Amy asked.

"How did you know about those?" Zoë asked.

"Tristan snooped through Russell's room."

"You're kidding," Zoë said. "He didn't have the right to do that."

"He owned the place and I think he felt that he could do what he wanted to," Amy said. "So did any of those beefcake nudes survive the ages?"

"Actually, two of them did. Both of them are of Russell, but no one knows who they are. They think they're of the local blacksmith. No one can believe the artist looked like that."

"I know," Amy said. "People today think we have the market cornered on beautiful men."

"Speaking of which," Faith said, "how did you and Tristan spend your last two days together?"

Amy smiled. "I want to hear how you've spent your last sixteen years. I see you're married but, somehow, I don't think it's to either Eddie or Tyler."

Zoë looked up from her drawing pad. "Don't tell me she's right."

"She is."

Zoë lifted her glass to Amy in tribute.

"Okay, that's enough about me," Amy said. "I want to hear about you."

"If Tyler hadn't died—"

"Been killed by your mother," Zoë said.

"All right, but I don't like to think about that," Faith said. "My mother was a woman of deep passions and I'll never know what really happened that day, but I'm sure it was spur of the moment. I'm sure she didn't plan to kill him."

"Dead is dead," Zoë said, her eyes on her drawing.

"Yes, and that's why I went back," Faith said. "If it hadn't been for Ty's premature death, I wouldn't have gone back to change anything."

"You're kidding," Zoë said.

"No. After I came back from living in a place where I was a useful woman, I knew what I wanted to do with my life," Faith said.

"And there were the seeds," Amy said. "You were concerned about them. They'd made it through one transport, but you weren't sure they'd stand another one."

"Exactly!" Faith said.

Zoë looked at her. "Are you telling me that you would have given up a chance to take away all the dreadful things that had been done to you just for a plant?"

"Yes," Faith said.

Zoë shook her head at her. "I'm almost glad Ty was killed if only to make you go back and rewrite your life."

"Me, too," Faith said. "I needed my youth to give the balm time to grow."

"Start when Ty came through your window," Amy said. "You told us that if you had a chance to do it again, you'd be packed and ready to leave with him."

"I was packed all right, but I wasn't leaving with any man." She looked at Amy. "Can you figure it out?"

"I think . . ." she began, then looked up. "I think the problem was that you thought you had only two men to choose from. One was a motorcycle-riding hillbilly, and the other was a tea-drinking rich boy."

Zoë looked at Faith.

"Is she right?"

"Perfectly," Faith said. "After we returned from the eighteenth century, I realized that I could never be happy with either man. If I married Ty, even knowing what I do now, I knew I wouldn't be happy with him. I had a vision of his working fourteen-hour days, seven days a week."

"All to prove that he was as good a man as Eddie," Amy said.

"Yes," Faith said. "I'm not sure what made me see it, maybe it was that back in Tristan's time, as Amy calls it, it was the first time that I was truly free. That sounds funny when you think of the centuries involved. We think women are free today, but were subjugated back then. For me, it was the opposite."

"But then, in this time, you had two mothers telling you what to do—for your entire life," Zoë said.

"It's going to be hard to believe, but I think the mothers had very little to do with it," Faith said. "I think

I grew up loving that two boys were in love with me. I thought about my childhood as best I could without wallowing in emotion and sentimentality."

She took a breath. "I think that I've always looked at my life entirely wrong. I always saw myself as a victim of my mother and later as the punching bag for Eddie's mother. But when I looked at things from afar, I saw that I was the one who caused the problems."

"You'll have to explain that to me," Zoë said, but Amy said nothing.

"I spent my whole childhood with two boys, Tyler and Eddie. I think it's just possible that I was the strong one when we were kids, and I think I may have adopted them in a motherly way."

"It's easy to mother the men in your life," Amy said. "It's one of my great faults."

"I didn't realize how motherly I was until I was in that orangery with William. I thought I was a martyr for taking care of Eddie all those years, but William made me realize that I like helping people."

Faith looked down at her hands. "I used to think that I overlooked the awful circumstances that Ty and Eddie lived in, but I came to realize that that's what I liked about them."

"They needed you," Amy said.

"Yes, they did. Ty was trapped in horrible circumstances in his family life, and even though Eddie looked to be better off, he wasn't. He just had more money."

"You thought you had to marry one of them out of guilt," Amy said.

"Right," Faith said. "I had taken them out of their bad families and we'd formed our own family."

"That doesn't sound so bad," Zoë said.

"Someday, you have to push your children out of the nest," Amy said. "I dread it. I want to buy houses for my sons that are next door to us. Even the thought of their going to college makes me ill."

"I agree," Faith said, "but I also know you well enough to know that, when the time comes, you won't hold your children back."

"No," Amy said, sighing. "I'm sure that when I have to, I'll get my courage together and let them go. However, I feel sorry for any girl who wants to marry one of *my* sons."

Faith and Zoë laughed.

Faith continued. "I knew that if I was going to give Eddie and Ty a real chance at life I had to leave them. I didn't plan to explain, just leave."

"Like me," Zoë said.

"Exactly. Sometimes words can't fix anything," Faith said, "and I knew this was such a case. If it had come to the point where my mother was willing to kill to make me marry the man of her choice, then I had to change everything."

"So what did you do?" Amy asked.

"You can't guess?" Zoë said.

"Maybe," Amy said, "but I'd rather hear what actually happened."

"When Ty climbed in my window that night, I wasn't there. And I wasn't there when Eddie came in and threw his jealous little fit. Instead, I went to Eddie's mother."

"You did what?!" Zoë said, her eyes wide. "I thought you hated her."

"I did. I knew all the awful things she'd done to me over the years I was married to her son. It hadn't happened yet and wasn't going to, but I still remembered them. But I also knew that she'd been right."

"You didn't love Eddie," Amy said.

"Yes she did," Zoë said. "She loved both of them."

"True," Faith said. "I loved Eddie like a brother, and I loved Ty like a sex machine. I had fun with him, but in the end I married Eddie."

"Why did you go to his mother?" Zoë asked.

Faith looked at Amy. "Do you know why?"

"I would think that you went to her for money."

"Don't tell me that's true," Zoë said. "I would have walked the streets before I asked her for money."

"That's because you can go into a gallery, show them your work, and instantly, you have a job."

"Not quite," Zoë said, looking up from her drawing. "It takes more work than that and I have a lot of supplies to buy."

Faith and Amy looked at her.

"Okay, so Russ bought them and, yes, I did sell rather

quickly to a gallery. Stop staring at me! It just seems to me that going to Eddie's mother to ask for money would be like my going to my sister to ask for money."

"Where did you get the hundred and fifty dollars that got you to New York?" Faith asked.

"Stole it from my sister," Zoë said, grinning. "But didn't she owe me?"

"And so did Eddie's mother," Faith said. "But I didn't just borrow money, I gave her a piece of the business I wanted to start."

"And what business was that?" Amy asked.

"Right," Faith said, "you've been in this house and haven't seen how I've changed the world."

"You changed the world?" Amy asked.

"Changed it a bit," Faith said as she got up and went to get her bag on the hall table. She reached inside and pulled out a jar of what looked to be face cream. It was a jar of dark blue glass, about two inches high, with a silver lid and silver writing on it. She handed it to Amy.

"I've never seen this before," Amy said. "Indigo," she read on the label. She unscrewed the lid and smelled it, then her eyes widened. "Beth. The seeds."

She glanced at Zoë and saw that she was staring at Faith with a look of astonishment on her face.

"Did I miss something?" Amy asked.

"Indigo?" Zoë asked. "You don't know about this stuff? No, right, you've been in here. That company is yours?"

"All except the seven percent that Eddie's mother

owns. I tried for five, but she held out for seven. She uses her millions to do charitable works in Eddie's name. He died on the same date he died when I was taking care of him."

"Destiny," Amy said, then, "Millions?"

Zoë laughed. "More like megamillions. It's hard to believe that you haven't seen these bottles on the store shelves. There's shampoo, face cream, you name it. It's a whole line and they're everywhere, on TV and in magazines. There isn't a movie star who doesn't use it." She looked at Faith. "If you run this company, how do you have time for a life?"

"I let a bunch of people in New York who wear suits all day run it. I just stay home with my kids. And . . ." She hesitated. "I run the charity part of my company. We give a lot of money away. And—"

Faith seemed to pause, as though for a drumroll. "One of the first things I bought was Tristan's house and the old medieval house next to it. I found out that after we left, William ran the cows out and restored the house, so it's still there today." Faith smiled. "I read that he never married, but he lived to be ninety-five. If you look deep in obscure books on landscaping, you'll see his name."

"That's great!" Zoë said.

"The houses are mine and I've spent a lot on putting them back to the way they were. When my kids are out of the house, I hope to have the time to oversee the re-creation of an eighteenth-century estate and open it to the public, but for right now, it's private housing. I don't get to stay there very often, so maybe you two would like to visit. Amy, would your kids like that?"

"They'd love it. All of us would. What about the tower?"

Faith shook her head. "Part of it was still there, but the glass roof was gone and of course there were no plants."

"You really did save them," Amy said.

"I want to know what happened between getting money from Eddie's mother to becoming a multimillionaire."

Faith smiled in memory. "I talked to Eddie's mother and I told her the truth, that I had come by some seeds from a plant that is extinct today and was mentioned in the Bible, and I wanted to grow it and make cosmetics with it. She wasn't interested until I told her I planned to move to California to grow the plant there."

"So she was paying you to get out of town," Zoë said.

"More or less. Actually, that's exactly what she was doing. The night before, she'd found the receipt for the engagement ring Eddie had bought me, and she knew what was going to happen. I took the ring off its chain and said I'd throw it into the deal. Gave her the diamond, I kept the chain." Faith reached under her collar and pulled out a pretty little gold chain. "I always wear it to remind me of Eddie and what might have been."

"What you escaped," Amy said.

"So how much did she give you?" Zoë asked.

"We put the money in a revolving account. She'd support me for the seven years I figured I needed to get the plants to a good size, and of course I had to buy land. In the end, it was quite a lot of money, but she's been repaid many times over."

"What happened in your personal life in California?" Amy asked.

"I met a man who I hadn't spent my childhood with and who I didn't mother. We got married, started Indigo, and along the way I had six children."

"Six!" Zoë said in horror.

"Six," Amy said in envy.

"We live in a beautiful house in the Napa Valley," Faith said, "and it's surrounded by acres of the Balm of Gilead. I've given the plant back to the Holy Lands," she added as though it meant nothing, even though it had been the happiest day of her life when she'd presented plants to their country of origin.

"What happened to Tyler?" Amy asked.

"He got married a few years after I left and he became a successful contractor. He built some very nice houses."

"Children?"

"Three," Faith said.

"And did you see him again?" Amy asked.

"Many times. My family and I visited my hometown often and we always saw him and Eddie and my mother. You won't believe this, but Eddie's mother and I became friends. She was great at business. I thought all her money came from her late husband, but I found out that that shrewd old woman was a whiz at the stock market. She's stayed at my house in Napa a dozen times. My kids love her."

Faith paused for a moment, then looked up. "One evening we were sharing a bottle of wine and she told me she wished she'd had a daughter-in-law like me."

"Did you strangle her?" Zoë asked.

"No, actually, her words made me cry. She didn't remember it, but I'd spent years working myself to death to try to make her like me, but she hadn't. But when I stopped trying, it happened."

"Too bad you could never tell Ty that you'd saved his life," Zoë said.

"I nearly forgot!" Faith said. "At my mother's funeral, he told a story that sent chills down my spine. He volunteered to give the eulogy and he told how my mother had saved his life. A few days after he crawled through my window—"

"And you weren't there," Amy said.

"Yes, by that time I'd already made my deal with Mrs. Wellman and I was getting ready to leave for California."

"How did Eddie and Tyler take your news that you were leaving town?" Zoë asked.

Faith shook her head. "Very well. In fact, they took it too well for my taste."

"As long as neither one of them got you," Amy said.

"You're right! I think I was the bone those two dogs

had fought over for most of their lives, and as long as neither of them won, they were okay. I don't like to think this, but in some ways I think they were relieved when I said I wasn't going to marry either of them."

"So what was your creepy funeral story?" Zoë asked. "How had your mom saved Tyler's life?"

"Ty said he went out to the cliffs as we used to call the local make-out place. I look back on it and I'd panic if my kids went there. It was really dangerous. There was a turnaround that was on the edge of a huge drop-off. We used to dare one another to look over because there were three cars at the bottom. It must have been a thousand feet down. Really scary."

Faith looked at Amy. "Ty got too close to the edge and fell over. He said it was the middle of the day, nobody was there, and he was hanging on to the edge with his fingertips. By a one-in-a-million chance, my mother showed up there. He yelled and she used a rope and Ty's truck to haul him up."

"Wow," Zoë said. "That makes my hair stand on edge."

"When your mother thought you might marry him, she hit him with a rock, and . . ." Amy said.

"Watched him fall to the bottom," Zoë said. "It's a good thing you went back."

"Yeah," Faith said. "A very good thing. You want to know something even more strange? After I left town, and after she saved his life, my mother and Ty became friends. He introduced her to his mother and when his construction company got going, he built them a new house, and I paid to furnish it. The two women lived together until my mother died. And Ty's friendship with Eddie stayed strong. He was a pallbearer at Eddie's funeral, and, yes, I was there too."

Faith looked at her watch. "I don't know about you young people, but I'm exhausted. I have a plane to catch tomorrow."

"Me, too," Zoë and Amy said in unison, then the three of them laughed.

Zoë turned her pad of paper around and showed what she'd drawn. It was Faith and Amy laughing together, glasses of wine in their hands. They looked as though they were the best friends in the world.

"Wonderful," Amy said. "Could I have a copy?"

"I'll have it framed and send it to you. We do plan to exchange addresses, don't we? I mean our new addresses."

"Mine's the same," Amy said, then looked away before she saw a look of sympathy cross their faces. She bid them good night and went to her bedroom.

As she showered, she thought about going home. It would be exactly the same, but Amy knew that she wasn't the same. She tried not to let it hurt her feelings, but the fact that neither Faith nor Zoë had said thank you to her for taking them back to the eighteenth century did hurt. If Amy hadn't insisted that they go back with her, Faith wouldn't have the seeds for her multimillion-dollar cosmetics company. And Zoë wouldn't have found her husband—and her backbone, Amy thought. It had taken a lot to make Zoë able to stand up to her bully of a sister.

But they hadn't said a word to Amy. That's all right, she thought. If they wanted to be selfish, let them. Amy had nothing to complain about. Tomorrow she was going to go home to her husband and sons, and she was going to be as happy as she had always been.

"I don't even know why I bothered to come here," she said as she got into bed. "Except that I saved Tristan. I did what I wanted to and that's what was important."

In spite of three glasses of wine, she had a difficult time going to sleep.

"*She doesn't know* a thing, does she?" Zoë whispered to Faith in the bathroom they shared.

"Nothing," Faith said, "and I felt bad for not telling her. She deserves to know."

"She'll find out, but I think her husband should tell her, not us."

"I'm sure you're right. If I didn't believe that, I wouldn't have agreed to keep my mouth shut."

Zoë dried her hands on the towel. "By the way, you were brilliant at not giving anything away. 'When did you get so good at stories?'" she said in a mocking tone. "I nearly lost it then."

"Quiet," Faith said. "She'll hear you. If you'd dealt with as many big shots in the business world as I have, you'd be good at lying too. We just have to remember to not give anything away tomorrow. We'll have a few hours together in the morning, then she belongs to her husband."

"Who knows nothing," Zoë said. "Didn't you find it unsettling that no one remembered what had happened? I asked my sister several questions about when I was in the hospital, but she just thought I was crazy."

"I feel sorry for Jeanne. This time around, she didn't have you and me as patients. I didn't hit my mother-in-law at the funeral of her son, and you didn't set fire to a car."

"No, this time it was all about Amy. Jeanne lent this summerhouse to a world-famous—" Zoë broke off at the look from Faith and lowered her voice. "Do you think Amy went to bed with Tristan?" Zoë whispered.

"I don't think we'll ever know that," Faith said, "and I don't think it's any of our business."

"Faith," Zoë said, "I know that Madame Zoya said that we weren't allowed to contact each other until we came here, but . . ."

"But what?"

"When I saw Amy's name, I couldn't help it. I sent her a gift."

"What kind of gift? No, wait, don't tell me. A picture of someone."

"Yes," Zoë said. "You don't think that will mess up anything, do you?"

"It doesn't seem to have. The truth is that I had to work hard not to contact her—and you. I wanted to jump up and down and say 'I know her' whenever I saw one of your paintings. I saw that you married a man named Russell, but I had no idea that he was a descendant of—"

"The man I loved?" Zoë said. "He's so much like him that sometimes it's freaky. I'm mad about him. But you! You're the great success! I had no idea that Indigo was yours. I'm truly impressed. But it's a good thing I didn't know or I would have looked you up on the Internet and found out who you married."

"Who I didn't marry," Faith said. "Zoë, I don't know how you'll take this, but my company has a new product line coming out and I've named it 'Amy.' I'm giving her a lot of the proceeds to do with as she wants."

"She'll give it to charities," Zoë said. "I hope you didn't think I'd be jealous of that. You and I owe Amy everything. If she hadn't taken us back with her . . ." Her eyes widened.

"I don't want to think about it," Faith said. "I would have married Tyler and had a second miserable life."

"And I would have spent my life feeling sorry for myself. By the way, I already sent Amy a letter saying she gets a portrait of her family from me every five years for life." She raised an eyebrow at Faith. "What if I start to do a portrait and see that she has a son who looks just like a certain famous American author?"

"I know just the herb to give you to keep you from laughing," Faith said. "I've had to use it at several board meetings."

Laughing together, they went to their bedrooms.

Twenty-six

❧

"I *will not* be disappointed," Amy said to herself as she waited in line to get off the plane. "I won't be disappointed or feel cheated. I did what I went there to do and that was all I needed to do. If I were a selfish person, I would have asked for something for myself, but I'm not so I didn't."

The man in line in front of her turned to glare at her.

"Sorry," she said, apologizing for talking out loud to herself.

When she got to the airport, as soon as she saw Stephen and the boys, all thoughts of getting "more" left her mind. The boys ran under the guard tape and nearly tackled her. She fell back against her rolling bag, and threw her arms around them, kissing them profusely.

"Can I get in here?" Stephen asked as he gave her a quick kiss, then took her bag and ushered the three of them back under the tape. "Is this it?"

"Are you kidding?" Amy said. "I have three more bags

full of . . ." She leaned down to the boys who were cling-
ing to her. "Presents!" They yelled so loud that people
frowned at them.

Stephen put his lips close to her ear. "I'd tell them to
calm down but I feel just as they do. I'd like to yell with
joy that you're home at last."

"I was gone just a few days," Amy said.

"I know, but for some reason it seemed like you were
gone forever. It's like it's been a lifetime since I saw you."

"I'm here now," she said. "And I'm not going to leave
again."

Stephen laughed. "That would mean you'd have to
go camping with us next year and you know how you
hate that."

Amy's mind filled with images. She had cooked
over an open fireplace for over a year. She could stick
her hand inside a wall oven and tell the temperature
within a few degrees. She'd had to deal with weevils in
the flour and maggots on the meat. She'd had to use an
outhouse.

"I think I might be persuaded to go camping with
you guys next year." She smiled at the expression on Stephen's face. "If I'm not a good camper, you can send me
back after one day." They had reached the baggage claim
area. "There are my bags," she added before he could say
anything.

They got the luggage to the car and Amy opened one
of them to give the boys what she thought of as "car
toys." They'd keep them quiet on the trip home. This

time they were those plastic boxes filled with hundreds of dull-tipped nails. The boys could make images of their body parts.

When they got in the car, Stephen took her hands in his to kiss them, then he drew back. "What in the world have you been doing?" He turned her hands palm up and looked at them in horror. There were cuts, half-healed blisters, calluses, scars, and skin so rough it could have been used to sand the paint off the car.

She pulled her hands out of his grasp. "Just because I went ridin' without my gloves one day . . ." she said in imitation of Scarlett O'Hara.

Stephen started the car and backed out of the parking space. "Wasn't the truth that she'd been working like a field hand?"

"And that's what I've been doing," Amy said as she reached in her bag and got out the jar of Indigo cream Faith had given her. When she'd handed it to her, Faith whispered, "All my products will always be free to you."

"You look different," Stephen said, driving and glancing at her. "Besides your cotton picker's hands, that is. Have you lost weight?"

"I lost weight before I left, but you never noticed," she said, lying. "I've had time to get over my sadness, and that's a big change."

"No, it's more than that. There's something different about you. I can't quite put my finger on it, but it's there."

"I'll let you try later."

"What?"

"To put your finger on it."

Stephen blinked at her a couple of times. "You didn't just make a sex joke, did you?"

"Maybe," she said, smiling enigmatically.

He seemed to be so shocked that he was silent, watching the road with intensity.

Was I such a prude before? Amy wondered, and the idea that what she'd been through had changed her made her smile. She remembered how shocked Faith had been at the state of William's bedroom. Bedbugs, head lice, fleas. When Faith told Amy about them, she'd expected her to be outraged. Now Amy remembered saying something about there being a problem, but she certainly hadn't been shocked.

"Are you laughing?" Stephen asked.

"Just at something one of the women I stayed with said."

"You got along with them then?"

"Yes, very well."

"The last time I saw you, you were acting like I was sending you to the guillotine. You didn't want to stay in the same house with a bunch of strangers."

"You know, I don't think I'll ever again worry about meeting strangers."

He glanced at her in puzzlement, then turned back to the road. The boys started yelling that she had to look at what they'd made, so she gave her attention to them.

When they got home, the boys tore into their other presents and Stephen took the fishing rod she'd bought him into the backyard to try it out, while Amy walked around her house. It was the same but it was wondrous to her. She ran her hand over her huge cookstove. Stainless steel burners that turned on with a knob. No one had to clean it, or keep the fire going all day. Her oven even had a rotisserie and she remembered the fire dogs they'd had at Tristan's house. They were iron cages that were powered by little greyhound dogs that ran around for an hour at a time. When Amy had first gone there, the dogs were made to stay in the cages for many hours. She had liberated them, and, like everyone else, they were given proper working hours.

Dishwasher, big mixer, food processor. She looked in wonder at an electrical socket, and turned the blender on and off a few times. Marvelous.

"I'm glad you came home, Mom," her oldest son said and threw his arms around her waist.

"Did you think I wouldn't?"

"I had a bad dream," he said, his face buried against her stomach.

Kneeling, she pulled him to her. "Were we in a strange house and was I searching for you and telling you to get up, that we had to get out of the house?"

He nodded against her shoulder.

"I had the same dream, and you know what? It was just a dream. You woke up and I'm here. Right?"

He nodded, but still wouldn't lift his head. "I love you and I'm glad you didn't stay there."

"Me too," she said.

He grinned at her, pushed out of her arms, and ran away to go yell with his brother.

When she stood up, Stephen was standing at the end of the counter. "He sees it too. Something about you is different."

"Maybe it's just that I'm clean," she said. "How long has it been since those boys had a bath?"

"How long were you gone?"

"Oh, Stephen," she said in mock disgust, "I expected more of you. Really! This is too much." She had her hands on her hips as she started out of the kitchen to get the boys.

He grabbed her about the waist and pulled her to him to give her a thorough kiss. "I missed you."

"I missed you too."

His hand wandered down the back of her. "Did Davy tell you about his dream?"

She nodded, her face buried in his shoulder. She'd nearly forgotten the smell of him. No one smelled like him.

"We were in the tent and he woke up screaming. He said that you were telling him to get up, to get out of the house. Even after he woke up, he kept saying that Mommy was lost. He hasn't been the same until now when he saw you here with us."

He pulled back to look at her. "Did something happen up there in Maine?"

"Yes and no," she said. "Nothing bad. I heard the life stories of some other women, and I realized that I like my life as it is."

"I hope so," he said. "I'd hate to change it just because of something that happened at some summerhouse in Maine. Why are you laughing?"

"Because I'm glad to be home. Now let me go so I can get those boys in the tub. I'm going to have to use lye soap on them."

"Lye soap?" he said. "Where did that come from?"

"It's great against fleas and bedbugs," she said as she grabbed one boy and ran after the other one.

❧❦

Amy was searching for Stephen. It had taken over two hours to get the family fed (Chinese takeout) and the boys scrubbed, then she'd had to wrestle them into pajamas. It took forty-five minutes of reading to get them settled. But after they'd at last fallen asleep, she'd spent thirty minutes just snuggling with them, holding their sleeping bodies. She hadn't realized how much she'd missed them.

When she went downstairs, Stephen was nowhere to be found.

"Stephen?" she called.

"In here."

She heard his voice but didn't know where it was coming from. It seemed to be coming from outside the dining room, but she didn't think he'd gone out.

It wasn't until she called him again and heard his voice a second time that she saw a door in the dining room that wasn't there before she went to Maine.

Tentatively, and a little bit concerned about what century waited behind the door, she opened it. She saw a large room, a study, that was done all in dark green and maroon. On the walls were photos she'd never seen before, of Stephen with people she didn't know.

Her husband was standing behind a huge, carved desk that looked as though it would fit in the White House, and he was going through a pile of mail.

"Sorry, babe," he said. "I promised myself I'd wait until tomorrow to do this, but it piled up while we were away."

Amy walked across a thick-piled Oriental carpet and looked at what he was throwing away. Every envelope was addressed to Dr. Stephen Hanford.

She picked up an envelope, sat down on the leather chesterfield, and looked at it. "Stephen?" she said softly.

"Yeah?"

She looked about the room more carefully. There were plaques on the wall, the kind that are given as awards. "What do you do for a living?"

"That's a funny question."

"Humor me," she said.

He looked up at her. "You know what I do as well as I do, since we married right after I finished my internship."

"Internship?"

"Amy, what's wrong with you? Okay," he said, but shaking his head at her. "I'm a cardiologist and you know that as well as I do. You've been with me every step of the way."

"A cardiologist," she said. "What about your father's trucking company?"

"Trucks? Amy, what were you girls smoking up there?" He put the mail down and went to sit beside her. "Okay, I'm game. What is it that you don't remember? My father is retired, but he was once the best cardiologist in the state. And no, being a great doctor didn't mellow him. He's still a pain in the neck. However, whenever I run into a problem I can't figure out, I still call Dad."

"Your father is a doctor?"

"Amy, you really are acting very strange. All of the men in my family are doctors. It's sort of a family tradition and has been for, oh, a few hundred years now. I can't vouch for what kind of doctors my ancestors back in England were. They probably did bloodletting and used lots of leeches."

"Your brothers are doctors?" she whispered. "Your beer-drinking, thrill-a-minute brothers are doctors?"

Stephen gave a sigh. "You know all this. Okay, so maybe it's like one of your books. My three brothers are all doctors and they travel all over the world. They helicopter in, climb mountains. If there's a disaster in the world, you can bet that one of my brothers will be there. They like excitement as much as they like life."

"Children? Wives?"

"Lots. There are so many ex-wives and children and stepchildren and half siblings that I can't keep track of them. But you've always been able to. Every year, you put on a Thanksgiving dinner for about fifty. You know all their names and relationships and you send them birthday gifts."

"I hope I can live up to my reputation," she said. The truth was that so much was swirling around in her mind that she couldn't seem to grasp it all. Tristan, doctors; doctors, Tristan. And she *had* changed her life. No, she'd changed Stephen's life. Somehow, her going back to one of Stephen's ancestors and saving his life, and, through Faith, introducing him to medicine, had filtered down through the centuries so that it was now a "tradition" in Stephen's family that all of them were doctors.

She had done exactly what she'd hoped to. She looked at Stephen. "Are you ready to go to bed?"

"Yeah," he said, then gave her a look that let her know what he had in mind.

At least some things haven't changed, she thought.

"I have to make one call, then I'll be up."

"Okay," Amy said as she started for the door, then she turned back. "Did you say 'your books'? As in *my* books?"

"Sure." He was looking down at the mail again. "Your books. The ones you write out there in your studio."

His words put Amy in such a state of shock that she couldn't say anything. She went to the kitchen, to the back door, and turned on the outside lights. There, at the back of their three-acre property, was what looked to be a little Victorian house. Beside the door were hooks with keys on them. The only one she didn't know had a key chain that said it was good to be queen. Amy knew that that was hers.

She took the key and went out to the house. She wasn't surprised to see that it was very much like the one in Maine owned by Primrose and Madame Zoya. When she opened the door, she smiled. The living room, down to the last fabric, was a duplicate of the room where she'd had tea with Primrose. Through an archway was another room and it was an exact copy of the room at the store where she'd found the book about the Hawthorne family. The only other room was the "with plumbing" one, the bathroom with a kitchenette in front of it. The bathroom countertop was covered with blue bottles and jars that said "Indigo."

She went back to the living room. In a bookcase to the right of the door, she found what she was looking for. There were eight books there with the author's name as Amy Hawthorne. Quickly, she read the blurbs and saw that they were books set in the eighteenth century. Inside were reprints of some reviews. One of them said that Amy's descriptions of the time period were so vivid that it was as though she'd been there.

She looked around the beautiful studio, and as she

did, memory seemed to flood into her mind. It was like when she'd suddenly found herself in the eighteenth century. She had been a newcomer there, yet she knew people and places.

She took one of the books with her name on it, her pen name, and held it to her. Yes, she was beginning to remember writing it, and even remember how many weeks it had spent on the *New York Times* Bestseller List. She glanced down and saw that the hero's name was Tristan.

When she looked back at the fireplace, she saw a portrait over the mantel. She knew where to turn on the light above the mantel. There was a portrait of Tristan, smiling at her in the way she'd seen a hundred times. The signature on the picture was, of course, Zoë's name.

"They knew about my books," Amy whispered. "They knew all the time." She smiled in memory of the way Zoë and Faith had kept secret what they must have known about her. In their relived lives, they'd seen her books on the stands, and Zoë had painted a portrait of Tristan and sent it to her. Amy looked at the little brass plaque on the bottom of the frame. It said "Nathaniel Hawthorne" and she laughed at the lie.

She had not only changed Stephen's life but her own as well. Maybe it was because in this second life her husband had a job that he was happy with, and it had released something inside her so she felt confident enough to write down the stories that ran through her head.

"I thought you wanted to go to bed," Stephen said from the doorway. "Don't tell me you're out here drooling over that guy again."

"I never drool," she said.

"Ha! I've never been jealous of any man except him," he said as he put his arms around her. "Sometimes I think that if he walked into this room you'd leave with him."

"Of course I wouldn't," she said as he bent to kiss her, and she knew that they'd never make it to the bedroom. "I would choose you over him."

As Stephen pushed her shirt off her shoulder, Amy glanced up at Tristan's portrait and she could swear he winked at her. She winked back, then gave her attention to her husband.

Turn the page for a preview of
Jude Deveraux's newest novel

Secrets

From Atria Books

Prologue

ASSIE HAD HEARD that drowning was the easiest form of death. She had no idea how anyone could know that, since whoever said it had lived, but as she drifted down in the deep end of the pool, she decided they were right. She could feel her long hair floating upward, and all weight left her twelve-year-old body. She wasn't trying to kill herself. No, she was just waiting for *him* to rescue her. But dying was interesting to think about. What if this really were the end? Smiling, she let her body relax into her thoughts. Never again would she have to hear her mother declare how easy Cassie's life had been while her mother's had been so difficult. "We stopped a war!" her mother, Margaret Madden, loved to say, referring to Vietnam. "No one else in history has ever done that!" Until she was ten, Cassie believed that her mother had single-handedly made the president of the United States remove the troops from the war that was never declared to be a war.

But when Cassie was ten, an old college friend of her mother had visited them, and when she'd heard Margaret bawling out her daughter, the friend started laughing. "Maggie," she said, and Cassie looked up in wonder because no one ever dared to call her mother "Maggie." "You never left your classes and you told us all that we were idiots to sit around on the grass smoking pot and protesting."

Needless to say, that was the end of that friendship, but it had been an enlightening experience for Cassie. That was when she found out that not every word that came out of her mother's mouth was the truth. She learned that just because someone delivered a statement with force and volume, didn't make it a fact. From that time on, she began to see her mother for what she was: a bully and a tyrant who believed that there was only one way to do anything, and that was the way *she* had done everything. To her mind, if her daughter wanted to grow up to be a successful person, then she had to conduct herself exactly as Margaret Madden had. That meant going to a top school, getting the best grades, then working her way up to the head of some mega corporation.

One time Cassie asked, "What about a husband and children?"

"Don't get me started," Margaret said, then said nothing else. But she had piqued Cassie's curiosity, so she began to secretly listen in on her mother's conversations. Most of the discussions revealed nothing of interest, but one day Cassie had the horror of hearing her mother say that her daughter had been conceived from a one-night stand with a man she hardly knew while she was on a business trip to Hong Kong. "Defective condom," Margaret had said without a hint of sentimentality. She was so disciplined that she hadn't realized she was pregnant until she was nearly five months along and it was too late for an abortion. Margaret said she'd done her best to ignore the pregnancy, and that she'd meant to turn the baby over to a childless colleague, but then her boss—the person she most admired—had said he was glad Margaret was going to be raising a child. It made her seem more human. When he gave her a sterling silver rattle from Tiffany, she decided to keep the kid.

As she did with all things, Margaret planned it carefully. She bought a house in upstate New York, hired a live-in housekeeper and a nanny, then turned the child over to them while she stayed in the city and clawed her way to the top.

Cassie saw her mother only on alternate weekends, and had spent most of her life terrified of her.

It was when her mother had been invited to a week-long seminar at Kingsmill Resort in Williamsburg, Virginia, that Cassie's life changed. She knew about her mother's career because Margaret Madden thought it was her duty to inform her daughter how to get ahead in the world. Margaret loved to tell how she had been raised in a middle-class household full of "morons" but that she had "risen above" them. She'd put herself through college, studying business administration, then got a job as a junior manager with a big office supply chain. In her sixth year there, the company was bought by a fledgling computer business, and Margaret was one of only three upper-employees kept. Within four years she was at the top of that company.

By the time she'd been out of college for fifteen years, she'd been in five corporations and had moved near the head of each one. She was creative and dedicated, and every waking second of her life was given to the company where she worked.

The trip to Williamsburg was to be pivotal. The company where she was second in command was about to be bought by an enormous conglomerate, and at the end of the week she was either going to be jobless or made executive vice president.

The only problem had been that Cassie's latest nanny had broken her ankle and the housekeeper was on vacation, so there was no one to take care of the child. Margaret had used the inconvenience to her advantage when she'd called her boss and said she so rarely got to see her beloved daughter, could she please take the child with her? The man had been pleasantly impressed and agreed readily.

Cassie and her mother were given one of the many pretty, two-bedroom guest condos, and Cassie had been left on her own. Her mother was busy "making contacts" as she called it, never friends, never anything just for pleasure, so she was unaware of where her daughter was.

It was the first time Cassie had really seen her mother's colleagues, and for a whole day she'd been fascinated.

There were over three hundred people at the conference and within hours they had assembled themselves into little groups where they put their heads together and whispered. When Cassie got near them, she heard "Madden," then they broke apart. It was as if they thought the girl had been brought there to spy for her mother.

Cassie spent her time wandering about the beautiful resort and watching and listening, something she was good at.

By the second day, she saw that there was one person who seemed to be different from the others. He was a tall young man with blue eyes, black hair, and a tiny cleft in his chin. She didn't know who he was or what he did, but he seemed to run the place. The CEOs of the two merging corporations both talked to him. He'd listen, then go away, and later he'd nod toward someone that something had been done.

Cassie thought he was the quiet in the eye of the storm. Tempers were high that week. There were big negotiations of who was going to stay and in what position, and who was leaving. Little cliques of men and women were everywhere, plotting and planning.

In the midst of it all was this young man, who was very calm. She watched him step into the middle of angry people, and within seconds, whatever he said to them made them quit shouting. Maybe it was a reaction to her hyper mother, who was always living in the future, constantly scheming about the next product that would sell millions, the next takeover, the next position up the ladder, but Cassie really liked this quiet man who could settle others down.

By the third day, Cassie began to study the young man. As much as possible, wherever he went, whatever he did, she was there. When he spoke, she put herself close enough to listen. Several times he turned quickly and winked at her, but he never once addressed her directly, and she was glad. She had no idea what she'd say if he did speak to her. What she liked the most was that he seemed to be at peace with himself and the world. She never once heard him talk about a "five-year plan."

By the fourth day, she knew she was in love with him, and as a result, her watching of him became more secretive. She hid in bushes as he played tennis and laughed with the other guests. On Saturday when he went sailing, she was nearby when he left and watching when he returned. She saw that every morning he went swimming before it was quite daylight, so early on Sunday, the last day, she waited for him by the pool. The fact that she couldn't swim very well was, to her mind, an asset. If she did begin to sink, he could save her.

Six came and went but he didn't show up. Cassie was in the deep end and she was getting tired. She hadn't had much sleep in the last few days because she'd been keeping vigil over him.

By six thirty, she knew she should get out of the pool. She'd decided he wasn't going to come, but then she heard voices from the direction of the house and she relaxed. He'd be there soon. She smiled in anticipation as she let her muscles go limp and sunk toward the bottom.

It was never her intention to actually drown, but as she

waited for him to come, as she thought about her mother, she forgot about time and place.

The next thing she knew, she opened her eyes and she was being kissed by . . . him. His lips, his eyes, his chin, his body were all near

hers and he was kissing her. Or giving her mouth-to-mouth, which was very nearly the same thing.

"She's alive!" Cassie heard a woman say, but she couldn't concentrate because she began coughing up a lot of water.

"Are you all right?" he asked, his hands on her shoulders, holding her as she choked and spit.

Cassie managed to nod that she was fine. As long as he was near her, she was sure that she'd always be all right.

Someone put a towel around her, and she looked up to see a pretty woman kneeling beside her. "You shouldn't go swimming alone," she said softly, tenderness in her eyes.

The man looked across Cassie to the woman. It didn't take much to figure out that they were together, a couple. If Cassie hadn't still been choking she would have burst into tears. She wanted to shout at the woman that he was *hers*! Hadn't she nearly died to prove that?

But Cassie said nothing of what she really thought. Life with her mother had taught her to keep her true feelings and emotions to herself. If people didn't agree with her mother, there were punishments.

"Don't tell my mother," Cassie managed to say at last, looking at him and avoiding the eyes of the woman.

Puzzled, the woman glanced at him.

"Margaret Madden," he said.

The woman let out her breath in a sympathetic sigh. "I didn't know ol' Maggie could have—" She cut off her sentence. "We won't tell," she reassured Cassie. "But maybe we should have a doctor look at you."

"No!" Cassie said, then jumped up to show them that she was all right. But she got dizzy and would have fallen if he hadn't caught her. For a moment she had the divine pleasure of feeling his arms around her. She was glad she hadn't died in the pool because if she had, she wouldn't have felt his lips on hers and his hands on her body.

The woman cleared her throat and he released Cassie.

She backed away, looking at them. They were a beautiful couple, the woman tall like he was, with her dark hair cut short and close to her head. She had on a swimsuit that showed off her long, lean, athletic body. She also probably played tennis and swam. *She* would never drown, Cassie thought, backing away from them. She was embarrassed now and afraid they'd ask why she was in the pool alone if she couldn't swim very well.

"I, uh . . . I have to go," she mumbled, then turned and ran toward the house. Behind her, she heard the man's baritone voice say something. The woman said, "Hush! She obviously has a crush on you and she deserves respect." Cassie heard the man say, "She's just a kid. She can't—"

Cassie heard no more. She wanted to die from the humiliation and embarrassment. She couldn't will herself to die, but she could stay in her room for the rest of the day.

She and her mother left the resort that evening, but while her mother said her farewells, Cassie had skulked in the corners, fearful of running into him again, afraid he and his girlfriend would laugh at her. She didn't see them. But as soon as she and her mother got into the company car, her mother launched into a lecture about how she'd been embarrassed by Cassie's rudeness. "You'll never achieve anything if you don't put yourself forward," Margaret said. "Lurking about in the shadows will achieve nothing. It's possible, even probable, that someday you'll be asking one of those people for a job. You should see that they remember you."

Cassie kept her head turned away. Her heart nearly stopped when she saw *them* strolling across the lawn, hand in hand. She was sure they'd already forgotten the child who had nearly drowned just that morning.

"Him!" Margaret said, looking at the handsome young couple. "He's part of the security hired for this meeting and he stuck his nose in where it didn't belong!" she said, a look of disgust on her face. "He told a senior VP that if he didn't contain his anger, he'd have to leave. I don't know who he thinks he is, but—"

"Shut up," Cassie said, her voice calm and quiet, but fierce. It was the first time in her life that she'd stood up to her overbearing mother. Cassie had survived because she'd figured out the meaning of "passive- aggressive" when she was three. But now she couldn't bear for her mother to say something against *him*.

As they drove by, he raised his hand to her and smiled.

Cassie smiled back and lifted her hand in return. Then the car turned a curve in the road and they were out of sight.

Margaret started with, "How dare you—" but when she caught the look on Cassie's young face, she stopped talking and picked up her briefcase from the floor.

When Cassie glanced up, the driver was looking at her in the rearview mirror and smiling. He was proud of her for telling Margaret Madden to back off.

Cassie turned to look out the window, and she smiled too. She wasn't sure what had happened but she knew that the week had changed her life.